Wedding Bell Wishes

KATE HARDY
ALISON ROBERTS
LYNNE MARSHALL

MILLS & BOON

First Published in Great Britain 2019
by Mills & Boon, an imprint of HarperCollins*Publishers*
1 London Bridge Street, London, SE1 9GF

WEDDING BELL WISHES © 2019 Harlequin Books S. A.

It Started At A Wedding... © 2015 Pamela Brooks
The Wedding Planner And The CEO © 2015 Alison Roberts
Her Perfect Proposal © 2015 Janet Maarschalk

ISBN: 978-0-263-27472-1

0119

MIX
Paper from
responsible sources
FSC™ C007454

This book is produced from independently certified FSC™
paper to ensure responsible forest management.

For more information visit: www.harpercollins.co.uk/green

Printed and bound in Spain
by CPI, Barcelona

IT STARTED
AT A WEDDING…

KATE HARDY

To the Mills & Boon True Love authors,
with much love and thanks for being
such brilliant colleagues and friends—
and for letting me bounce mad ideas off them!

CHAPTER ONE

No.

This couldn't be happening.

The box had to be there.

It *had* to be.

But the luggage carousel was empty. It had even stopped going round, now the last case had been taken off it. And Claire was the only one standing there, waiting with a small suitcase and a dress box—and a heart full of panic.

Where was her best friend's wedding dress?

'Get a grip, Claire Stewart. Standing gawping at the carousel isn't going to make the dress magically appear. Go and talk to someone,' she told herself sharply. She gathered up her case and the box containing the bridesmaid's dress, and went in search of someone who might be able to find out where the wedding dress was. Maybe the box had accidentally been put in the wrong flight's luggage and it was sitting somewhere else, waiting to be claimed.

Half an hour of muddling through in a mixture of English and holidaymakers' Italian got her the bad news. Somewhere between London and Naples, the dress had vanished.

The dress Claire had spent hours working on, hand-stitching the tiny pearls on the bodice and the edge of the veil.

The dress Claire's best friend was supposed to be wearing at her wedding in Capri in two days' time.

Maybe this was a nightmare and she'd wake up from it in a second. Surreptitiously, Claire pinched herself. It hurt. Not good, because that meant this was really happening. She was in Naples with her luggage, her own bridesmaid's dress...and no wedding dress.

There was nothing else for it. She grabbed her mobile phone, found a quiet corner in the airport and called Ashleigh.

Whose phone was switched through to voicemail.

This definitely wasn't the kind of news Claire could leave on voicemail; that would be totally unfair. She tried calling Luke, Ashleigh's fiancé, but his phone was also switched through to voicemail. She glanced at her watch. It was still so early that they were probably in the middle of breakfast and they'd probably left their phones in their room. OK. Who else could she call? She didn't have a number for Tom, Luke's best man. Sammy, her other best friend, who was photographing the wedding, wasn't flying to Italy until tomorrow, after she'd finished a photo-shoot in New York. The rest of the wedding guests were due to arrive on the morning of the wedding.

Which left Ashleigh's brother. The man who was going to give Ashleigh away. The man who played everything strictly by the rules—and Claire had just broken them. Big time. He was the last person she could call.

But he wasn't in Capri yet, either. Which meant she had time to fix this.

What she needed was a plan.

Scratch that. What she *really* needed was coffee. She'd spent the last two weeks working all hours on Ashleigh's dress as well as the work she was doing for a big wedding show, and she'd skimped on sleep to get everything done in time. That, plus the ridiculously early flight she'd taken out here this morning, meant that she was fuzzy and unfocused.

Coffee.

Even thought she normally drank lattes, this called for desperate measures. She needed something strong and something fast. One espresso with three sugars later, Claire's head was clear enough to work out her options. It meant more travelling—a lot more travelling—but that didn't matter. Claire would've walked over hot coals for Ashleigh. She was more than Claire's best friend; she was the sister Claire would've chosen.

She tried calling Ashleigh again. This time, to Claire's relief, her best friend answered her mobile phone.

'Claire, hi! Are you in Naples already?'

'Um, yes. But, Ash, there's a bit of a problem.'

'What's wrong?'

'Honey, I don't know how to soften this.' There wasn't a way to soften news like this. 'Is Luke with you?'

'Ye-es.' Ashleigh sounded as if she was frowning with concern. 'Why?'

'I think you're going to need him,' Claire said.

'Now you're really worrying me. Claire? What's happened? Are you all right?'

'I'm fine.' Claire had no option but to tell her best friend the news straight. 'But I'm so sorry, Ash. I've really let you down. Your dress. It's gone missing somewhere between here and London.'

'What?'

'I've been talking to the airline staff. They phoned London for me. They said it's not in London, and it's definitely not in Naples. They're going to try and track it down, but they wanted us to be prepared for the fact that they might not be able to find it before the wedding.'

'Oh, my God.' Ashleigh gave a sharp intake of breath.

'I know. Look—we have options. I don't have time to make you another dress like that one, even if I could get the material and borrow a sewing machine. But we can go looking in Naples and find something off the peg, something I can maybe tweak for you. Or I can leave the bridesmaid's dress and my case here in the left luggage, and get the next flight back to London. I'm pretty much the same size as you, so I'll Skype you while I try on every single dress in my shop and you can pick the ones you like best. Then I'll get the next flight back here, and you can try the dresses on and I'll do any alterations so your final choice is perfect.'

Except it wouldn't be perfect, would it?

It wouldn't be the dress of Ashleigh's dreams. The dress Claire had designed especially for her. The dress that had gone missing.

'And you'll still be the most beautiful bride in the world, I swear,' Claire finished, desperately hoping that her best friend would see that.

'They lost my dress.' Ashleigh sounded numb. Which wasn't surprising. Planning the wedding had opened up old scars, so Ashleigh had decided to get married abroad—and the dress had been one of the few traditions she'd kept.

And Claire had let her down. 'I'm so, so sorry.'

'Claire, honey, it's not your fault that the airline lost my dress.'

That wasn't how Sean would see it. Claire had clashed with Ashleigh's brother on a number of occasions, and she knew that he didn't like her very much. They saw the world in very different ways, and Sean would see this as yet another example of Claire failing to meet his standards. She'd failed to meet her own, too.

'Look, I was the one bringing the dress to Italy. It was my responsibility, so the fact it's gone wrong is my fault,' Claire pointed out. 'What do you want to do? Meet me here in Naples and we'll go shopping?'

'I'm still trying to get my head round this. My *dress*,' Ashleigh said, sounding totally flustered—which, considering that Ashleigh was the calmest and most together person Claire knew, was both surprising and worrying.

'OK. Forget Naples. Neither of us knows the place well enough to find the right wedding shops anyway, so we'll stick with London. Have a look on my website, email me with a note of your top ten, and we'll talk again when I'm back in the shop. Then I'll bring your final choices on the next flight back.' She bit her lip. 'Though I wouldn't blame you for not trusting me to get it right this time.'

'Claire-bear, it's not your fault. Luke's here now—he's worked out what's going on and he's just said he'd marry me if I was wearing a hessian sack. The dress isn't important. Maybe we can find something in Capri or Sorrento.'

Ashleigh was clearly aiming for light and breezy, but Claire could hear the wobble in her best friend's voice. She knew what the dress meant to Ashleigh: the one big tradition she was sticking to for her wedding day. 'No,

Ash. It'll take us for ever to find a wedding shop. And what if you don't like what they have in stock? That's not fair to you. I know I'll have something you like, so I'm going to get the next flight back to London. I'll call you as soon as I get there,' she said.

'Claire, that's so much travelling—I can't make you do that.'

'You're not making me. I'm offering. You're my best friend and I'd go to the end of the earth for you,' Claire said, her voice heartfelt.

'Me, too,' Ashleigh said. 'OK. I'll call the spa and move our bookings.'

So much for the pampering day they'd planned. A day to de-stress the bride-to-be. Claire had messed that up, too, by losing the dress. 'I'm so sorry I let you down,' Claire said. 'I'd better go. I need to get my luggage stored and find a flight.' And she really hoped that there would be a seat available. If there wasn't... Well, she'd get to London somehow. Train, plane, ferry. Whatever it took. She wasn't going to let Ashleigh down again. 'I'll call you when I get back to London.'

'Please don't tell me something's come up and you're not going to make it in time for the wedding.'

'Of course not,' Sean said, hearing the panic in his little sister's voice and wondering what was wrong. Was this just an attack of last-minute nerves? Or was she having serious second thoughts? He liked his future brother-in-law enormously, but if Ashleigh had changed her mind about marrying him, then of course Sean would back her in calling off the wedding. All he wanted was to see Ashleigh settled and happy. 'I was just calling to see if you needed me to bring any last-minute things over with me.'

'Oh. Yes. Of course.'

But she sounded flustered—very unlike the calm, sensible woman he knew her to be. 'Ashleigh? What's happened?'

'Nothing.'

But her response was a little too hasty for Sean's liking. He deliberately made his voice gentle. 'Sweetie, if there's a problem, you know you can always talk to me. I'll help you fix it.' OK, so Ashleigh was only three years younger than he was, and he knew that she was perfectly capable of sorting out her own problems— but he'd always looked out for his little sister, even before their parents had been killed in the crash that had turned their lives upside down six years ago. 'Tell me.'

'The airline lost my dress,' Ashleigh said. 'But it's OK. Claire's gone back to London to get me another one.'

Sean paused while it sank in.

There was a problem with his sister's wedding.

And Claire Stewart was smack in the middle of the problem.

Why didn't that surprise him?

'Wasn't Claire meant to be bringing the dress with her?' he asked.

'It wasn't her fault, Sean.'

No. Of course not. It would never be Miss Follow-Your-Heart's fault that something went wrong and everyone else had to pick up the pieces.

But he wasn't going to spoil his sister's wedding by picking a fight with her best friend. At least, not in front of Ashleigh. He fully intended to discuss the matter with Claire herself—sooner, rather than later. 'OK. Is there anything else you need?'

'No, it's fine.'

But his little sister didn't sound fine. She sounded shaky. 'Is Luke there with you?' he asked.

'Yes. He said the dress didn't matter and he'd marry me if I was wearing a hessian sack. He says it's our marriage that matters, not the trappings.'

Sean mentally high-fived his brother-in-law-to-be. And thank God Luke was so sensible and reliable. Ashleigh's last boyfriend had been selfish, thoughtless and flaky—and he'd just so happened to be the best friend of Claire's boyfriend at the time. Which figured. Claire always seemed to leave chaos in her wake.

'I could've told you that, sweetheart. Luke's a good bloke and he loves you to bits. Look, I'll be there later tonight, OK? If there's anything you need, anything at all, just call me. And I'm with Luke. Even if you're wearing a hessian sack, you're going to be the most beautiful bride ever.' The bride his father should've been giving away. His throat tightened. If only. But the crash had happened and they'd had to make the best of it ever since. And Sean was determined that his little sister was going to have the wedding she really wanted. He'd *make* it happen.

'Thanks, Sean.' She blew out a breath. 'I'm fine. Really. This is just a little hiccup and Claire's fixing it.'

Yes, Sean thought grimly, because he'd make quite sure that Claire did exactly that.

'See you tonight,' she said.

'See you tonight.'

Sean checked his diary when he'd put down the phone. All his meetings that afternoon could be moved. Anything else, he could deal with in Capri. A quick word with his PA meant that everything would be sorted. And then he called Claire.

Her phone went straight through to voicemail.

So that meant either she was on the phone already, her phone was switched off completely, or she'd seen his name on the screen and wasn't answering because she was trying to avoid him. OK, then; he'd wait for her at the shop. And he'd make absolutely sure that Ashleigh's dress didn't get lost, this time round.

It didn't take Sean long to get to the terraced house in Camden which held Dream of a Dress on the ground floor and Claire's flat on the top storey. Although the sign on the door said 'closed', he could see light inside—meaning that Claire was there, or whoever she'd employed to man the shop in her absence. Either would do.

He rang the doorbell.

No reply.

OK. Play dirty it was, then. This time, he leaned on the doorbell until a figure hurried through to the door.

A figure wearing a wedding dress.

Claire narrowed her eyes at him when she opened the door. Though he noticed that she didn't ask him why he was here. Clearly she had a pretty good idea that he already knew she'd lost his sister's wedding dress and he wasn't happy about the situation.

'I'm Skypeing Ash right now,' she said quietly. 'And I don't want her upset any more today, so can we leave the fight until she's chosen another dress and I've said goodbye to her?'

Claire clearly realised that they were about to have a fight. A huge one. But Sean agreed with her about not rowing in front of his sister. Right now, Ashleigh's feelings had to come first. 'OK.'

'Good. Come in. If you want a drink, feel free to make yourself something. There's tea, coffee and mugs in the cupboard above the kettle, though I'm afraid there's only long-life milk.' She gestured to a doorway which obviously led to the business's kitchen.

'Thank you,' he said. Though he wasn't about to accept any hospitality from Claire Stewart, even if it was do-it-yourself hospitality.

'If you'll excuse me, I have a wedding dress to sort out.' She gave him a level look. 'And I'm modelling the dresses for Ash, which means I'll need to change several times—so I'd appreciate it if you didn't come through to the back until I'm done.'

'Noted,' he said.

She locked the shop door again, still keeping the 'closed' sign in place, and vanished into the back room. Feeling a bit like a spare part—but wanting to know just how Claire had managed to lose a wedding dress—Sean waited in the main area of the shop until she walked back out, this time dressed in faded jeans and a strappy top rather than a wedding dress.

'No coffee?' she asked.

'No.'

She folded her arms. 'OK. Spit it out.'

'Firstly, does Ashleigh actually have a dress?' he asked.

'There are three she likes,' Claire said. 'I'm taking them all over to Capri as soon as I can get a flight. Then she can try them on, and I'll make any necessary alterations in time for the wedding.'

'What I don't understand is how you managed to lose her dress in the first place.' He shook his head in exasperation. 'Why wasn't it with you in the plane?'

'Believe it or not,' she said dryly, 'that was my original plan. I cleared it with the airline that I could put the boxes with her dress and mine in the overhead storage compartments, and if there was room they'd hang Ash's dress on a rail in the stewardesses' cabin. I packed both the dresses in boxes that specifically met the airline's size guidelines. Your waistcoat and cravat, plus Luke's and Tom's, are packed in with my dress.'

So far, so sensible. But this was Claire—the woman who was chaos in high heels with a snippy attitude. 'But?'

'It turned out there were three other brides on the flight. One of whom was a total Bridezilla and demanded that her dress should be the one in with the stewardesses. There was a massive row. In the end, the captain intervened and ordered that all the bridal dresses should go in the hold with the rest of the luggage—even those belonging to people who weren't involved in the argument with Bridezilla. He wouldn't even let us put the dresses in the overhead lockers. The atmosphere on the plane was pretty bad.' She shrugged. 'The airline staff have looked in London and in Naples, and there's no sign of the box with Ash's dress. They're still checking. It might turn up in time. But it probably won't, so these dresses are my contingency plan—because I don't intend to let Ash down. Ever.'

It hadn't been *entirely* Claire's fault, Sean acknowledged. But, at the same time, she *had* been the one responsible for the dress, and right now the dress was missing. 'Why didn't you buy a seat for the dress?'

'They said I couldn't—that if I wanted the dress to come with me, it would have to be treated as additional cabin luggage. Which,' she pointed out, 'is what I organised and what I paid for.' Her blue eyes were icy as she added, 'And, just in case you think I'm perfectly OK about the situation, understand that I've spent weeks working on that dress and I'm gutted that my best friend doesn't get to wear the dress of her dreams—the dress

I designed especially for her. But moaning on about the situation isn't going to get the dress back. I'd rather do something practical to make sure Ash's wedding goes as smoothly as possible. So, if you'll excuse me, I have three wedding dresses to pack and a flight to book.' She shrugged again. 'But, if it makes you feel better, do feel free to storm and shout at me.'

Funny how she was the one in the wrong, but she'd managed to make him feel as if *he* were the one in the wrong, Sean thought.

Though she had a point. Complaining about the situation or losing his temper with her wouldn't make the dress magically reappear. And Claire had spent most of today travelling—two and a half hours each way on a plane, plus an hour each way on a train and waiting round in between. Now she was just about to fly back to Italy: yet more travelling. All for his sister's sake.

Claire Stewart was trying—in both senses of the phrase. But maybe he needed to try a bit harder, too.

'Do you want me to find you a flight while you pack the dresses?' he asked.

She looked at him as if he'd just grown two heads.

'What?' he asked.

'Are you actually being *helpful*?' she asked. 'To *me*?'

He narrowed his eyes at her. 'Don't make it sound as if I'm always the one in the wrong.'

'No. That would be me,' she said. 'In your regimented world view.'

'I'm not regimented,' he said, stung. 'I'm organised and efficient. There's a difference.'

Her expression suggested otherwise.

'I was,' he pointed out, 'trying to call a truce and work with you. For Ashleigh's sake.'

She looked at him for a long, long time. And then

she nodded. 'Truce. I can do that. Then thank you—it would save me a bit of time if you could find me a flight. I don't care which London airport it's from or how much it costs—just let me know as soon as they need paying and I'll come to the phone and give them my credit card details. But please put whichever airline in the picture about what happened to the dress this morning, and I want cast-iron guarantees that *these* dresses are going to make it out to Italy with me. Otherwise I'll be carving their entire check-in staff into little pieces with a rusty spoon.'

He couldn't help smiling. 'Spoons are blunt.'

'That,' she said, 'is entirely the point. Ditto the rusty.'

'You really care about Ashleigh, don't you?' he said.

'Sean, how can you not already know that?' Claire frowned. 'She's been my best friend for more than half my lifetime, since I moved to the same school as her when I was thirteen. I think of Ash practically as my sister.'

Which would technically make her his sister, too. Except Sean didn't have any sibling-like feelings towards Claire. What he felt for Claire was…

Well, it was a lot easier to think of it as dislike. When they weren't being scrupulously polite to each other, they clashed. They had totally opposite world views. They were totally incompatible. He wasn't going to let himself think about the fact that her hair was the colour of a cornfield bathed in sunshine, and her eyes were the deep blue of a late summer evening. And he certainly wasn't going to let himself think about the last time he'd kissed her.

'Of course. I'll get you a flight sorted.'

Though he noticed her movements while he was on the phone. Deft and very sure as she packed each dress in tissue paper to avoid creases, put it inside a plastic cover to protect it from any damage and then in a box. As if she'd done this many times before. Which, he realised, she probably had.

He'd never seen Claire at work before. Apart from when she'd measured the three men in the wedding party for their waistcoats, and that had been at Ashleigh and Luke's house. He'd been too busy concentrating on being polite and anodyne to her for his sister's sake to take much notice of what she was actually doing.

And, OK, it was easy to think of dress designers as a bit kooky and not living in the same world as the rest of the population. The outlandish outfits on the catwalks in Milan and the big fashion shows left him cold and wondering what on earth was going on in the heads of the designers—real people just didn't wear stuff like that. But the woman in front of him seemed businesslike. Organised. Efficient.

Like someone who belonged in his world.

He shook himself. That was just an illusion. Temporary. Claire didn't belong in his world and he didn't belong in hers. They'd be civil to each other over the next few days, purely for Ashleigh's sake, and then they'd go back to avoiding each other.

Safely.

CHAPTER TWO

As CLAIRE WORKED on packing up the dresses, she found herself growing more and more aware of Sean. He looked every inch the meticulous businessman in a made-to-measure suit, handmade shirt, and perfectly polished shoes; as part of her job, Claire noticed details like that. Sean wouldn't have looked out of place on a catwalk or in a glossy magazine ad.

And he was actually helping her—working with her as a team. Which was rarer than a blue moon. They didn't get on.

Apart from a few occasions, and some of those were memories that still had the ability to make Claire squirm. Such as Ashleigh's eighteenth birthday party. Claire's life had imploded only a couple of weeks before and, although she'd tried so hard to smile and be happy for her best friend's sake, she'd ended up helping herself to too much champagne that evening to blot out the misery that had threatened to overwhelm her.

Sean had come to her rescue—and Claire had been young enough and drunk enough to throw herself at him. Sean had been a perfect gentleman and turned her down, and her adult self was glad that he'd been so decent, but as a teenager she'd been hideously embarrassed by the whole episode and she'd avoided him like the plague for months and months afterwards.

Then there was his parents' funeral, three years later. Claire had been there to support Ashleigh—just as Ashleigh had supported Claire at her own mother's funeral—and she'd glanced across at Sean at a moment when he'd looked utterly lost. Wanting to help, Claire had pushed past the old embarrassment and gone to offer him her condolences. Sean hadn't been quite approachable enough for her to give him a hug, so she'd simply squeezed his hand and said she was sorry for his loss. At the time, her skin had tingled at the contact with his—but the timing was so inappropriate that she hadn't acted on it.

They'd fought again when Ashleigh had decided not to join the family business. Sean had blamed Claire for talking Ashleigh out of what he clearly saw as her duty. OK, so Claire had been a sounding board and helped Ashleigh work out what she really wanted to do, encouraging her to follow her dreams; but surely Sean had wanted his sister to be happy instead of feeling trapped and miserable in a job she really didn't want to do? And surely, given that his parents had died so young, he understood how short life was and how you needed to make the most of every moment? It wasn't as if being a maths teacher was some insecure, fly-by-night job. And Ash was a really gifted teacher. She loved what she did and her pupils adored her. It had been the right decision.

The problem was, Sean had always been so overprotective. Claire could understand why; he was Ashleigh's elder brother and had been the head of the family since he was twenty-four. But at the same time he really needed to understand that his sister was perfectly capable of standing on her own two feet and making her own way in the world.

She forced herself to concentrate on packing the dresses properly, but she couldn't help noticing the deep tone of Sean's voice, his confidence and sureness as he talked to the airline.

Most of the time Claire didn't admit it, even to herself, but she'd had a secret crush on Sean when she'd been fourteen. Which was half the reason why she'd thrown herself at him at Ashleigh's birthday party, three years later.

Another memory seeped back in. Ashleigh's engagement party to Luke. Sean had asked her to dance; Claire had been well aware that he was only being polite for his sister's sake. Which was the same reason why she'd agreed to dance with him. Though, somewhere between the start and the middle of the song, something had changed. Claire couldn't even blame it on the champagne, because she hadn't been drinking. But something had made her pull back slightly and look up at Sean. Something had made her lips part slightly. And then he'd dipped his head and kissed her.

The kiss had shaken her right to the core. Nobody had ever made her feel like that with a single kiss—as if her knees had turned to mush and she needed to cling to him to keep herself upright. It had panicked her into backing away and cracking some inane joke, and the moment was lost.

Since then, she'd been scrupulously polite and distant with Sean. But in unguarded moments she wondered. Had he felt that same pull of attraction? And what if…?

She shook herself. Of course not. Apart from the fact that her judgement when it came to men was totally rubbish, she knew that Sean just saw her as his baby sister's super-annoying best friend, the woman he ended up bickering with every time they spoke to each other for more than five minutes. It rankled slightly that he still didn't take her seriously—surely the fact that she'd had her own business for the last three years and kept it going through the recession counted for *something*?

Then again, she didn't need to prove anything to him. She was perfectly comfortable with who she was and what she'd achieved.

She finished packing the last box.

'Any luck with my flight?' she asked when Sean ended his call.

'There's good news and bad,' he said.

'OK. Hit me with the bad first.'

He frowned. 'Why?'

'Because then I've faced the worst, and there's still something good to look forward to.'

He looked surprised, as if he'd never thought of it in that way before. 'OK. The bad news is, I can't get you a flight where they'll take the dresses on board.'

The worst-case scenario. Well, she'd just have to deal with it. 'Then if planes are out, I'll just have to go by train.' She thought on her feet. 'If I get the Eurostar to Paris, there'll be a connecting train to Milan or Rome, and from there to Naples. Though it means I probably won't get to Capri until tomorrow, now.'

'Hold on. I did say there was good news as well,' he reminded her. 'We can fly to Naples from London.'

She frowned, not understanding. 'But you just said you couldn't get me a seat where they'll take the dresses.'

'Not on a commercial flight, no. But I have a friend with a private plane.'

'You have *what*?'

'A friend with a private plane,' he repeated, 'who's willing to take us this afternoon.'

'Us.' The word hit her like a sledgehammer and she narrowed her eyes at him. 'Are you saying that you don't trust me to take the dresses on my own?'

'You need to go to Naples. I need to go to Naples. So it makes sense,' he said, 'for us to travel together.'

She noticed that he hadn't answered her question. Clearly he didn't trust her. To be fair to him, she had already lost his sister's wedding dress—but it hadn't been entirely her fault. 'But don't you already have a flight booked?'

'I cancelled it,' he said. 'I promised Ashleigh I'd be there tonight or I would've offered you my original booking and flown in later. This seemed like the best solution to the problem.'

'You have a friend with a private plane.' She still couldn't get over that one. 'Sean, normal people don't have friends with private planes.'

'You barely accept that I'm human, let alone normal,' he pointed out.

And they were heading towards yet another fight. She grimaced. 'Sorry. Let's just rewind and try this again. Thank you, Sean, for coming to the rescue and calling in whatever favour you had to call in to get me a flight to Naples. Please tell your friend that if he ever needs a wedding dress or a prom dress made, I'll do it for nothing.'

'I'll tell her,' Sean said dryly.

Her. Girlfriend? Probably not, Claire thought. Ashleigh was always saying that Sean would never settle down and never dated anyone for more than three weeks in a row. So maybe it was someone who'd gone to university with him, or a long-standing business acquaintance. Not that she had any right to ask.

'Thanks,' she said. 'So what time does the flight leave?'

'When we want it to, give or take half an hour,' he said. 'My car's outside. I just need to drop it back home and collect my luggage.' He looked at her. 'You might as well come with me.'

Gee, what an invitation, Claire thought. But she wasn't going to pick a fight with him now. He'd already gone above and beyond. It was for Ashleigh's sake rather than hers, she knew, but she still appreciated it. 'Ready when you are.'

He drove them back to his house and parked outside. His luggage was in the hallway, so it only took a few seconds for him to collect it; Claire noticed that he didn't invite her in. Fair enough. It was his space. Though she was curious to know whether his living space was as organised and regimented as the rest of him.

They took the tube through to London City airport. Claire used the noise of the train as an excuse not to make conversation, and she knew that he was doing exactly the same. Being with Sean wasn't easy. He was so prickly. He had to have a charming side, or he wouldn't have made such a success of running the family business—clients wouldn't want to deal with him. But the sweetness of the toffee that Farrell's produced definitely didn't rub off on him where Claire was concerned.

The check-in process was much faster than Claire was used to; then again, she didn't know anyone with a private plane. It was more the sort of thing that a rock star would have, not a wedding dress designer. The plane was smaller than she'd expected, but there was plenty of room to stretch out and the seats were way, way more comfortable than she was used to. She always travelled economy. This was another world.

'Welcome aboard,' the pilot said, shaking their hands. 'Our flight today will be about two and a half hours. If you need anything, ask Elise.'

Elise turned out to be their stewardess.

And, most importantly, Elise stored the dress boxes where Claire could see them. This time, she could be totally sure that none of the dresses would be lost.

'Do you mind if I…?' Sean gestured to his briefcase.

Claire would much rather work than make small talk with him, too. 'Sure. Me, too,' she said, and took a sketchpad from her bag. She'd had a new client yesterday who wanted a dress at short notice, plus there was the big wedding show in two months' time—a show where Claire was exhibiting her very first collection, and she was working flat out to get enough dresses ready in time. Six wedding dresses plus the bridesmaids' outfits to go with each, as well as colour coordinating the groom's outfit with each set. She could really do with an extra twenty-four hours in a day for the next few weeks—twenty-four hours when she didn't need to sleep. But, as that wasn't physically possible, she'd have to settle for drinking too much coffee and eating too much sugary stuff to get her through the next few weeks.

As he worked, Sean was aware of the quick, light strokes of Claire's pencil against her sketchpad. Clearly she was working on some preliminary designs for someone else's dress. When the sound stopped, he looked over at her.

She'd fallen asleep mid-sketch, her pencil still held

loosely in one hand, and there were deep shadows beneath her eyes.

Right at that moment, she looked vulnerable. And
Sean was shocked by the sudden surge of protectiveness.

Since when did he feel protective about Claire Stewart?

That wasn't something he wanted to think about too
closely. So he concentrated on his work and let her sleep
until the plane landed. Then he leaned over and touched
her shoulder. 'Claire, wake up.'

She murmured something and actually nestled closer,
so her cheek was resting against his hand.

It was his second shock of the afternoon, how her
skin felt against his. It made him feel almost as if he'd
been galvanised. Very similar to that weird sensation
when she'd measured him for the waistcoat—even
though her touch had been as professional and emo-
tionless as any tailor's, it had made him feel strange to
feel the warmth of her fingers through his shirt.

Oh, help.

Sexual attraction and Claire Stewart were two things
that definitely didn't go together, in his book.

OK, so there had been that night, all those years
ago—but Claire had been seventeen and his mother had
dispatched him to rescue the girl and get her safely to
bed back at their house. Of course he'd been tempted
when she'd tried to kiss him—he was a man, not an
automaton—but he also knew that he was responsible
for her, and no way would he ever have taken advantage of her.

And the times since when their eyes had met at one
of Ashleigh's parties…

Well, she'd normally had some dreadful boyfriend

or other in tow. In Sean's experience, Claire's men were always the type who'd claim that artistic integrity was much more important than actually earning a living. Sean didn't have much time for people who wouldn't shoulder their fair share of responsibility and expected other people to bail them out all the time, but he still wouldn't encourage their girlfriend to cheat on them. He'd never made a move.

Except, he remembered with a twinge of guilt, for the night Ashleigh had got engaged to Luke. He'd asked Claire to dance—solely for his sister's sake. But then Claire had looked up at him, her blue eyes huge and her mouth parted, and he'd reacted purely on instinct.

He'd kissed her.

A kiss that had shaken him to the core. It had shaken him even more when he analysed it. No way could he feel like *that* about Claire Stewart. She was his total opposite. It would never, ever work between them. They'd drive each other crazy.

He'd been too shocked to say a word, at first, but then she'd made some terrible joke or other and he'd somehow managed to get his common sense back. And he'd blanked out the memory.

Except now it was back.

And he had to acknowledge that the possibility of something happening between himself and Claire had always been there. Right now, the possibility hummed just a little harder. Probably because he hadn't dated anyone in the last three months—this was a physical itch, he told himself, and Claire definitely wasn't the right woman to scratch said itch. Their approach to life was way too different for it ever to work between them.

'Claire.' This time, he shook her a little harder, the

way he would've liked to shake himself and get his common sense back in place.

She woke with a jolt. She blinked, as if not quite sure where she was, and he saw her expression change the second that she realised what had happened. 'Sorry,' she said. 'I didn't intend to fall asleep. I hope I didn't snore too loudly.'

He could tell that this was her way of trying to make a joke and ease the tension between them. Good idea. He'd follow her lead on that one. 'Not quite pneumatic drill mode,' he said with a smile.

'Good.'

Like him, she thanked the pilot and the stewardess for getting them there safely. And then they were in the bright Italian sunshine, so bright that they both needed to use dark glasses. And Sean was secretly glad of the extra barrier. He didn't want Claire guessing that she'd shaken his composure, even briefly.

And no way was he going to let her struggle with three dress boxes. 'I'll take these for you.'

She rolled her eyes. 'They're not that heavy, Sean. They're just a bit bulky.'

'Even so.'

'I can manage.'

Did she think that he was being sexist? 'I'm taller than you and my arms are longer,' he pointed out. 'So it makes sense for me to carry the boxes.'

'Then I'll carry your suitcase and briefcase.'

He'd almost forgotten just how stubborn she could be. But, at the same time, he had a sneaking admiration for her independence. And he always travelled light in any case, so his luggage wouldn't be too heavy for her.

On the way from the plane to the airport terminal, Claire said to Sean, 'Perhaps you can let me have your friend's name and address, so I can send her some flowers.'

'Already done,' he said.

'From you, yes. I want to send her something from *me*.'

'Sure,' he said easily. 'I'll give you the details when we get to the hotel.'

'Thank you.' She paused. 'And I need to pick up my case and the bridesmaid's dress. I checked them in to the left luggage, this morning.'

'Wait a second.' He checked his phone. 'Good. Jen—my PA—has booked us a taxi from here to Sorrento and arranged the hydrofoil tickets.'

They went through passport control, then collected Claire's luggage. He waited while she checked with the airline whether Ashleigh's original dress had turned up yet. He knew from her expression that there was still no luck.

The taxi driver loaded their luggage into the car. Claire and Sean were sitting together in the back seat. She was very aware of his nearness, and it made her twitchy. She didn't want to be this aware of Sean. And how did you make small talk with someone who had nothing in common with you?

She looked out of the window. 'Oh, there's Vesuvius.' Looming over the skyline, a brooding hulk of a mountain with a hidden, dangerous core.

'You went there with Ashleigh, didn't you?' he asked.

'And Sammy. Three years ago. It was amazing—like nothing any of us had ever seen before. It was what I imagine a lunar landscape would look like, and we squeaked like schoolkids when we saw steam coming out of the vents.' She smiled at the memory. 'I think that's why Ash chose to get married in Capri, because she fell in love with the island when we came here and had a day trip there.'

They both knew the other reason why Ashleigh hadn't planned to get married in the church where she and Sean had been christened and their parents had got married—because their parents were buried in the churchyard and it had been too much for Ashleigh to bear, the idea of getting married inside the church while her parents were outside.

'It's a nice part of the world,' Sean said.

'Very,' Claire replied. She ran out of small talk at that point and spent the rest of the journey looking out of the window at the coastline, marvelling at the houses perched so precariously on the cliffsides and the incredible blueness of the sea. At the same time, all her senses seemed to be concentrating on Sean. Which was insane.

Finally the taxi dropped them at the marina in Sorrento. Claire waited with their luggage while Sean collected their tickets—and then at last they boarded the hydrofoil and were on their way to Capri.

There were large yachts moored at the marina. As they drew closer she could see the buildings lining the marina, painted in brilliant white or ice cream shades. There were more houses on the terraces banking up behind them, then the white stone peak of the island.

Once they'd docked, they took the funicular railway up to the Piazzetta, then caught a taxi from the square; she noticed that the cars were all open-topped with a stripy awning above them to shade the passengers. So much more exotic than the average convertible.

The taxi took them past more of the brilliant white buildings, in such sharp contrast to the sea and the sky.

There were bougainvillea and rhododendrons every-where, and terracotta pots full of red geraniums. Claire had always loved the richness and depth of the colours on the south European coast.

At last, they reached the hotel.

'Thank you for arranging this,' she said as they collected their keys. 'And you said you'd give me your friend's details?' She grabbed a pen and paper, ready to take them down as Sean gave them to her. 'Thanks. Last thing—milk, white or dark chocolate?'

'I have no idea. You're sending her chocolate?'

'You've already sent flowers.' She smiled. 'I guess you can't really send anyone confectionery, with your business being in that line.' Admittedly Farrell's specialised in toffee rather than chocolates, but it would still be a bit of a *faux pas*. 'I'll play it safe and send a mixture.'

'Good plan,' he said. 'See you later.'

He'd made it clear that he didn't plan to spend much time with her. Which suited Claire just fine—the less time they were in each other's company, the less likelihood there was of another fight.

She let the bellboy help her carry her luggage to her room. She'd barely set the dress boxes on the bed in her room when there was a knock on the door.

'Come in,' she called with a smile, having a very good idea who it would be.

Ashleigh walked in—physically so like Sean, with the same dark eyes and dark hair, but a million times easier to be with and one of Claire's favourite people in the whole world. Claire hugged her fiercely. 'Hey, you beautiful bride-to-be. How are you?'

Ashleigh hugged her back. 'I'm so glad to see you! I can't believe you've been flying back and forth between England and Italy all day. That's insane, Claire, even for you.'

Claire shrugged. 'You're worth it. Anyway, I'm here now.' She held her friend at arm's length. 'You look gorgeous. Radiant. Just as you should be.'

'And you look shattered,' Ashleigh said, eyeing her closely. 'You were up before dawn to get your first flight here.'

'I'm fine. I, um, had a bit of a nap on the plane,' Claire admitted.

'Good—and you must be in dire need of something to eat and a cold drink.'

'A cold drink would be nice—but, before we do anything else, I need you to try on these dresses so I can get the alterations started.' Claire hugged her again. 'I'm so sorry that it's all gone so wrong.'

'It wasn't your fault,' Ashleigh said loyally.

That wasn't how Sean saw it, but Claire kept that thought to herself.

Ashley tried on the dresses and looked critically at herself in the mirror. Finally, she made her decision. 'I think this one.'

'Good choice,' Claire said.

Thankfully, the dress didn't need much altering. Claire took the dressmaking kit from her luggage and pinned the dress so it was the perfect fit.

'You're not doing any more work on that tonight,' Ashleigh said firmly. 'It's another day and a half until the wedding, and you've been travelling all day, so right now I want you to chill out and relax.'

'I promise you, I plan to have an early night,' Claire said. 'But I still need to check the waistcoats on the men. And I would kill for a shower.' All the travelling had made her feel tired, as well as sticky; running some cool water over her head might just help to keep her awake a bit longer.

'Sort the men's fitting tomorrow after breakfast,' Ashleigh said. 'Just have your shower, then come and meet us on the terrace when you're done. I'll have a long, cold drink waiting for you. With lots and lots of ice.'

'That sounds like heaven,' Claire said gratefully.

When Ashleigh had gone, Claire hung up all the dresses and waistcoats, and had a shower. Then she joined her best friend, her husband-to-be and their best man on the terrace. To her relief, Sean wasn't there.

'He had some phone calls to make,' Ashleigh explained. 'You know Sean. He always works crazy hours.'

Probably, Claire thought, because he'd been thrown in at the deep end when he'd had to take over the family business at the age of twenty-four after their parents had been killed in a car crash. Working crazy hours had got him through the first year, and it was a habit that had clearly stuck. 'Well—cheers,' she said, and raised her glass as the others echoed her toast.

Somehow Claire managed to avoid Sean for most of the next day; their only contact was just after breakfast, when she did the final fitting of the waistcoats and checked that they went perfectly with the suits and shirts. She was busy for most of the day making the last-minute alterations to Ashleigh's dress, and when she was finished Sean was still busy making phone calls and analysing reports.

Then again, the sheer romance of the island of Capri would be wasted on a man like Sean, Claire thought. He was too focused on his work to notice the gorgeous flowers or the blueness of the sea. So much so that she'd half expected him not to join them for the surprise that she and Luke had organised for Ashleigh that evening; when he joined them in the taxi, she had to hide her amazement.

'So where are we going?' Ashleigh asked.

'You'll see. Patience, Miss Farrell,' Claire said with a grin. Actually, it was something that she was looking forward to and dreading in equal measure, but she knew that it was something her best friend would love, so she'd force herself to get over her fears. It was just a shame that Sammy wasn't there to join them as her flight from New York had been delayed. Which meant that, instead of being able to let Sammy defuse the awkwardness between herself and Sean, Claire was going to have to make small talk with him—because she could hardly talk only to the best man and the groom-to-be and ignore Sean completely.

Finally they arrived at the chairlift.

'Oh, fabulous!' Ashleigh hugged Claire and then her husband-to-be. 'I love this place. I didn't think we'd get time to do this.'

'It was Claire's idea,' Luke said with a smile. 'She said sunset at the top of Monte Solaro would be incredibly romantic.'

'Especially because it's outside the usual tourist hours and we'll have the place all to ourselves. I can't believe you arranged all this.' Ashleigh looked thrilled. 'Thank you so much, both of you.'

Twelve minutes, Claire reminded herself as she was helped onto the chair. It would only take twelve minutes to get from the bottom of the chairlift to the very top of the island. She wasn't going to fall off. It was perfectly safe. She'd done this before. Thousands and thousands of tourists had done this before. The chairs were on a continuous loop, so all she had to do was let them help her jump off at the top. It would be *fine*.

Even so, her palms felt slightly damp and she clung on to the green central pole of her chair for dear life. Thankfully, her bag had a cross-body strap, so she didn't have to worry about holding on to that, too. Her hands ached by the time she reached the top, but she managed to get off the chair without falling flat on her face.

Just as she and Luke had arranged, there was a table at the panoramic viewpoint overlooking the *faraglioni*, the three famous vertical columns of rock rising out of the sea. There was a beautiful arrangement of white flowers in the centre of the table, and white ribbons on the wicker chairs. When they sat down, the waiter brought over a bottle of chilled Prosecco and canapés.

'Cheers. To Ashleigh and Luke—just to say how much we love you,' Claire said, lifting her glass, and the others echoed the toast.

'I really can't believe you did this.' Ashleigh was beaming, and Claire's heart swelled. The night before the wedding, when Ashleigh should've been happily fussed over by her mum…Claire had wanted to take her best friend's mind off what she was missing, and she and Luke had talked over the options. The scary one had definitely been the best decision.

'It wasn't just me. It was Luke as well,' Claire said, wanting to be fair. 'It's just a shame Sammy couldn't make it.'

'She'll be here tomorrow,' Tom said confidently.

'You know, some brides actually get married up here,' Ashleigh said. 'Obviously they're not going to walk for an hour uphill in a wedding dress and high heels, so they ride on the chairlift. I've seen photographs where the bride carried her shoes in one hand and her bouquet in the other.'

'And I suppose Claire showed them to you,' Sean said.

Claire didn't rise to the bait, but she wished she hadn't already done the final fitting of his waistcoat, because otherwise she would've had great pleasure in being totally unprofessional and sticking pins into him.

'No,' Ashleigh said. 'Actually, she talked me out of it.'

'Because the design of your dress means you wouldn't fit in the seat properly and I didn't want your dress all creased in the photographs,' Claire said with a smile.

Ashleigh laughed. 'More like because you wouldn't be able to hang on to your shoes and your flowers and cling on to the central bar for dear life all at the same time.'

Claire laughed back. 'OK, so I'm a wuss about heights—but I would've done it if that's what you'd really wanted, Ash. Because it's your day, and what *you* want is what's important.' Her words were directed at her best friend, but she looked straight into Sean's eyes, making it very clear that she meant every word.

He had the grace to flush.

It looked as if he'd got the message, then. Ashleigh came first and they'd put their differences aside for her sake.

Luke and Tom chatted easily, covering up the fact that Claire and Sean were barely speaking to each other. And gradually Claire relaxed, letting herself enjoy the incredibly romantic setting. They watched as the sun began to set over the sea; mist rose around the distant islands as the sky became striped with yellow and pink and purple, making them seem mysterious and other-worldly.

Claire took a few shots with her camera; she knew they wouldn't be anything near as good as Sammy's photographs, but it would at least be a nice memory. She glanced at Sean; he looked as if he was lost in thought, staring out at the sunset. Before she quite realised what she was doing, she took the snap.

Later that evening, back in her hotel room, she reviewed her photographs. There were some gorgeous shots of the sunset and the sea, of Ashleigh and Luke and Tom. But the picture she couldn't get out of her head was the impulsive one she'd taken of Sean. If they'd never met before, if there were no history of sniping and backbiting between them, she would've said he was the most attractive man she'd ever met and she would've been seriously tempted to get together with him.

But.

She'd known Sean for years, he was far from an easy man, and she really didn't need any complications in her life right now.

'Too much Prosecco addling your brain, Claire Stewart,' she told herself with a wry smile. 'Tomorrow, you're on sparkling water.'

Tomorrow.

Ashleigh's wedding day.

And please, please, let it be perfect.

CHAPTER THREE

'MISS STEWART?' THE woman from the airline introduced herself swiftly on the phone. 'I'm very pleased to say we've found the dress box that went missing.'

It took a moment for it to sink in. They'd actually found Ashleigh's original dress?

'That's fantastic,' Claire said. She glanced at her watch. Ashleigh's wedding wasn't until four o'clock. Which meant she had enough time to get the hydrofoil across to Sorrento and then a taxi to the airport to collect the dress, and she'd be back in time to get the dress ready while Ashleigh was having her hair and make-up done. Thankfully, she'd brought her portable steam presser with her in her luggage, so although the dress would be quite badly creased by now, she'd be able to fix it. 'Thank you very much. I'll be with you as soon as possible.'

'And if you could bring some identification with you, it would be helpful,' the airline assistant added.

'I'll bring my passport,' Claire said. Even before she'd said goodbye and ended the call, she was unlocking the safe in her wardrobe and taking her passport out.

When she went to tell Ashleigh the good news, Sean was there.

'It'd be quicker to get the dress couriered here,' he said.

'I've already lost the dress once. If you think I'm taking the risk of that happening again…' Claire shook her head. 'No chance.'

It also meant she had a bulletproof excuse to avoid Sean for the next few hours. Though that was slightly beside the point. She kissed Ashleigh's cheek. 'I'll text you when I've picked it up and I'm on my way back. But I'll be back well before it's time to have our hair and make-up done, I promise.'

Ashleigh hugged her back. 'I know. And thanks, Claire.'

'Hey. That's what best friends are for,' she said with a smile.

When Claire collected the dress, the box was in perfect condition, so she didn't have to worry that the contents had been damaged in any way. It didn't matter any more where the dress had been; the important thing was that she had it now, and Ashleigh would wear the dress of her dreams on her wedding day.

'Miss Stewart? Before you go,' the airline assistant said, 'I have a message for you. You have transport back to Capri. Would you mind coming this way?'

'Why?' Claire asked, mystified. She'd planned to get another taxi back to Sorrento, and then the hydrofoil across to Capri.

Before the airline assistant could answer, Claire's phone pinged with a message. 'Sorry, would you mind if I check this?' she asked, just in case it was Ashleigh.

To her surprise, the message was from Sean.

Transport arranged. Don't argue. Ashleigh worrying. Need to save time.

Sean had arranged transport for her? She swallowed hard. She knew Sean had done this for his sister's sake, not for hers, but it was still such a nice thing to do.

And the transport wasn't a taxi back to Sorrento. It was a helicopter. And the pilot told her that the flight from Naples to Capri took less time than the hydrofoil from Sorrento to Capri, so Sean had saved her the time of the taxi journey on top of that.

She texted back swiftly. Thank you. Tell her the dress is absolutely fine. Let me know how much I owe you for the transport. She knew Sean's opinion of her was already low and she was absolutely not going to let him think she was a freeloader, on top of whatever else he thought about her. She'd always paid her own way.

A text came back from him.

Will tell her. Transport on me.

Oh, no, it wasn't. Dress my responsibility, so *I* will pay. Not negotiable, she typed back pointedly. No way was she going to be in debt to Sean.

She'd half expected a taxi to meet her at the helipad, but Sean was in the reception area, waiting for her. He was wearing formal dark trousers and a white shirt— Claire didn't think he actually owned a pair of jeans— but for once he wasn't wearing a tie. His concession to casual dress, perhaps.

He looked gorgeous.

And he was totally off limits. She really needed to get a grip. Like *now*.

'What are you doing here?' she asked.

'Transport,' he said, gesturing to an open-topped sports car in the car park.

She didn't have much choice other than to accept. 'Thank you.' She looked at him. 'Is Ash OK?'

'She's fine,' he reassured her.

'Good.'

'And I owe you an apology.'

Claire frowned, surprised. Sean was apologising to her? 'For what?'

'Sniping at you last night—assuming that you'd given Ashleigh that crazy idea of getting married at the top of the mountain and going up by chairlift.'

'Given that I'm scared of heights,' she said dryly, 'I was quite happy to talk her out of that one on the grounds of dress practicalities.'

'But you went up on the chairlift last night.'

She shrugged. 'Luke and I wanted to distract her and we thought that would be a good way.'

'Yeah.'

She looked at him. He masked his feelings quickly, but she'd seen the flash of pain in his eyes. On impulse, she laid her hand on his arm. 'It must be hard for you, too.'

He nodded. 'It should be Dad walking down the aisle with her, not me.' His voice was husky with suppressed emotion. 'But things are as they are.'

'Your parents would be really proud of you,' she said.

'Excuse me?' His voice had turned icy.

She took her hand off his arm. 'OK. It's not my place to say anything and I wasn't trying to patronise you. But I thought a lot of your parents. Your mum in particular was brilliant when my mum died. And they would've been proud of the way you've always been there for Ash, always supported her—well, *almost* always,' she amended. To be fair, he'd been pretty annoyed about Ashleigh's change of planned career. He hadn't supported it at first.

'She's my little sister. What else would I do?'

It was a revelation to Claire. Sean clearly equated duty with love, or mixed them to the point where they couldn't be distinguished. And discussing this was way beyond her pay grade. She changed the subject again. 'So how much do I owe you for the flight?'

'You don't.'

'I've already told you, the dress is my responsibility, so I'll pay the costs. But thank you for organising it, especially as it means Ash isn't worrying any more.'

'We'll discuss it later,' he said. 'Ashleigh comes first.'

'Agreed—but that doesn't mean I'm happy to be in your debt,' she pointed out.

'I did this for Ashleigh, not for you.'

'Well, *duh*.' She caught herself before she said something really inflammatory. 'Sean, I know we don't usually get on too well.' That was the understatement of the year. 'But I think we're going to have to make the effort and play nice while we're on Capri.'

He slanted her a look that said very clearly that he didn't believe she could keep it up.

If she was honest, she wasn't sure she could keep it up, either. Or that Sean could, for that matter. But they were at least going to make the effort. Though they had a cast-iron excuse not to talk to each other for the next few minutes, because he needed to concentrate on driving.

She put the dress box safely in the back of the car, took her sunhat from her bag and jammed it on her head so it wouldn't be blown away, then sat in the front seat next to Sean. She still had her dark glasses on from the helicopter flight, so the glare of the sun didn't bother her.

Sean was a very capable driver, she noticed, even though he was driving on the right-hand side of the road instead of the left as he was used to doing in England. The road was incredibly narrow and winding, with no verges and high stone walls at the edges; it was busy with vans and scooters and minibuses, and every so often he had to pull over into the tiniest of passing places. If Claire had been driving, she would've been panicking that the car would end up being scraped on one of those stone walls; but she knew that she was very safe with Sean. It was an odd feeling, having to rely on someone she normally tried to avoid. And even odder that for once she didn't mind.

'Is there anything you need for the dress?' he asked as they pulled up outside the hotel.

'Only my portable steam presser, which I brought with me on my first trip.'

He looked confused. 'Why do you need a steam presser?'

'This dress has been in a box for three days. Even though I was careful when I packed it, there are still going to be creases in the material, and I don't have time to hang the dress in a steamy bathroom and wait for the creases to fall out naturally. And an ordinary iron isn't good enough to give a professional finish.'

'OK. Let me know if you need anything organised.'

He probably needed some reassurance that it wasn't going to go wrong, she thought. 'You can come and have a sneak peek at the dress, if you want,' she said.

'Isn't that meant to be bad luck?'

'Only if you're the bridegroom. Remember that the

dress needs pressing, so you won't be seeing it at its best,' she warned, 'but it will be perfect by the time Ash puts it on.'

Sean looked at Claire. Her sunhat was absolutely horrible, a khaki-coloured cap with a peak to shade her eyes; but he supposed it was more sensible than going out bareheaded in the strong mid-morning sun and risking sunstroke.

He wondered if she'd guessed that he wanted reassurance that nothing else was going to go wrong with the dress—just as she'd clearly noticed that moment when the might-have-beens had shaken his composure. She'd been a bit clumsy about it, but she hadn't pushed him to talk and share his feelings. She'd been kind, he realised now, and that wasn't something he associated with Claire Stewart. It made him feel weird.

But, if she could make the effort, then so could he. 'Thanks. I would appreciate that.'

'Let's go, then,' she said.

He followed her up to her room. Everywhere was neat and tidy. Funny, he'd expected the room to be as messy and chaotic as Claire's life seemed to be—even though her shop had been tidy. But then he supposed the shop would have to be tidy or it would put off potential clients.

She put the dress box on the bed. 'Right—how much do I owe you for that flight?'

'We've already discussed that,' he said, feeling awkward.

'No, we haven't, and I don't want to be beholden to you.'

'Ashleigh is my sister,' he reminded her.

'I know, and she's my best friend—but I still don't want to be beholden to you.'

He frowned. 'Now you're being stubborn.'

'Pots and kettles,' she said softly. 'Tell me how much I owe you.'

Actually, he liked the fact that she was so insistent on paying her fair share. It showed she had integrity. Maybe he'd been wrong to tar her with the same brush as her awful boyfriends. Just because she had a dreadful taste in men, it didn't necessarily mean that she was as selfish as they were—did it? 'OK.' He told her a sum that was roughly half, guessing that she'd have no idea how much helicopter transfers would cost.

'Fine. Obviously I don't have the cash on me right at this very second,' she said, 'but I can either do a bank transfer if you give me your account details, or give you the cash in person when we're back in England.'

'No rush. I'll give you my bank details, but making the transfer when you get back to England will be fine,' he said.

'Good. Thank you.' She opened the box, unpacked the dress, and put it on a hanger.

The organza skirt was creased but Sean could already see how stunning the ivory dress was. It had a strapless sweetheart neckline, the bodice was made of what he suspected might be handmade lace, and it looked as if hundreds of tiny pearls had been sewn into it. It was worthy of something produced by any of the big-name designers.

And Claire had designed this for his little sister. She'd made it all by hand.

Now he understood why she'd called her business that ridiculous name, because she was delivering exactly what her client wanted—a dream of a dress.

Clearly his lack of response rattled her, because she folded her arms. 'If you hate it, fine—but remember that this is what Ash wanted. And I'm giving you fair warning, if you tell Ash you hate it before she puts it on, so she feels like the ugliest bride in the world instead of like a princess, then you're so getting the rusty spoon treatment.'

'I don't hate it, actually. I'm just a bit stunned, because I wasn't expecting it to be that good,' he admitted.

She dropped into a sarcastic curtsey. 'Why, thank you, kind sir, for the backhanded compliment.'

'I didn't mean it quite like that,' he said. 'I don't know much about dresses, but that looks as if it involved a lot of work.'

'It did. But she's worth every second.'

'Yeah.' For a moment, he almost turned to her and hugged her.

But this was Claire 'Follow Your Heart' Stewart, the mistress of chaos. Their worlds didn't mix. A hug would be a bad, bad idea. 'Thanks for letting me see the dress,' he said. 'I'd better let you get on.'

'Tell Ash her dress is here safely, and I'll come and find her the second it's ready.'

He nodded. 'Will do.'

Once Claire was satisfied with the dress, she took it through to Ashleigh's room. Sammy opened the door. 'Claire-bear! About time, too,' she said with a grin. 'Losing the dress. Tsk. What kind of dressmaker does that?'

'Don't be mean, Sammy,' Ashleigh called. 'I'd cuff her for you, Claire, but I have to sit still and let Aliona take these rollers out of my hair.'

Claire hung up the dress, then enveloped Sammy with a hug. 'Hello to you, too. How was your flight?'

'Disgusting,' Sammy said cheerfully, 'but when I've finished taking photographs tonight then I'm going to drink Prosecco until I don't care any more.'

'Hangover on top of jet lag. Nice,' Claire teased. 'It's so good to see you, Sammy.'

'You, too. And oh, my God. How amazing is that dress? You've really surpassed yourself this time, Claire.'

Claire smiled in acknowledgement. 'I'm just glad we got it back.'

The hotel's hairdresser and make-up artist cooed over the dress, too, and then Claire submitted to being prettied up before putting on her own dress and then helping Ashleigh with hers.

Sammy posed them both for photographs on the balcony. 'Righty. I need to do the boys, now,' she said when she'd finished. 'See you at the town hall.'

'OK?' Claire asked when Sammy had gone.

Ashleigh gulped. 'Yes. Just thinking.'

'I know.' It would be similar for Claire, if she ever got married: she'd be missing her mum, though her dad would be there—*if* he approved of Claire's choice of man—and her mum's family would be there, with Ashleigh and Sammy to support her.

Not that Claire thought she'd ever get married. All the men she'd ever been involved with had turned out to be Mr Wrong. Men she'd thought would share her dreams, but who just couldn't commit. Men who'd been so casual with her emotions that she'd lost trust in her judgement.

'But I think they're here in spirit,' Claire said softly.

'They loved you so much, Ash. And Luke can't wait to make you his bride. You've got a good guy, there.'

'I know. I'm lucky.' Ashleigh swallowed hard.

'Hey. If you cry and your make-up runs, Sean will have my guts for garters,' Claire said. She went into a dramatic pose. 'Help! Help! Save me from your scary big brother!'

To her relief, it worked, and Ashleigh laughed; she was still smiling when Sean knocked on her door to say they needed to go.

CHAPTER FOUR

SEAN HAD ALREADY seen the dress—albeit not at its best—but seeing his little sister wearing it just blew him away. The ivory dress emphasised Ashleigh's perfect hour-glass shape by skimming in at the waist, then falling to the floor in soft folds. Her dark hair was drawn back from her face and pinned at the back as a base for her veil, and then flowed down in soft curls. She wore a discreet and very pretty tiara with sparkling stones and pearls to reflect the pearls in the bodice. And finally she was carrying a simple posy of dusky lavender roses, the same colour as Claire's dress; the stems were tightly bound with ivory ribbon.

'You look amazing, Ashleigh,' he said. 'Really amazing.'

Then he glanced at Claire. Again, he was shocked. He hadn't seen the bridesmaid's dress before, though he'd had a fair idea that it would be dusky lavender, the same colour as his waistcoat and the rose in his buttonhole. Although it, too, was strapless and had a sweetheart neckline, it was much plainer than Ashleigh's dress and ended at the knee. Claire's hair was dressed in a similar style to his sister's, though without a veil and with a discreet jewelled headband rather than a tiara. Her roses were ivory rather than lavender, as a counterpoint to the bride's bouquet, and her satin high heels were dyed to match her dress.

If he'd seen her across a crowded room as a complete stranger, he would've been drawn to her immediately. Approached her. Asked her out.

He pushed the thought away. This was Claire. He *did* know her. And, if they hadn't made a truce for Ashleigh's sake, they would've been sniping at each other within the next five minutes. She was absolutely not date material.

'Ready?' he asked.

'Ready,' they chorused.

The official civil ceremony was held at the town hall in Anacapri. Only the main people from the wedding party were there: Ashleigh and Luke, with Luke's best friend, Tom, as the best man, Claire as the bridesmaid and one of the witnesses, and himself as the other witness. Sammy was there, too, to take photographs.

After everything had been signed, the two open-topped cars took them to the private villa where the symbolic ceremony was being held and the rest of their family and friends were waiting to celebrate with them.

Luke and Tom went ahead to wait at the bridal arch, which was covered with gorgeous white flowers.

Then Ashleigh stood at the edge of the red carpet, her arm linked through Sean's. He could feel her trembling slightly. Nervous, excited and a little sad all at the same time, he guessed. 'Ashleigh, you're such a beautiful bride,' he said softly. 'Our parents would be so proud of you right now.'

Ashleigh nodded, clearly too overcome to speak, and squeezed his arm as if to say, 'You, too.'

'Come on. Let's get the party started,' he said, and

gave the signal to the traditional Neapolitan guitar and mandolin duo.

Their version of Pachelbel's 'Canon' was perfect. And Sean was smiling as he walked his little sister down the aisle to marry the man she loved.

Claire had seen the photographs and knew that the garden where Ashleigh and Luke were getting married was spectacular, but the photographs really hadn't done the place justice. The garden was breathtaking, overlooking the sea; lemon trees grew around the edge of the garden, their boughs heavy with fruit, and the deep borders were filled with rhododendrons and bougainvillea. There seemed to be butterflies everywhere. A symbol of good luck and eternal love, she thought.

She took the bouquet from Ashleigh and held it safely during the ceremony, and she had to blink back the tears as Ashleigh and Luke exchanged their vows, this time in front of everyone. She glanced at Sean, who was standing beside her, and was pleased to see that for once he was misty-eyed, too. And so he should be, on Ashleigh's wedding day, she thought, and she looked away before he caught her staring at him.

Everyone cheered when the celebrant said, 'You may now kiss the bride,' and Luke bent Ashleigh back over his arm to give her a show-stopping kiss.

'Let them have it, guys,' Sammy called as Ashleigh and Luke started to walk back down the aisle, and the confetti made from white dried flower petals flew everywhere.

Once the formal photographs had been taken, waiters came round carrying trays filled with glasses of Prosecco. Ashleigh and Luke headed the line-up to welcome their guests; and then, finally, it was time for the meal. Ashleigh had chosen a semi-traditional top table layout, so Claire as the chief bridesmaid was at one end, next to Luke's father. As Sean was standing in for the bride's father, he was at the other end, between Ashleigh and Luke's mother. And there were enough people between them, Claire thought, for them to be able to smile and hide their relief at not having to make small talk.

It was an amazing table, under a pergola draped with white wisteria. Woven in between the flowers were glass baubles, which caught the light from the tea-light candles set in similar glass globes on the table, and reflected again in the mirrored finish of the table. The sun was already beginning to set, and Claire had never seen anything so romantic in her life. And the whole thing was topped off by the traditional Neapolitan guitar and mandolin duo who played and sang softly during the meal.

If she ever got married, Claire thought, this was just the kind of wedding she'd want, full of love and happiness and so much warmth.

Finally, after the excellent coffee and tiny rich Italian desserts, it was time for the speeches. Luke's was sweet and heartfelt, Tom's made everyone laugh, but Sean's made her blink back the tears.

He really did love Ashleigh. And, for that, Claire could forgive the rest.

The cake—a spectacular four-tier confection, which Claire knew held four different flavours of sponge— was cut, and then it was time for the dancing.

Ashleigh and Luke had chosen a song for their bridal dance that always put a lump in her throat—'Make You Feel My Love'—and she watched them glide across the temporary dance floor. The evening band played it in waltz time, and Claire knew that Luke had been taking private lessons; he was step-perfect as he whirled Ashleigh round in the turns. The perfect couple.

Tradition said that the best man and the chief bridesmaid danced together next, and Claire liked Tom very much indeed; she was pleased to discover that he was an excellent dancer and her toes were perfectly safe with him.

'I love the dresses,' Tom said. 'If I wasn't gay, I'd *so* date you—a woman who can create such utter beauty. You're amazing, Claire.'

She laughed and kissed his cheek. 'Aww, you're such a sweetie, Tom. Thank you. But I wouldn't date you because I have terrible taste in men—and you're far too nice to be one of *my* men.'

He laughed. 'Thank *you*, sweetie. You'll find the right guy some day.'

'If I could find someone who'd make me as happy as Luke makes Ash,' she said softly, 'I'd consider myself blessed.'

'Me, too,' Tom said. 'And the other way round. They're perfect for each other.'

'They certainly are,' she said with a smile, though at the same time there was a nagging ache in her heart. Would she ever find someone who'd make her happy, or was she always destined to date Mr Wrong?

Sean knew it was his duty—as the man who'd given the bride away—to dance with the chief bridesmaid at some point. For a second, he stood watching Claire as she danced with Luke's father. She was chatting away, looking totally at ease. And then Sean registered what the band was playing: 'Can't Take My Eyes Off You'. He was shocked to realise that it was true: he couldn't take his eyes off Claire.

Which was absolutely not a good thing.

Claire Stewart was the last woman he wanted to get involved with.

And yet he had to acknowledge that he was drawn to her. There was something about her. He couldn't pin it down, which annoyed him even more—he couldn't put his feelings in a pigeonhole, the way he usually did. And that made her dangerous. He needed to stay well away from her.

Though, for tonight, he had to do the expected thing and make the best of it.

As the song came to an end, he walked over. 'I guess we need to play nice for Ashleigh.'

'I guess,' she said.

Even as the words came out of his mouth, he knew he was saying the wrong thing, but he couldn't stop himself asking, 'So is one of your awful boyfriends joining you later?'

'If that's your idea of nice,' Claire said, widening her eyes in what looked like annoyance, 'I'd hate to see how caustic your idea of snippy would be.'

He grimaced, knowing that he was in the wrong this time. 'Sorry. I shouldn't have put it quite like that.'

'Not if you were being nice. Though,' she said, 'I do admit that I have a terrible taste in men. I always seem to pick Mr Wrong.' She shrugged. 'And the answer's no, nobody's joining me. I'm happily single right now. And I'm way too busy at work right now to get involved with someone.'

Was that her way of telling him she wasn't interested? Or was she just giving him the facts?

Her perfume wasn't one he recognised; it was something mysterious and deep. Maybe that was what was scrambling his brain, rather than her nearness. Scrambling his brain enough to make him think that she was the perfect fit. The way she felt, in his arms…

'So isn't one of your sweet-but-temporary girlfriends joining you later?' Claire asked.

Ouch. Though Sean knew he deserved the question. He'd started it. 'No. Becca and I broke up three months ago. And I'm busy at work.' Which was his usual excuse for ending a relationship before things started to get too close.

'Two peas in a pod, then, us,' she said with a grin.

'I always thought we were chalk and cheese.'

She laughed. 'I was going to say oil and vinegar. Except they actually go together.'

'And we don't,' Sean said. 'So would you be the vinegar or the oil?'

'Difficult to say. A bit of both, really,' she said. 'I make things go smoothly for my clients. But I'm sharp with people who have an attitude problem. You?'

'Ditto,' he said.

This was *weird*.

They were actually laughing at themselves. Together. Not sniping at each other.

And this felt sparky. Fun. He was actually enjoying Claire's company—something that he'd never thought would happen in a million years.

This was the second song in a row they were dancing to. The music was slower. Softer. And, although he knew it was a seriously bad idea, he found himself drawing Claire closer. Swaying with her.

Oh, help, Claire thought. She'd been here before. Today, she'd paced herself and only drunk a couple of small glasses of Prosecco, well spaced out with sparkling water. But she could still remember the first night she'd kissed Sean Farrell. The way his mouth had felt against hers before he'd pulled away and given her a total dressing-down about being seventeen years old and in a state where an unscrupulous man could've taken advantage of her.

And again, at Ashleigh and Luke's engagement party, where they'd ended up dancing way too close and then Sean had kissed her, his mouth warm and sweet and so tempting that it terrified her.

Right now, it would be all too easy to let her hands drift up over his shoulders, curl round the nape of his neck, and draw his mouth down to hers. Particularly as they were no longer on the dance floor, in full view of the rest of the guests; at some point, while they'd been dancing together, they'd moved away from the temporary dance floor. Now they were in a secluded area of the garden. Just the two of them in the twilight.

'Claire.' His voice was a whisper.

And she knew he was going to kiss her again.

He dipped his head and brushed his mouth against hers, very lightly. It felt as if every nerve-end had been galvanised. He did it again. And again. This time, Claire gave in and slid her hands into his hair. His arms tightened round her and he continued teasing her mouth with those light, barely there kisses that made her want more. Maybe she made some needy little sound, because then he was really kissing her, and it felt as if fireworks were exploding all around them.

When he broke the kiss, she was shaking.

'Claire.' He sounded dazed.

That made two of them.

Part of her wanted to do this. To go with him—her room or his, it wouldn't matter. She knew they both needed a release from the tension of the last few days.

But the sensible part of her knew that doing that would make everything so much worse. How would they face each other in the morning? They certainly didn't have a future. Yes, Sean was reliable, unlike most of her past boyfriends—but he was also too regimented for her liking. Everything had to go within his twenty-year plan. Which was fine for a business, but it wasn't the way she wanted to live her personal life. She wanted to take time to smell the roses. Spontaneity. A chance to seize the day and enjoy whatever came her way. Live life to the full.

'We need to stop,' she said. While she could still be sensible. If he kissed her once more, she knew she'd say yes. So she'd say the word while she could still actually pronounce it. 'No.'

'No.' He looked at her, his eyes haunted. For a second, he looked so vulnerable. She was about to crack and place her palm against his cheek to comfort him, to tell him that she'd changed her mind, when she saw his expression change. His common sense had snapped back into place. 'You're absolutely right,' he said, and took a step back from her.

'I have bridesmaid stuff to do,' she said. It wasn't strictly true—the rest of the evening was all organised—but it was an excuse that she thought would save face for both of them.

'Of course,' he said, and let her go.

Even as she walked away, Claire regretted it. Her old attraction to Sean had never quite gone away, no matter how deeply she thought she'd buried it or how much she denied it to herself.

But she knew it had been the right thing to do. Because no way could things work out between her and Sean, and she'd had enough of broken relationships and being let down. Keeping things platonic was sensible, and the best way to avoid heartbreak.

Claire spent the rest of the evening socialising with the other guests, encouraging the younger ones to dance. All the time, she was very aware of exactly where Sean was in the garden, but she didn't trust herself not to make another stupid mistake. She'd got it wrong with him in the past. She couldn't afford to get it wrong in the future.

Finally, she went back to the hotel with the last few guests, kicked off her high heels, and curled up in one of the wrought iron chairs on the balcony of her room, looking out at the moon's sparkling path on the sea. She'd been sitting there for a while when there was a knock at her door.

She wasn't expecting anyone, especially this late at night—unless maybe someone had been taken ill and needed help?

She padded over to the door, still in bare feet, and blinked in surprise when she saw Sean in the doorway. 'Is something wrong?'

'Yes,' he said.

She went cold. 'Ash?'

'No.'

Then she saw that he'd removed his jacket and cravat. He looked very slightly dishevelled, and it made him much more approachable. And much, much harder to resist.

He was also carrying a bottle of Prosecco and two glasses.

'Sean?' she asked, completely confused.

'I think we need to talk,' he said.

Again, for a split second, she glimpsed that vulnerability in his eyes. How could she turn him away when she had a good idea of how he was feeling—the same way she was feeling herself? 'Come in,' she said, and closed the door behind him.

'I saw you sitting on your balcony,' he said.

She nodded. 'I was a bit too wired to sleep, so I thought I'd look out over the sea and just chill for a bit.'

'Good plan.' He gestured to her balcony. 'Shall we?'

Sean, the sea and moonlight. A dangerous combination. It would be much more sensible to say no.

'Yes,' she said.

He uncorked the bottle with a minimum of fuss and without spilling a drop of the sparkling wine, then poured them both a glass.

Claire held hers up in a toast. 'To Ashleigh and Luke,' she said, 'and may they have every happiness in their life together.'

'Absolutely,' he said, clinking his glass against hers. 'To Ashleigh and Luke.'

'So you're too wired to sleep, too?' she asked.

He nodded. 'I was walking in the hotel gardens. That's when I saw you sitting on the balcony.'

'So why do we need to talk, Sean?'

He blew out a breath. 'You and me.'

The idea sent a shiver of pure desire through her.

'I think it's been a long time coming,' he said softly.

'But we don't even like each other. You think I'm a flake, and I think you're…well…a bit *too* organised,' she said, choosing her words carefully.

'Maybe,' he said, 'because it's easier for us to think that of each other.'

She took a sip of Prosecco, knowing that he was right but not quite wanting to admit it. 'You turned me down.'

'Nearly ten years ago? You know why,' he said. 'I think we've both grown up and got past that.'

'I guess.' She turned her glass round. 'Though I'm not in a hurry to put myself back in that situation.'

'You won't be,' he said softly. 'Because you're not seventeen any more, you're not drunk, and I'm not responsible for you.'

The three barriers that had been in the way, back then. It had hurt and embarrassed her at the time, but later Claire had appreciated how decent he'd been. Not that they'd ever discussed it. It was way too awkward for both of them.

But, now he'd said it, she needed to know. 'Back then, if I hadn't been drunk, if I'd been eighteen, and if you hadn't been responsible for me—would you have…?'

'Let you seduce me?' he asked.

She nodded.

His breath shuddered through him. 'Yes.'

Heat curled in her belly. That night, she'd wanted him so desperately. And, if the circumstances had been different, he would have made love with her. Been her first lover.

All the words were knocked out of her head. Because all she could think about was the way he'd kissed her tonight in the garden, and the way he looked right now. Sexy as hell.

'Ashleigh's engagement,' he said softly. '*You* turned *me* down, that time.'

'Because I was being sensible.' She paused. 'This isn't sensible, either.'

'I know. But your perfume's haunted me all evening,' he said, his voice low and husky and drenched in desire. 'Your mouth. And you've been driving me crazy in that dress.'

She made a last-ditch attempt at keeping the status quo. 'This is a perfectly demure bridesmaid's dress,' she said. 'It's down to my knees.'

'And I can't stop thinking about what you might be wearing under it.'

Her breath hitched. 'Can't you, now?'

The same heat that curled in her belly was reflected in his eyes. 'Going to show me?' he invited.

'We're on my balcony. Anyone could see us. *You* saw me,' she pointed out.

'Then maybe,' he said, 'we should go inside. Draw the curtains.'

She knew without a shadow of a doubt what was going to happen if they did.

There would be repercussions. Huge ones.

But the old desire had lanced sharply through her, to the point where she didn't care about the repercussions any more. 'Yes.'

Without a word, he stood up and scooped her out of her chair. Carried her into the room and set her down on her feet. He turned away just long enough to close the curtains, then pulled her into his arms and kissed her

That first kiss in the garden had been tentative, sweet. This was like lighting touchpaper, setting her on fire. By the time he broke the kiss, they were both shaking.

'Show me,' he said softly.

She reached behind her back to the zip and slid it down; then she held the dress to her.

He raised an eyebrow. 'Shy?'

She shook her head. 'I'm waiting for you to get rid of your waistcoat and undo your shirt.'

He looked puzzled, and she explained, 'Because, if we're going to do this, it's going to be equal. Both of us. All the way.'

'All the way,' Sean repeated huskily. He removed his waistcoat, then undid his shirt and pulled it out of the waistband of his trousers. 'Better?'

'Much better. It makes you look touchable,' she said.

'Good—because I want you to touch me, Claire. And I want to touch you.' He gestured to her dress. 'Show me.'

She felt ridiculously shy and almost chickened out; but then took a deep breath and stepped out of the dress before hanging it on the back of a chair.

'Now that I wasn't expecting—underwear to match your dress.' He closed the gap between them and traced the outline of her strapless lacy bra with the tip of his finger.

'I had it dyed at the same time as my shoes,' she said.

'Attention to detail—I like that,' he said approvingly.

She slid her palms against his pectoral muscles. 'Very nice,' she said, and let her hands slide down to his abdomen. 'A perfect six pack. I wasn't expecting that.'

'I don't spend the whole day in a chair. The gym gives me time to think about things,' he said.

'Good plan.' She slipped the soft cotton from his shoulders.

'So now I'm naked to the waist, and you're not. You said we were in this together, Claire.'

'Then do something about it,' she invited.

Sean smiled, unclipped her bra and let the lacy garment fall to the floor. Then scooped her up, carried her to the bed, and Claire stopped thinking.

CHAPTER FIVE

CLAIRE'S MOBILE SHRILLED. Still with her eyes closed, she groped for the phone on the bedside table. 'Hello?'

'C'mon, sleepyhead! You went to bed before I did—you can't *still* be snoozing,' Sammy said cheerfully. 'There's a pile of warm pastries and a bowl of freshly picked, juicy Italian peaches down here with our name on them. And the best coffee ever.'

Breakfast.

Claire had arranged to meet Sammy for breakfast.

And right now she was still in bed. *With Sean.* Whose arms were still wrapped round her, keeping her close.

'Uh—I'll be down as soon as I can,' Claire said hastily. 'If you're hungry, start without me.'

'Don't blame me if the pastries are all gone by the time you get here. See you soon,' Sammy said, her voice full of laughter.

'Who was that?' Sean asked when Claire put the phone down.

'Sammy. We arranged to have breakfast together this morning.' Claire dragged in a breath. 'Except…Sean, I…' She frowned. 'And now I'm being incoherent and stupid, and that isn't me.'

'Lack of sleep,' he said, nuzzling her shoulder. 'Which is as much my fault as yours.'

Oh, help. When he was being sweet and warm like this, it made her want what she knew she couldn't have. And she really had to be sensible about this. 'Sean—we really can't do this,' she blurted out.

'Do what?'

'Be together. Or let anyone know about what happened last night.' She twisted round to face him. 'You and me—you know it would never work out between us in a month of Sundays. We're too different. You have a twenty-year plan for everything, and I hate being boxed in like that. We'd drive each other bananas.'

'So, what? We're going to pretend last night didn't happen?' he asked.

'That'd probably be the best thing,' she said. 'Because then it won't be awkward when Ash asks us both over to see the wedding photos and what have you.'

'Uh-huh.' His face was expressionless.

And now she felt horrible. Last night had been a revelation about just how much attention Sean paid to things and how good he'd made her feel. And it had been better between them than she'd ever dreamed it would be as a starry-eyed teenager. If only they weren't so different, she'd be tempted to start a proper relationship with him. Seriously tempted. But she knew it wasn't going to work out between them, and she didn't want her oldest friendship to become collateral damage of a fling that didn't last. She swallowed hard. 'Last night… You made it good for me. Really good.'

'Dear John—it's not you, it's me,' he intoned, raising an eyebrow.

'It's both of us, and you know it,' she said. 'You hate the fact that I follow my heart. I know what you call me, Sean.' Just as she was pretty sure that he knew what she called him.

He shrugged. 'I guess you're right.'

So why did it make her feel so bad—so *guilty*? 'I'm not dumping you, and you're not dumping me, because we were never really together in the first place,' she said. 'We'd be a disaster as a couple.'

'Probably,' he agreed.

'Sammy's waiting for me downstairs. I don't get to see her that much, with her job taking her away so much. I promised her I'd be there. I really have to go,' Claire said, feeling even more awkward. She wanted to stay. She wanted to pretend that she and Sean were two completely different people and that it would have a chance of working out between them.

But she had to face the facts. Tomorrow they'd both be back in London. And no way could things work between them there. Their lives were too opposite, and they just wouldn't fit.

'I know I'm being rude and bratty and everything else, but would you mind, um, please closing your eyes while I grab some clothes and have the quickest shower in the world?' she asked.

'It's a little late for shyness,' he said dryly, 'given that we saw every millimetre of each other last night.'

Not just saw, either. The memory made her face hot. They'd touched. Stroked. Kissed.

'Even so,' she said.

'As you wish.' He rolled over and closed his eyes. 'Let me know when it's safe to look.'

'I'm sorry. I really wish things could be different,' she said, meaning it. 'But this is the best way. A clean break.'

'Apart from the fact that my little sister is your best friend, and we'll still have to see each other in the future.'

'And we'll do exactly the same as we've done for years and years,' she said. 'We'll be polite to each other for her sake, and avoid each other as much as we can.'

'Uh-huh.'

'Like you said, last night—well, it's been a long time coming. And now we've done it and it's out of our systems.' Which was a big, fat lie, so it was just as well that he couldn't see her face. She had a nasty feeling that Sean Farrell would never be completely out of her system. Especially now she knew what it was like to kiss him properly. To touch him. To make love with him.

She shook herself and grabbed some clothes. 'It's OK to look,' she said as she closed the bathroom door.

She showered and dressed in record time. When she walked back into the bedroom, Sean was already dressed and sitting on the bed, waiting for her. Well, he would. He had impeccable manners. 'Thank you,' she said. 'Um—I guess I'll see you in London when Ash gets back. And I'll sort out the money I owe you for that helicopter flight.'

Downstairs, Sammy was pouring a cup of coffee from a cafetière when Claire walked over to her table. 'So who was he?' she asked.

'Who was what?' Claire asked.

'The guy who kept you awake last night and gave you that hickey on the left-hand side of your neck.'

Claire clapped a hand to her neck and stared at her friend in utter dismay. She hadn't noticed a hickey while she was in the bathroom—well, not that she'd paid much attention to the mirror, because she'd been too busy panicking about the fact that Sean Farrell was naked and in her bed, and she'd just messed things up again.

And he'd given her a hickey?

Oh, no. She hadn't had a hickey since she was thirteen, and her dad had been so mad at her that she'd never repeated that particular mistake. Until now.

When Claire continued to be silent, Sammy laughed. 'Gotcha. There's no hickey. But clearly I wasn't far wrong and there *was* a guy last night.'

'You don't want to know,' Claire said.

'I wouldn't be fishing if I didn't,' Sammy pointed out.

'It was a one off. And I feel suitably ashamed, OK? I said I wouldn't date any more Mr Wrongs.'

'Forgive me for saying, but you didn't have a date for Ash's wedding,' Sammy said. 'So I think he doesn't count as one of your Mr Wrongs.'

'Oh, he does. You couldn't get more wrong for me than him,' Claire said feelingly. More was the pity.

'Was the sex good?'

'Sammy!' Claire felt the colour hit her face like a tidal wave.

Her friend was totally unrepentant. 'Out of ten?'

Claire groaned. 'I need coffee.'

'Answer the question, Claire-bear.'

'Eleven,' Claire muttered, and helped herself to coffee, sugaring it liberally.

'Then maybe,' Sammy said, 'he might be worth working on. Sort out whatever makes him Mr Wrong.'

'That'd be several lifetimes' work,' Claire said wryly.

'Your call. Pastries or peaches?'

Claire couldn't help smiling. Only Sammy would ask something so outrageous followed by something so practical and mundane. 'I thought you'd already scoffed all the pastries? But if there are any left I'll have both,' she said.

'Attagirl.' Sammy winked at her. 'And I hope you

don't have a hangover. Because we're taking that boat out to the Blue Grotto this afternoon before we catch our flights—I've got a commission.'

'Do you ever stop working?' Claire asked.

'About as much as you do,' Sammy said with a grin. 'Anyway, mixing work and play means you get to fit twice as much into your day—and you enjoy it more.'

'True.'

'Pity about Mr Wrong.'

Yeah.

And Claire really wasn't looking forward to facing Sean, the next time they met. Somehow, before then she needed to get her emotions completely under control.

Claire enjoyed her trip to the Blue Grotto, and the colours and textures gave her several ideas for future dress designs; but on the plane home she found herself thinking about Sean. He'd been a very focused lover, very considerate. She still felt guilty about the way she'd called a halt to it, but she knew she'd done the right thing. Sean planned things out to the extreme, and she preferred to follow her heart, so they'd never be able to agree on anything.

Back at her flat, she unpacked and put the laundry on, checked her mail and her messages, and made notes for what she needed to do in the morning. Though she still couldn't get Sean out of her head. When she finally fell asleep, she had the most graphic dream about him—one that left her hot and very bothered when her alarm went off on the Monday morning.

'Don't be so ridiculous. Sean Farrell is completely off limits,' she told herself firmly, and went for her usual pre-breakfast run. Maybe that would get her common sense back in working order. But even then she couldn't stop thinking about Sean. How he'd made her feel. How she wanted to do what they'd done all over again.

After her shower, she opened her laptop and logged in to her bank account so she could transfer the money she owed Sean for the flight into his account. And, once that was done, she knew she wouldn't need any contact with him until Ashleigh and Luke were back from honeymoon. By which time, her common sense would be back.

She hoped.

She went down to open the shop, then headed for her workroom at the back to start work on the next dress she needed to make for the wedding show. She'd just finished cutting it out when the old-fashioned bell on her door jangled to signal that someone was coming through the front door.

She came out from the workroom to see a delivery man carrying an enormous bunch of flowers. 'Miss Stewart?' he asked.

'Um, yes.'

'For you.' He smiled and handed her the flowers. 'Enjoy.'

'Thank you.'

It wasn't her birthday and she wasn't expecting any flowers. Or maybe they were from Ashleigh and Luke to say thanks for her help with the wedding. She absolutely loved dusky pink roses; the bouquet was stuffed with them, teamed with sweet-smelling cream freesias and clouds of fluffy gypsophila. She'd never seen such a gorgeous bouquet.

She opened the envelope that came with it and felt her eyes widen with shock; she recognised the strong, precise handwriting immediately, because she'd seen it on cards and notes at Ashleigh's flat over the years.

Saw these and thought of you. Sean.

He'd sent her flowers.

Not just any old flowers—glorious flowers.

And he hadn't just asked his PA to do it, either. The handwriting was his, so he'd clearly gone to the florist in person, and maybe even chosen the flowers himself.

Sean Farrell had sent her flowers.

Claire couldn't quite get her head round that.

Why would he send her flowers?

She didn't quite dare ring him to ask him. So, once she'd put them in water, she took the coward's way out and texted him.

Thank you for the flowers. They're gorgeous.

He took his time replying, but eventually the text came through. Glad you like them.

Where was he going with this?

Before she could work out a way to ask without sounding offensive, her phone beeped again to signal the arrival of another text.

Thank you for the flight money. Bank just notified me. Do you have an appointment over lunch?

Why? No, that sounded grudging and suspicious. She deleted the message and started again. No worries, and no, she typed back.

You do now. See you at your shop at one.

What? Was he suggesting a lunch date? Dating her? But—but—they'd agreed that the thing between them would be a disaster if they let it go any further.

Sean, we can't.

But he didn't reply. And she was left in a flat spin.

By the time the bell on the front door jangled and she went through to the shop to see Sean standing there— and he'd turned her sign on the door to 'closed', she no-ticed—she was wound up to fever pitch.

'What's this about, Sean?' she asked.

'I thought we could have lunch together.'

'But…' Her voice faded. They'd already agreed that this was a bad idea—hadn't they?

'I know,' he said softly, and walked over towards her.

He was dressed in another of his formal well-cut suits, with his shoes perfectly shined and his silk tie perfectly knotted; he was a million miles away from the sensual, dishevelled man who'd spent the night in her bed in Capri. And yet he was every bit as delec-table. Even though he wasn't even touching her, being this close to him made all her senses go on red alert.

'I can't get you out of my head,' he said.

Well, if he could be brave enough to admit it, so could she. She swallowed hard. 'Me, neither,' she said.

'So what do we do about this, Claire?' he asked. 'Be-cause I have a feeling this isn't going away any time soon.'

'That night in Capri was supposed to—well—get it out of our systems,' she reminded him.

'And it didn't work,' he said. 'Not for me.'

His admission warmed her and terrified her at the same time.

'Claire?' he asked softly.

He deserved honesty. 'Me, neither.'

He leaned forward and brushed his lips against hers, ever so gently. And every nerve end on her mouth sizzled.

He tempted her. Oh, so much. But it all came back to collateral damage.

'We have to be sensible,' she said. 'And why am I the one saying this, not you? You're the one with—'

'—the twenty-year plan,' he finished. 'For the record, it's five years. Not twenty.'

'Even so. You have your whole life planned out.'

'There's nothing wrong with being responsible and organised,' he said.

'There's nothing wrong with being spontaneous, either,' she retorted.

He smiled. 'Not if it's like Saturday night, no.'

Oh, why had he had to bring that up again? Now her temperature was spiking. Seriously spiking. 'We're too different,' she said. 'You're my best friend's brother.'

'And?'

'There's a huge risk of collateral damage. I can't take that risk.' The risk of losing Ashleigh. Claire had already lost too much in her life. She wasn't prepared to risk losing her best friend as well. 'If it goes wrong between us. *When* it goes wrong between us,' she amended.

'Why are you so sure it will go wrong?'

That was an easy one. 'Because my relationships always go wrong.'

'Because you pick the kind of man who doesn't commit.'

She didn't have an answer to that. Mainly because she knew he was right.

'You pick men who say they're free spirits. And you

think that'll work because you're a free spirit, too. Except,' he said softly, 'they always let you down.'

Claire thought of her last ex. The one who'd let her down so much that she'd temporarily sworn off relationships. He definitely hadn't been able to commit. She'd found him in bed with someone else—and then she'd discovered that he was cheating on both of them with yet *another* woman. Messy and a half.

And the worst thing was that he'd assumed she'd be OK with it, because she was a free spirit, too... It had been a wake-up call. Claire had promised herself that never again would she date someone who could be so casual with her feelings. But it had shaken her faith in her judgement of men. In a room full of eligible men, she was pretty sure she'd pick all the rotten ones.

'I guess,' she said. 'And anyway, what about you? You never date anyone for longer than three weeks.'

'It's not quite that bad.'

'Even so, that's not what I want, Sean. Three weeks and you're out. That's just...' She grimaced. 'No.'

'I'm always very clear with my girlfriends. That it's for fun, that I'm committed to the factory and won't have time to...' His voice faded.

'Actually, that makes you the kind of man who won't commit,' she said softly. 'Like every other man I date.'

Sean had never thought of himself in that way before. He'd thought of the way he conducted his relationships as protecting his heart. Not letting himself get too involved meant not risking losing someone. He'd already lost too much in his life, and he didn't want to lose any more. So he'd concentrated on his career rather than on his relationships. Because the business was *safe*. Staying in control of his emotions kept his heart safe.

'What do you want, Sean?' she asked.

Such an easy answer—and such a difficult one. Though he owed her honesty. 'You. I can't think beyond that at the moment,' he admitted. And that was scary. Claire had accused him of having a twenty-year plan; although it wasn't anywhere near that long-range, he had to admit that he always planned things out, ever since his parents had died and he'd taken over the family business.

Planning had helped him cope with being thrown in at the deep end and being responsible for everything, without having the safety net of his father's experience to help him. And planning meant that everything was always under control. Just the way he liked it.

She bit her lip. 'I've got a wedding show in two months. My first collection. This could make all the difference to my career—this could be what really launches me into the big time. I'm hoping that one of the big wedding fashion houses might give me a chance to work with them on a collection. So I really don't have time for a relationship right now.'

'And I've just finished fighting off a takeover bid from an international conglomerate who wanted to add Farrell's to their portfolio,' he said. 'The vultures are still circling. I need to concentrate on the business and make absolutely sure they don't get another opening. If anything, I need to expand and maybe float the company on the stock market to finance the expansion. It's going to take all my time and then some.'

'So we're agreed: this is the wrong time for either of us to start any kind of relationship. By the time it *is* the right time, we'll both be back to our senses and we'll know it'd be the wrong thing to do anyway.'

That was something else she'd thrown at him—he

was the sensible one, the one who planned things out and was never spontaneous. So why wasn't he the one making this argument instead of her? Why had he sent her flowers and moved an appointment so he could see her for lunch?

It was totally crazy. Illogical.

And he couldn't do a thing to stop it.

Which exhilarated him and terrified him at the same time. With Claire, there was a real risk of losing control. And if he wasn't in control…what then? The possibilities made his head spin.

The only thing he could do now was to state the facts. 'I want you,' he said softly. 'And I think you want me.'

'So, what? We have a stupid, crazy, insane affair?'

He grimaced. 'Put like that, it sounds pretty sleazy.'

'But that's what you're offering.'

Was it? 'No.'

She frowned. 'So what *are* you suggesting, Sean?'

'I don't know,' he said. And it was a position he'd never actually been in before. He'd always been the one to call the shots. The one who initiated a relationship and the one who ended it. He shook his head, trying to clear it. But nothing changed. It was still that same spinning, out-of-control feeling. Like being on the highest, fastest, scariest fairground ride. 'All I know is that I want you,' he said.

'There's too much at stake. No.'

'Unless,' he said, 'we have an agreement.'

Her eyes narrowed. 'What kind of agreement?'

'We see each other. Explore where this thing goes. And then, whatever happens between us, we're polite to each other in front of Ashleigh. Nobody gets hurt. Especially her.'

'Can you guarantee that?' she asked softly.

'I can guarantee that I'll always be polite to you in front of Ashleigh.' He paused. 'The rest of it—I don't think anyone could guarantee that. But maybe it's worth the risk of finding out.' Risk. Something he didn't usually do unless it was precisely calculated. This wasn't calculated. At all. He needed his head examined.

'Maybe,' she said.

He curled his fingers round hers. His skin tingled where it touched her. 'Come and have lunch with me.'

She smiled then. Funny how it made the whole room light up. That wasn't something he was used to, either.

'OK,' she said. 'I just need to get my bag.'

'Sure.' He waited for her; then, when she'd locked the shop door behind them, he took her hand and walked down the street with her.

CHAPTER SIX

CLAIRE WAS WALKING hand in hand with Sean Farrell. Down the high street in Camden. On an ordinary Monday lunchtime.

This was surreal, she thought.

And she couldn't quite get her head round it.

But his fingers were wrapped round hers, his skin was warm against hers, and it was definitely happening rather than being some kind of super-realistic dream—because when she surreptitiously pinched herself it hurt.

'So what do you normally do for lunch?' Claire asked.

'I grab a sandwich at my desk,' he said. 'In the office, we put an order in to a local sandwich shop first thing in the morning, and they deliver to us. You?'

'Pretty much the same, except obviously I eat it well away from my work area so I don't risk getting crumbs or grease on the material and ruining it,' she said.

'So we both work through lunch. Well, that's another thing we have in common.'

There was a gleam in his eye that reminded her of the first thing they had in common. That night in Capri. She went hot at the memory.

'So how long do you have to spare?' he asked.

'An hour, maybe,' she said.

'So that's enough time to walk down to Camden Lock, grab a sandwich, and sit by the canal while we eat,' he said.

'Sounds good to me.' The lock was one of her favourite places; even though the area got incredibly busy in the summer months, she loved watching the way the narrow boats floated calmly down the canal underneath the willow trees. 'But this is a bit strange,' she said.

'How?'

'I've been thinking—we've known each other for years, and I know hardly anything about you. Well, other than that you run Farrell's.' His family's confectionery business, which specialised in toffee.

'What do you want to know?' he asked.

'Everything. Except I don't know where to start,' she admitted. 'Maybe we should pretend we're speed-dating.'

He blinked. 'You've been speed-dating?'

'No. Sammy has, though. I helped her do a list of questions.'

'What, all the stuff about what you do, where you come from, that sort of thing?' At her nod, he said, 'But you already know all that.'

'There's other stuff as well. I think the list might still be on my phone,' she said.

'Let's grab some lunch, sit down and go through your list, then,' he said. 'And if we both answer the questions, that might be a good idea—now I think about it, I don't really know that much about you, either.'

She smiled wryly. 'I can't believe we're doing this. We don't even like each other.'

He glanced down at their joined hands. 'Though we're attracted to each other. And maybe we haven't given each other a proper chance.'

From Claire's point of view, Sean was the one who hadn't given her a chance; but she wasn't going to pick a fight with him over it. He was making an effort, and she'd agreed to see where this thing took them. It was exhilarating and scary, all at the same time. Exhilarating, because this was a step into the unknown; and scary, because it meant trusting her judgement again. Her track record where men were concerned was so terrible that…

No. She wasn't going to analyse this. Not now. She was going to see where this took them. Seize the day.

They walked down to Camden Lock, bought bagels and freshly squeezed orange juice from one of the stalls, and sat down on the edge of the canal, looking out at the narrow boats and the crowd.

Claire found the list on her phone. 'Ready?' she asked.

'Yup. And remember you're doing this, too,' he said.

'OK. Your favourite kind of book, movie and music?' she asked.

He thought about it. 'In order—crime, classic film noir and anything I can run to. You?'

'Jane Austen, rom-coms and anything I can sing to,' she said promptly.

'So we're not really compatible there,' he said.

She wrinkled her nose. 'We're not that far apart. I like reading crime novels, too, but I like historical ones rather than the super-gory contemporary stuff. And classic noir—well, if Jimmy Stewart's in it, I'll watch it. I love *Rear Window*.'

'I really can't stand Jane Austen. I had to do *Mansfield Park* for A level, and that was more than enough for me,' he said with a grimace. 'But if the rom-com's witty and shot well, I can sit through it.'

She grinned. 'So you're a bit of a film snob, are you, Mr Farrell?'

He thought about it for a moment and grinned back. 'I guess I am.'

'OK. What do you do for fun?'

'You mean you actually think I might have fun?' he asked.

She smiled. 'You can be a little bit too organised, but I think there's more to you than meets the eye—so answer the question, Sean.'

'Abseiling,' he said, his face totally deadpan.

She stared at him, trying to imagine it—if he'd said squash or maybe even rugby, she might've believed him, but abseiling? 'In London?' she queried.

'There are lots of tall buildings in London.'

She thought about it a bit more, and shook her head. 'No, that's not you. I think you're teasing me.' Especially because he knew she was scared of heights.

'Good call,' he said. And his eyes actually *twinkled*.

Sean Farrell, teasing her. She would never have believed that he had a sense of humour. 'So what's the real answer?' she asked.

'Something very regimented,' he said. 'Sudoku.'

'There's nothing wrong with doing puzzles,' she said. Though trust Sean to pick something logical.

'What about you? What do you do for fun?' he asked.

Given how he'd teased her, he really deserved this. She schooled her face into a serious expression. 'Shopping. Preferably for shoes.' Given what she did for a living, that would be totally plausible. 'Actually, I have three special shoe wardrobes. Walk-in ones.'

'Seriously?' He looked totally horrified.

'About as much as you go abseiling.' She laughed. 'I like shoes, but I'm not that extreme. No, for me it's cooking for friends and watching a good film and talking about it afterwards.'

'OK. We're even now,' he said with a smile. 'So what do you cook? Anything in particular?'

'Whatever catches my eye. I love magazines that have recipes in them, and it's probably one of my worst vices because I can never resist a news stand,' she said. 'What about you?'

'I can cook if I have to,' he said. 'Though I admit I'm more likely to take someone out to dinner than to cook for them.'

She shrugged. 'That's not a big deal. It means you'll be doing the washing up, though.'

'Was that an offer?' he asked.

'Do you want it to be?' she fenced.

He held her gaze. 'Yes. Tell me when, and I'll bring the wine.'

There was a little flare of excitement in her stomach. They were actually doing this. Arranging a date. Seeing each other. She could maybe play a little hard to get and make him wait until Friday; but her mouth clearly had other ideas, because she found herself suggesting, 'Tonight?'

'I'd like that. I've got meetings until half past five, and some paperwork that needs doing after that—but I can be with you for seven, if that's OK?' he asked.

'It's a date,' she said softly.

He took her hand and brought it up to his mouth. Keeping eye contact all the way, he kissed the back of her hand, just briefly, before releasing it again; it made Claire feel warm and squidgy inside. Who would've thought that Sean Farrell was Prince Charming in disguise? Not that she was a weak little princess who needed rescuing—she could look after herself perfectly well, thank you very much—but she liked the charm. A lot.

'Next question,' he said.

'OK. What are you most proud of?' she asked.

'That's an easy one—my sister and Farrell's,' he said.

His family, and his family business, she thought. So it looked as if Sean Farrell had a seriously soft centre, just like the caramel chocolates his factory made along with the toffee.

'How about you?' he asked.

'The letters I get from brides telling me how much they loved their dress and how it really helped make their special day feel extra-special,' she said.

'So you're actually as much of a workaholic as you think I am?'

'Don't sound so surprised,' she said dryly. 'I know you see extreme things on a fashion catwalk and the pages of magazines, but it doesn't mean that designers are all totally flaky. I want my brides to feel really special and that they look like a million dollars, in a dress I've made just for them. And that means listening to what their dream is, and coming up with something that makes them feel their dream's come true.'

'Having seen the dress you made for Ashleigh, I can understand exactly why they commission you,' he said. 'Next question?'

'What are you scared of?'

'Easy one. Anything happening to Ashleigh or the business.'

But he didn't meet her eye. There was clearly something else. Something he didn't want to discuss.

'You?' he asked.

'Heights. I'm OK in a plane, but chairlifts like that

one in Capri make my palms go sweaty. Put it this way, I'm never, ever going skiing. Or abseiling.'

'Fair enough. Next?'

She glanced down at her phone to check. 'Your most treasured possession.'

'I can show you that.' He took his wallet out of his pocket, removed two photographs and handed them to her. One was of himself with Ashleigh, and the other was himself on graduation day with his parents on either side of him. Claire had a lump in her throat and couldn't say a word when she handed them back.

'You?' he asked.

'The same,' she whispered, and took her own wallet from her bag. She showed him a photograph of herself and her parents on her seventeenth birthday, and one of her with Ashleigh and Sammy and the Coliseum in the background.

He took her hand in silence and squeezed it briefly. Not that he needed any words; she knew he shared her feelings.

She put the photographs away. 'Next question—is the glass half full or half empty?'

'Half full. You?'

'Same,' she said, and glanced at her watch. 'We might have to cut this a bit short. Last one for now. Your perfect holiday?'

'Not a beach holiday,' he said feelingly. 'That just bores me silly.'

'You mean, you get a fit of the guilts at lying on a beach doing nothing, and you end up working.'

'Actually, I'm just not very good at just sitting still and doing nothing,' he admitted.

'So you'd rather have an active holiday?'

'Exploring somewhere, you mean?' He nodded. 'That'd work for me.'

'Culture or geography?'

'Either,' he said. 'I guess my perfect holiday would be Iceland. I'd love to walk up a volcano, and to see the hot springs and learn about the place. You?'

'I like city breaks. I have a bit of an art gallery habit, thanks to Sammy,' she explained. 'Plus I love museums where they have a big costume section. I should warn you that I really, really love Regency dresses. And I can spend hours in the costume section, looking at all the fine details.'

'So you see yourself as Lizzie Bennett?'

'No,' she said, 'and I'm not looking for a Darcy—anyway, seeing as you hate Austen, how come you know more than just the book you did for A level?'

'Ex-girlfriends who insisted on seeing certain films more than once, and became ex very shortly afterwards,' he said dryly.

'Hint duly noted,' she said. 'I won't ever ask you to watch *Pride and Prejudice* with me. Even though it's one of my favourite films.'

'Nicely skated past,' he said, 'but let's backtrack—you said you like holidays where you go and look at vintage clothes. And you said you look at details, so I bet you take notes and as many photos as you can get away with. Isn't that partly work?'

'Busted.' She clicked her fingers and grinned. 'I have to admit, I don't really like beach holidays, either. It's nice to have a day or two to unwind and read, but I'd rather see a bit of culture with friends. I really loved my trips in Italy with Ash and Sammy.'

'So what's your perfect holiday?' he asked.

'Anywhere with museums, galleries and lots of nice

little places to eat. Philadelphia and Boston are next on my wish list.'

'This is scary,' he said. 'A week ago I would've said we were total opposites.'

She thought about it. 'We still are. We have a few things in common—probably more than either of us realised—but you like things really pinned down and I like to go with the flow.' She smiled. 'And I bet you have an itinerary on holiday. Down to the minute.'

'If you don't know the opening times and days for a museum or what have you, then you might go to see it when it's closed and not get a chance to go back,' he pointed out. 'So yes, I do have an itinerary.'

'But if you go with the flow, you discover things you wouldn't have known about otherwise,' she pointed out.

'Let's agree to disagree on that one.' He glanced at his watch. 'We'd better head back.'

'You don't have to walk me back, Sean. Go, if you have a meeting.'

'I was brought up properly. I'll walk you back,' he said.

'I'm planning a slight detour,' she warned.

He looked a little wary, but nodded. 'We'll do this your way, then.'

Her detour was to an ice cream shop where the ice cream was cooled with liquid nitrogen rather than by being put in a freezer. 'I love this place. The way they make the ice cream is so cool,' she said, and laughed. 'Literally.'

'It's a little gimmicky,' he said.

'Just wait until you taste it.'

To her surprise, he chose the rich, dark chocolate. 'I would've pegged you as a vanilla man,' she said.

'Plain and boring?'

'Not necessarily. Seriously good vanilla ice cream is one of the best pleasures in the world—which is why I just ordered it.'

'True. But remember what I do for a living. And my favourite bit of my job is when I work with the R and D team. Am I really going to pass up chocolate?'

This was a side of Sean she'd never really seen. Teasing, bantering—*fun*. And she really, really liked that.

She watched him as he took a spoonful of ice cream. He rolled his eyes at her to signal that he thought she was overselling it. And then she saw his pupils widen.

'Well?' she asked.

'This is something else,' he admitted. 'I can forgive the gimmicky stuff. Good choice.'

'And if you hadn't gone with the flow, you wouldn't have known the place was there.' She grinned. 'Admit it. I was right.'

'You were right about the ice cream being great. That's as far as I go.' He held her gaze. 'For now.'

It should've been cheesy and made her laugh at him. But his voice was low and sexy as hell, and there was the hint of a promise in his words that made her feel hot all over, despite the ice cream. It was enough to silence her, and she concentrated on eating her ice cream on the walk back to her shop.

'Well, Ms Stewart,' he said on her doorstep. 'I'll see you later. Though there is something you need to attend to.'

She frowned. 'What's that?'

'You have ice cream on the corner of your mouth.' Just as she was about to reach up and scrub it away, he stopped her. 'Let me deal with this.'

And then he kissed the smear of sweet confection away. Slowly. Sensually. By the time he'd finished, Claire was close to hyperventilating and her knees felt weak. Sean was kissing her *in the street*. This was totally un-Sean-like behaviour and it put her in a flat spin.

'Later,' he whispered, and left.

Although Claire spent the rest of the day alternately talking to customers and working on the dress, in the back of her head she was panicking about what to cook for him. She had no idea what he liked. She could play safe and cook chicken—she was fairly sure that he wasn't a vegetarian. Wryly, she realised that this was when Sean's 'plan everything down to the last microsecond' approach would come in useful.

She could text him to check what he did and didn't like. But that meant doing it his way and planning instead of being spontaneous—and she didn't want to give him the opportunity to say 'I told you so'. Then again, she didn't want to cook a meal he'd hate, or something he was allergic to, so it would be better to swallow her pride.

She texted him swiftly.

Any food allergies I need to know about? Ditto total food hates.

The reply came back.

No and no. What's for dinner?

She felt safe enough to tease him.

Whatever I feel like cooking. Carpe diem.

When he didn't reply she wondered if she'd gone too far. Then again, he'd said that he was going to be in meetings all afternoon. She shrugged it off and concentrated on making the dress she'd cut out that morning.

Though by the end of the afternoon she still hadn't decided what to cook. She ended up having a mad dash round the supermarket and picked up chicken, parma ham, asparagus and soft cheese so she could make chicken stuffed with asparagus, served with tiny new potatoes, baby carrots and tenderstem broccoli.

Given that Sean was a self-confessed chocolate fiend, she bought the pudding rather than making it from scratch—tiny pots of chocolate ganache, which she planned to serve with raspberries, as their tartness would be a good foil to the richness of the chocolate.

Once she'd prepared dinner, she fussed around the flat, making sure everywhere was tidy and all the important surfaces were gleaming. Then she changed her outfit three times, and was cross with herself for doing so. Why was she making such a big deal out of this? She'd known Sean for years. He'd seen her when she had teenage spotty skin and chubby cheeks. And this was her flat. It shouldn't matter what she wore. Jeans and a strappy vest top would be fine.

Except they didn't feel fine. Sean was always so pristine that she'd feel scruffy.

In the end, she compromised with a little black dress but minimal make-up and with her hair tied back. So he'd know that she'd made a little more effort than just dragging on a pair of jeans and doing nothing with her hair, but not so much effort that she was making a big deal out of it.

The doorbell rang at seven precisely—exactly

what she'd expected from Sean, because of course he wouldn't be a minute late or a minute early—and anticipation sparkled through her.

Dinner.

And who knew what else the evening would bring?

CHAPTER SEVEN

HE WAS ACTUALLY *NERVOUS*, Sean realised.

Which was crazy.

This was Claire. He'd known her for years. There was nothing to be nervous about. Except for the fact that this was a date, and in the past they'd never really got on. And the fact that, now he was getting to know her, he was beginning to realise that maybe she wasn't the person he'd thought she was.

Would it be the same for her? He had no idea.

He took a deep breath and rang the doorbell.

When she opened the door, she was barefoot and wearing a little black dress, and her hair was tied back at the nape with a hot pink chiffon scarf. He wanted to kiss her hello, but was afraid he wouldn't be able to stop himself—it had been tough enough to walk away at lunchtime. So instead he smiled awkwardly at her. 'Hi. I wasn't sure what to bring, so I brought red and white.'

'You really didn't need to, but thank you very much.' She accepted the bottles with a smile. 'Come up.'

She looked so cool, unflustered and sophisticated. Sean was pretty sure that she wasn't in the slightest bit nervous, and in turn that made him relax. This was just dinner, the getting-to-know-you stuff. And he really should stop thinking about how easy it would be to untie that scarf and let her glorious hair fall over her shoulders, then kiss her until they were both dizzy.

He followed her up the stairs and she ushered him in to the kitchen.

'We're eating in here, if that's OK,' she said. 'Can I get you a drink? Dinner will be ten minutes.'

'A glass of cold water would be fabulous, thanks.' At her raised eyebrows, he explained, 'It's been a boiling hot day and I could really do with something cold and non-alcoholic.'

'Sure.' She busied herself getting a glass and filled it from the filter jug in the fridge, adding ice and a frozen slice of lime. When she handed the glass to him, her fingers brushed against his; it sent a delicious shiver all the way down his spine.

Her kitchen was a place of extremes. The work surfaces had all been used, and it looked as if most of her kitchen equipment had been piled up next to the sink. The fridge was covered with magnets and photos, and a cork board on one wall had various cards and notes pinned to it, along with what looked like a note of a library fine. Chaos. And yet the bistro table was neatly set for two, and there was a compact electric steamer on the worktop next to the cooker, containing the vegetables. So there was a little order among the chaos.

Much like Claire herself.

'Something smells nice,' he said.

'Dinner, I hope,' she said, putting the white wine into the fridge.

He handed her a box. 'I thought these might be nice with coffee after dinner.'

'Thank you.' She smiled. 'Toffee, I assume?'

'Samples,' he said, smiling back. 'There have to be some perks when you're dating a confectioner.'

'Perks. Hmm. I like the sound of that, though if we're talking about a lot of calories here then I might have to start doubling the length of my morning run.' She did a cute wrinkly thing with her nose that made his knees go weak, then looked in the box. 'Oh, you brought those lovely soft caramel hearts! Fabulous. Thank you.'

Clearly she liked those; he made a mental note, and hoped she wouldn't be disappointed with what these actually were. 'Not *quite*,' he said.

'What are they, then?'

'Wait until coffee. Is there anything I can do to help?'

'No, you're fine—have a seat.' She gestured to the bistro table, and he sat down on one of the ladder-back chairs.

Small talk wasn't something Sean was used to doing with Claire, and he really wasn't sure what to say. It didn't help that he was itching to kiss her; but she was bustling round the kitchen, and he didn't want to distract her and ruin the effort she'd put into making dinner. 'It's a nice flat,' he said.

She nodded. 'I like it here. The neighbours are lovely, the road's quiet, and yet I'm five minutes away from all the shops and market stalls.'

Work. An excellent subject, he thought. They could talk about that. 'So how did the dressmaking go today? Are you on schedule for your big show?'

'Fine, thanks, and I think I am. How about your meetings?'

'Fine, thanks.' Then it finally clicked that she wasn't as cool and calm as she seemed. She was being super-polite. So did that mean that she felt as nervous about this as he did? 'Claire, relax,' he said softly.

'Uh-huh.' But she still looked fidgety, and he noticed that she didn't sit down with him. Was she just feeling a little shy and awkward because of the newness of their situation, or was she having second thoughts?

'Have you changed your mind about this?' he asked, as gently as he could.

'No-o,' she hedged. 'It's not that.'

'What is it, then?'

'I'm usually a reasonable cook.' She bit her lip. 'What if it all goes wrong tonight?'

Nervous, then, rather than second thoughts. And suddenly his own nerves vanished. He stood up, walked over to her and put his arms round her. 'I'm pretty sure it'll be just fine. If it's not, then it doesn't matter. I'll carry you to your bed and take your mind off it—and then I'll order us a pizza instead.' He kissed the corner of her mouth, knowing he was dangerously close to distracting her, but wanting to make her feel better. 'Claire, why are you worrying that the food's going to be bad tonight?'

'Because it's *you*,' she said.

Because she thought he'd judge her? He had to acknowledge that he'd judged her in the past—and not always fairly. 'You already know I'd rather wash up or take someone out to dinner than cook for them, so I'm in no position to complain if someone cooks me something that isn't Michelin-star standard.'

'I guess.' She blew out a breath. 'It's just… Well, this is you and me, and it feels…'

He waited. What was she going to say? That it felt like a mistake?

'Scary,' she finished.

He could understand that. Claire fascinated him; yet, at the same time, this whole thing scared him witless. Her outlook was so different from his. She didn't have a totally ordered world. She followed her heart. If he let her close—what then? Would he end up with his heart broken? 'Me, too,' he said.

The only thing he could do then was to kiss her, to stop the fear spreading through him, too. So he covered her mouth with his, relaxing as she wrapped her arms round him, too, and kissed him back. Holding her close, feeling the warmth of her body against his and the sweetness of her mouth against his, made his world feel as if the axis was in the right place again.

A sharp ding made them both break apart. 'That was the steamer. It means the vegetables are done,' Claire said, looking flustered and adorably pink.

'Is there anything I can do to help?' he asked again.

This time, to his relief, she stopped treating him like a guest who had to be waited on. 'Could you open the wine? The corkscrew's in the middle drawer.'

'Sure. Would you prefer red or white?'

'We're having chicken, so it's entirely up to you.'

He looked at her. 'You'd serve red wine with chicken?'

'Well, hey—if you can cook chicken in red wine, then you can serve it with red wine.'

He wrinkled his nose at her. 'Am I being regimented again?'

'No. Just a teensy bit of a wine snob,' she said with a grin. 'You need to learn to go with the flow, Sean. *Carpe diem.* Seize the day. It's a good motto to live by.'

'Maybe.' By the time he'd taken the wine from her fridge, found the corkscrew in the jumble of her kitchen drawer, uncorked the bottle and poured them both a glass, she'd served up.

He sat down opposite her and raised his glass. 'To us, and whatever the future might bring.'

'To us,' she echoed softly, looking worried and uncertain—vulnerable, even—and again he felt that weird surge of protectiveness towards her. It unsettled him, because he didn't generally feel like that about his girl-friends.

'This is really lovely,' he said after his first mouthful. Chicken, stuffed with soft cheese and asparagus, then wrapped in parma ham. Claire Stewart was definitely capable in the kitchen, and he could tell that this had been cooked from scratch. He'd assumed that she'd be the sort to buy ready-made meals from the supermarket; clearly that wasn't the case.

'Thank you.' She acknowledged his compliment with a smile.

'But you're not reasonable.'

She frowned. 'Excuse me?'

'You called yourself a reasonable cook,' he said. 'You're not. You're more than that.'

'Thank you. Though I wasn't fishing for compliments.' She shrugged. 'I used to like cooking with my mum. Not that she ever followed a recipe. She'd pick something at random, and then she'd tweak it.'

'So I'm guessing that you didn't follow a recipe for this, did you?' he asked.

'I cooked us dinner. It's not exactly rocket science,' she drawled.

Why had he never noticed how deliciously sarcastic she could be?

'What?' she asked

He blinked. 'Sorry. I'm not following you.'

'You were smiling. What did I say that was so funny?'

'It was the way you said it.' He paused. 'Do you have any idea how delectable you are when you're being sarcastic?'

It was her turn to blink. 'Sarcasm is sexy?'

'It is on you.'

She grinned. 'Well, now. I think tonight has just got a whole lot more interesting. Are you on a sugar rush, Sean?'

'Excuse me?'

'Working where you do, you have toffee practically on tap. Eat enough of the stuff and you'll be on a permanent sugar rush. Which, I think, must be the main reason why you're complimenting me like this tonight.'

No. It was because it was as if he'd just met her for the first time. She wasn't the girl who'd irritated him for years; she was a woman who intrigued him. But he didn't want to sound soppy. 'Honey,' he drawled, 'the only sugar I want right now is you.'

She laughed at him. 'Now you've switched to cheese.'

'No. You're the one who's served cheese.' He indicated the stuffing for the chicken. 'And very nice it is, too.'

Her mouth quirked. 'Keep complimenting me like this, and…'

'Yeah?' he asked, his voice suddenly lower. What was she going to do? Kiss him? That idea definitely worked for him.

'Oh, shut up and eat your dinner,' she said, looking flustered.

'Chicken,' he said, knowing that she'd pick up on the double use of the word—and he was seriously enjoying fencing with her. Why had he never noticed before that she was bright and funny, and sexy as hell?

Probably because he'd had this fixed idea of her as a difficult girl who attracted trouble. That was definitely true in the past, but now…Now, she wasn't who he'd always thought she was. She'd grown up. Changed.

And he really liked the woman he was beginning to get to know.

She served pudding next—a seriously rich chocolate ganache teamed with tart raspberries. 'Come and work for my R and D department,' he said, 'because I think you'd have seriously good ideas about flavouring.'

She smiled. 'I know practically nothing about making toffee, and if I make banoffee pie I always buy a jar of *dulce de leche* rather than making my own.'

'That's a perfectly sensible use of your time,' he said.

She grinned. 'It's not so much that you have to boil a can of condensed milk for a couple of hours and keep an eye on it.'

'What, then?'

'I had a friend who tried doing it,' she explained. 'The can exploded and totally wrecked her kitchen.'

'Ouch.' He grimaced in sympathy, and took another spoonful of pudding. 'This is a really gorgeous meal, Claire.'

'I didn't make the ganache myself—it's a shop-bought pudding.'

'I don't care. It's still gorgeous. And I appreciate the effort. Though, for future reference, you could've ordered in pizza and I would've been perfectly happy,' he said. 'I just wanted to spend time with you.'

'Me, too,' she said softly. 'But I wanted to—well…'

Prove to him that she wasn't the flake he'd always thought she was? 'I know. And you did.'

And how weird it was that he could follow the way she thought. Scary, even. She was the last woman in the world he'd expected to be so in tune with.

Once he'd helped her clear away, she said, 'I thought we could have coffee in the living room.'

'Sounds good to me.'

'OK. You can go through and put on some music, if you like,' she suggested.

Claire's living room had clearly been hastily tidied, judging by the edges of the magazines peeking from the side of her sofa—he remembered her telling him that she was addicted to magazines; but the flowers he'd sent her that morning were in a vase on the coffee table, perfectly arranged. Clearly she liked them and hadn't just been polite when she'd thanked him for them earlier. And, given the pink tones in the room, he'd managed to pick her favourite colours.

Her MP3 player was in a speaker dock. He took it out and skimmed through the tracks. Given what she'd said at lunchtime, he'd expected most of the music to be pop, but he was surprised to see how much of it was from the nineteen-sixties. In the end, he picked a general compilation and switched on the music.

She smiled when she came in. 'Good choice. I love the Ronettes.' She sang a snatch of the next line.

'Aren't you a bit young to like this stuff?' he asked.

'Nope. It's the sort of stuff my gran listens to, so I grew up with it—singing into hairbrushes, the lot,' she said with a smile. 'Best Friday nights ever. Totally girly. Me, Mum, Gran, Aunt Lou and my cousins. Popcorn, waffles, milkshake and music.'

It was the first time she'd talked about her family. 'So you're close to your family?' he asked.

'Yes. I still clash quite a bit with my dad,' she said, 'but that's hardly tactful to talk about that to you.'

'Because I'm male?'

'Because,' she said softly, 'I'd guess that, like Ash, you'd give anything to be able to talk to your dad. And here am I grumbling about my remaining parent.

Though, to be fair, my dad is nothing like yours was. Yours actually *listened*.'

Fair point. He did miss his parents. And, when the whole takeover bid had kicked off, Sean would've given anything to be able to talk about it to his dad. But at the same time he knew that relationships were complicated. And it was none of his business. Unless Claire wanted to talk about it, he had to leave the subject alone.

She'd brought in a tray with a cafetière, two mugs, a small jug of milk and the box he'd given her earlier. 'Milk and sugar?' she asked.

'Neither, thanks. I like my caffeine unadulterated,' he said with a smile.

Claire, he noticed, took hers with two sugars and a lot of milk. Revolting. And it also made him worry that she wouldn't like the samples he'd brought; she probably preferred white chocolate to dark. Then again, he'd been wrong about a lot of things where Claire was concerned.

'Right. This box of utter yumminess. Whatever else I might have said about you in the past,' she said, 'I've always said that you make seriously good toffee.'

Honesty compelled him to say, 'No, my staff do. I'm not really hands-on in the manufacturing department.'

'Now that surprises me,' she said. 'I would've pegged you as the kind of manager who did every single job in the factory so you knew exactly what all the issues are.'

'I have done, over the years,' he said. 'Everything from the manufacturing to packing the goods, to carrying the boxes out for delivery. And every single admin role. And, yes, I worked with the cleaning team as well. Nowadays, I have regular meetings with each department and my staff know that I want to know about any problems they have and can't smooth out on their own.'

'Attention to detail.'

Her voice sounded almost like a purr. And there was a suspicious glow of colour across her cheeks.

'Claire?'

'Um,' she said. 'Just thinking. About Capri. About...'

And now he was feeling the same rush of blood to the head. 'Close your eyes,' he said.

Her breathing went shallow. 'Why?'

'Humour me?'

'OK.' She closed her eyes.

He took one of the dark salted caramel chocolates from the box and brushed it against her lips. Her mouth parted—and so did the lashes on her left eye.

'No peeking,' he said.

In return, she gave him an insolent smile and opened both eyes properly. 'So we're playing, are we, Mr Farrell?'

'We are indeed, Ms Stewart. Now close your eyes.' He teased her mouth with the chocolate and made her reach for it before finally letting her take a bite.

'You,' she said when she'd eaten it, 'have just upped your game considerably. I love the caramel-filled hearts, but these are spectacular.'

'You liked them?' Funny how that made him feel so good.

'Actually, I think I need another one, to check.'

He laughed. 'Oh, really?'

'Yes, really.' She struck a pose.

No way was he teasing her with chocolate when she looked like that, all pouting and dimpled and sexy as hell. Instead, he leaned over and kissed her.

The next thing he knew, they were both lying full length on the sofa and she was on top of him, his arms were wrapped tightly round her, and one of his hands was resting on the curve of her bottom.

'You're telling me that was chocolate?' she dead-panned.

'Maybe. Maybe not.' He moved his hand, liking the softness of her curves. 'Claire. You're…'

'What?'

'Unexpectedly luscious,' he said. 'None of this was supposed to happen.'

'Says the man who made me close my eyes and lean forward to take a bite of chocolate. Giving him a view straight down the front of my dress, if I'm not mistaken.'

'It was a very nice view,' he said, and shifted slightly so she was left in no doubt of his arousal.

'This is what chocolate does to you?' she asked.

'No. This is what *you* do to me.'

She leaned forward and caught his lower lip between hers, teasing him. 'Indeed, Mr Farrell.'

'Yeah.' He was aware that his voice sounded husky. She'd know from that exactly how much she affected him.

'So did you come prepared?' she asked.

He couldn't speak for a moment. And then he looked into her eyes. 'Are you suggesting…?'

'Capri, redux?' She held his gaze and nodded.

He blew out a breath. 'I didn't come prepared.'

'Tsk. Not what I expected from Mr Plan-Everything-Twenty-Years-in-Advance,' she teased.

'How do you manage to do that?' he asked plaintively.

'Do what?'

'Make me feel incredibly frustrated and make me want to laugh, all at the same time?'

'Go with the flow, sweetie,' she drawled.

He kissed her again. 'OK. Tonight wasn't about expectations. It wasn't about sending you flowers this morning so you'd sleep with me tonight. It was about getting to know you better.'

'Platonic, you mean?'

'I'd like to be friends.'

'Uh-huh.' She sounded unaffected, but he'd seen that little vulnerable flicker in her expression and he didn't let her move. He pulled her closer.

'I didn't say *just* friends. I want to be your lover as well.'

Her pupils went gratifyingly large.

'But I didn't come prepared because I'm not taking you for granted.'

To his surprise, he saw a sheen of tears in her eyes. 'Claire? What's wrong?'

She shook her head. 'I'm being wet.'

'Tell me anyway.'

'That's not how it usually is, for me,' she admitted.

Not being taken for granted? He brushed his mouth very gently against hers. 'That's because you've been dating the wrong men, thinking they're Mr Right.'

'I always thought you'd be Mr Wrong,' she admitted.

'And I always thought you'd be Ms Wrong,' he said. 'But maybe we should give each other a little more of a chance.'

'Maybe,' she said softly. 'But next time—I think I'm going to be prepared.'

'You and me, both.' He nuzzled the curve of her neck. 'Careful, Claire. You might turn into a bit of an *über*-planner if you keep this up.'

As he'd hoped, she laughed. 'And you might start going with the flow without having to be reminded.'

He laughed back. 'I think we need to move. While we still both have some self-control.'

'Good plan.' But when she climbed off him, he didn't

let her move away and sit in a different chair. He kept hold of her hand and drew her down beside him.

'This works for me,' he said. 'Just simply holding hands with you.'

For a moment, she went all dreamy-eyed. 'Like teenagers.'

'What?'

She shook her head. 'Ah, no. I'm not confessing that right now.'

Confessing what? He was intrigued. 'I could,' he suggested sweetly, '*make* you confess. Remember, I'm armed with seriously good chocolate.'

She drew his hand up to her mouth and kissed each knuckle in turn. 'But I also happen to know you're a gentleman. So you won't push me right now.'

So even when she hadn't liked him, she'd recognised that he had integrity and standards and knew that she was safe with him? That warmed him from the inside out. 'I won't push you right now,' he agreed. He handed her the box. 'Help yourself.'

'Salted caramel in dark chocolate. Fabulous. Are they all like that?'

'No. There's a Seville orange version and an espresso.'

'Nice choices. And you said earlier they were samples.' She looked thoughtful. 'So are you experimenting with new lines?'

'Possibly.'

She rolled her eyes. 'Sean, I'm hardly going to rush straight off to one of your competitors and sell them the information.'

'Of course you're not.' He frowned. 'Do you think I'm that suspicious?'

'You sounded it,' she pointed out.

'It's an experiment, moving into a slightly different form of toffee,' he said, 'but I need to put them through some focus groups first and see what my market thinks.'

'Ah, research. Looking at growing your market share.' She smiled. 'So either you sell the same product to more people, or you sell more products to the same people.'

At his raised eyebrow, she sighed. 'I'm not a total dimwit, you know. I've had my own business for three years.'

'I know, and it's not just that. Ashleigh told me you turned down an unconditional offer from Cambridge for medicine, and I know you wouldn't get that sort of offer if you weren't really bright.' He looked at her. 'I always wondered why you became a wedding dress designer instead of a doctor.'

She looked sad. 'It's a long story, and I don't really want to tell it tonight.'

Because she didn't trust him not to judge her? 'Fair enough,' he said coolly.

'I wasn't pushing you away, Sean,' she said. 'I just don't want to talk about it right now.'

'So what do you want, Claire?' He couldn't resist the question.

'Right now? I want you to kiss me again. But we've both agreed that's, um, possibly not a good idea.'

'Because I'm not prepared, and neither are you. So we'll take a rain check,' he said.

'How long?' She slapped a hand to her forehead. 'No. I didn't ask that and you didn't hear me.'

'Right. And I wasn't thinking it, either,' he retorted. 'When?'

'Wednesday?'

Giving them two days to come to their common sense. 'Wednesday,' he agreed. 'I would offer to cook for you, except you'd get a sandwich at best.'

She laughed. 'I can live with sandwiches.'

'No, I mean a proper date.'

'Planned to the nth degree, Sean-style?' she asked.

Why did planning things rattle her so much? In answer, he kissed her. Hard. And she was breathless by the time she'd finished.

'That was cheating,' she protested.

'Yeah, yeah.' He rubbed the pad of his thumb along her lower lip. 'And?'

'Go home, Sean, before we do something stupid.'

'Rain check,' he said. 'Wednesday night. I'll pick you up at seven.' He leaned forward and whispered in her ear, 'And, by the time I've finished with you, you won't remember what your name is or where you are.'

Her voice was gratifyingly husky when she said, 'That had better be a promise.'

'It is.' He stole one last kiss. 'And I always keep my promises. Which reminds me—I have washing-up duties.'

'I'll let you off,' she said.

'The deal was, you'd cook and I'd wash up.'

'Do you really think it's a good idea for us to be that close to each other, in the presence of water, and while neither of us is, um, prepared?'

He didn't quite get the reference to water, but he agreed with the rest of it. 'Good point. Rain check on the washing up, then, too?'

She laughed. 'No need. I have a dishwasher. It's horribly indulgent, given that I live on my own, but it's nice when I have friends over for dinner.' She paused, and added in a softer, sexier, deeper tone, 'Or my lover.'

Which sounded as if she was going to invite him back.

And that set his pulse thrumming.

'Right.' He couldn't resist one last kiss, one that sent his head spinning and left her looking equally dazed. 'Enjoy the chocolate,' he said. And then he left, while he was still capable of being sensible.

CHAPTER EIGHT

SEAN SENT CLAIRE a text later that evening.

Sweet dreams.

Yes, she thought, because they'd be of him. She typed back, You, too x.

He'd turned out to be unexpectedly sweet, so different from how he'd always been in the past. He was still a little regimented, but there was huge potential for him to be…

She stopped herself. No. This time she wasn't going to make the same old mistake. She wasn't going into this relationship thinking that Sean might be The One, that there would definitely be a happy-ever-after. OK, so he wasn't like the men she usually dated; but that didn't guarantee a different outcome for this relationship, either.

And this was early days. Sean had a reputation for not dating women for very long; the chances were, this would all be over in another month. Claire knew that she needed to minimise the potential damage to her heart and make sure that her best friend didn't get caught in any crossfire. Which meant keeping just a little bit of distance between them.

Even though Claire tried to tell herself to be sensible, she still found herself anticipating Wednesday. Wondering if he'd kiss her again. Wondering if they'd end up at his place or hers. Wondering if this whole thing blew his mind as much as it did hers.

Wednesday turned out to be madly busy, and Claire spent a long time on the phone with one of her suppliers, sorting out a mistake they'd made in delivering the wrong fabric—and it was going to cost her time she didn't have. A last-minute panic from one of her brides took up another hour; and, before she realised it, the time was half past six.

Oh, no. She still needed to shower, wash her hair, change and do her make-up before Sean arrived. She called him, hoping to beg an extra half an hour, but his line was busy. Swiftly, she tapped in a text as she went up the stairs to her flat.

Sorry, running a bit late. See you at half-seven?

She pressed 'send' and dropped the phone on her bed before rummaging through her wardrobe to find her navy linen dress.

She'd just stepped out of the shower and wrapped a towel round her hair when her doorbell rang.

No. It couldn't be Sean. It couldn't be seven-thirty already.

Well, whoever it was would just have to call back another time.

The bell rang again.

Arrgh. Clearly whoever it was had no intention of being put off. If it was a cold-caller, she'd explain firmly and politely that she didn't buy on the doorstep.

She blinked in surprise when she opened the door

to Sean. 'You're early!' And Sean was never early and never late; he was always precisely on time.

'No. We said seven.'

She frowned. 'But I texted you to say I was running late and asked if we could make it half past.'

'I didn't get any text from you,' he said.

'Oh, no. I'm so sorry.' She blew out a breath. 'Um, come up. I'll be twenty minutes, tops—make yourself a coffee or something.'

'Do you want me to make you a drink?'

She shook her head. 'I'm so sorry.'

He stole a kiss. 'Stop apologising.'

'I'll be as quick as I can,' she said, feeling horribly guilty. Why hadn't she kept a better eye on the time? Or called him rather than relying on a text getting through?

She had to dry her hair roughly and tie it back rather than spending time on a sophisticated updo, but she was ready by twenty-five past seven.

'You look lovely,' he said.

'Thank you.' Though she noticed that he'd glanced at his watch again. If only he'd lighten up a bit. It would drive her crazy if he ran this evening to schedule, as if it were a business meeting. 'Where are we going?' she asked brightly.

'South Bank.'

'Great. We can play in the fountains,' she said with a smile. 'It's been so hot today that it'd be nice to have a chance to cool down.'

He simply glanced at his suit.

And she supposed he had a point. Getting soaked wouldn't do the fabric any favours. Or her dress, for that matter. But the art installations on the South Bank were *fun*.

'I called the restaurant to say we'd be late,' he said.

Sean and his schedules. Though if they didn't turn up when they were expected, the restaurant would be perfectly justified in giving their table to someone else, so she guessed it was reasonable of him. 'Sorry,' she said again.

This was the side of Sean she found harder to handle. Mr Organised. It was fine for business; but, in his personal life, surely he could be more relaxed?

They caught the tube to the South Bank—to her relief, the line was running without any delays—and the restaurant turned out to be fabulous. Their table had a great view of the river, and the food was as excellent as the view. Claire loved the fresh tuna with mango chilli salsa. 'And the pudding menu's to die for,' she said gleefully. 'It's going to take me ages to choose.'

'Actually, we don't have time,' Sean said, looking at his watch,

'No time for pudding? But that's the best bit of dinner out,' she protested.

'We have to be somewhere. Maybe we can fit pudding in afterwards,' he said.

Just as she'd feared, Sean had scheduled this evening down to the last second. If she hadn't been running late in the first place, it might not have been so much of a problem. But right now she was having huge second thoughts about dating Sean. OK, so he managed to fit a lot in to his life; but all this regimentation drove her crazy. They were too different for this to work.

'So why exactly do we have to rush off?' she asked.

'For the next bit of this evening,' he said.

'Which is?'

'A surprise.'

Half past eight was too late for a theatre performance to start, and if they'd been going to the cinema she thought he would probably have picked a restaurant nearer to Leicester Square. She didn't work out what he'd planned until they started walking towards the London Eye. 'Oh. An evening flight.'

'It's the last one they run on a weeknight,' he confirmed. 'And we have to pick up the tickets fifteen minutes beforehand. Sorry I rushed you through dinner.'

At least he'd acknowledged that he'd rushed her. And she needed to acknowledge her part in the fiasco. 'If I hadn't been running late, you wouldn't have had to rush me.' She bit her lip. 'I'm beginning to think you might be right about me being chaotic. I should've checked that the text had gone or left you a voicemail as well.'

'It's OK. Obviously you had a busy day.'

She nodded. 'There were a couple of glitches that took time to sort out,' she said. 'And I'm up to my eyes in the wedding show stuff.'

'It'll be worth it in the end,' he said.

'I hope so. And I had a new bride in to see me this morning. That's my favourite bit of my job,' Claire said. 'Turning a bride-to-be's dreams into a dress that will suit her and make her feel special.'

'That's why you called your business "Dream of a Dress", then?' he asked.

'Half of the reason, yes.'

'And the other half?' he asked softly.

'Because it's my dream job,' she said.

He looked surprised, as if he'd never thought of it that way before. 'OK. But what if a bride wants a dress that you know wouldn't suit her?'

'You mean, like a fishtail dress when she's short and curvy?' At his nod, she said, 'You find out what it is she loves about that particular dress, and see how you can adapt it to something that will work. And then you need tact by the bucketload.'

'Tactful.' He tipped his head on one side and looked at her. 'But you always say what you think.'

'I do. But you can do that in a nice way, without stomping on people.'

The corners of his mouth twitched. 'I'll remember that, the next time you don't mince your words with me.'

She laughed back. 'You're getting a bit more bearable, so I might be nicer to you.'

He bowed his head slightly. 'For the compliment.' Then he took her hand and lifted it to his mouth, pressed a kiss into her palm, and folded her fingers round it.

It made her knees go weak. To cover the fact that he flustered her, she asked, 'How was your day?'

'Full of meetings.'

No wonder he found it hard to relax and go with the flow. He was used to a ridiculously tight schedule.

But at least he seemed to relax more once they were in the capsule and rising to see a late summer evening view of London. Claire was happy just to enjoy the view, with Sean's arm wrapped round her.

'I was thinking,' he said softly. 'I owe you pudding and coffee. I have good coffee back at my place.'

'Would there be caramel hearts to go with it?' she asked hopefully.

'There might be,' he said, the teasing light back in his eyes.

This sounded like a spontaneous offer rather than being planned, she thought. So maybe it could make up for the earlier part of the evening. 'That sounds good,' she said. 'Coffee and good chocolate. Count me in.'

And, to her pleasure, he held her hand all the way

back to his place. Now they weren't on a schedule any more, he was less driven—and she liked this side of him a lot more.

The last time Claire had been to Sean's house, she'd waited on the path outside while he picked up his luggage. This time, he invited her in. She discovered that his kitchen was very neat and tidy—as she'd expected—but it clearly wasn't a cook's kitchen. There were no herbs growing in pots, no ancient and well-used implements. She'd guess that the room wasn't used much beyond making drinks.

His living room was decorated in neutral tones. Claire was pleased to see that there were lots of family photographs on the mantelpiece, but she noticed that the art on the walls was all quite moody.

'It's Whistler,' he said, clearly realising what she was looking at. 'His nocturnes—I like them.'

'I would've pegged you as more of a Gainsborough man than a fan of tonalism,' she said.

He looked surprised. 'You know art movements?'

'I did History of Art for GCSE,' she said. 'Then again, I guess those paintings are a lot like you. They're understated and you really have to look to see what's there.'

'I'm not sure,' he said, 'if that was meant to be a compliment.'

'It certainly wasn't meant to be an insult,' she said. 'More a statement of fact.'

He poured them both a coffee, added sugar and a lot of milk to hers, and gestured to the little dish he'd brought on the tray. 'Caramel hearts, as you said you liked them.'

'I do.' She smiled at him, appreciating the fact that he'd remembered and made the effort.

'You can put on some music, if you like,' he suggested, indicating his MP3 player.

She skimmed through it quickly and frowned. 'Sean, I don't mean to be horrible, but all your playlists are a bit—well...'

'What?' he asked, sounding puzzled.

'They're named for different types of workouts, so I'm guessing all the tracks in each list have the same number of beats per minute.'

'Yes, but that's sensible. It means everything's arranged the way I want it for whatever exercise I'm doing.'

'I get that,' she said, 'but don't you enjoy music?'

He frowned. 'Of course I do.'

'I can't see what you listen to for pleasure. To me this looks as if you only play set music at set times.' Regimented again. And this time she couldn't just let it go. 'That works for business but, Sean, you can't live your personal life as if it's a business.'

'Right,' he said tightly.

So much for reaching an understanding. She sighed. 'I'm not having a go at you. I'm just saying you're missing out on so much and maybe there's another way of doing things.'

'Let's agree to disagree, shall we?'

Sean had closed off on her again, Claire thought with an inward sigh—and now she could guess exactly why his girlfriends didn't last for much longer than three weeks. He'd drive them crazy by stonewalling them as soon as they tried to get close to him, and then either he'd gently suggest that they should be just friends, or they'd give up trying to be close to him.

She also knew that telling him that would be the quickest way of ending things between them; and from the few glimpses she'd had she was pretty sure that, behind his walls, the real Sean Farrell was someone really worth getting to know.

'OK, I'll back off,' she said. 'But you have absolutely nothing slushy and relaxing on here.'

He coughed. 'In case you hadn't noticed, I'm male.'

She'd noticed, all right.

'I don't do slushy,' he continued. 'But...' He took the MP3 player gently from her and flicked rapidly through the tracks.

When the music began playing, she recognised 'Can't Take My Eyes Off You', but it was a rock version of the song.

'The band played this at Ashleigh's wedding,' he said, 'and I found myself looking straight at you—that's why I asked you to dance.'

'And there was I thinking it was because it was traditional,' she deadpanned.

'No. I just wanted to dance with you.'

His honesty disarmed her. Just when he'd driven her crazy and she was thinking of calling the whole thing off, he did something like this that made her melt inside.

He drew her into his arms, and Claire was surprised to discover that, even though the song was fast, they could actually dance slowly to it.

'And then, when I was dancing with you,' he continued, 'I wanted to kiss you.'

She found herself moistening her lower lip with her tongue. 'Do you want to kiss me now, Sean?'

'Yes.' He held her gaze. 'And I want to do an awful lot more than just kiss you.'

Excitement thrummed through her, but she tried to play it cool. 'Could you be more specific?'

'I want to take that dress off,' he said, 'lovely as it is. And I want to kiss every inch of skin I uncover.'

'That sounds like a good plan,' she said. 'So what do I do?'

He smiled. 'I'm surprised you don't already know that one. Isn't it what you're always saying? Be spontaneous. Follow your heart. Go with the flow.'

'So that means,' she said, 'I get to take that prissy suit off you?'

'Prissy?' he queried. 'My suit's *prissy*?'

'It's beautifully cut, but it's so neat and tidy. I'd like to see you dishevelled,' she said, 'like you were that morning in Capri.'

'Would that be the morning you threw me out of your bed?'

'Yes, and don't make me feel guilty about it. That was mainly circumstances,' she said.

'Hmm.'

'Besides, I can't throw you out of your own bed,' she pointed out.

'Now that's impeccable logic.' He frowned. 'Though, actually, if you said no at any point I hope you realised I'd stop.'

She stroked his face. 'Sean, of course I know that. You're…'

'Dull?'

She shook her head. 'I was going to say honourable.'

He brushed the pad of his thumb across her lower lip, making her skin tingle. 'You normally call me regimented.'

'You can be. You were tonight, and I nearly left you to it and went home.' She smiled. 'But there's a huge difference between regimented and dull.'

'Is there?'

'Let me show you,' she said. 'Take me to bed.'

'I thought you'd never ask.'

To her surprise, he scooped her up and actually carried her up the stairs. She half wanted to make a snippy comment about him being muscle-bound, to tease him and push him, but at the same time she didn't want to spoil the moment. She was shocked to discover that she actually quite liked the way he was taking charge and being all troglodyte.

Once they were in his room, he set her down on her feet.

His bedroom was painted in shades of smoky blue—very masculine, with a polished wooden floor, a rug in a darker shade that toned with the walls and matched the curtains, and limed oak furniture. But what really caught Claire's eye was his bed. A sleigh bed, also in limed oak, and she loved it. She'd always wanted a bed like that, but there really wasn't the room for that kind of furniture in her flat. Sean's Victorian terraced house was much more spacious and the bed was absolutely perfect.

'The last time you took your dress off for me,' he said, 'your underwear matched. Does it match today?'

'That's for me to know,' she said, 'and for you to find out.'

'Is that a challenge?'

'In part. It's also an offer.' She paused. 'Um, before this goes any further, do we have Monday's problem?'

'We absolutely do not,' he confirmed.

'Good.' Because she was going to implode if she had to wait much longer.

He drew the curtains and turned on the bedside light; it was a touch lamp, so he was able to dim the glow. Then he sat on the edge of the bed. 'Show me,' he invited.

She unzipped her dress and stepped out of it, then hung it over the back of a chair.

'What?' she asked, seeing the amusement in his face.

'You're a closet neat freak,' he said.

'No. Just practical. This is linen. It creases very, very badly. And I'm not walking out of here looking as if I've just been tumbled in a haystack.'

He gave her a slow, sexy smile. 'I like that image. Very much. You, tumbled in a haystack.'

She shook her head. 'It's not at all romantic, you know. Straw's prickly and itchy and totally unsexy.'

'And I assume you know that because you've, um, gone with the flow?'

'Listen, I haven't slept with everyone I've dated, and I certainly haven't slept with anyone else as fast as I fell into bed with *you*,' she said, folding her arms and giving him a level stare.

He stood up, walked over to her and brushed his mouth against hers. 'I'm not calling you a tart, Claire. We both have pasts. It's the twenty-first century, not the nineteen-fifties. I'm thirty and you're twenty-seven. I'd be more surprised if we were both still virgins.' He traced the lacy edge of her bra with one fingertip. 'Mmm. Cream lace. I like this. You have excellent taste in clothing, Ms Stewart.'

'It's oyster, not cream,' she corrected.

He grinned. 'And you have the cheek to call me prissy.'

'Details,' she said. 'You need to get them right.'

'We're in agreement there.'

She coughed.

'What?' he asked.

'I'm in my underwear. You can see that it matches,

so I've done my half of the bargain. And right now, Mr Farrell, I have to say that you're very much overdressed.'

'So strip me, Claire,' he said, opening his arms to give her full access to his clothes.

It was an offer she wasn't going to refuse.

Afterwards, curled in Sean's arms, Claire turned her face so she could kiss his shoulder. 'I'd better go.'

'Not yet. This is comfortable.' He held her closer. 'Stay for a bit longer. I'll drive you home.'

So Sean the super-efficient businessman was a cuddler? Ah, bless, Claire thought. And, actually, she rather liked it. It made him that much more human. 'OK,' she said, and settled back against him.

Funny how they didn't really need to talk. Just being together was enough. It was *peaceful*. Something else she would never have believed about herself and Sean; but she liked just being with him. When he wasn't being super-organised down to the last microsecond. And it seemed that he felt the same.

So maybe, just maybe, this wasn't all going to end in tears.

When she finally got dressed and he drove her home, he parked outside her flat. 'So. When are you free next?' he asked.

'Sunday?' she suggested. 'I have the shop on Saturday.'

'Sunday works for me.'

'You organised tonight, so I'll organise Sunday,' she said. 'And that means doing things my way.'

'Going with the flow.' He looked slightly pained.

'It means being spontaneous and having fun,' she said. 'I'll pick you up at nine. And I won't be late.'

'No?' he asked wryly.

'No.' She kissed him. 'The first bit of tonight was, um, a bit much for me. But I loved dinner. I loved the London Eye and just being with you. Those kind of things works for me. It's just...' She shook her head. 'Schedules are for work. And I keep my work and my personal life separate.'

'Hmm,' he said, and she knew he wasn't convinced. But then he made the effort and said, 'I enjoyed being with you.'

But the fact she'd been late had really grated on him. He didn't have to tell her that.

He kissed her lightly. 'I'll walk you to your door.'

'Sean, it's half a dozen paces. I think I'm old enough to manage.'

He spread his hands. 'As you wish.'

'I'm not pushing you away,' she said softly. 'But I don't need protecting—the same as you don't.' She already had one overprotective male in her life, and that was more than enough for her. And it was half the reason why she'd always chosen free-spirited boyfriends who wouldn't make a fuss over everything or smother her.

Though maybe she'd gone too far the other way, because they'd all been disastrous.

But could Sean compromise? Could they find some kind of middle ground between them? If not, then this was going to be just as much a disaster as her previous relationships.

'Thank you for caring,' she said, knowing that his heart was in the right place—he just went a bit too far, that was all. 'I'll see you Sunday.'

'Spontaneous. Go with the flow.'

'You're learning. *Carpe diem*,' she said with a smile, and kissed him. 'Goodnight.'

CHAPTER NINE

WHEN CLAIRE WENT to pick Sean up on Sunday morning he was wearing formal trousers, a formal shirt and a tie. At least this time it wasn't a complete suit, but it still didn't work for what she wanted to do. And they looked totally mismatched, given that Claire was wearing denim shorts, a strappy vest and matching canvas shoes. Sean looked way too formal.

'Do you actually own a pair of jeans?' she asked.

'No.'

It was just as well she'd second-guessed. 'Right, then.' She delved into her tote bag and brought out a plastic carrier bag bearing the name of a department store.

'What's this?' he asked.

'Pressie. For you.' When he still looked blank, she added, 'The idea is that you wear it. As in right now.'

He looked in the bag. 'You bought me a pair of jeans?'

'Give the monkey a peanut,' she drawled.

'How do you know my size?'

She rolled her eyes. 'I measured you for a wedding suit, remember?'

He sighed. 'Claire, you didn't need to buy me a pair of jeans.'

'You don't own any. So actually, yes, I did.'

He looked at her, and she sighed. 'Sean, don't be difficult about this. I bought you a present, that's all. It's what people do when they date.'

He still didn't look convinced.

'Look, you bought me those gorgeous flowers, and I don't think you'd enjoy it if I bought you flowers—well, not that I think you *can't* buy a man flowers,' she clarified, 'but I don't think you're the kind of man who'd really appreciate them.'

'Probably not,' he admitted.

'Most people would buy their man some chocolate, but I can hardly give chocolate to someone who owns a confectionery company, can I? Which leaves me pretty stuck for buying you a gift. It's just an ordinary pair of jeans, Sean. Nothing ridiculously overpriced. So come on. Do something you haven't done since you were a teenager,' she coaxed, 'and wear the jeans. And swap those shoes for your running shoes.'

'My running shoes?' he queried.

She nodded. 'Because I bet you don't have a pair of scruffy, "go for a walk and it doesn't matter if they're not perfectly polished" shoes.'

'There's nothing wrong with looking smart at work,' he protested.

'I know, but you're not at work today, Sean. You're playing. You can keep the shirt, but lose the tie.'

'Bossy,' he grumbled, but he did as she asked. By the time he'd changed into the jeans and his running shoes, he looked fantastic—much more approachable. *Touchable.* Claire was glad she'd picked a light-coloured denim that looked slightly worn. It really, really suited him.

She folded her arms and looked at him.

'What now?' he asked. 'I'm not wearing the tie.'

'But your top button is still done up. Fix it, and roll your sleeves up.'

'Claire…'

'We did your date your way,' she said. 'And you agreed that we'd do this one my way.'

'This is the giddy limit,' he said, and for a moment she thought he was going to refuse; but finally he indulged her.

'That's almost perfect,' she said, then sashayed over to him, reached up to kiss him, and then messed up his hair.

'Why did you do that?' he asked, pulling back.

'It's the "just got out of bed" look. Which makes you look seriously hot,' she added. 'Like you did in Capri.'

He gave her a predatory smile. 'So if you think I look hot…'

'Rain check,' she said. 'Because we're going out and having fun, first.'

There was a bossy side to Claire, Sean thought, that he'd never seen before. The whole idea of giving up control—that just wasn't how he did things.

Claire Stewart was dangerous with a capital D where his peace of mind was concerned.

'This is your car?' He looked at the bright pink convertible Mini stencilled with daisies that was parked on the road outside his house. 'Oh, you are kidding me.'

'What's wrong with my car?' She put her finger into the keyring and spun her keys round.

What was wrong with the car? Where did he start?

He closed his eyes. 'OK. I know, I know, go with the flow.' He groaned and opened his eyes again. 'But, Claire. *Pink.* With daisies. Really?'

Finally she took pity on him. 'I borrowed it from a friend. I don't have a car of my own at the moment.'

'Then we could go wherever it is in mine,' he suggested hopefully.

'Nope—we're doing this my way.' She gave him another of those insolent grins. 'Actually, my friend wants to sell this. I was thinking about buying it from her.'

He pulled a face, but said nothing.

'Very wise, Sean, very wise,' she teased.

She tied her hair back with a scarf, added some dark glasses that made her look incredibly sexy, and then added the disgusting khaki cap he remembered from Capri and which cancelled out the effect of the glasses. Once they were sitting in the car, she put the roof down, connected her MP3 player, and started blasting out sugary nineteen-sixties pop songs. Worse still, she made him sing along; and Sean was surprised to discover that he actually knew most of the songs.

By the time they got to Brighton, he'd stopped being embarrassed by the sheer loudness of the car and was word-perfect on the choruses of all her favourite songs.

'Brighton,' he said.

'Absolutely. Today is "Sean and Claire do the seaside",' she said brightly.

'And this isn't planned out?'

She rolled her eyes. 'Don't be daft—you don't plan things like going to the seaside. You go with the flow and you have *fun*.' She parked the car, then took his hand and they strolled across to the seafront.

This was so far removed from what he'd normally do on a Sunday. He might sit in his garden—perfectly manicured by the man he paid to mow the lawn, weed the flower beds, and generally make the area look tidy—but nine times out of ten he'd be in his study, working.

He couldn't even remember the last time he went to the seaside. With one of his girlfriends, probably, but he hadn't paid much attention.

But with Claire, he was definitely paying attention.

He hung back slightly. 'Those are very *short* shorts.' And it made him want to touch her.

She just laughed. 'I have great legs—I might as well show them off before they go all wrinkly and saggy when I'm old.'

'You're...' He stopped and shook his head.

'I'm what, Sean?'

'A lot of things,' he said, 'half of which I wouldn't dare utter right now.'

'Chicken,' she teased.

'Discretion's the better part of valour,' he protested.

She laughed and took him onto the pier. They queued up to go on the fairground rides.

'You couldn't get fast-track tickets?' he asked.

She rolled her eyes. 'Queuing is part of the fun.'

'How?' he asked. In his view, queuing was a waste of time. If something was worth visiting, you bought fast-track tickets; otherwise, you didn't bother and you used your time more wisely.

'Anticipation,' she said. 'It'll be worth the wait.'

He wasn't so sure, but he'd agreed to do this her way. 'OK.'

But then they queued for the roller coaster.

'I thought you hated heights?'

'I do, but it'll be worth it if it loosens you up a little,' she said. 'It's OK to stop and smell the roses, Sean. If anything it'll enrich the time you spend on your business, because you'll look at things with a wider perspective.'

'Playing the business guru now, are you?'

'I don't play when it comes to business,' she said, 'but I do remember to play in my free time.'

'Hmm.'

He wasn't that fussed about the thrill rides, but for her sake he pretended to enjoy himself.

They grabbed something quick to eat, then went over to the stony, steeply sloping beach next. The sea was such an intense shade of turquoise, they could have been standing on the shore of the Mediterranean rather than the English Channel. He'd never seen the sea in England look so blue. And this, he thought, was much more his style than waiting in a queue for a short thrill ride that did nothing to raise his pulse.

Claire, on the other hand, could seriously raise his pulse...

'Shoes off,' she said, removing her own canvas shoes, 'and roll up your jeans.'

'You're so bossy,' he grumbled.

She grinned. 'The reward will be worth it.'

'What reward?'

She fluttered her eyelashes at him. 'Wait and see.'

He had to admit that it was nice walking on the edge of the sea with her, his shoes in one hand and her hand in his other. The sound of the waves rushing onto the pebbles and the seagulls squawking, the scent of the sea air and the warmth of the sunlight on his skin. Right at that moment, he'd never felt more alive.

It must have shown in his face, because she said softly, 'Told you it was rewarding.'

'Uh-huh.' He smiled at her. 'Talking of rewards...' He leaned forward and kissed her. But what started out as a sweet, soft brush of her lips against his soon turned hot.

He pulled back, remembering that they were in a

public place and with families around them. 'Claire. We need to…'

'I know.' Her fingers tightened round his. 'And this was what I wanted today. For you to let go, just a little bit, and have some fun with me.'

'I *am* having fun,' he said, half surprised by the admission.

'Good.' Her face had gone all soft and dreamy and it made him want to kiss her again—later, he promised himself.

When they'd finished paddling, they had to walk on the pebbles to dry off—Claire clearly hadn't thought to bring a towel with her—and then she said, 'Time for afternoon tea. And I have somewhere really special in mind.'

'OK.' He didn't mind going with the flow for a while, especially as it meant holding her hand. There was something to be said about just wandering along together.

As they walked into the town, he could see the exotic domes and spires of Brighton Pavilion.

Another queue, he thought with a sigh. It was one of the biggest tourist attractions in the area. Again, if she'd planned it they could've bought tickets online rather than having to queue up. He hated wasting time like this.

But, when they got closer, he realised there was something odd. No queues.

A notice outside the Pavilion informed them that the building was closed for urgent maintenance. Just for this weekend.

Sean just about stopped himself pointing out that if Claire had planned their trip in advance, then she would've known about this and she wouldn't have been disappointed.

'Oh, well,' she said brightly. 'I'm sure we can find a nice tea shop somewhere and have a traditional cream tea.'

Except all the tea shops nearby were full of tourists who'd had exactly the same idea. There were queues.

'Sorry. This is, um, a bit of a disaster,' she said.

Yes. But he wasn't going to make her feel any worse about it by agreeing with her. *'Carpe diem,'* he said. 'Maybe there's an ice cream shop we can go to instead.'

'Maybe,' she said, though he could tell that she was really disappointed. He guessed that she'd wanted to share the gorgeous furnishings of the Pavilion with him—and there had probably been some kind of costume display, too.

They wandered through the historic part of the town, peeking in the windows of the antiques shops and little craft shops, and eventually found a tea shop that had room at one of the tables. Though as it was late afternoon, the tea shop had run out of scones and cream.

'Just the tea is fine, thanks,' Sean said with a smile.

They had a last walk along the beach, then Claire drove them home. 'Shall I drop you back at your house, or would you like to come back to my place and we can maybe order in some Chinese food?' she asked.

Given what she'd said to him by the sea, Sean knew what she wanted to hear. 'I think,' he said, 'we'll go with the flow.'

Her smile was a real reward—full of warmth and pleasure rather than smugness. 'We won't go home on the motorway, then,' she said. 'We'll find a nice little country pub where we can have dinner.'

Except it turned out that every pub they stopped at didn't do food on Sunday evenings.

'I can't believe this,' she said. 'I mean—it's the summer. Prime tourist season. Why on earth wouldn't any of them serve food on Sunday evenings?'

Sean didn't have the heart to ask why she hadn't planned it better. 'Go back on to the motorway,' he said. 'We'll get a takeaway back in London.'

'I'm so sorry. Still, at least we can keep the roof down and enjoy the sun on the way home,' Claire said.

Which was clearly all she needed to say to jinx it, because they were caught in a sudden downpour. By the time she'd found somewhere safe to stop and put the car's soft top back up, they were both drenched. 'I'm so sorry. That wasn't supposed to happen,' Claire said, biting her lip.

'So we were literally going with the flow. Of water,' Sean said, and kissed her.

'What was that for?' she asked.

'For admitting that you're not always right.' He stole another kiss. 'And also because that T-shirt looks amazing on you right now.'

'Because it's wet, you mean?' She rolled her eyes at him. 'Men.'

He smiled. 'Actually, I wanted to cheer you up a bit.'

'Because today's been a total disaster.'

'No, it hasn't. I enjoyed the sea.'

'But we didn't get to the Pavilion, we missed out on a cream tea, I couldn't find anywhere for dinner and we just got drenched.' She sighed. 'If I'd done things your way, it would've been different.'

'But when I planned our date, we ended up rushing and that was a disaster, too,' he said softly. 'I think we might both have learned something from this.'

'That sometimes you need to plan your personal life?' she asked.

'And sometimes you need to go with the flow,' he said. 'It's a matter of compromise.'

'That works for me, too. Compromise.' And her smile warmed him all the way through.

On the way back to London, he asked, 'So are you seriously going to buy this car?'

'What's wrong with it?'

'Apart from the colour? I was thinking, it's not very practical for transporting wedding dresses.'

'I don't need a car for that. I'm hiring a van for the wedding show,' she said.

'So why don't you have a car?' he asked.

'I live and work in London, so I don't really need one—public transport's fine.'

'You needed a car today to take us to the seaside,' he pointed out.

'Not necessarily. We could have gone by train,' she said.

'But then you wouldn't have been able to sing your head off all the way to Brighton.'

'And we wouldn't have got wet on the way home,' she agreed ruefully.

'We really need to get you out of those wet clothes,' he said, 'and my place is nearer than yours.'

'Good point,' she said, and drove back to his.

Sean had the great pleasure of peeling off her wet clothes outside the shower, then soaping her down under the hot water. When they'd finished, he put her clothes in the washer-dryer while she dried off. And then he had the even greater pleasure of sweeping her off her feet again, carrying her to his bed, and making love with her until they were both dizzy.

Afterwards, she was all warm and sweet in his arms. He stroked her hair back from her face. 'You were going to tell me how come you're not a doctor.'

'It just wasn't what I wanted to do,' she said.

'But you applied to study medicine at university.'

She shifted onto her side and propped herself on one elbow so she could look into his face. 'It was Dad's dream, not mine. It's a bit hard to resist pressure from your parents when you're sixteen. Especially when your father's a bit on the overprotective side.' She wrinkled her nose. 'Luckily I realised in time that you can't live someone else's dream for them. So I turned down the places I was offered and reapplied to design school.'

He frowned. 'But you were doing science A levels.'

'And Art,' she said. 'And the teacher who taught my textiles class at GCSE wrote me a special reference, explaining that even though I hadn't done the subject at A level I was more than capable of doing a degree. At my interview, I wore a dress I'd made and I also took a suit I'd made with me. I talked the interviewers through all the stitching and the cut and the material, so they knew I understood what I was doing. And they offered me an unconditional place.'

He could see the pain in her eyes, and drew her closer. 'So what made you realise you didn't want to be a doctor?'

'My mum.' Claire dragged in a breath. 'She was only thirty-seven when she died, Sean.' Tears filmed her eyes. 'She barely made it past half the proverbial three score years and ten. In the last week of her life, when we were talking she held my hand and told me to follow my dream and do what my heart told me was the right thing.'

Which clearly hadn't been medicine.

Not knowing what to say, he just stroked her hair.

'Even when I was tiny, I used to draw dresses. Those paper dolls—mine were always the best dressed in class. I used to sketch all the time. I wanted to design dresses. Specifically, wedding dresses.'

He had a feeling he knew why she tended to fight with her father, now.

Her next words confirmed it. 'Dad said designers were ten a penny, whereas being a doctor meant I'd have a proper job for life.' She sighed. 'I know he had my best interests at heart. He had a tough upbringing, and he didn't want me ever to struggle with money, the way he did when he was young. But being a doctor was *his* dream, not mine. He said I could still do dressmaking and what have you on the side—but no way would I have had the time, not with the crazy hours that newly qualified doctors work. It was an all or nothing thing.' She grimaced. 'We had a huge fight over it. He said I'd just be wasting a degree if I studied textile design instead, and he gave me an ultimatum. Study medicine, and he'd support me through uni; study textiles, and he was kicking me out until I came to my senses.'

That sounded like the words of a scared man, Sean thought. One who wanted the best for his daughter and didn't know how to get that through to her. And he'd said totally the wrong thing to a teenage girl who'd just lost the person she loved most in the world and wasn't dealing with it very well. Probably because he was in exactly the same boat.

'That's quite an ultimatum,' Sean said, trying to find words that wouldn't make Claire think he was judging her.

'It was pretty bad at the time.' She paused. 'I talked to your mum about it.'

He was surprised. 'My mum?'

Claire nodded. 'She was lovely—she knew I was going off the rails a bit and I'd started drinking to blot out the pain of losing Mum, so she took me under her wing.'

Exactly what Sean would've expected from his mother. And now he knew why she'd been so insistent that he should look after Claire, the night of Ashleigh's eighteenth birthday party. She'd known the full story. And she'd known that she could trust Sean to do the right thing. To look after Claire when she needed it.

Claire smiled grimly. 'The drinking was also the worst thing I could have done in Dad's eyes, because his dad used to drink and gamble. I think that was half the reason why I did it, because I wanted to make him as angry as he made me. But your mum sat me down and told me that my mum would hate to see what I was doing to myself, and she made me see that the way I was behaving really wasn't helping the situation. I told her what Mum said about following my dream, and she asked me what I really wanted to do with my life. I showed her my sketchbooks and she said that my passion for needlework showed, and it'd be a shame to ignore my talents.' She smiled. 'And then she talked to Dad. He still didn't think that designing dresses was a stable career—he wanted me to have what he thought of as a "proper" job.'

'Does he still think that?' Sean asked.

'Oh, yes. And he tells me it, too, every so often,' Claire said, sounding both hurt and exasperated. 'When I left the fashion house where I worked after I graduated, he panicked that I wouldn't be able to make a go of my own business. Especially because there was a recession on. He wanted me to go back to uni instead.'

'And train to be a doctor?'

'Because then I'd definitely have a job for life.' She wrinkled her nose. 'But it's not just about the academic side of things. Sure, I could've done the degree and the post-grad training. But my heart wouldn't have been in it, and that wouldn't be fair to my patients.' She sighed. 'And I had a bit of a cash flow problem last year. I took a hit from a couple of clients whose cheques bounced. I still had to pay my suppliers for the materials and, um...' She wrinkled her nose. 'I could've asked Dad to lend me the money to tide me over, but then he would've given me this huge lecture about taking a bigger deposit from my brides and insisting on cash or a direct transfer to my account. Yet again he would've made me feel that he didn't believe in me and I'm not good enough to make it on my own. So I, um, sold my car. It kept me afloat.'

'And have you changed the way you take money?'

She nodded. 'I admit, I learned that one the hard way. Nowadays I ask for stage payments. But there's no real harm done. And Dad doesn't know about it so I avoided the lecture.' Again, Sean could see the flash of pain in her eyes. 'I just wish Dad believed in me a bit more. Gran and Aunty Lou believe in me. So does Ash.'

'So do I,' Sean said.

At her look of utter surprise, he said softly, 'Ashleigh's wedding dress convinced me. I admit, I had my doubts about you. Especially when you lost her dress. But you came up with a workable solution—and, when the original dress turned up, I could see just how talented you are. Mum was right about you, Claire. Yes, you could've been a perfectly competent doctor, but you would've ignored your talents—and that would've been a waste.'

Her eyes sparkled with tears. 'From you, that's one hell of a compliment. And not one I ever thought I'd hear. Thank you.'

'It's sincerely meant,' he said. 'You did the right thing, following your dreams.'

'I know I did. And I'm happy doing what I do. I'm never going to be rich, but I make enough for what I need—and that's important.' She paused. 'But what about you, Sean? What about your dreams?'

'I'm living them,' he said automatically.

'But supposing Farrell's didn't exist,' she persisted. 'What would you do then?'

'Start up another Farrell's, I guess,' he said.

'So toffee really is your dream?' She didn't sound as if she believed him.

'Of course toffee's my dream. What's wrong with that?' he asked.

'You're the fourth generation to run the business, Sean,' she said softly. 'You have a huge sense of family and heritage and integrity and duty. Even if you didn't really want to do it, you wouldn't walk away from your family business. Ever.'

It shocked him that she could read him so accurately. Nobody else ever had. She wasn't judging him; she was just stating facts. 'I like my job,' he protested. He *did*.

'I'm not saying you don't,' she said softly. 'I'm just asking you, what's your dream?'

'I'm living it,' he said again. Though now she'd made him question that.

It was true that he would never have walked away from the business, even if his parents hadn't been killed. He'd always wanted to be part of Farrell's. It was his heritage.

But, if he was really honest about it, he'd felt such

pressure to keep the business going the same way that his father had always run things. After his parents had died in the crash, he'd needed to keep things stable for everyone who worked in the business, and keeping to the way things had always been done seemed the best way to keep everything on a stable footing.

He'd been so busy keeping the business going. And then, once he'd proved to his staff and his competitors that he was more than capable of running the business well, he'd been so busy making sure that things stayed that way that he just simply hadn't had the time to think about what he wanted.

Just before his parents' accident, he'd been working on some new product ideas. Something that would've been his contribution to the way the family business developed. He'd loved doing the research and development work. But he'd had to shelve it all after the accident, and he'd never had time to go back to his ideas.

Though it was pointless dwelling on might-have-beens. Things were as they were. And the sudden feeling of uncertainty made him antsy.

Sean had intended to ask Claire to stay, that night; but right at that moment he needed some distance between them, to get his equilibrium back. 'I'd better check to see if your clothes are dry.'

They were. So it was easy to suggest making a cold drink while she got dressed. Easier still to hint that it was time for her to go home—particularly as Claire took the hint. He let her walk out of the door without kissing her goodbye.

And he spent the rest of the evening wide awake, miserable and regretting it. She'd pushed him and he'd done what he always did and closed off, not wanting her to get too close.

But her words went round and round in his head. *What's your dream?*

The problem was, you couldn't always follow your dreams. Not if you had responsibilities and other people depended on you.

Everybody has a dream, Sean.

What did he really want?

He sat at his desk, staring out of the window at a garden it was too dark to see. Then he gritted his teeth, turned back to his computer and opened a file.

Dreams were a luxury. And he had a business to run—one that had just managed to survive a takeover bid. Dreams would have to wait.

CHAPTER TEN

SEAN SPENT THE next day totally unable to concentrate.

Which was ridiculous because he never, but never, let any of his girlfriends distract him from work.

But Claire Stewart was different, and she got under his skin in a way that nobody ever had before. He definitely wasn't letting her do it, but it was happening all the same—and he really didn't know what to do about it.

Part of him wanted to call her because he wanted to see her; and part of him was running scared because she made him look at things in his life that he'd rather ignore.

And he still couldn't get her words out of his head. *Everybody has a dream, Sean.* Just what was his?

He still hadn't worked out what to say to her by the evening, so he buried himself in work instead. And he noticed that she hadn't called him, either. So did that mean she, too, thought this was turning out to be a seriously bad idea and they ought to end it?

And then, on Tuesday morning, his PA brought him a plain white box.

'What's this?' he asked.

Jen shrugged. 'I have no idea. I was just asked to give it to you.'

There was no note with the box. He frowned. 'Who brought it?'

'A blonde woman. She wouldn't give her name. She said you'd know who it was from,' Jen said.

His heart skipped a beat.

Claire.

But if Claire had actually come to the factory and dropped this off personally, why hadn't she come to see him?

Or maybe she thought he'd refuse to see her. They hadn't exactly had a fight on Sunday evening, but he had to acknowledge that things had been a little bit strained when she'd left. Maybe this was her idea of a parley, the beginning of some kind of truce.

And hadn't she said about not sending him flowers and how you couldn't give chocolates to a confectioner?

'Thank you. I have a pretty good idea who it's from,' he said to Jen, and waited until she'd closed the door behind her before opening the box.

Claire had brought him cake.

Not just cake—the most delectable lemon cake he'd ever eaten in his life.

He gave in and called her business line.

She answered within three rings. 'Dream of a Dress, Claire speaking.'

'Thank you for the cake,' he said.

'Pleasure.'

Her voice was completely neutral, so he couldn't tell her mood. Well, he'd do things her way for once and ask her straight out. 'Why didn't you come in and say hello?'

'Your PA said you were in a meeting, and I didn't really have time to wait until you were done.'

'Fair enough.' He paused. He knew what he needed to say, and he was enough of a man not to shirk it. 'Claire, I owe you an apology.'

'What for?'

'Pushing you away on Sunday night.'

'Uh-huh.'

He sighed, guessing what she wanted him to say. 'I still can't answer your question.'

'Can't or won't?'

'A bit of both, if I'm honest,' he said.

'OK. Are you busy tonight?'

'Why?' he asked.

'I thought we could go and smell some roses.'

Claire-speak for having some fun, he guessed.

'Can you meet me at my place?'

'Sure. Would seven work for you?'

'Fine. Don't eat,' she said, 'because we can probably grab something on the way. Some of the food stalls at Camden Lock will still be open at that time.'

Clearly she intended to take him for a walk somewhere. 'And is this a jeans and running shoes thing?' he checked.

'You can wear your prissiest suit and your smartest shoes—whatever you like, as long as you can walk for half an hour or so and still be comfortable.'

When Sean turned up at her shop at exactly seven o'clock, Claire was wearing a navy summer dress patterned with daisies and flat court shoes. Her hair was tied back with another chiffon scarf—clearly that was Claire's favoured style—but he was pleased that she didn't add her awful khaki cap, this time. Instead, she just donned a pair of dark glasses.

They walked down to Camden Lock, grabbed a burger and shared some polenta fries, then headed along the canalside towards Regent's Park. He'd never really explored the area before, and it was a surprisingly pretty walk; some of the houses were truly gorgeous, and all the while there were birds singing in the trees and the calm presence of the canal.

'I love the walk along here. It's only ten minutes or so between the lock and the park,' she said.

And then Sean discovered that Claire had meant it literally about coming to smell the roses when she took him across Regent's Park to Queen Mary's Garden.

'This place is amazing—it's the biggest collection of roses in London,' she told him.

There were pretty bowers, huge beds filled with all different types of roses, and walking through them was like breathing pure scent; it totally filled his senses.

'This is incredible,' he said. 'I didn't think you meant it literally about smelling the roses.'

'I meant it metaphorically as well—you must know that WH Davies poem, "What is this life if full of care, We have no time to stand and stare,",' she said. 'You have to make time for things like this, Sean, or you miss out on so much.'

He knew she had a point. 'Yeah,' he said softly, and tightened his fingers round hers.

He could just about remember coming to see the roses in Regent's Park as a child, but everything since his parents' death was a blur of work, work and more work.

Six years of blurriness.

Being with Claire had brought everything into sharp focus again. Though Sean wasn't entirely sure he liked what he saw when he looked at his life—and it made him antsy. Claire was definitely dangerous to his peace of mind.

She drew him over to look at the borders of delphiniums, every shade of white and cream and blue through to almost black.

'Now these I *really* love,' she said. 'The colour, the shape, the texture—everything.'

He looked at her. 'So you're a secret gardener?'

'Except doing it properly would take time I don't really have to spare,' she said. 'Though, yes, if had a decent-sized garden I'd plant it as a cottage garden with loads of these and hollyhocks and foxgloves, and tiny little lily-of-the-valley and violets.'

'These ones here are exactly the same colour as your eyes.'

She grinned. 'Careful, Sean. You're waxing a bit poetic.'

Just to make the point, he kissed her.

'Tsk,' she teased. 'Is that the only way you have to shut me up?'

'It worked for Benedick,' he said.

'*Much Ado* is a rom-com—and I thought you said you didn't like rom-coms?'

'I said I didn't mind ones with great dialogue—and dialogue doesn't get any better than Beatrice.' He could see Claire playing Beatrice; he'd noticed that she often had that deliciously acerbic bite to her words.

'And it's a good plot,' she said, 'except Hero ends up with a man who isn't good enough for her. I hate the bit where Claudio shames her on their wedding day, and it always makes me want to yell to her, "Don't do it!" at the end when she marries him.'

'They were different times and different mores, though I do know what you mean,' he said. 'I wouldn't want Ashleigh to marry a weak, selfish man.'

She winced. 'Like Rob Riverton. And I introduced her to him.'

'Not one of your better calls,' Sean said.

'I know.' She looked guilty. 'I did tell her to dump

him because he wasn't good enough for her and he didn't treat her properly.'

A month ago, Sean wouldn't have believed that. Now, he did, because he'd seen for himself that Claire had integrity. 'Claire,' he said, yanked her into his arms and kissed her.

'Was that to shut me up again?' she asked when he broke the kiss.

'No—it was because you're irresistible.'

She clearly didn't know what to say to that, because it silenced her.

They walked back along the canalside to Camden, hand in hand; then he bought them both a glass of wine and they sat outside, enjoying the late evening sunshine before walking back to her flat.

'Do you want to come in?' she asked.

'Is that wise?'

'Probably not, but I'm asking anyway.'

'Probably not,' he agreed, 'but I'm saying yes.'

They sat with the windows open, the curtains open and music playing; there was a jug of iced water on the coffee table, and she'd put frozen slices of lime in the jug. Sean was surprised by how at home he felt here; the room was decorated in very girly colours, compared to his own neutral colour scheme, but he felt as if he belonged.

'It's getting late. I ought to go,' he said softly. 'I have meetings, first thing.'

'You don't have to go,' Claire said. 'You could stay.' She paused. 'If you want to.'

'Are you sure?'

'I'm sure.'

In answer, he closed her curtains and carried her to her bed.

* * *

The next morning, Claire woke before her alarm went off to find herself alone in bed, and Sean's side of the bed was stone cold. She was a bit disappointed that he hadn't even woken her before he left, or put a note on the pillow. Then again, he'd said that he had early meetings. He'd probably left at some unearthly hour and hadn't wanted to disturb her sleep.

At that precise moment he walked in, carrying a tray with two paper cups of coffee and a plate of pastries. 'Breakfast is served, my lady.'

'You went out to buy us breakfast? That's—that's so *lovely*,' she said, sitting up, 'but you really didn't have to. I have fruit and yoghurt in the fridge, plus bread and granola in the cupboard.'

'I noticed a bakery round the corner from yours. I thought croissants might be nice, and I'm running a bit short on time so I bought the coffee rather than making it.'

'That sounds to me like an excuse for having decadent tendencies,' she teased.

He laughed back. 'Maybe.'

He sat on the bed and shared the almond-filled croissants with her. 'You thought I'd gone without saying goodbye, didn't you?'

'Um—well, yes,' she admitted.

'I wouldn't do that to you. I would at least have left you a note.' He finished his coffee and kissed her lightly. 'Sorry. I really *do* have to go now. Can I call you later?'

'I'd like that.' Claire wrapped herself in her robe so she could pad barefoot to the kitchen with him and kiss him goodbye at her front door.

She still couldn't quite get over the fact he'd gone out to buy them a decadent breakfast. And he'd stayed last night. This thing between them was moving so incredibly fast; it scared and exhilarated her at the same time. She guessed it would be the same for Sean. But would it scare him enough to make him push her away again, the way he had the other night? Or would he finally let her in?

They were both busy during the week, but Sean texted her on Friday.

Do you have any appointments over lunch?

Sorry, yes.

And, regretfully, she wasn't playing hard to get. She really did have appointments that she couldn't move.

OK. Are you busy after work?

Yes, but that was something she could move.

Why?

Am trying to be like you and plan a spontaneous date.

She couldn't help laughing. Planning and spontaneity didn't go together.

OK.

Cinema? he suggested.

Depends. Is popcorn on offer?

Could be... he texted back.

Deal. Time and place?

Can pick you up.

She wanted to keep at least some of her independence.

Saves time if I meet you there.

OK. Will check out films and text you where and when.

Claire had expected him to choose some kind of noir movie, but when she got to the cinema and met him with a kiss she discovered that he'd picked a rom-com.

'Is this to indulge me?' she asked.

'I've seen this one before. The structure's good and the acting's good,' he said.

'You're such a film snob,' she teased, but it warmed her that he'd thought of what she'd enjoy rather than imposing his choices on her regardless.

They sat in the back row, holding hands, and Claire enjoyed the film thoroughly. Back at his place afterwards, they were curled in bed together, when Sean said, 'I had a focus group meeting today.'

She remembered the samples he'd given her. 'Did it go how you wanted?'

'Not really,' he said. 'We need a rethink.'

'For what it's worth, I've always thought that your caramel hearts would be great as bridal favours. That's the sort of thing my brides always ask me if I know about, because not everyone likes the traditional sugared almonds.'

'Bridal favours?' he queried.

'Uh-huh—the hearts could be wrapped in silver or

gold foil, and you can offer a choice of organza bags with them in say white, silver or gold, so brides can buy the whole package. They could be ordered direct from your website, or you could offer the special bridal package through selected shops.'

He nodded. 'That's brilliant, Claire. Thank you. I never even considered that sort of thing.'

'Why would you, unless you were connected to a wedding business?' she pointed out.

'I guess not.'

'So why didn't the focus group like the salted caramels? I thought they were fabulous.'

'It's a move too far from the core business. Farrell's has produced hard toffee for generations. We're not really associated with chocolates, apart from the caramel hearts—which were my mum's idea.'

'Are you looking to move away from making toffee, then?'

'Yes and no,' he said. 'What I want to do is look at other sorts of toffee.'

She frowned. 'Am I being dense? Because toffee's—well—toffee.'

'Unless it's in something,' he said. 'Toffee popcorn, like the one you chose tonight at the cinema. Or toffee ice cream.'

'You weren't concentrating on the film, were you?' she asked. 'You were thinking about work.'

'I was thinking about you, actually,' he said. 'But the toffee popcorn did set off a lightbulb in the back of my head.' He wrinkled his nose. 'If I took the business in that direction, it'd mean buying a whole different set of machinery and arranging a whole different set of staff training. I'd need to be sure that the investment would be worth the cost and Farrell's would see a good return on the money.'

'Unless,' she said, 'you collaborated with other manufacturers—ones who already have the factory set-up and the staff. Maybe you could license them to use your toffee.'

'That's a great idea. And I could draw up a shortlist of other family-run businesses whose ideas and ethos are the same as Farrell's. People who'd make good business partners.'

'That's your dream, isn't it?' she asked softly. 'To keep your heritage—but to put your own stamp on it.'

'I guess. Research and development was always my favourite thing,' he admitted. 'I wanted to look at developing different flavours of toffee. Something different from mint, treacle, orange or nut. I was thinking cinnamon or ginger for Christmas, or maybe special seasonal editions of the chocolate hearts—say a strawberries and cream version for summer.'

'That's a great idea,' she said. 'Maybe white chocolate.'

'And different packaging,' he said. 'Something to position Farrell's hearts as the kind of thing you buy as special treats.'

'You could sell them in little boxes as well as big ones,' she said. 'For people who want a treat but don't want a big box.'

He kissed her. 'I'm beginning to think that I should employ you on my R and D team.'

'Now that,' she said, 'really wouldn't work. I'm used to doing things my way and I'd hate to have to go by someone else's rules all the while. Besides, I don't want you bossing me about and I think we'd end up fighting.'

He wrinkled his nose. 'I don't want to fight with you, Claire—I like how things are now.'

'Me, too,' she admitted.

'Make love, not war—that's a great slogan, you know.'

She grinned. 'Just as long as it's not all talk and no action, Mr Farrell.'

He laughed. 'I can take a hint.' And he kissed her until she was dizzy.

CHAPTER ELEVEN

OVER THE NEXT couple of weeks, Claire and Sean grew closer. Claire didn't get to see Sean every evening, but she talked to him every day and found herself really looking forward to the times they did see each other. And even on days when things were frustrating and refused to go right, or she had a client who changed her mind about what she wanted at least twice a day, it wasn't so bad because Claire knew she would be seeing Sean or talking to him later.

And he indulged her by taking her to one of her favourite places—the Victoria and Albert Museum. She took him to see her favourite pieces of clothing, showing him the fabrics, the shapes and the stitching that had inspired some of her own designs. When they stopped for a cold drink in the café, she looked at him.

'Sorry. I rather went into nerd mode. You should have told me to shut up.'

He smiled. 'Actually, I really enjoyed it.'

'But I was lecturing you, making you look at fiddly bits and pieces that probably bored you stupid.'

'You were lit up, Claire. Clothing design is your passion. And it was a privilege to see it,' he said softly. He reached across the table, took her hand and drew it to his lips. 'Don't ever lose that passion.'

He'd accepted her for who she was, Claire thought with sudden shock. The first man she'd ever dated who'd seen who she was, accepted it, and encouraged her to do what she loved.

In turn, Sean gave her a personal guided tour of the toffee factory. 'I'm afraid the white coat and the hair covering are non-negotiable,' he said.

'Health and safety. This is a working factory. And the clothes are about function, not form—just as they should be,' she said.

'I guess.' He took her through the factory, explaining what the various stages were and letting her taste the different products.

'I love the fact you're still using your great-grandparents' recipe for the toffee,' she said. 'And the photographs.' She'd noticed the blown-up photographs from years before lining the walls in the reception area. 'It's lovely to see that connection over the years.'

'A bit like you,' he said, 'and the way you hand-decorate a dress exactly the same as they would've done it two hundred years ago.'

'I guess.'

They were halfway through when Sean's sales manager came over.

'Sean, I'm really sorry to interrupt,' he said, smiling acknowledgement at Claire. 'I'm afraid we've got a bit of a situation.'

'Hey—don't mind me,' Claire said. 'The business comes first. I can do a tour at any time.'

'Thanks,' Sean said. 'What's the problem, Will?'

'I had the press on the phone earlier, talking about the takeover bid,' Will said. 'I explained that it's not happening and Farrell's is carrying on exactly as before, but someone's clearly been spreading doubts among our biggest customers, because I've been fielding phone calls ever since. And one of our customers in particular says he wants to talk to the organ grinder, not the monkey.'

'You're my sales manager,' Sean said. 'Which makes you as much of an organ grinder as I am.'

Will looked awkward. 'Not in Mel Archer's eyes.'

'Ah. *Him.*' Sean grimaced. 'Claire, would you mind if I let Will finish the tour with you?'

'Sure,' she said.

'I'll talk to Archer and explain the situation to him,' Sean said. 'And I'll make it very clear to him that I trust my senior team to do their jobs well and use their initiative.'

'Sorry.'

'It's not your fault,' Sean said. 'I'll see you later, Claire.'

She smiled at him. 'No worries. I'll wait for you in reception.'

'Sorry. It's the monkey rather than the organ grinder for you, too,' Will said.

She smiled. 'Sean says you're an organ grinder. That's good enough for me.'

Will finished taking her round and answered all her questions. Including ones she knew she probably shouldn't ask but couldn't help herself; this was a chance to see another side of Sean.

'So have you worked for Sean for long?' she asked Will.

'Three years,' Will said. 'And he's probably the best manager I've ever worked with. He doesn't micromanage—he trusts you to get on and do your job, though he's always there if things get sticky.'

'Which I guess they would be, in a toffee factory,' Claire said with a smile.

Will laughed. 'Yeah. Pun not actually intended. What I mean is he knows the business inside out. He's there if you need support, and if there's a problem you can't solve he'll have an answer—though what he does is ask you questions to make you think a bit more about it and work it out for yourself.'

So her super-efficient businessman liked to teach people and develop his staff, too. And it was something she knew he wouldn't have told her himself.

From the half of the tour Sean had given her and the insights Will added, Claire realised that maybe Sean really was living his dream; he really did love the factory and his job, and not just because it was his heritage and he felt duty-bound to preserve it for the next generation. Though she rather thought that if he'd had a choice in the matter, he would've worked in the research and development side of the business.

'He's a good man,' she said, meaning it.

When Ashleigh and Luke returned from their honeymoon, they invited Claire over to see the wedding photographs. She arrived bearing champagne and brownies. Sean was there already, and she gave him a cool nod of acknowledgement before cooing over the photographs and choosing the ones she wanted copies of.

A little later, he offered to help her make coffee. 'Have I done something to upset you?' he asked softly when they were alone in Ashleigh's kitchen.

'No.' Clare frowned. 'What makes you think that?'

'Just you seemed a little cool with me tonight.'

'In front of Ash, yes—she expects me to be just on the verge of civil with you. If I'm nice to you, she's going to guess something's going on, and I don't want her to know about this.' Claire took a deep breath. 'She's already asked me a couple of questions, and I told her we came to a kind of truce in Capri—once you realised it wasn't my fault her wedding dress disappeared—and you were one step away from grovelling.'

'You told her I was *grovelling*?'

Claire grinned. 'She just laughed and said grovelling isn't in your vocabulary, and she'd give it a week before we started sniping at each other again.'

He moved closer. 'I'm definitely not grovelling, but I'm not sniping either.' He paused. 'In fact, I'd rather just kiss you.'

'I'd rather that, too,' she said softly, 'but I'm not ready for Ash to know about this yet.'

'So I'm your dirty little secret?'

'For now—and I'm yours,' she said.

At the end of the evening, Sean said, 'Claire, it's raining—I'll give you a lift home to save you getting drenched.'

'This is quite some truce,' Ashleigh said, giving them both a piercing look. 'Though you probably won't make it back to Claire's before the ceasefire ends.'

'I won't fight if she doesn't,' Sean said. 'Claire?'

'No fighting, and thank you very much for the offer of the lift.'

Ashleigh narrowed her eyes at both of them, but didn't say any more.

'Do you have any idea how close you were to breaking our cover?' Claire asked crossly on the way home. 'I'm sure Ash has guessed.'

'What's your problem with anyone knowing about you and me?' Sean asked.

'Because it's still early days. And, actually, unless my calendar's wrong, you'll be dumping me in the next few days anyway.'

'How do you work that out?'

'Because, Sean Farrell, you never date anyone for more than three weeks in a row.'

'I don't dump my girlfriends exactly three weeks in to a relationship,' he said. 'That's a little old and a little unfair.'

'But you dump them,' Claire persisted.

'No, I break up with them nicely and I make them feel it's their decision,' he corrected.

'When it's actually yours.'

He shrugged. 'If it makes them feel better about the situation, what's the problem?'

'You're impossible.'

He laughed. 'Ashleigh said we wouldn't make it back to your place before we started fighting. She was right.'

'I'm not fighting, I'm just making a statement of facts—and don't you dare kiss me to shut me up,' she warned.

'I can't kiss you when I'm driving,' Sean pointed out, 'so that's a rain check.'

'You really are the most exasperating...' Unable to think of a suitable retort, she lapsed into silence.

'Besides,' he said softly, 'you'd be bored to tears with a yes-man or a lapdog.'

'Lapdog?' she asked, not following.

'"When husbands or when lapdogs breathe their last." Alexander Pope,' he explained helpfully.

She rolled her eyes. 'I forgot you did English A level.'

'And dated a couple of English teachers.'

'Would one of those have been the one who made you see a certain rom-com more than once?'

'Yes. At least you haven't done that.'

'You're still impossible,' she grumbled.

'Yup,' he said cheerfully.

'And, excuse me, you just missed the turning to my place.'

'Because we're not going to your place. We're going to mine.'

'But I have a bride coming in first thing tomorrow morning for a final fitting,' she protested.

'I have a washer-dryer, an alarm clock, a spare unused toothbrush, and I'll run you home after breakfast.'

She sighed. 'You've got an answer for everything.'

'Most things,' he corrected, and she groaned.

'I give up.'

'Good,' he said.

He stripped her very slowly once he'd locked his front door behind them, put her clothes in the laundry, then took her to bed. And he was as good as his word, finding her a spare toothbrush, making her coffee in the morning, making sure her clothes were dried, and taking her home.

She kissed him lingeringly in the car. 'See you later. And thanks for the lift.'

Ashleigh dropped by at lunchtime.

'Well, hello, stranger—long time, no see,' Claire teased. 'What is it, a little over twelve hours?'

'We're having lunch,' Ashleigh said. 'Now.'

'Why does this feel as if you're about to tell me off?' Claire asked.

'Because I am. When did this all happen?'

Claire tried to look innocent. 'When did all what happen?'

'You know perfectly well what I mean. You and my brother. And don't deny it. You're both acting totally out of character round each other.'

'He just gave me a lift home last night,' Claire said,

crossing her fingers under the table. It had been a lot more than that.

'Hmm.' Ashleigh folded her arms and gave Claire a level stare.

Claire gave in. 'Ash, it's early days. And you know Sean; it's probably not going to last.'

'Why didn't you tell me?'

'Because when it all goes wrong I don't want our friendship to be collateral damage.'

Ashleigh hugged her. 'Idiot. Nothing would stop me being friends with you.'

'Sean doesn't want you to be collateral damage, either,' Claire pointed out.

Ashleigh rolled her eyes. 'I won't be, and don't you go overprotective on me like my big brother is—remember I'm older than you.'

'OK,' Claire said meekly.

'I thought something was up when he helped you make coffee, and then when he offered you a lift home...I knew it for sure,' Ashleigh said.

'It's still really, really early days,' Claire warned.

'But it's working,'

'At the moment. We still fight, but it's different now.' Claire smiled. 'Sean's not quite as regimented as I thought he was.'

Ashleigh laughed. 'Not with you around, he won't be.'

'And he's stopped calling me the Mistress of Chaos.'

'Good, because you're not.' Ashleigh hugged her again. 'I can't think of anyone I'd like more as my sister-in-law. I've always thought of you as like my sister anyway.'

'We haven't been together long,' Claire warned, 'so I'm not promising anything.'

'I think,' Ashleigh said, 'that you'll be good for each other.'

'Promise me you won't say anything? Even to Luke?'

'It's a bit too late for Luke,' Ashleigh said, 'but I won't say anything to Sean.'

'Thank you. And you'll be the first to know if things move forward. Or,' Claire said, 'when we break up.'

In the two weeks before the wedding show Claire was crazily busy and had almost no free time for dates. Sean took over and brought in takeaways to make sure she ate in the evenings; he also made her take breaks before her eyes started hurting, and gave her massages when her shoulders ached.

Even though part of Claire thought he was being just a little bit overprotective, she was grateful for the TLC. 'I really appreciate this, Sean.'

'I know, and you'd do the same for me if I had an exhibition,' he pointed out. 'By the way, I'm in talks with a couple of manufacturers about joint projects and licensing. Talking to you and brainstorming stuff like that,' he said, 'really helped me see the way I want the company to go in the future.'

'Following your dreams?'

'Maybe,' he said with a smile, and kissed her.

The week before the wedding show, Claire took Sean to meet her family—her father, her grandmother, Aunt Lou and her cousins. Clearly she'd talked to them about him, Sean thought, because they already seemed to know who he was and lots about him. Then he realised that they knew Ashleigh and his background was the same as hers.

Even though they were warm and welcoming and

treated him as if he were one of them, chatting and laughing and teasing him, he still felt strange. His grandparents would've been older than Claire's and had died when he was in his teens. This was the first time for years that Sean had been in a family situation where he wasn't being the protective big brother and the head of the family, and it made him feel lost, not knowing quite where he was supposed to fit in.

It didn't help that Claire's father grilled him mercilessly about his intentions towards Claire. Sean could understand it—he shared Jacob's opinion of Claire's previous boyfriends, at least the ones that he'd met— but it still grated that he'd be judged alongside them.

And he could also see what Claire meant about her dad not believing in her. Jacob didn't see the point of spending time and money making six sets of wedding clothes that hadn't actually been ordered by clients, and he'd said a couple of times during the evening that he couldn't see how Claire would possibly get a return on her investment. Claire had smiled sweetly and glossed over it, but Sean had seen that little pleat between her brows that only appeared when she was really unhappy about something. Clearly she was hurt by the way her father still didn't believe in her.

Well, maybe he could give Jacob Stewart something to think about. 'I always do trade shows,' he said. 'They're really good for awareness—and it makes new customers consider stocking you when they see the quality of your product.'

'Maybe,' Jacob said.

'I don't know if you saw the dress Claire made for my sister, but it was absolutely amazing. She's really good at what she does. And what gives her the extra edge is that she loves what she does, too. That gives her clients confidence. And it's why they tell all their friends about her. Her referral rate is stunning.'

Jacob said nothing, but raised an eyebrow.

Sean decided not to push it any further—the last thing he wanted was for Jacob to upset Claire any further on the subject and knock her confidence at this late stage—but he had to hide a smile when he saw the fervent thumbs-up that Claire's grandmother and aunt did out of Jacob's viewpoint.

Though he was quiet when he drove Claire home.

'I'm sorry, Sean. I shouldn't have asked you to meet them—it's too early,' she said, guessing why he was quiet and getting it totally wrong. 'It's just, well, they'll all be coming to the wedding show and I thought it'd be better if you met them before rather than spring it on you then.'

'No, it was nice to meet them,' he said. 'I liked them.' He wanted to shake her father, but judged it not the most tactful thing to say.

'They liked you—and Dad approved of you, which has to be a first.'

He couldn't hide his surprise. 'Even though I argued with him?'

'You batted my corner,' she said. 'And I appreciate that. I think he did, too. Dad's just…a bit difficult.'

'He'll come round in the end,' Sean said. 'When he sees your collection on the catwalk, he'll understand.'

'Hardly. He's a guy. So he's not the slightest bit interested in dresses,' Claire said, though to Sean's relief this time she was smiling rather than looking upset. 'I just have to remember not to let it get to me.'

'You're going to be brilliant,' Sean said. 'Come on. Let's go to bed.'

She smiled. 'I thought you'd never ask…'

* * *

Over the next week, Claire worked later and later on last-minute changes to the wedding show outfits, and the only way Sean could get her out of her workroom for dinner was to haul her manually over his shoulder and carry her out of the room.

'You need to eat to keep your strength up, and you can't live off sandwiches for the next week,' he told her, 'or you'll make yourself ill.'

'I guess.' She blinked as she took in the fact that her kitchen was actually being used and something smelled gorgeous. 'Hang on, dinner isn't a takeaway.'

'It's nothing fancy, either,' Sean said dryly, 'but it's home-cooked from scratch and there are proper vegetables.' He gave her a rueful smile. 'And at least you have gadgets that help.'

'My electric steamer. Best gadget ever.' She smiled back and stroked his face. 'Sean, thank you. It's really good of you to do this for me.'

'Any time, and you know you'd do the same if I was the one up to my eyes in preparation for a big event, so it's not a big deal.' He kissed her lightly. 'Sit down, milady, because dinner will be served in about thirty seconds.'

But when he'd dished up and they were eating, he noticed that she was pushing her food around her plate. 'Is my cooking that terrible? You don't have to be polite with me—leave it if you hate it.'

'It's wonderful. I'm just tired.' She made an effort to eat.

He tried to distract her a little. 'So do you have a dream of a dress?'

'Not really,' she said.

'So all these years when you've sketched wedding

dresses, you never once drew the one you wanted for yourself?'

'I guess it would depend when and where I got married—if it was on a beach in the Seychelles I wouldn't pick the same dress, veil or shoes as I'd pick for a tiny country church in the middle of winter in, say, the far north of Scotland.'

'I guess,' he said. 'So which kind of wedding would you prefer?'

'It's all academic,' she said.

He could guess why she wasn't answering him—she was obviously worried he'd think she was hinting and had expectations where he was concerned.

'Is that why the outfits in your wedding collection are so diverse?'

'Yes—four seasonal weddings, one vintage-inspired outfit, and one that's more tailored towards a civil wedding,' she explained.

'That's a good range,' he said. 'It will show people what you can do.'

'I hope so.' For a second she looked really worried and vulnerable.

'Claire, you know your stuff, you're good at what you do and your work is really going to shine at the show.' He reached over to squeeze her hand. 'I believe in you.'

'Thank you, though I wasn't fishing for compliments.'

'I know you weren't, and I was being sincere.'

'Sorry.' She wrinkled her nose. 'Ignore me. It's just a bit of stage fright, or whatever the catwalk equivalent is.'

'Which is totally understandable, given that it's your first show.' He cleared their plates away. 'Let me get you some coffee.'

She gave him a tired smile. 'Sorry, I'm really not pulling my weight in this relationship right now.'

'Claire, you're so busy you barely have time to breathe. I'm not going to give you a hard time about that; I just want to take some of the weight off your shoulders,' he said.

'Then thank you. Coffee would be lovely.'

He made two mugs of coffee and set them on the table. 'This is decaf,' he said, 'because I think you're already going to have enough trouble getting to sleep and the last thing you need is caffeine.'

'I guess.'

And he hoped that what he was about to do would distract her enough to let her fall asleep in his arms tonight and stop worrying quite so much about the wedding show.

He rescued the box he'd stowed in her fridge earlier—a box containing a very important message. He checked behind the door that he hadn't accidentally disturbed the contents of the box and mixed up the order of the lettered chocolates, then brought them out and placed the box on the table in front of her.

She gave him a tired smile. 'Would these be some of your awesome salted caramels? Or are you trying out new stuff on me as your personal focus group?'

'Open the box and see,' he invited.

She did so, and her eyes widened as she read the message. When she looked back at him, he could see the sheen of tears in her eyes. *'Sean.'*

'Hey. They say you should say it with flowers, but I know you like to be different, so I thought I'd say it in chocolate.' He'd iced the letters himself. *I love you Claire.* He paused. 'Or maybe I just need to say it.' He swallowed hard. Funny how his throat felt as if it were filled with sand. 'I've never said this to anyone before. I love you, Claire. I think I probably have for years, but the idea of letting anyone close scared me spitless. You know you asked me what scared me? *That*. Deep down guess I was worried that I'd end up losing my partner like I lost my parents, so it was easier to keep you at a distance.'

'So what changed?' she asked.

'Capri,' he said. 'Seeing the way you just got on with things and sorted out the problems when Ashleigh's dress went missing. And then dancing with you. I really couldn't take my eyes off you—it wasn't just the song. I tried to tell myself that it was just physical attraction, but it's more than that. So very much more.'

'Oh, Sean.' She blinked back the tears.

And now he just couldn't shut up. 'And in these last few weeks, getting to know you, I've seen you for who you really are. You're funny and you're brave and you're bossy, and you think outside the box, and—you know your speed dating question thing, about what you're looking for in a partner? I can answer that, now. I'm looking for *you*, Claire. You're everything I want.' He gave her a wry smile. 'Though my timing's a bit rubbish, given that you're up to your eyes right now.'

'Your timing's perfect,' she said softly. 'You know, I had a huge crush on you when I was fourteen, but you were my best friend's older brother, which made you off limits. And you always made me feel as if I was a nuisance.'

'You probably were, when you were a teenager.'

She laughed. 'Tell it to me straight, why don't you?'

He laughed back. 'You wouldn't have it any other way, and you know it—I love you, Claire.'

'I love you, too, Sean.' She pushed her chair back, came round to his side of the table, wrapped her arms round him and kissed him. 'Over the last few weeks

I've got to know you and you're not quite who I thought you were, either. You're this human dynamo but you also think on your feet. You're not regimented and rule-bound.'

'No?'

'Well, maybe just a little bit—and you do look good in a suit.' She smiled at him. 'Though how I really like you dressed is in faded jeans, and a white shirt with the sleeves rolled up. It makes you much more touchable.'

'Noted,' he said.

He could see that she was so tired, she didn't even have the energy to drink her coffee. So he carried her to bed, cherished her, and let her fall asleep in his arms. He wasn't ready to sleep yet; it was good just to lie in the dark with her in his arms, thinking. How amazing it was that she felt the same way about him. So maybe, just maybe, this was going to work out.

CHAPTER TWELVE

ON THE MORNING of the wedding show, Claire was up before six, bustling around and double-checking things on her list.

Then her mobile phone rang. Sean couldn't tell much from Claire's end of the conversation, but her face had turned white and there was a tiny pleat above her nose that told him something was definitely wrong.

When she ended the call, she blew out a breath. 'Sorry, I'm going to have to neglect you and make a ton of phone calls now.'

'What's happened?'

'That was the modelling agency.' She closed her eyes for a moment. 'It seems that the six male models that I booked through the agency are all really good friends. They went out together for a meal last night, and they've all gone down with food poisoning so they can't do the show.'

'So the agency's going to send you someone else?'

She shook her head. 'All their models are either already booked out or away. So they're very sorry to let me down, but it's due to circumstances beyond their control and they're sure I'll understand, and of course they'll return my fee.'

The sing-song, patronising tone in which she replayed the conversation told Sean just how angry Claire was—and he wasn't surprised. She'd been very badly let down.

'I'll just have to go through my diary and beg a few favours, and hope that I can find six men willing to stand in for the models.' She raked a hand through her hair. 'And I need to look at my list and see where I can cut a few corners, because I'll have to alter their clothes to fit the stand-ins, and…' She shook her head, looking utterly miserable.

He put his arms round her and hugged her. 'You need five. I'll do it.'

She stared at him as if the words hadn't quite sunk in. '*You'll* do it?'

'Well, obviously I don't know the first thing about a catwalk,' he said, 'so someone's going to have to teach me how to do the model walk thing. But everyone's going to be looking at the clothes and not the model in any case, so I guess that probably doesn't matter too much.'

'You'll do it,' she repeated, sounding disbelieving.

'Is it that much of a stretch to see me as a model?' he asked wryly.

'No, it's not that at all. You'd be *fabulous*. It's just that—it's a pretty public thing, standing on a catwalk at a wedding show with everyone staring at you, and it's so far from what you normally do that I thought you'd find it too embarrassing or awkward or…' She tailed off. 'Oh, my God, Sean. You'd really do that for me?'

'Yes,' he said firmly.

'Thank you.' She hugged him fiercely. 'That means I only have to find five.'

'You've already got enough to do. I'll find them for you,' he said. 'I reckon we can count on Luke and Tom, and I have a few others in mind. Just tell me the rough heights and sizes you need, and I'll ring round and sort it out.'

'Your height and build would be perfect, but I can adjust things if I need to—the men's outfits are easier to adjust than the women's, so I guess I'm lucky that it was the male models and not the female ones or the children who had to bail out on me. Sean, are you really sure about this?'

'Really,' he confirmed. 'I'm on Team Claire, remember? Now go hit that shower, I'll have coffee ready by the time you're out, and I'll start ringing round.'

She hugged him. 'Have I told you how wonderful you are? Five minutes ago it felt as if the world had ended, and now...'

'Hey—you'd do the same for me,' he pointed out.

Half an hour later, Sean had it all arranged. Luke and Tom agreed immediately to stand in, plus Tom's partner. Sean called in his best friend and his sales manager from the factory, and they all agreed to meet him and Claire at the wedding show two hours before it started, so Claire could do any last-minute necessary alterations to their outfits. Then he made Claire sit down and eat breakfast, before helping her to load everything into the van she'd hired for the day.

'Sure we've got all the wedding dresses?' he asked before he closed the van doors. 'Though I guess we're going to Earl's Court rather than Capri, so we should be OK.'

'Not funny, Sean.' She narrowed her eyes at him.

He kissed her lightly. 'That was misplaced humour and I apologise. It's all going to be fine, Claire. Just breathe and check your list.'

'Sorry, I'm being unfair and overly grouchy. Ignore

me.' She looked over her list. 'Everything's ticked off and loaded, so we're ready to roll.'

'At least we've got the bumps out of the way this side of the catwalk. It's all going to be fine now.' He kissed her again. 'By the way, I meant to tell you, I've got some extra giveaways for you. Will from the office is bringing them to the show.'

'Giveaways?' Her eyes went wide. 'Oh, no. I completely forgot about giveaways. I meant to order some pens. I've been so focused on the outfits that it totally slipped my mind.'

'You have business cards?'

'Yes.'

'Grab them,' he said, 'and we'll get a production line stuffing them at the show.'

'Stuffing what?' She looked at him blankly.

'My genius girlfriend talked about wedding favours. I had some samples run up, with white organza bags and gold foil on the caramel hearts. The bag is just the right size to put your business card in as well—and don't worry about the pens. Everyone will remember the chocolate.'

'Sean, that's above and beyond.'

'No, it's supporting you,' he corrected, 'and it also works as a test run for me, so we both win. Let's get this show on the road.'

At the wedding show, people were busy setting up exhibition stands and the place was bustling. Claire was busy measuring her new male models and doing alterations; then, when the female models arrived, she filled them in on the situation and got them to teach the men how to walk. Her stand was set up with showbooks of her designs, and her part-time shop assistant Iona was there to field enquiries and take contact details of people who were interested in having a consultation about a wedding dress. Will had brought the organza bags and chocolates with him, so Sean had a production line of people stuffing bags with the chocolates and Claire's business card. He knew how much was riding on this.

And it also worried him. Claire had already had to deal with extra problems that weren't of her making today. If this didn't go to plan, all her hard work would have been for nothing.

What he wanted to do was to make sure that the people she wanted to see her collection actually saw it. She'd already mentioned the names of some of the fashion houses who were going to be there. A little networking might just give them the push they needed to make sure they saw Claire's work.

While Claire was making last-minute fixes to the dresses, Sean slipped away quietly to find the movers and shakers of her world. Claire had just about finished by the time he returned.

'Everything OK?' he asked.

'Yes.' She smiled at him. 'You're amazing and I love you. Now go strut your stuff.'

The dresses all looked breathtaking. He knew how much work had gone into them, along with Claire's heart and soul. Please let the reviewers be kind rather than snarky, he begged silently. Please let her get the kudos she deserved. Please let the fashion houses keep their word and come to see her. Please let them give her a chance.

Claire's hands were shaking visibly. Ashleigh was sitting next to her; she took Claire's hands and held them tightly. 'Breathe. It's going to be just fine.'

'They all look amazing,' Claire's grandmother added.

'You're going to wow the lot of them,' Aunt Lou said, reaching over to pat her shoulder.

Only Jacob was silent, but Claire hadn't really expected anything from her dad; she knew that fashion shows weren't his thing. The fact that he'd actually turned up meant that he was on her side for once—didn't it?

But finally the catwalk segment of the show began. Her collection was first. The models came down the catwalk, one group at a time: the bride, groom and bridesmaids. Autumn. Winter. Spring. Summer. Sean, looking incredibly gorgeous in morning dress and a top hat with his vintage-inspired bride beside him; her heart skipped a beat when he caught her eye and smiled at her. The contemporary civil wedding.

And then finally, the whole collection of six stood on the stage in a tableau. Claire became aware of music, lights—and was that applause?

'You did it, love,' her grandmother said and hugged her. 'Listen to everyone clapping. They think you're as fantastic as we do.'

'We did it.' Claire was shaking with a mixture of relief and adrenaline. She swallowed hard. 'I need to get back to my stand.'

'Iona can cope for another five minutes,' Aunt Lou said with a smile. 'Just enjoy this bit.'

A woman came over to join them. 'Claire Stewart?' she asked.

Claire looked up. 'Yes.'

'Pia Verdi,' the woman introduced herself, and handed over her business card.

Claire's eyes widened as she took in the name of one of the biggest wedding dress manufacturers in the country.

'I like what I've just seen up there, and I'd like to

talk to you about designing a collection for us,' Pia said. 'Obviously you won't have your diary on you now, but call my PA on Monday morning and we'll set up a meeting.'

'Thank you—I'd really like that,' Claire said.

The one thing she'd been secretly hoping for—her chance in the big league. To design a collection that would be sold internationally and would have her name on it.

She just about managed to keep it together until Sean—who'd clearly changed out of his wedding outfit at top speed—came out. He picked her up and spun her round, and she laughed.

'We did it, Sean.'

'Not me. You're the one who designed those amazing outfits.'

'But you supported me when I needed it. Thank you so, so much.' She handed him the business card and grinned her head off. 'Look who wants to talk to me next week!'

'They're offering you a job?' he asked.

'Better than that—they're asking me to talk to them about designing a collection. So I'll get my name out there, but I still get to do my brides and design one-offs as well. It's the icing on the cake. Everything I wanted. I'm so happy.'

'That's brilliant news.' He hugged her. 'I'm so proud of you, Claire. You deserve this.'

'Thanks.' She beamed at him. 'Though I'd better come down off cloud nine and get back to the stand. It's not fair to leave Iona on her own.'

'I'm so glad Pia Verdi came to see you,' he said.

She frowned as his words sank in. 'Hang on. Are you telling me you know her?'

'Um, not exactly.'

Her eyes narrowed as she looked at him. 'Sean?'

He blew out a breath. 'I just networked a bit while you were sorting stuff out, that's all.'

Claire went cold. 'You *networked*?'

'I just told her that your collection was brilliant and she needed to see it.'

Bile rose in Claire's throat as she realised what had actually happened. So much for thinking that she'd got this on her own merit. That her designs had been good enough to attract the attention of one of the biggest fashion houses.

Because Sean had intervened.

Without him talking to her, Pia Verdi probably wouldn't even have bothered coming to see Claire's collection.

And, although part of Claire knew that he'd done something really nice for her, part of her was horrified. Because what this really meant was that Sean was as overprotective as her father. Whatever Sean had said, he didn't really believe in her: he didn't think that she could make it on her own, and he thought she'd always need a bit of a helping hand. To be looked after.

Stifled.

So what she'd thought was her triumph had turned out to be nothing of the kind.

'You spoke to Pia Verdi,' she repeated. 'You told her to come and see my collection.'

He waved a dismissive hand. 'Claire, it was just a little bit of networking, that's all. You would've done the same for me.'

'No.' She shook her head. 'No, I wouldn't have thought that I needed to interfere. Because I *know* you can do things on your own. I *know* that you'll succeed without having someone to push you and support you. And you…' She blew out a breath. 'You just have to be in control. All the time. That's not what I want.'

'Claire, I—'

'No,' she cut in. 'No. I think you've just clarified something for me. Something important. I can't do this, Sean. I can't be with someone who doesn't consult me and who always plays things by the book—*his* book.' She shook her head. 'I'm sorry. I know you meant well, but…this isn't what I want.' She took a deep breath. There was no going back now. 'It's over.'

'Claire—'

She took a backward step, avoiding his outstretched hand. 'No. Goodbye, Sean.'

She walked away with her head held high. And all the time she was thinking, just how could today have turned from so spectacularly wonderful to so spectacularly terrible? How could it all have gone so wrong?

Even though her heart was breaking, she smiled and smiled at everyone who came to her exhibition stand. She talked about dresses and took notes. She refused help from everyone to pack things away at the end of the show and did it all herself; by then, her anger had burned out to leave nothing but sadness. Sean had taken her at her word and left, which was probably for the best; but her stupid heart still wished that he were there with her.

Well, too late. It was over—and they were too different for it to have worked out long term. So this summer had just been a fling. One day she'd be able to look back on it and remember the good times, but all she could think of now was the bitterness of her disappointment and how she wished he'd been the man she thought he was.

* * *

Stupid, stupid, *stupid*.

Sean hated himself for the way the light had gone from Claire's eyes. Because he'd been the one to cause it. He'd burst her bubble big-time—ruined the exuberance she'd felt at her well-deserved success. He'd meant well—he'd talked to Pia Verdi and the others with the best possible intentions—but now he could see that he'd done completely the wrong thing. He'd taken it all away from Claire, and he'd made her feel as if the bottom had dropped out of her world.

It felt as if the bottom had fallen out of his world, too. He'd lost something so precious. He knew it was all his own fault; and he really wasn't sure he was ever going to be able to fix this.

He definitely couldn't fix it today; he knew he needed to give her time to cool down. But tomorrow he'd call her. Apologise. Really lay his heart on the line—and hope that she'd forgive him and give him a second chance.

CHAPTER THIRTEEN

IT SHOULD HAVE been a night of celebration.

Not wanting to jinx things before the wedding show, Claire hadn't booked a table at a restaurant in advance; though she'd planned to take her family, Sean, Ashleigh and Luke out to dinner that evening, to thank them for all the support they'd given her in the run-up to the show.

But now the food would just taste like ashes; and she didn't want her misery to infect anyone else. So she smiled and smiled and lied her face off to her family and her best friend, pretending that her heart wasn't breaking at all. 'I'm fine. Anyway, I need to get the van back to the hire company, and start sorting out all these enquiries...'

Finally she persuaded them all to stop worrying about her, and left in the van on her own. But, by the time she'd dropped all the outfits back at her shop, delivered the van back to the hirer and caught the tube back to her flat, she felt drained and empty. Dinner was a glass of milk—which was just about all she could face—and she lay alone in her bed, dry-eyed and too miserable to sleep and wishing that things were different.

Had she been unfair to Sean?

Or were her fears—that he'd be overprotective and stifling in the future, and they'd be utterly miserable together—justified?

Claire still hadn't worked it out by the time she got up at six, the next morning. It was ridiculously early for a Sunday, but there was no point in just lying there and brooding. Though she felt like death warmed up after yet another night of not sleeping properly, and it took three cups of coffee with extra sugar before she could function enough to take a shower and wash her hair.

Work seemed to be about the best answer. If she concentrated on sketching a new design, she wouldn't have room in the front of her head to think about what had happened with Sean. And maybe the back of her head would come up with some answers.

She hoped.

She was sketching in her living room when her doorbell rang.

Odd. She wasn't expecting anyone to call. And she hadn't replied to any of the messages on her phone yet, so as far as everyone else was concerned she was probably still asleep, exhausted after the wedding show.

And who would ring her doorbell before half past eight on a Sunday morning, anyway?

She walked downstairs and blinked in surprise when she opened the door.

Sean was standing there—dressed in jeans and a white shirt rather than his normal formal attire—and he was carrying literally an armful of flowers. She could barely see him behind all the blooms and the foliage of delphiniums, stocks, gerberas and roses.

She blinked at him. 'Sean?'

'Can I come in?' he asked.

'I...' Help. What did she say now?

'I'll say what I've got to say on your doorstep, if I have to,' he said. 'But I'd rather talk to you in private.'

She wasn't too sure that she wanted an audience, either. 'Come up,' she said, and stood aside so he could go past and she could close the door behind them.

'Firstly,' he said, 'I wanted to say sorry. And these are just...' He stopped, glanced down at the flowers and then at her. 'I've gone over the top, haven't I?'

'They're gorgeous—though I'm not sure if I have enough vases, glasses and mugs to fit them all in,' she said.

'I just wanted to say sorry. And I kind of thought I needed to make a big gesture, because the words aren't quite enough. And I know you love flowers. And...' His voice trailed off.

'You're carrying an entire English cottage garden there.' She was still hurt that he didn't truly believe in her, but she could see how hard he was trying to start making things right. And as he stood there in the middle of all the flowers, looking completely like a fish out of water...how could she stay angry with him?

'Let's get these gorgeous flowers in water before they start wilting.' She went into the kitchen and found every receptacle she had, and started filling them with water. 'They're lovely. Thank you. Where did you get them?' she asked. 'Covent Garden flower market isn't open on Sundays.'

'Columbia Road market,' he said. 'I looked up where I could get really good fresh flowers first thing on a Sunday morning.'

She thought about it. 'So you carried all these on the tube?'

'Uh-huh.' He gave her a rueful smile. 'I had to get someone to help me at the ticket barrier.'

He'd gone to a real effort for her. And he'd done something that would've made people stare at him—something she knew would've made him feel uncomfortable.

So this apology was sincerely meant. But she still needed to hear the words.

When they'd finished putting the flowers in water—including using the bowl of her kitchen sink—she said, 'Do you want a coffee?'

'No, thanks. I just need to talk to you,' he said. He took a deep breath. 'Claire, I honestly didn't mean to hurt you. I just wanted to help. But I realise now that I handled it totally the wrong way. I interfered instead of supporting you properly and asking you what you needed me to do. I made you feel as if you were hopeless and couldn't do anything on your own—but, Claire, I *do* believe in you. I knew your designs would make any of the fashion houses sit up and take notice. But the wedding show was so busy, I didn't want to take the risk that they wouldn't get time to see your collection and you wouldn't get your chance. That's the only reason I went to talk to Pia Verdi.'

His expression was serious and completely sincere. She knew he meant what he said.

And she also knew that she owed him an apology, too. They were *both* in the wrong.

'I overreacted a bit as well,' she said. 'I'd been working flat out for weeks and, after the way everything had gone wrong from the first…well, I think it just caught me at the wrong time. Now I've had time to think about it, I know your heart was in the right place. You meant well. But yesterday I felt that you were being overprotective and stifling, the way Dad is, because you don't think I can do it on my own. You think that I need looking after all the time.'

'Claire, I'm not your father. I know you can do it on your own,' he said softly. 'And, for the record, I don't think you need looking after. Actually, I think it would drive you bananas.'

'It would.' She took a deep breath. 'I want an equal partnership with someone who'll back me and who'll let me back them.'

'That's what I want, too,' Sean said.

Hope bloomed in her heart. 'Before yesterday—before things went wrong—that's what I thought we had,' she said.

'We did,' he said. 'We *do*.'

She bit her lip. 'I've hurt you as much as you hurt me. I was angry and unfair and ungrateful, I pushed you away, and I'm sorry. And, if I try to think first instead of reacting first in future, do you think we could start again?'

'So Ms Follow-Your-Heart turns into a rulebook devotee?' Sean said. 'No deal. Because I want a partner who thinks outside the box and stops me being regimented.'

'You're not regimented—well, not *all* the time,' she amended.

'Thank you. I think.' He looked at her. 'I can't promise perfection and I can't promise we won't ever fight again, Claire.'

'It wouldn't be normal if we didn't ever fight again,' she pointed out.

'True. I guess we just need to learn to compromise. Do things the middle way instead of both thinking that our way's the only way.' He opened his arms. 'So. You and me. How about it?'

She stepped into his arms. 'Yes.'

'Good.' He kissed her lingeringly. 'And we'll talk more in future. I promise I won't think I know best.'

'And I promise I won't go super-stubborn.'

He laughed. 'Maybe we ought to qualify that and say we'll *try*.'

'Good plan.'

He arched an eyebrow. 'Are you going to admit that planning's good, outside business?'

She laughed. 'That would be a no. Most of the time. Are you going to admit that being spontaneous means you have more fun?'

He grinned. 'Not if I'm hungry and I've just been drenched in a downpour.'

'Compromise,' she said. 'That works for me.'

'Me, too.' He kissed her again. 'And we'll make this work. Together.'

EPILOGUE

Two months later

CLAIRE WAS WORKING on the preliminary sketches for her first collection for Pia Verdi when her phone beeped.

She glanced at the screen. Sean. Probably telling her that he was going to be late home tonight, she thought with a smile. Although they hadn't officially moved in with each other, they'd fallen into a routine of spending weeknights at her place and weekends at his.

V and A. Thirty minutes. Be there.

Was he kidding?
Three tube changes! Takes thirty minutes PLUS walk to station, she typed back.

And of course he'd know she knew this. The Victoria and Albert Museum was her favourite place in London. She'd taken him there several times and always lingered in front of her favourite dress, a red grosgrain and chiffon dress by Chanel. She never, ever tired of seeing that dress.

Forty minutes, then.

Half a minute later, there was another text.

Make it fifty and change into your blue dress. The one with the daisies.

Why?

Tell you when you get here.

She grinned. Sean was clearly in playful mode, so this could be fun. But why did he want to meet her at the museum? And why that dress in particular?

She still didn't have a clue when she actually got to Kensington. She texted him from the museum entrance: Where are you?

Right next to your favourite exhibit.

Easy enough, she thought, and went to find him.

He was standing next to the display case, dressed up to the nines: a beautifully cut dark suit and a white shirt, but for once he wasn't wearing a tie. That little detail was enough to soften the whole package. Just how she liked it.

'OK. I'm here.' She gestured to her outfit. 'Blue dress. Daisies. As requested, Mr Farrell.'

'You look beautiful,' he said.

'Thank you. But I'm still trying to work out why you wanted to meet me here.'

'Because I'm just about to add to your workload.'

She frowned. 'I don't understand.'

He dropped to one knee. 'Claire Stewart, I love you with all my heart. Will you marry me?'

'I...' She stared at him. 'Sean. I can't quite take this in. You're really asking me to marry you?'

'I'm down on one knee and I used the proper form,' he pointed out.

This was the last thing she'd expected on a Thursday afternoon in her favourite museum. 'Sean.'

'I've been thinking about it for the last month. Where else could you ask a wedding dress designer to marry you, except in her favourite place in London? And next to her favourite exhibit, too?'

Now she knew why he'd asked her to wear his favourite dress: to make this just as special for him. And why he'd said he was adding to her workload—because now she'd have a very special wedding dress to design. Her own.

She smiled. 'Sean Farrell, I love you with all my heart, too. And I'd be thrilled to marry you.'

He stood up, swung her round, and kissed her thoroughly. Then he took something from his pocket. 'We need to formalise this.'

She blinked. 'You bought me a ring?'

'Without consulting you? No chance. This is temporary. Go with the flow. *Carpe diem*,' he said, and slid something onto the ring finger of her left hand.

When she looked at it, she burst out laughing. He'd made her a ring out of unused toffee wrappers.

'We'll choose the proper one together,' he said. 'Just as we'll make all our important decisions together.'

'An equal partnership,' she said, and kissed him. 'Perfect.'

* * * * *

THE WEDDING PLANNER
AND THE CEO

ALISON ROBERTS

CHAPTER ONE

'*No?*'

The smile was sympathetic but the head-shake emphasised the negative response and the receptionist's raised eyebrows suggested that Penelope must have known she was dreaming when she thought her request might be considered reasonable.

'There must be *someone* I could speak to?' It was harder to say no face to face than over the phone, which was, after all, why she'd taken time out of her crazy schedule to fight London traffic and come to the company's head office in person.

In desperation?

'There's really no point.' The receptionist's smile faded slightly. 'You might be able to engage a cowboy to let off a few fireworks on a week's notice but to get the kind of show the best company in the country has to offer, you have to book in advance. *Months* in advance.'

'I didn't have months. My bride only decided she wanted fireworks this morning. I'm talking Bridezilla, here, you know?'

There was a wary edge to the receptionist's gaze

now. Was she worried that Penelope might be capable of following her client's example and throwing an epic tantrum?

'I understand completely but I'm sorry, there's still nothing I can do to help. For future reference, you can book online to make an appointment to talk to one of our sales reps.'

'I don't want to talk to a sales rep.' Penelope tapped into the extra height her four-inch heels provided. 'I want to talk to your manager. Or director. Or whoever it is that runs this company.'

The smile vanished completely. 'We have a chief executive officer. All Light on the Night is an international company. An *enormous* international company. We do shows like the Fourth of July on the Brooklyn Bridge in New York. New Year's Eve on the Sydney Harbour Bridge in Australia.' Her tone revealed just how far out of line Penelope had stepped. 'You might very well want to talk to him but there's no way on earth Ralph Edwards would be interested in talking to *you*.'

'Really? Why not?'

The curiosity sounded genuine and it came from a male voice behind Penelope. The effect on the young woman in front of her was astonishing. The receptionist paled visibly and her mouth opened and closed more than once, as if she was trying to recall all the vehement words that had just escaped.

Penelope turned to see a tall man and registered dark hair long enough to look tousled, faded denim jeans and...cowboy boots? One of the sales reps, perhaps?

'She...doesn't have an appointment.' The receptionist was clearly rattled. 'She just walked in and wants to book a show. A *wedding*...'

The man's gaze shifted to Penelope and made her want to smooth the close fit of her skirt over her hips even though she knew perfectly well it couldn't be creased. Or raise a hand to make sure no errant tresses had escaped the French braiding that described a perfect crescent from one side of her forehead to meet the main braid on the back of her head.

'Congratulations.' His voice had a rich, low timbre. It made Penelope think of gravel rolling around in something thick and delicious. Like chocolate.

'Sorry?' Was he congratulating her on her choice of this company?

'On your engagement.'

'Oh...it's not *my* wedding.'

That was a dream too distant to be visible even with a telescope at the moment. And there was no point even picking up a telescope until she knew what it was she was looking for, and how could she know that until she discovered who she really was and what she was capable of? Come to think of it, this was the first step towards that distant dream, wasn't it? The first time she was taking a leap out of any known comfort zone. Doing something *she* wanted—just for herself.

'I'm an event manager,' she said, after the barely perceptible pause. 'It's my client who's getting married.'

'Ah...' The spark of polite interest was fading rapidly. 'You've come to the right place, then. I'm sure Melissa will be able to help you with whatever arrangements you want to make.'

Melissa made a choked sound. 'She wants the show next Saturday, Mr Edwards.'

Mr Edwards? The terribly important CEO of this huge international company wore faded jeans and cowboy boots to work? Penelope was clearly overdressed but she couldn't let it faze her enough to lose this unexpected opportunity.

One that was about to slip away. She saw the look that implied complete understanding and went as far as forgiving the company receptionist for her unprofessional exchange with a potential client. She also saw the body language that suggested this CEO was about to retreat to whatever top-floor executive sanctuary he'd unexpectedly appeared from.

'I'll give her a list of other companies that might be able to help,' Melissa said.

'I don't want another company.' The words burst out with a speed and emphasis that took Penelope by surprise. 'I…I have to have the best and…and you're the best, aren't you?'

Of course they were. The entire wall behind the receptionist's desk was a night sky panorama of exploding fireworks. Pyrotechnic art with a combination of shape and colour that was mind-blowing.

The man's mouth twitched. Maybe he'd been surprised, too. 'We certainly are.' Amusement reached his eyes with a glint. Very dark eyes, Penelope noticed. As black as sin, even. Her pulse skipped and sped up. There was only one thing to do when you found yourself so far out of your depth like this. Aim for the surface and kick hard.

'It might be worth your while to consider it.' She snatched a new gulp of air. 'This is a celebrity wedding. The kind of publicity that can't be bought.' She managed a smile. 'I understand you specialise in huge shows but New Year's Eve and the Fourth of July only happen once a year, don't they? You must need the smaller stuff as well? This could be a win-win situation for both of us.'

An eyebrow quirked this time. Was he intrigued by her audacity? Was that a sigh coming from Melissa's direction?

'You have a managerial board meeting in fifteen minutes, Mr Edwards.'

'Give me ten,' Penelope heard herself saying, her gaze still fixed on him. 'Please?'

She looked like some kind of princess. Power-dressed and perfectly groomed. The spiky heels of her shoes looked like they could double as a lethal weapon and he could imagine that the elegant, leather briefcase she carried might be full of lengthy checklists and legally binding contracts.

She was the epitome of everything Rafe avoided like the plague so why on earth was he ushering her into his office and closing the door behind them? Perhaps he was trying to send a message to the junior staff that even difficult clients needed to be treated with respect. Or maybe there had been something in the way she'd looked when he'd suggested it was her own wedding she'd come here to organise.

A flicker of…astonishment? He'd probably have the

same reaction if someone suggested he was about to walk down the aisle.

Maybe not for the same reasons, though. The kind of people he had in his life were as non-conformist as he was, whereas this woman looked like she'd already have the preferred names picked out for the two perfectly behaved children she would eventually produce. One girl and one boy, of course. She might have them already, tidied away in the care of a nanny somewhere, but a quick glance at her left hand as she walked past him revealed an absence of any rings so maybe it had been embarrassment that it was taking so long rather than astonishment that had registered in that look.

No. More likely it was something about the way she'd said 'please'. That icy self-control with which she held herself had jarred on both occasions with something he'd seen flicker in her face but the flicker that had come with that 'please' had looked like determination born of desperation and he could respect that kind of motivation.

'Take a seat.' He gestured towards an area that had comfortable seating around a low coffee table—an informal meeting space that had a wall of glass on one side to show off the fabulous view of the Wimbledon golf course.

Not that she noticed the gesture. Clearly impressed to the point of being speechless, she was staring at the central feature of the penthouse office. A mirror-like tube of polished steel that was broken in the middle. The layer of stones on the top of the bottom section had flames flickering in a perfect circle.

He liked it that she was so impressed. He'd designed this feature himself and he was proud of it. But he didn't have time for distractions like showing off.

'Ms...?'

'Collins. Penelope Collins.'

'Rafe Edwards.' The handshake was brief but surprisingly firm. This time she noticed his invitation and he watched her seat herself on one of the couches. Right on the edge as if she might need to leap up and flee at any moment. Legs angled but not crossed.

Nice legs. Was that subtle tug on the hem of her skirt because she'd noticed him noticing? Rafe glanced at his watch and then seated himself on the opposite couch. Or rather perched on his favourite spot, with a hip resting on the broad arm of the couch.

'So...a celebrity wedding?'

She nodded. 'You've heard of Clarissa Bingham?'

'Can't say I have.'

'Oh... She's a local Loxbury girl who got famous in a reality TV show. She's marrying a football star. Blake Summers.'

'I've heard of *him*.'

'It's a huge wedding and we were lucky enough to get the best venue available. Loxbury Hall?'

'Yep. Heard of that, too.'

Her surprise was evident in the way she blinked—that rapid sweep of thick, dark eyelashes. He could understand the surprise. Why should he know anything about a small town on the outskirts of the New Forest between here and Southampton? Or an eighteenth-century manor house that had been used as a function venue for the last decade? He wasn't about to tell her that this location did, in fact, give him a rather close connection to this upcoming event.

'It could be the last wedding ever held there because the property's just been sold and nobody knows whether the new owner will carry it on as a business venture.'

'Hmm.' Rafe nodded but his attention was straying. This Penelope Collins might not be remotely his type but any red-blooded male could appreciate that she was beautiful. Classically beautiful with that golden blonde hair and that astonishing porcelain skin. Or maybe not so classical given that her eyes were brown rather than blue. Nice combination, that—blonde hair and brown eyes—and her skin had a sun-kissed glow to it that suggested an excellent spray tan rather than risking damage from the real thing. She was probably no more than five feet three without those killer heels and her drink of choice was probably a gin and tonic. Or maybe a martini with an olive placed perfectly in the centre of the toothpick.

'Sorry…what was that?'

'It's the perfect place for a fireworks show. The terrace off the ballroom looks down at the lake. There'll be six hundred people there and major magazine coverage. I could make sure that your company gets excellent publicity.'

'We tend to get that from our larger events. Or special-effects awards from the movie industry. There are plenty of smaller companies out there that specialise in things like birthday parties or weddings.'

'But I want this to be spectacular. The *best*…'

She did. He could see that in her eyes. He'd had that kind of determination once—the need to get to the top and be the very best, and it hadn't been easy, especially that first time.

'Is this your first wedding?'

Her composure slipped and faint spots of pink appeared on her cheeks. 'I run a very successful catering company so I've been involved in big events for many years. Moving to complete event design and execution *has* been a more recent development.'

'So this *is* your first wedding.'

She didn't like the implied putdown. Something like defiance darkened her eyes and the aura of tension around the rest of her body kicked up a notch.

'The event is running like clockwork so far. Everything's in place for the ceremony and reception. The entertainment, decorations and catering are locked in. Clarissa is thrilled with her dress and the photographers are over the moon by the backdrops the venue offers. We even have the best local band playing live for the dancing. You must have heard of Diversion?'

Rafe's breath came out in an unexpected huff. Another connection? This was getting weird.

'It was all going perfectly until this morning, when Clarissa decided they had to have fireworks to finish the night. She had a complete meltdown when I told her that it was probably impossible to organise at such late notice.'

Rafe had dealt with some meltdowns from clients so he knew how difficult it could be, especially when your reputation might be hanging by a thread. Maybe Penelope was reliving some of the tension and that was what was giving her voice that almost imperceptible wobble. A hint of vulnerability that tugged on something deep in his gut with an equally almost imperceptible 'ping'.

'When it got to the stage that she was threatening to pull the plug on the whole wedding, I said I'd make some enquiries.'

'So you came straight to the top?' The corner of Rafe's mouth lifted. 'Have to say your style is impressive, Ms Collins.'

He'd done the same thing himself more than once.

'I know I'm asking a lot and it probably is impossible but at least I can say I tried and…and maybe you can point me in the direction of an alternative company that might be able to do at least a reasonable job.'

There was a moment's silence as Rafe wondered how to respond. Yes, he could send her hunting for another company but nobody reputable would take this on.

'Have you any idea what's involved with setting up a professional fireworks show?'

She shook her head. She caught her bottom lip between her teeth, too, and the childlike gesture of trepidation was enough to make Rafe wonder just how much of her look was a front. And what was she trying to hide?

'Long-term planning is essential for lots of reasons. We have to have meetings with the client to discuss budgets and the style and timing of the show.'

'The budget won't be an issue.'

'Are you sure? We're talking over a thousand pounds a minute here.'

'I'm sure.' She sounded confident but he'd seen the movement of her throat as she'd swallowed hard.

'The show gets fired to music. That has to be chosen and then edited and correlated to the pyrotechnic effects. The soundtrack has to be cued and programmed into a computer.'

Once upon a time, Rafe had done all these jobs himself. Long, hard nights of getting everything perfect on an impossible schedule. The memories weren't all bad, though. That kind of hard work had got him where he was today.

'The fireworks have to be chosen and sourced. The site has to be mapped and the display layout planned for firing points. There are safety considerations and you have to allow for a fallout range that could be over a hundred metres. You have to get permits. And this all has to happen before you start setting up—fusing all the fireworks together in the correct sequence, putting electric matches in each fuse run, and then testing the whole package to make sure it's going to work.'

'I understand.' There was a stillness about her that suggested she was preparing to admit defeat. 'And you were right. I had no idea how much work was involved. I'm sorry...' She got to her feet. 'It was very kind of you to take the time to explain things.'

The door to the office opened as she finished speaking. Melissa poked her head around the edge.

'They're waiting for you in the boardroom, Mr Edwards.'

Rafe got to his feet, too. Automatically, he held out his hand and Penelope took it. It was a clasp rather than a shake and, for some bizarre reason, Rafe found himself holding her hand for a heartbeat longer than could be considered professional.

Long enough for that odd ping of sensation he'd felt before to return with surprising force. Enough force to be a twist that couldn't be dismissed. A memory of what it was like to be struggling and then come up against a brick wall? Or maybe articulating all the steps of the challenge of delivering a show had reminded him that he'd been able to do all that himself once. Every single job that he now employed experts in the field to do on his behalf.

He could do it again if he wanted. Good grief, he ran one of the biggest pyrotechnic companies in the world—he could do whatever he wanted.

And maybe…he wanted to do *this*.

He had everything he'd always dreamed of now but this wasn't the first time he'd felt that niggle that something was missing. Wasn't the best way to find something to retrace your footsteps? Going back to his roots as a young pyrotechnician would certainly be retracing footsteps that were long gone. Had he dropped something so long ago he'd forgotten what it actually was?

'There is one way I might be able to help,' he found himself saying.

'A personal recommendation to another company?' Hope made her eyes shine. They had a dark outline to their pupils, he noticed. Black on brown. A perfect ring to accentuate them. Striking.

'No. I was thinking more in terms of doing it myself.'

Her breath caught in an audible gasp. 'But…all those things you said…'

'They still stand. Whether or not it's doable would depend on cooperation from your clients with any restrictions, such as what fireworks we happen to have in stock. The site survey and decisions on style and music would have to be done immediately. Tomorrow.'

'I could arrange that.' That breathless excitement in her voice was sweet. 'What time would you be available?'

'It's Saturday. We don't have any major shows happening and I make my own timetable. What time would your clients be available?'

'We'll be on site all day. They have a dance lesson in the morning and we're doing a ceremony rehearsal in the afternoon. Just come anytime that suits. Would you like me to email you a map?'

'That won't be necessary. By coincidence, I'm familiar with the property, which is another point in favour of pulling this off. The site survey wouldn't be an issue.'

The massive image of exploding fireworks was impossible to miss as Penelope left the office but it was more than simply a glorious advertisement now. For a heartbeat, it felt like she was actually *there*—seeing them happen and hearing the bone-shaking impact of the detonations.

Excitement, that was what it was. Ralph Edwards might look like a cowboy but he was going to help her get the biggest break she could ever have. Clarissa's wedding was going to finish with the kind of bang that would have her at the top of any list of desirable wedding planners. On her way to fame and fortune and a lifelong career that couldn't be more perfect for her. She would be completely independent and then she'd be able to decide what else she might need in her life.

Who else, maybe…

Thanks to the traffic, the drive back to Loxbury was going to take well over two hours, which meant she would be up very late tonight, catching up with her schedule. She could use the time sensibly and think ahead about any potential troubleshooting that might be needed.

Or she could think about fireworks instead. The kind of spectacular shapes and colours that would be painted against the darkness of a rural sky but probably seen by every inhabitant of her nearby hometown and have images reproduced in more than one glossy magazine.

As the miles slid by—despite an odd initial resistance—Penelope also found herself thinking about the tousled cowboy she would have to be working with in the coming week to make this happen. He had to be the most unlikely colleague she could have imagined. Someone she would have instinctively avoided like the plague under normal circumstances, even. But if he could help her make this wedding the event that would launch her career, she was up for it.

Couldn't wait to see him again, in fact.

CHAPTER TWO

'No, no, Monsieur Blake. Do not bend over your lady like that, or you will lose your balance and you will both end up on the floor. Step to the side and bend your knee as you dip her. Keep your back *straight*.'

Blake Summers abruptly let go of his bride-to-be but Clarissa caught his arm. 'Don't you dare walk out on me again. How are we ever going to learn this dance if you keep walking away?'

He shook his arm free. 'I can't do it, babe. I told you that. I. Don't. Dance.'

'But this our *wedding* dance.' The tone advertised imminent tears. 'Everyone will be watching. Taking photos.'

'This whole thing is all about the photos, isn't it? I'm up to *here* with it.' Muscles in the young football star's arm bunched as he raised a fist well above head level. 'You know what? If I'd had any idea of how much crap this would all involve I would have thought twice about asking you to marry me.'

'Oh, my God…' Clarissa buried her face in her hands and started sobbing. Penelope let out a long sigh. She felt rather inclined to follow her example.

The dance teacher, Pierre, came towards her with a wonderfully French gesture that described exactly how frustrated he was also becoming.

'It's only a simple dance,' he muttered. 'We've been here for an hour and we have only covered the first twenty seconds of the song. Do you know how long Monsieur Legend's "All of Me" goes for?' He didn't wait for Penelope to respond. 'Five minutes and eight seconds—that's how long. *C'est de la torture.*'

Blake's expression morphed from anger to irritation and finally defeat. 'I'm sorry, babe. I didn't mean it. Really.' He put his arms around Clarissa. 'I just meant we could have eloped or something and got away from all the fuss.'

'You did mean it.' Clarissa struggled enough to escape his embrace. 'You don't want to marry me.' She turned her back on him and hugged herself tightly.

'I do. I love you, babe. All of me, you know, loves all of you.'

Clarissa only sobbed louder. This was Penelope's cue to enter stage left. She walked briskly across the polished wood of the floor and put an arm around her client's shoulders.

'It's okay, hon. We just need to take a break.' She gave a squeeze. 'It's such an emotional time in the final run-up to such a big day. Things can seem a bit overwhelming, can't they?'

Clarissa nodded, sniffing loudly.

'And we've got a whole week to sort this dance out. Just a few moves that you can repeat for the whole song, isn't that right, Pierre?'

Pierre shrugged. 'As you say. Only a few moves.'

Penelope turned her most encouraging smile on the groom-to-be. 'You're up for that, aren't you, Blake? You do know how incredibly sexy it is for a man to be able to dance, even a little bit, don't you?'

'Dancing's for pansies,' Blake muttered.

Penelope's smile dimmed. She could feel a vibe coming from Pierre's direction that suggested she might be about to lose her on-call dance teacher.

'How 'bout this?' she suggested brightly. 'We'll put the music on and Pierre will dance with Clarissa to show you what you'll look like on the night. So you can see how romantic it will be. How gorgeous you'll both look.'

Blake scowled but Clarissa was wiping tears from her face with perfectly French-manicured fingertips. The sideways glance at the undeniably good-looking dance teacher was flirtatious enough for Penelope to be thankful that Blake didn't seem to notice.

'Fine.' He walked towards the tall windows that doubled as doors to the flagged terrace. Penelope joined him as Pierre set the music up and talked to Clarissa.

'Gorgeous view, isn't it?'

'I guess. The lake's okay. I like those dragons that spout water.'

'The whole garden's wonderful. You should have a look around while the weather's this nice. There's even a maze.'

The notes of the romantic song filled the space as Pierre swept Clarissa into his arms and began leading her expertly through the moves. Blake crossed his arms and scowled.

'It's easy for her. She's been doing salsa classes for years. But she expects me to look like *him*? Not going to happen. Not in this lifetime.'

Penelope shook her head and smiled gently. 'I think all she wants is to be moving to the song she's chosen in the arms of the man she loves.'

A sound of something like resignation came from Blake but Penelope could feel the tension lift. Until his head turned and he stiffened again.

'Who's that?' he demanded. 'I told you I didn't want anyone watching this lesson. I feel like enough of an idiot as it is. If that's a photographer, hoping to get a shot of me practising, he can just get the hell out of here.'

Penelope turned her head. The ballroom of Loxbury Hall ran the length of the house between the two main wings. There were probably six huge bedrooms above it upstairs. Quite some distance to recognise a shadowy figure standing in the doorway that led to the reception hall but she knew who it was instantly. From the man's height, perhaps. Or the casual slouch to his stance. That shaft of sensation deep in her belly had to be relief. He'd kept his word.

She could trust him?

'It's Ralph Edwards!' she exclaimed softly. 'I told you he was coming some time today. To discuss your fireworks?'

'Oh…yeah…' Blake's scowl vanished. 'Fireworks are cool.' He brightened. 'Does that mean I don't have to do any more dancing today?'

'Let's see what Pierre's schedule is. We'd have time

for another session later. After the meeting with the florist maybe. Before the rehearsal.'

It was another couple of minutes before the song ended. Clarissa was following Pierre's lead beautifully and Penelope tried to focus, letting her imagination put her client into her wedding dress. To think how it was going to look with the soft lighting of hundreds of candles. The song was a great choice. If Blake could end up learning the moves well enough to look a fraction as good as Pierre, it was going to be a stunning first dance.

Details flashed into her mind, like the best places to put the huge floral arrangements and groups of candles to frame the dance floor. Where the photographers and cameramen could be placed to be inconspicuous but still get great coverage. Whether it was going to work to have the wrist loop to hold the train of Clarissa's dress out of the way. She scribbled a note on the paper clipped to the board she carried with her everywhere on days like this so that none of these details would end up being forgotten.

The dress. Candles. Flowers. There was so much to think about and yet the thing she was most aware of right now was the figure standing at the ballroom doorway, politely waiting for the music to finish before interrupting. Why did his presence make her feel so nervous? Her heart had picked up speed the moment she'd seen him and it hadn't slowed any since. That initial twinge of relief had shattered into butterflies in her stomach now, and they were twisting and dancing rather like Clarissa was.

Not that the feeling was altogether unpleasant. It reminded her of the excitement that strong physical attraction to someone could produce.

Was she physically attracted to Ralph Edwards?

Of course not. The very idea was so ridiculous she knew that wasn't the cause. No. This nervousness was because the fireworks show wasn't a done deal yet and there could be another tantrum from Clarissa to handle if the meeting didn't go well.

It had to go well. Penelope held the clipboard against her chest and clutched it a little more tightly as the music faded.

Rafe was quite content to have a moment or two to observe.

To bask in the glow of satisfaction he'd had from the moment he'd driven through the ornate gates of this historic property.

A property he now owned, for heaven's sake.

Who would have thought that he'd end up with a life like this? Not him, that's for sure. Not back in the day when he'd been one of a busload of disadvantaged small children who'd been brought to Loxbury Hall for a charity Christmas party. He'd seen the kind of kingdom that rich people could have. People with enough money to make their own rules. To have families that stayed together and lived happily ever after.

Yes. This was a dream come true and he was loving every minute of it.

He was loving standing here, too.

This room was stunning. A few weeks ago he'd had to use his imagination to think of what it might be like with music playing and people dancing on the polished floor. Reality was even better. He was too far away to get more than a general impression of the girl who was dancing but he could see enough. A wild cascade of platinum blonde waves. A tight, low-cut top that revealed a cleavage to die for. Enhanced by silicone, of course, but what did that matter? She was a true WAG and Blake Summers was a lucky young man.

What a contrast to Ms Collins—standing there clutching a clipboard and looking as tense as a guitar string about to snap. You'd never get her onto a dance floor as a partner, that's for sure. His buoyant mood slipped a little—kind of reminding him of schooldays when the bell sounded and you had to leave the playground and head back to the classroom.

Never mind. As she'd pointed out herself, this could well be the last time the reception rooms of Loxbury Hall would be used as a public venue and there was a kind of irony in the idea that he could be putting on a fireworks show to mark the end of that era for the house and the start of his own occupation.

Remarkably fitting, really.

Rafe walked towards her as the music faded. Was her look supposed to be more casual, given that it was a weekend? If so, it hadn't worked. Okay, it was a shirt and trousers instead of a skirt but they were tailored and sleek and she still had that complicated rope effect going on in her hair. Did she sleep like that and still not have a hair out of place in the morning?

Maybe she didn't sleep at all. Just plugged herself in to a power point for a while.

Good thing that he was close enough to extend a hand to the young man standing beside Penelope. That way, nobody could guess that his grin was due to private amusement.

'I'm Rafe Edwards,' he said. 'Saw that winning goal you scored on your last match. Good effort.'

'Thanks, man. This is Clarissa. Clarrie, this is Ralph Edwards—the fireworks guy.'

'Rafe, please. I might have Ralph on my birth certificate but it doesn't mean I like it.' His smile widened as Clarissa batted ridiculously enhanced eyelashes at him and then he turned his head.

'Gidday, Penny. How are you?'

'Penelope,' she said tightly. 'I actually like the name on *my* birth certificate.'

Whoa…could she get any more uptight? Rafe turned back to the delicious Clarissa and turned on the charm.

'How 'bout we find somewhere we can get comfortable and have a chat about what I might be able to do for you?'

Clarissa giggled. 'Ooh…yes, *please*…'

'Why don't we go out onto the terrace?' Penelope's tone made the suggestion sound like a reprimand. 'I just need to have a word with Pierre and then I'll join you. I'll organise some refreshment, too. What would you like?'

'Mineral water for me,' Clarissa said. 'Sparkling.'

'A cold beer,' Blake said. 'It's turning into a scorcher of a day.'

'I'm not sure we've got beer in the kitchen at the moment.'

Blake groaned.

'My apologies,' Penelope said. 'I'll make sure it's available next time.' She scribbled something on her clipboard.

'Coffee for me, thanks,' Rafe said. 'Strong and black.'

The look flashed in his direction was grateful. 'That we *can* do. Would you like a coffee, too, Blake?'

'Have to do, I s'pose. At least we're gonna get to talk about something cool. Do we get to choose the kind of fireworks we want?'

'Sure. We need to talk about the music first, though.' Rafe led the way through the French doors to the terrace. 'I'm guessing you want something romantic?'

Music wasn't being discussed when Penelope took the tray of drinks out to the group. Rafe had a laptop open and Blake and Clarissa were avidly watching what was on the screen.

'Ooh…that one. We've got to have that. What's it called?'

'It's a peony. And this one's a chrysanthemum. And this is a golden, hanging willow. It's a forty-five-shot cake so it goes for a while.'

'Nice. I like them loud.' Blake was rubbing his hands together. 'Man, this is going to be epic.'

'With it being your wedding, I was thinking you might want something a bit more romantic.' Rafe tapped his keyboard. 'Look at this for an opening, maybe.'

'OMG.' Clarissa pressed a hand to her open mouth. 'You can do love hearts? For *real*?'

'Sure can. And look at this. Horsetails look a lot like bridal veils, don't you think?'

Clarissa hadn't looked this happy since the first fitting of her wedding dress. Before she'd started to find tiny imperfections that had to be dealt with.

'I want it to be romantic,' she breathed. 'And I've got the perfect song. Whitney Houston's "I Will Always Love You".'

Blake rolled his eyes and shook his head. Rafe lifted an eyebrow. 'Nice, but the tempo could be a bit on the slow side. Maybe a better song to dance to than accompany fireworks?'

'It's soppy,' Blake growled. 'We need something loud. Fun. Wasn't the whole idea to end the night with a bang?'

Clarissa giggled. 'Oh…we will, babes, don't you worry about that.'

Blake grinned. 'You're singing my song already.'

Rafe's appreciative grin faded the moment he caught Penelope's gaze. He took a sip of his coffee.

'What about Meat Loaf?' Blake suggested. '"I'd Do Anything For Love"?'

'Not bad. Good beats to time to effects.'

'No.' Clarissa shook her head firmly.

Penelope was searching wildly for inspiration. 'Bon Jovi? "Livin' On A Prayer"? Or the Troggs? "Wild Thing"?'

'Getting better.' Rafe nodded. The look he gave her this time held a note of surprise. Did he think she wasn't into music or something? 'Let's keep it going. Bon Jovi's a favourite of mine. What about "Always"?'

The words of the song drifted into Penelope's head. Along with an image of it being passionately sung. And even though it was Rafe she was looking at, it was no excuse to let her mind drift to imagining him with wild, rock-god hair. Wearing a tight, black singlet and frayed jeans. Saying he would cry for the woman he loved. Or die for her...

Phew...it was certainly getting hot. She fanned herself with her clipboard and tried to refocus. To push any image of men in frayed jeans and singlets out of her head. So not her type.

She liked designer suits and neat haircuts. The kind of up-and-coming young attorney look, like her last boyfriend who'd not only graduated from law school with honours but was active in a major political party. Disappointing that it had turned out they'd had nothing in common—especially for her grandparents—but she didn't have time for a relationship in her life right now anyway.

She didn't have time to pander to this group's inability to reach an agreement either, but she couldn't think of any way to speed things up and half an hour later they were still no closer to making a definitive choice.

Further away, perhaps, given that both Clarissa and Blake were getting annoyed enough to veto any suggestion the other made and getting steadily snarkier about it. Any moment now it would erupt into a full-blown row and the hint of annoyance in Rafe's body language would turn into disgust and he'd walk away from a job he didn't actually need.

Penelope was increasingly aware that time was running out. They had a meeting with the florist coming up, Pierre was going to return for another dance lesson and there was a rehearsal with the celebrant in the garden at four p.m.

'Did you have anything else you needed to do while you're here?' she asked Rafe.

'A bit of a survey.' He nodded. 'I need to get a feel for the layout and check where I'd position things. I'm thinking a barge on the other side of the lake but I'll be able to get a good view if I go upstairs and—' He stopped abruptly. 'Is that a problem?'

'We're not allowed upstairs,' Clarissa confided. 'Apparently it's one of the biggest rules about using this venue.'

'Is that right?'

It was no surprise that Rafe wasn't impressed by a set of rules and his tone suggested he wouldn't hesitate in breaking them. She could imagine how well it would go down if she forbade the action and she certainly didn't want to get him offside any more than he was already, thanks to the sparring young couple.

If he had to go upstairs in order to be able to do his job, maybe she'd just have to turn a blind eye and hope for the best. At least she could plead ignorance of it actually happening if word got out and she could probably apologise well enough to smooth things over if the owners were upset.

'How long will your survey take?' The words came out more crisply than she'd intended.

'Thirty-nine minutes.' He grinned. 'No, make that forty-one.'

He wasn't the only person getting annoyed here. 'In that case, let's meet back here in forty-five minutes,' Penelope said. 'Blake—take Clarissa to the Loxbury pub and you can get your cold beer and a quick lunch and see if you can agree on a song. This fireworks show isn't going to happen unless we lock that in today. Isn't that right, Ralph?'

His look was deadpan.

'Sorry. Rafe.'

'That's right, Penelope. We're on a deadline that's tight enough to be almost impossible as it is.' He smiled at Clarissa. 'You want your red hearts exploding all over the sky to start the show. What if I told you we could put both your names inside a love heart to finish?'

Clarissa looked like she'd just fallen in love with this new acquaintance. She tugged on Blake's arm with some urgency. 'Come on, babes. We've *got* to find a song.'

'I'll have a think, too,' Penelope called after them. 'I've got my iPod and I need a bit of a walk.'

There was a third-floor level on each of the wings of the house, set back enough to provide an upstairs terraced area. Rafe fancied one of these rooms as his bedroom and that was where he headed. He already knew that he'd have the best view of the lake and garden from that terrace. It took a few minutes to get there. Was he crazy, thinking he could actually live in a place this big?

By himself?

He had plenty of friends, he reminded himself as he stepped over the braided rope on the stairs marking the boundary of public access. The guys in the band would want to make this place party central. And it wasn't as if he'd be here that much. He had his apartments in New York and London and he was looking at getting one in China, given that he spent a lot of time there sourcing fireworks. He'd need staff, too. No way could he manage a house this size. And he'd probably need an entire team of full-time gardeners, he decided as he stepped out onto the bedroom terrace. Just clipping the hedges of that maze would probably keep someone busy for weeks.

In fact, there was someone in there right now. Rafe walked closer to the stone pillars edging the terrace and narrowed his eyes. The figure seemed to know its way through the maze, moving swiftly until it reached the grass circle that marked the centre.

Penelope. Of course it was. Hadn't she said she needed a walk? She stopped for a moment with her head down, fiddling with something in her hand. Her iPod? And then she pressed her fingertips against her ears as though she was listening carefully to whatever music she had chosen.

Rafe should have been scanning the grounds on the far side of the lake and thinking about positioning things like the scissor lift he'd need to hold the frame for the lancework of doing the names in fireworks to end the show. Instead, he found himself watching Penelope.

She was kicking her shoes off, which was probably sensible given that heels would sink into that grass. But then she did something that made Rafe's jaw drop.

Blew whatever it was he'd been thinking of her right out of the water.

She started dancing.

Not just the kind of unconscious jiggle along with the beat either. She was dancing like she thought no one could see her which was probably exactly what she did think, tucked into the centre of that maze with its tall, thick hedges.

Rafe leaned into the corner of the terrace, any thoughts of planning a show escaping irretrievably. His eyes narrowed as he focused on the slim figure moving on her secret stage.

An amused snort escaped him. No wonder she needed to hide herself away. She was rubbish at dancing. Her movements were uncoordinated enough to probably make her a laughing stock on a dance floor.

But then his amusement faded. She was doing something she believed was private and she was doing it with her heart and soul. Maybe she didn't really know how to dance but she was doing more than just hearing that music—she was a part of it with every cell of her body.

Rafe knew that feeling. That ability to lose yourself in sound so completely the rest of the world disappeared. Music could be an anaesthetic that made even the worst kind of pain bearable.

Impossible not to remember wearing headphones and turning the sound level up so loud that nothing else existed. So you couldn't hear the latest row erupting in the new foster home that meant you'd be packed up before long and handed around again like some unwanted parcel.

Impossible not to still feel grateful for that first set of drums he'd been gifted so many years ago. Or the thrill of picking up a saxophone for the first time and starting the journey that meant he could do more than simply listen. That meant he could become a part of that music.

It was another world. One that had saved him from what this one had seemed doomed to become.

And he was getting the same feeling from watching Penelope being uninhibited enough to try and dance.

What was that about?

He'd sensed that what you could see with Penelope Collins wasn't necessarily real, hadn't he? When she'd admitted she knew nothing about setting up a fireworks show. Watching her now made him more sure that she was putting up a front to hide who she really was.

Who was the person that was hiding?

Or maybe the real question here was why did he want to know?

He didn't.

With a jerk, Rafe straightened and forced his gaze sideways towards the lake and the far shore. Was there enough clearance from the trees to put a scissor lift or two on the ground or would the safety margins require a barge on the water? He'd bring one of the lads out here first thing tomorrow and they could use a range finder to get accurate measurements but he could trust his eye for now. And he just happened to have an aerial photograph of the property on his laptop, too. Pulling a notepad and the stub of a pencil from the back pocket of his jeans, he started sketching.

By the time he'd finished what he'd wanted to do he

was five minutes late for the time they'd agreed to meet back on the terrace. Not that it made him hurry down the stairs or anything but he wouldn't have planned to stop before he turned into the ballroom and headed for the terrace. The thought only occurred to him when he saw the iPod lying on the hall table, on top of that clipboard Penelope carried everywhere with her.

If he took a look at what she'd played recently, could he pick what it was that she'd been dancing to? Get some kind of clue to solve the puzzle of who this woman actually was?

Clarissa and Blake were late getting back from lunch and, judging by the looks on their faces, they hadn't managed to agree on the music to accompany their fireworks show.

Which meant that Rafe would most likely pull the plug on doing it at all.

He came through the French doors from the ballroom at the same time as the young couple were climbing the stairs from the garden.

'Did you decide?' Rafe asked.

'We tried,' Clarissa groaned. 'We really did…' Her face brightened. 'But then we thought you're the expert. We'll let you decide.'

Penelope bit back the suggestion she'd been about to make. Throwing ideas around again would only take them back to square one and this was a potentially quick and easy fix.

But Rafe lifted an eyebrow. 'You sure about that? Because I reckon I've found the perfect song.'

'What is it?'

'Doesn't matter,' Blake growled. 'You promised you wouldn't argue this time.'

'Have a listen,' Rafe said, putting his laptop on the table and flipping it open. He tapped rapidly on the keyboard. 'I think you might like it.'

It only took the first two notes for Penelope to recognise the song and it sent a chill down her spine. The very song she'd been about to suggest herself. How spooky was *that*?

'Ohhh…' Clarissa's eyes were huge. 'I *love* this song.'

'Who is that?' Blake was frowning. 'Celine Dion?'

Rafe shook his head. 'This is the original version. Jennifer Rush. She cowrote "The Power of Love" in 1984.'

It was the version that Penelope preferred. The one she had on her iPod. The one she'd been dancing to in her private space in the centre of the maze only half an hour or so ago, when she'd taken that much-needed break.

'It's got some great firing points. Like that…' Rafe's hands prescribed an arc as the crescendo started. 'And we can use the extended version to give us a good length of time. Fade it away to leave your names in the heart hanging over the lake.'

He wasn't looking at Penelope. He didn't even send a triumphant glance in her direction as Clarissa and Blake enthusiastically agreed to the song choice.

Which was probably just as well. Penelope had no idea what her expression might look like but it had to include an element of shock. Surely it had to be more than coincidence and she didn't believe in telepathy but it was impossible not to feel some sort of weird connection happening here. How awful would it be if she looked like Clarissa had when he'd told her he could finish the show by putting their names in a love heart? As though she'd just fallen head over heels in love with the man?

Not that it really mattered. The *pièce de résistance* of the wedding that was going to launch her new career was starting to come together and the choice of song was perfect.

With a lot of hard work and a little bit more luck, this whole wedding was going to be perfect.

CHAPTER THREE

SO FAR, SO GOOD.

They couldn't have wished for a better day weather-wise for what the local media was already billing the wedding of the year. The blue stretch of summer sky was broken only by innocent cotton-wool puffs of cloud and it was warm enough for the skimpy dresses most of the women seemed to be wearing. More importantly, the breeze was gentle enough not to ruin any elaborate hairdos or play havoc with a bridal veil.

The vintage champagne every guest had been offered on arrival was going down a treat and people were now beginning to drift towards the rows of chairs draped with white satin and tied with silver bows. Penelope saw someone open the small gauze bag she'd found on her seat and smile as she showed her partner the confetti that was made up of tiny, glittery silver stars.

How much bigger were those smiles going to be when they were watching the kind of stars that would explode across the sky as the finale to this event? Rafe had arrived as early as Penelope had, driving onto the estate in the chill mist of a breaking dawn. She'd seen him and the technicians he'd brought with him, in their fluorescent vests, working in the field on the far side of the lake at various times over the hectic hours since then. Just orange dots of humanity, really, at this distance, but she was sure it was Rafe who was directing the forklift manoeuvring the pallets from the back of a truck at one point and, much later, the towing of a flat barge to float on the lake.

Because that was the kind of job a boss would do, she told herself. It had nothing to do with that odd tingle of something she had no intention of trying to identify. A tingle that appeared along with that persistent image of the man in frayed jeans and a black singlet she had conjured up. An image that had insisted on haunting her dreams over the last week, leaving her to wake with the odd sensation that something was simply not *fair*...

Heading back inside the house, she popped into the kitchen to check that her team was on top of the catering. Judging by the numerous silver platters of hors d'oeuvres lined up ready for the lull while photographs would be taken after the ceremony, they were right on schedule.

'Any worries, Jack?'

'Apart from an eight-course sit-down dinner for two hundred and supper for six hundred? Nah...it's all good.' The older man's smile was reassuring. 'I've got this side of the gig covered. Go and play with your bride.'

'I do need to do that. But I'll be back later. Keep an apron for me.'

'Are you kidding? That dress is far too fancy to get hidden by any apron.'

'It's not too much, is it?' Penelope glanced down at the dark silver sheath dress she had chosen. A lot of effort had gone into what she hoped would be her signature outfit as she occupied an unusual space in a wedding party that was more than simply hired help but less than invited guest. The dress was demure with its long sleeves and scooped neckline that only showed a hint of cleavage. The skirt was ballet length and fell in soft swirls from thigh level but it did fit like a glove everywhere else and it had a soft sparkle that would probably intensify under artificial or candle light.

Jack grinned. 'You look like the director of the nation's most successful event managing company. Make sure they get some photos of you for one of those flash magazines. Now—stop distracting me. Get out of my kitchen and go and keep our first event ticking. Isn't Princess Clarissa about due for another meltdown?'

'Oh, God, I hope not.' With a worried frown, Penelope headed for a ground-floor room in the west wing that had been set aside for the bride and bridesmaids to get dressed in. A room in the east wing was where the groom and his entourage were waiting. That would be the next stop, to make sure they were in position on time. Penelope checked her watch. Only twenty minutes away. The countdown was on.

She took a deep breath. At least she didn't have to worry about the catering side of things. Jack—her head chef—had worked with her ever since she'd advertised for someone to come on board with a fledgling catering company nearly ten years ago. His own restaurant might have failed despite his talent with food but together they'd built a company to be proud of and it had been his idea for her to take the risky move of taking on event management.

Dreaming about something and even making endless lists of the things that she'd have to keep on top of hadn't really prepared her for the reality of it, though. The catering was only one aspect. Had the celebrant arrived yet? Were the photographers behaving themselves? How were the band going in setting themselves up? She'd seen the truck parked around the back an hour or more ago and people unloading a drum kit and amplifiers but what if they couldn't find enough power points? There was a lighting expert who was coming to supervise the safe positioning and lighting of all those candles and would then be in charge for any spotlighting of key people. He hadn't arrived as far as she knew but they weren't due to meet until after the actual ceremony.

At some point, she would have to find Rafe, too, and make sure that he was happy with his set-up. The fireworks were scheduled to go off at one a.m. to mark the end of the party and there was plenty of security personnel discreetly in place to make sure nobody went into forbidden areas and that everybody left Loxbury Hall when they were supposed to.

It was possible that this was the moment when the tension was at its highest. The moment before the carefully timed show that was going to be the wedding of the year kicked off. With her heart in her mouth, Penelope opened the door of the bride's dressing room. Clarissa—in a froth of white—was standing serenely in the centre of the room with a champagne flute in her hand.

She was surrounded by her six bridesmaids who were in same shade of orange as one of the colours of Blake's football club. One of the girls sent another champagne cork hurtling towards the ceiling with a loud pop and the shriek of happy giggles was deafening. The flash of the camera from the official photographer showed he was capturing every joyous moment.

The hairdresser and make-up artists and their teams were packing up an enormous amount of gear. Hair straighteners, heated rollers and cans of spray went into one set of suitcases. Pots of foundation, dozens of brushes and cards of false eyelashes were heading for another. Penelope smiled at the women.

'I think you deserve to join the celebration. They all look fabulous.' She stepped closer and lowered her voice, although it was hardly necessary as the chatter and laughter as the glasses were being refilled were enough to make any conversation private. 'Any problems?'

Cheryl's smile said it all. 'Bit of a mission to get every one of Clarissa's curls sitting just right but we got there in the end. Thank goodness for industrial-strength hairspray.'

The spirals of platinum blonde hair hung to the bride's waist at the back, easily visible through the sheer mist of an exquisitely embroidered veil. Tresses at the front had been twisted and clipped into a soft frame that supported the tiara holding the veil, as well as offering an anchor for a dozen or more small silver stars. A star made of diamonds sparkled on the perfect spray tan of Clarissa's décolletage—a gift from Blake that had inspired one of the themes for the wedding. Beneath that, the heavily beaded corset bodice of the dress made the most of what had to be close to the top of the bride's assets.

'What d'ya think, Penelope?'

'I think you couldn't look more perfect, Clarrie. It's just as well Blake's got all those groomsmen to hold him up when he sees you walking down the aisle.' She took another quick glance at her watch. 'Five minutes and we'll need you all in position in the reception hall. I'm just going to make sure the boys are out of the building and that those photographs as you come out will be the first glimpse of your dress that the world gets.'

It was Penelope who waited with Clarissa in the main entrance, signalling each pair of bridesmaids when it was their turn to walk out of the huge doorway, down the sweep of wide steps and start the journey along the carpet that led to the raised gazebo where the celebrant was waiting, flanked by the males of the wedding party. Clarissa's song choice of Whitney Houston that had been rejected for the fireworks show was perfect for this entrance but it needed careful timing to make sure the bride arrived beside her groom before the song finished.

Penelope waited until all the heads turned to watch Clarissa take her final position, facing Blake and holding both his hands. Nobody saw her as she quietly made her way to the shade of an ancient oak tree, well away from the audience but close enough to hear the ceremony, thanks to the lapel microphone the celebrant was wearing.

A brief respite from the tension of the day was more than welcome. A private moment to collect her thoughts and remember to breathe.

Except it didn't stay private for long. A figure materialised beside her in the shade. A dark figure. And Penelope forgot to breathe for rather too long.

Had Rafe dressed up for the occasion? He was wearing black jeans today, and a black T-shirt that had a faded image of what was probably an album cover from a forgotten era. The cowboy boots were the same, though, and they were in harmony with a battered, wide-brimmed leather hat that any cowboy would have treasured.

He was dressed for his work and clearly comfortable with being on the hired-help side of the boundary Penelope was balancing on but right now her position in this gathering was unimportant. This short period of time was a limbo where nothing mattered other than the vows the wedding couple were exchanging. This tiny patch of the famous Loxbury Hall gardens was a kind of limbo as well. An island that only she and Rafe were inhabiting.

He was as dark as she was pale. As scruffy as she was groomed. As relaxed as she was tense. Black and white. Total opposites.

It should be making her feel very uncomfortable but it wasn't.

There was a curl of something pleasant stealing through Penelope's body. Try as she might to deny it, the surprise of his company was sprinkled with a condiment that could—quite disturbingly—be delight.

* * *

He'd had something on the tip of his tongue to justify the choice of joining Ms Collins in the shade of this tree. Had it been something about it being the best vantage point to observe the ceremony and that he had the time because everything else that could be a distraction in the background had to be put on hold for the duration? Not that his team had much else to do. Everything was in place and all that was needed between now and about midnight was a rehearsal to check that all the electronic components were in functioning order.

Or maybe it had been something about how well the event was going so far. That it was everything the perfect wedding should be.

No wonder the ability to produce words seemed to have failed him for the moment. This was everything the perfect wedding *shouldn't* be. The epitome of the circus that represented conforming to one of society's expected rules of declaring commitment and faithfulness. A rule that was rarely kept, so why bother with the circus in the first place?

Or perhaps the loss of a conversational opening had something to do with being this close to Penelope?

He'd spotted her discreet position from the edge of the lake where he'd initially positioned himself to be out of sight of the guests. That silvery dress she was wearing shone like a new moon in the dense shade of this ancient tree and…and it was possibly the most stunning dress he'd ever seen. Weird, considering there was no more cleavage to be seen than a tiny, teasing line just where that sun-kissed skin began to swell.

Rafe dragged his gaze away, hopefully before she was aware of his appreciation because the glance had been so swift. Her hair looked different today, too. Softer. She still had those braids shaping the sides of her head but the length of it was loose at the back, falling in a thick ringlet instead of another braid. It was longer than he remembered, almost touching the small of her back in that second, silver skin. What would happen, he found himself wondering, if he buried his fingers in that perfect silky spiral and pulled it apart? Would her whole back get covered with golden waves?

What was more likely to happen was that he would infuriate this would-be queen of event management by messing up her hair. She might not be holding a clipboard right now but the tension was still palpable. She was in control. On top of every moment and ready to troubleshoot any problem with the efficiency of a nuclear blast.

Clarissa's breathlessly excited whisper was being amplified by strategically placed microphones. 'I, Clarissa Grace Bingham, take thee, Blake Robert Summers, to be my lawfully wedded husband. To have and to hold…'

Finally, he found something to say.

'Sounds like she's the happiest girl on earth right now.'

'Of course she is. This is her wedding day. Every girl's dream.'

'Really?' Rafe couldn't help the note of scepticism. 'Does anyone really believe that those vows mean anything these days?'

Uh-oh... Maybe he should have ruffled the spiral of hair down her back instead of dropping some kind of verbal bomb. The look he received made him feel like he'd just told a kid that Santa Claus didn't really exist.

'I believe it,' Penelope said.

She did. He could see it in her eyes. A fierce belief that it meant something. Something important. He couldn't look away. He even found himself leaning a little closer as a soft word of query escaped his lips.

'Why?'

Oh, help... His eyes weren't really as black as sin, were they? The mottled light sifting down through the leaves of the tree was enough to reveal that they were a dark brown, with flecks of gold that made them more like a very deep hazel. And the way he was looking at her...

The eye contact had gone on far too long to be polite but Penelope couldn't break the gaze. It felt physical—almost as though he was holding her in his arms. No... it went deeper than that. He was holding something that wasn't physical. Touching something that was deep inside. The part of her that couldn't be seen.

But Rafe was seeing it and it made her feel... vulnerable?

Nobody had ever looked at her like this. As if they could see that dark, secret part of her. As if the world wouldn't end if the door got opened and light flooded in.

And he wanted to know why she believed in something he clearly had no time for. Marriage. Could he see that she *had* to believe in it? Because there was something about it that held the key to putting things right?

The exchange of vows had been completed on the stage of the gazebo and the applause and raucous whistling told her that the first kiss was happening. The flash of cameras going off was there, like stars in the periphery of her vision, but Penelope still couldn't look away from Rafe's gaze.

'It's about the promise,' she found herself saying softly. 'It's not about the dress or the flowers or…or even the fireworks.'

He raised an eyebrow.

'I don't mean they're not important. That's what weddings are all about. Celebrating the promise.' Penelope drew in a breath. She'd said enough and she should be using the time to make sure the photographers had everything they needed for the next part of the programme. And that Jack was ready to keep the guests entertained with food and wine for as long as it took. 'I can't wait to see the show,' she added with a placating smile. 'I know it'll be fabulous.'

'Oh, it will.' Rafe nodded. 'I'll make sure you get the best spot to watch it, shall I?'

'Won't you be busy? Pushing buttons or something?'

'There's pretty much only one button to push. On my laptop. The rest is automatic.'

'No problems setting up? It is all done?'

'Yes, ma'am.' He tipped his hat. 'We're about to double-check everything and that'll be it until show time.'

'That's great. Thank you so much.' Penelope could see guests starting to move. Reaching for those bags of confetti stars and preparing to shower the bride and groom as they went down the aisle together. She stepped away to move closer but Rafe's voice stopped her.

'That promise,' he said quietly. 'The one you believe in. What is it, exactly?'

Startled, she turned her head. 'Security,' she responded. 'Family. It's the promise of a safe place, I guess. Somewhere you know you'll always be loved.'

There was something soft in his eyes now. Something sad?

'You're one of the lucky ones, then.'

'Because I believe in marriage?'

'Because you know what it's like to have a family. Parents. You know what it's like to live in that safe place.'

And he didn't? Something huge squeezed inside her chest and made her breath come out in a huff. She understood that yearning. Her life might look perfect from the outside but she wanted him to know that she understood. That they had a connection here that very few people could have. They might be complete opposites but in that moment it felt like they were the opposite sides of the same coin.

'I've never had parents. My mother abandoned me as a baby and then died. I have no idea who my father is.' Good grief...why on earth was she telling him this much? She backed off. 'You're right, though. I *was* lucky. My grandparents brought me up. I had everything I could possibly want.'

She saw the change in his eyes. He was backing off, too. Had he thought she understood but now saw her as one of the privileged? One who couldn't possibly have any idea of what it was like not to have that safe place?

Penelope didn't want to lose that tiny thread of connection. She was the one who needed that understanding, wasn't she? Because nobody had ever understood.

'Almost everything,' she added, her voice no more than a sigh. She swallowed past the tightness in her throat. 'Maybe if my parents had believed in marriage they could have looked after each other and things would have been different.' She bit her lip as the admission slipped out. 'Better…'

'You don't know that.' That softness in his gaze had changed. There was a flash of anger there. A world of pain. 'Things could have been worse.' Rafe tugged on the rim of his hat, blocking off his gaze. 'Catch you later,' he muttered as he turned away. 'When it's show time.'

The next hours were a blur. Penelope felt like she needed to be in six places at once to make sure everything was flowing smoothly but the adrenaline of it all kept her going without pause. A reporter from the magazine that had the exclusive, first coverage of the event even asked for a quick interview and photographs.

'You do realise you're going to be inundated with work after this, don't you? Every celebrity who's planning a wedding in the foreseeable future is going to want something this good.'

There was fear to be found hiding in the excitement of how well it was all going.

'We're a boutique company. I'm not ever going to take on more clients than I can personally take care of.'

'You've organised this all yourself?'

'I have a partner who's in charge of the catering today. Come and meet Jack. With dinner over, he should have a minute or two to spare. You could get a great picture of him in his chef's whites in the kitchen. He deserves the publicity as much as I do.'

'Let's get one of you two together.' The journalist made a note on her pad. 'Are you, like, a couple?'

Penelope shook her head as she smiled. 'No. Jack has a family. I'm happily single. Career-woman, through and through, that's me.'

That was certainly the image she wanted to portray, anyway. There was no reason for anybody to ever feel sorry for Penelope Collins.

Not any more.

By midnight, the band had been playing for two hours and the party in the ballroom was still in full swing. The drums pulsed in Penelope's blood and the music was so good it was an effort not to let her body respond. It was just as well she was kept too occupied to do more than make a mental note to download some of Diversion's tracks so she could listen again in private.

People were getting drunk now. Emergency cleaning was needed more than once in the restrooms and an ambulance was discreetly summoned to the service entrance to remove one unconscious young woman. Another one was found sobbing in the garden and it fell to Penelope to sit and listen to the tale of romantic woe and calm the guest enough to rejoin the revelry. Then she escaped to the kitchens for a while and insisted on an apron so she could spend a few minutes helping to prepare the supper that would be served on the terrace, timed to finish as the fireworks started.

And then it would all be over, bar the massive job of clearing up, most of which would happen tomorrow. All the tension and exhaustion of the last weeks and days and hours would be over. What was that going to feel like? Would she crawl home and crash or would she still be buzzing this time tomorrow?

Her head was spinning a little now, which suggested that it might be a good thing if she crashed. Maybe that glass of champagne with Jack a few minutes ago to toast their success had been a bad thing. At least it was quieter in the vast spaces of Loxbury Hall. The dance music was finished and people were crowded onto the terrace, enjoying a last glass or two of champagne, along with the delicious canapés on offer. The bride and groom had gone off to change into their going-away outfits and the vintage car, complete with the rope of old tin cans, was waiting at the back, ready to collect them from the front steps as soon as the fireworks show ended.

It was almost time for those fireworks. Penelope hadn't seen Rafe since that weirdly intense conversation under the tree. She hadn't even thought of him.

No. That wasn't entirely true. That persistent image of him was never far away from the back of her mind. And hadn't it got a bit closer right about the time she'd described herself as 'happily single' to that journalist?

And now he was here again, still wearing that hat, with a laptop bag slung over his shoulder. Right outside the kitchen door, when Penelope had hung up her apron and slipped back into the entrance hall so that she could go and find a place to watch the show.

'Ready?'

Words failed her. She could hear an echo of his voice from that earlier conversation.

I'll make sure you get the best spot to watch...

He'd kept his word. Again. She'd known she could trust him, hadn't she, when he'd turned up for that first meeting here?

Having that trust confirmed, on top of being drawn back into where she'd experienced the feeling that they were somehow connected on a secret level, was a mix so powerful it stole the breath, along with any words, from Penelope's body.

All she could do was nod.

A corner of his mouth lifted. 'Come on, then.'

He held out his hand.

And Penelope took it. His grip was strong. Warm. A connection that was physical. Real, instead of the one that was probably purely only in her own imagination, but if she hadn't already been sideswiped by that visceral force, she would never have taken his hand.

Who in their right mind would start holding hands with a virtual stranger? One who had a 'bad boy' label that was practically a neon sign? What good girl would be so willing to follow him?

Not her. Not in this lifetime. She could almost hear her grandmother's voice. The mantra of her life. Her greatest fear.

'You'll end up just like your mother, if you're not very careful.'

How could it feel so good, then? Kind of like when she knew no one could see her and she could let loose and dance...

No one could see her now. Except Rafe. It was like being in one of her dreams, only she wasn't going to end up feeling that something wasn't fair because she didn't have to wake up any time soon. She had to almost skip a step or two to keep up with his long stride but then she tugged back on the pressure. Silly to feel fear at breaking such a little rule when she was already doing something so out of character but maybe it was symbolic.

'We can't go *upstairs*.'

'We have to. I need to get the best view of the show. I've got people on the ground I can reach by radio if there's any problem but I have to be able to see.' He stepped over the thick red rope. 'It's okay. I'm not really breaking the sacred rules. I've cleared it with the owner.'

He sounded completely convincing. Maybe Penelope just wanted to believe him. Or perhaps the notion of going somewhere forbidden—in his company—was simply too enticing. She could probably blame that glass of champagne for giving in so readily. Or maybe it was because she was letting herself give in to the pulse of something too big to ignore. It might not look like it from the outside, but she was already dancing.

Up the stairs. Along a wide hallway. Past an open door that revealed a luxurious bathroom. Into...a *bedroom*? Yes, there was a four-poster bed that looked about as old as Loxbury Hall itself. It also looked huge and…dear Lord…irresistibly inviting. As if it was the exact destination she'd been hoping this man would lead her to.

Shocked, Penelope jerked her hand free of Rafe's but he didn't seem to notice. He was opening French doors with the ease of knowing exactly where the latches were and then he glanced over his shoulder as they swung open.

'Come on, then. You won't see much in there.'

Out onto the flagged terrace, and the chill of the night air went some way to cooling the heat Penelope could feel in her cheeks. Hopefully, the heat deeper in her body would eventually cool enough to disappear as well.

Rafe checked in with his team by portable radio. Some were as close as it was safe to be to the action, with fire extinguishers available if something went seriously wrong. They would be working alongside him when the show was over, checking for any unexploded shells and then clearing up the rubbish of spent casings and rolling up the miles of cables to pack away with the rest of the gear.

For the next ten minutes, though, there was nothing to do but watch and see how the hard work of the last few days had come together. Rafe set up his laptop, activated the program that synched the music and effects and kept the radio channel open to have the ground team on standby for the countdown. Speakers had been set up along the terrace and the first notes of the song caught everybody's attention.

And then the first shells were fired and the sky filled with expanding, red hearts. The collective gasp from the crowd on the terrace below was loud enough to hear over the music for a split second before the next shell was detonated. The gasp from the woman in the silver dress beside him shouldn't have been loud enough to hear but, suddenly, it was Penelope's reaction that mattered more than anything else.

For the first time in his life in professional pyrotechnics, Rafe found he wasn't watching the sky but he could still gauge exactly what was happening. He could feel the resonance of the explosions in his bones and he could see the colours reflected on Penelope's face. He could see much more than that as well. He could see the amazement, a hint of fear and the sheer thrill of it all. He could feel what it was that had sucked him into this profession so long ago with an intensity that he hadn't realised had become blurred over the years.

And he was loving it.

Penelope had seen fireworks before. Of course she had. She'd always been a little frightened of them. They were so loud. So unpredictable. Too dangerous to really enjoy.

But she felt safer here. She was with the person who was controlling the danger so she could let go of that protective instinct that kept her ready to run in an instant if necessary. She could let herself feel the boom of the explosions in her body instead of bracing herself against them. She could watch the unfurling of those astonishing colours and shapes against the black sky.

She could even watch the new shells hurtling upwards with an anticipation that was pure excitement about what was about to come.

She didn't want it to end. This was the ultimate finale to the biggest thing she had accomplished so far in her life. The wedding was done and dusted and it had been all she had hoped and dreamed it would be. She could let go of all that tension and bask in the satisfaction of hard work paying off.

It had to end, though. The music was beginning to fade. The huge red heart that looked as if it was floating in the middle of the lake came alive with the names of Clarrie and Blake appearing in white inside. The cheering from the crowd below was ecstatic and Penelope felt the same appreciation. Unthinking, she turned to Rafe to thank him but words were not enough in the wake of that emotional roller-coaster.

She stood on tiptoe and threw her arms around his neck.

'That was *amazing*. Thank you *so* much…'

The silver dress felt cool and slippery as his hands went automatically to the hips of the woman pressed against him but he could feel the warmth of her skin beneath the fabric.

This was the last thing Rafe had expected her to do.

He'd been reliving the passion of his job through watching her reaction to the show. Now, with this unexpected touch, he was reliving the excitement of touching a woman as if it were the first time ever. Was this the thing he'd lost? It was a sensation he hadn't even known he'd been pursuing so he couldn't have known it had been missing for so long, but surely it couldn't be real? If he kept on touching her, it would end up being the same as all the others. Or would it?

She drew back and she was smiling. Her eyes were dancing. She looked more alive than Rafe had ever seen her look.

She looked more beautiful than any woman had the right to look.

He had to find out if there was any more to this magic. If he kissed her, would it feel like the first time he'd ever kissed a woman he'd wanted more than his next breath?

He was going to *kiss* her.

Penelope had a single heartbeat to decide what she should do. No. There was no decision that needed to be made, was there? What she should do was pull away from this man. Apologise for being overly effusive in her thanks and turn and walk away.

It wasn't about what she should do. It was about what she *wanted* to do. And whether—for perhaps the first time in her life—she could allow herself to do exactly that. Were the things she had denied herself for ever *really* that bad? How would she know if she never even took a peek?

It was just a kiss but waiting for it to happen was like watching one of those shells hurtle into the darkness, knowing that it would explode and knowing how exciting it would be when it did.

The anticipation was unbearable. She *had* to find

out. Had to open the door to that secret place and step inside.

And the moment his lips touched hers, Penelope knew she was lost. Nothing had ever felt like this. Ever. The softness that spoke of complete control. Gentleness that was a glove covering unimagined, wild abandon.

Not a word was spoken but the look Rafe gave her when they finally stopped kissing asked a question that Penelope didn't want to answer. If she started thinking she would stop feeling and she'd never felt anything like this. It wasn't real—it had to be some weird alchemy of exhaustion and champagne, the thrill of the fireworks and the illicit thrill of an invitation to go somewhere so forbidden—but she knew it would never happen again and she couldn't resist the desire to keep it going just a little longer.

It was bliss. A stolen gift that might never be offered again.

Maybe it wasn't really so astonishing that this woman was capable of such passion. He'd seen her dancing, hadn't he? When she'd thought no one could see her. By a stroke of amazingly good fortune he was sharing that kind of space with her right now. Where nobody could see them. Where whatever got kept hidden so incredibly well was being allowed out to play. Maybe it was true that he wouldn't have chosen a woman like this in a million years but it was happening and he was going to make the most of every second.

Because the magic was still there. Growing stronger with every touch of skin on skin. It was like the first time. Completely new and different and…and just *more*. More than he'd ever discovered. More than he'd ever dreamed he could find.

He took Penelope to paradise and then leapt over the brink to join her. For a long minute then, all he could do was hold her as he fought to catch his breath and wait for his heart to stop pounding. As he tried—and failed—to make sense of the emotions tumbling through his head and heart. Ecstasy and astonishment were mixed with something a lot less pleasant. Bewilderment, perhaps?

A sense of foreboding, even?

What the hell had just happened here?

And what on earth was going to happen next?

CHAPTER FOUR

THE HOUNDS OF HELL were chasing Penelope's car as she drove away from Loxbury Hall.

How awful had that been?

What an absolute, unmitigated train crash.

She'd felt the moment of impact and it had been, undoubtedly, the most shocking sensation of her life. There she'd been, lying in Rafe's arms, floating in a bubble of pure bliss—knowing that there was no place in the world that would ever feel this good.

This safe…

And then she'd heard it. Her grandmother's voice.

'What have you done, Penelope? Oh, dear Lord…it's your mother all over again…you wicked, wicked girl…'

Her worst fear. She'd spent her whole life resisting the temptation to give in to doing bad things and she'd just thrown it all away.

For *sex*… Lust. One of those deadly sins.

Her partner in crime hadn't helped.

'It was only sex, babe.' The look on his face hadn't helped. *'Okay, it was great sex but, hey…it's still no big deal. Don't get weird about it.'*

He had *no* idea how big a deal it was for her.

'It's not as if you have to worry about getting pregnant.'

As if using a condom made it okay. Maybe it did in the world he came from. The world she'd avoided for ever. Sex, drugs and rock 'n' roll.

Her mother's world.

Oh, she'd held it together for a while. Long enough to get her clothes on and retreat from that bedroom with some dignity at least. She'd gone to the downstairs cloakroom, relieved to find that the only people around were the clean-up crew and members of the band, who were still dismantling their sound system. She'd sat in a cubicle for a long time, hoping that the shaking would ease. That the memory of what it had been like in Rafe's arms would fade. Or that she would be able to reassign it as something as horrible as it should be instead of the most incredible experience she'd ever had.

One that she knew she might desperately want to have again.

No-o-o...

She couldn't be that girl. She wouldn't let herself.

Jack had taken one look at her face when she'd gone to the kitchen and simply hugged her.

'It's over, love. You get to go home and get some sleep. I'll finish up here. I've already packed the leftovers into your car. Those kids at the home are going to get a real treat for Sunday lunch this week.' He'd tightened his hug. 'You've done it. Awesome job. You can be very proud of yourself.'

Jack had no idea either, did he?

Somehow, she got home to the small apartment over the commercial kitchen that had been the base for her business for those first years. It was more of a test kitchen now and a back-up for when they needed things they didn't have the time or space to produce in the bigger kitchens that were Jack's domain, but it was full of memories and Penelope loved it with a passion. She transferred the containers of food to the cool room and then slammed the door to the street shut behind her and locked it, hoping to shut those hounds outside. But they followed her upstairs and she could see them circling her bed, waiting to move in for the kill.

One of them had her grandmother's face. Cold and disgusted. With sharp teeth ready to shave slivers of flesh from her bones with every accusation.

One of them had Rafe's face. With eyes that glowed with desire and a lolling tongue that promised pleasures she'd never dreamed of. It stopped and gave her what looked like a grin as she unzipped the silver dress and it felt like it was Rafe's hands that were peeling the fabric from her body all over again.

Where did that heat come from? Coursing through her body like an electric shock that was delicious instead of painful?

Oh, yeah…it was the bad blood. Of course it was. How else could it move so fast and infuse every cell of her body?

Penelope balled the dress and threw it into the corner. So much for it being her trademark wedding outfit. She'd never be able to wear it again.

She'd never be able to sleep if she got into her bed

either. The thought of lying there in the dark with those mental companions was unbearable. Even exhaustion wouldn't be enough protection.

Pyjamas were a good idea, though. Comfortable and comforting. Her current favourites were dark blue, with a pattern of silver moons and stars. A soft pair of knitted booties on her feet and Penelope was already feeling better. All she needed now was a cup of hot chocolate and the best thing about making that was that she could be in her kitchen and that was a comfort zone all of its own.

Or was it?

Encased in the upright, clear holder on the gleaming expanse of the stainless-steel bench was a recipe for cake. Red velvet cake. The cake she'd promised her grandmother she would provide for the dinner party tomorrow night to celebrate Grandad's birthday. No, make that tonight because Sunday had started hours and hours ago.

Before the fireworks. Before she'd blown up the foundations of her life by doing something so reckless she had no idea how to process any possible repercussions.

Easier not to think. To go on autopilot and do what she could do better than anyone. Opening cupboards, Penelope took out bowls and measuring cups and cake tins. She turned an oven on and went to the cool room and then the pantry to collect all the ingredients she would need.

Flour and cocoa. Unsalted butter and eggs and buttermilk. Caster sugar and red paste food colouring. She

could think about the icing later. Cream cheese for between the layers, of course, but the decoration on top
would have to be spectacular to impress her grandmother. Maybe a whole bouquet of the delicate frosted
roses that she was famous for.

It would take hours. Maybe so long she would have
to leave her kitchen and go straight to her Sunday gig
of making lunch for the residents of the Loxbury Children's Home. Another comfort zone.

How good was that?

It wasn't easy to identify the prickle of irritation because it had been a long time since Rafe Edwards had
felt…guilty?

He didn't *do* guilt. He'd learned at a very young age
that it was only justified if you hurt somebody intentionally and that was something else he never did. He
refused to feel guilty for breaking rules that weren't
going to damage anything bar the egos of people who
thought they had the right to control what you did because they were more important. Better educated, or
richer, or simply older.

The snort that escaped as he pulled his jeans back on
was poignant. The age factor hadn't mattered a damn
since he'd been sixteen. Nearly two decades since anyone had been able to make his life unbearable simply
because they were old enough to have authority.

Back then, he'd get angry at being caught rather than
feel guilty about what rule he'd broken. And maybe
there was a smidge of anger to be found right now. Annoyance, for sure. Penelope had wanted it as much as he

had, so why had she looked as if the bottom had fallen out of her world the moment her desire-sated eyes had focused again?

Yep. Annoyance had been why he'd baited her. Why he'd made no attempt to cover himself as he'd lain there with his arms hooked over the pillows behind him. Why he'd tried to dismiss what had happened as nothing important. Had he really said it was no big deal because she hadn't been in danger of getting pregnant?

It had been lucky he'd found that random condom in his pocket. Would either of them have been able to stop what had been happening by the time he'd gone looking? That was a scary thought. Unprotected sex was most certainly one of the rules that Rafe never broke because there was a real risk of someone getting hurt. A kid. Someone so vulnerable it was something he never even wanted to have to think about. Didn't want to have to remember…

Robot woman had returned as she'd scrambled into her clothes. Man, Penelope Collins was uptight. No wonder he'd avoided her type for ever. This aftertaste was unpleasant. A prickle under his skin that didn't feel like it was going to fade any time soon.

He didn't bother straightening the bed before he left the room. He owned the room now. And the bed, seeing as he'd bought the place fully furnished. It was the room he intended on using as his bedroom when he moved in but…dammit…would he ever be able to sleep in there without remembering that astonishing encounter?

And maybe that was where that irritation was coming from. Because he knew it was an encounter he was never going to get the chance to repeat.

Which was crazy because he didn't want to. Why would anybody want to if it left you feeling like this?

It was probably this disturbance to his well-being that made it take a second glance to recognise the man coming out of the ballroom when he got downstairs.

Or maybe it went deeper than that?

More guilt?

This was an old friend. One of the few good mates from the past that he hadn't spent nearly enough time with in recent years because his life had taken him in such a different direction. Such an upward trajectory.

This felt awkward. Was there a chance of being seen as completely out of their league? Too important to hang out with them any more?

But there was relief to be found here, too, being drawn back into a part of his past he would never choose to abandon. A comfort zone like no other, and that was exactly what he needed right now.

And it appeared as if he was welcome, judging by the grin that split the man's face as he caught sight of Rafe.

'Hey, man… What the heck are you doin' here?'

'Scruff. Hey… Good to see you. Here, give me that.' Rafe took one of the huge bags that held part of the drum kit. 'I heard you and the boys. You're still sounding great.'

'Thanks, man. Still missing your sax riffs in some of those covers. Like that one of Adele's. If we'd known you were going to be here we would have hauled you on stage.'

The tone was light but there was a definite under-
current there. Rafe hadn't been imagining the barrier
he'd inadvertently erected with his neglect. Or maybe
it was more to do with how successful he'd become.
How rich…

'I was a bit busy. That fireworks show? Put that together myself. Haven't done the hands-on side of the
business for years. It was fun.'

'It was awesome.' Scruff dumped the gear he was
carrying beside the van parked on the driveway. He
leaned against the vehicle to roll a cigarette and when
it was done he offered it to Rafe.

'Nah, I'm good. Given it up, finally.'

'For real? Man…' Scruff lit the cigarette and took a
long draw, eyeing Rafe over the smoke. The awkwardness was there again. He was different. Their relationship was different. 'Given up all your other vices, too?'

'Nah…' Rafe grinned. 'Some things are too good
to give up.'

Like sex.

Scruff's guffaw and slap on the arm was enough to
banish the awkwardness. And then other band members joined them and Scruff's delight in rediscovering
a part of Rafe that he recognised was transmitted—
unspoken—with no more than a glance.

Rafe was only too happy to take the rebukes of how
long it had been. To apologise and tell them all how
great it was to see them. Reunion time was just what
he needed to banish that prickle.

The one that told him sex was never going to be anything like the same again.

Unless it was with Penelope Collins?

The enthusiasm of the other members of Diversion gained momentum as they finished packing their gear into the truck. 'Bout time you got yourself back where you belong. Party tomorrow night… No, make that *tonight*. You up for it?'

'You bet.'

Diversion's lead singer, Matt, grinned. 'We'd better send out some more invites. I can think of a few bods who'll want to see you again.'

Scruff snorted. 'Yeah…like the Twickenham twins.'

The sudden silence let him know that the boys were eyeing each other again. Still wondering how different he might be. It seemed important to diffuse that tension. To get into that comfort zone more whole-heartedly.

'Oh, no…' Rafe shook his head. 'They're still hanging around? Do they still dress up as cowgirls?'

'Sure do.' Scruff gave him a friendly punch on the arm. 'And they're gonna be mighty pleased to see you, cowboy.'

The prickle was fading already. With a bit of luck, normal service was about to be resumed. 'Bring it on. Just tell me where and when.'

The Loxbury Children's Home, otherwise known as Rainbow House, was on the opposite side of the city from Loxbury Hall and its style was just as different as the location. The building had no street appeal, with the haphazard extensions that had taken place over time and maintenance like painting that was well overdue, and the garden was littered with children's toys and a playground that had seen better days.

But it felt like home, and Maggie and Dave, the house parents, welcomed Penelope with the same enthusiasm as they'd done years ago—that very first time she'd turned up with the tentative offer of food left over from a catering event. The same age as her grandparents, Maggie and Dave were the parents Penelope had never had. The house, noisy with children and as messy and lived in as the garden, was so different from where she'd grown up that, for a long time, she'd felt guilty for enjoying it so much.

She'd gone back, though. Again and again. Maggie hadn't discovered for a long time that she actually cooked or baked things when there weren't enough leftovers to justify a weekly drop-off. When she did, she just gave Penelope one of those delicious, squishy hugs that large women seemed to be so good at.

'It's you we need more than free food, pet. Just come. Any time.'

It wasn't enough to just visit. Helping Maggie in the kitchen was the time she loved the best. Cooking Sunday lunch with her favourite person in the world was a joy and what had become a weekly ritual was never broken.

She'd got to know a lot of the children now, too. The home offered respite care to disabled children and temporary accommodation to those in need of foster homes. There were the 'boomerang' kids who sadly bounced between foster homes for one reason or another and some long-term residents that places could never be found for. The home was always full. Of people. And love.

'Oh, my… Is that fillet steak?'

'It is. Jack over-catered for the wedding last night. It came with wilted asparagus and scalloped potatoes but I thought the kids might like chips and maybe peas.'

'Good idea. What a treat. Well, you know where the peeler is. Let's get on with it. Don't you have some special do at your folks' place tonight?'

'Mmm. Grandad's birthday. There's no rush, though. I'm only doing dessert and I've made a cake. I don't need to turn up before seven-thirty.'

Maggie beamed. 'Just as well. The kids have got a play they want to put on for you after lunch. Have to warn you, though, it's a tad tedious.'

'Nothing on how tedious the dinner party's going to be. I'm almost thirty, Maggie, and I still get 'the look' if I use the wrong fork.'

Penelope rinsed a peeled potato under the tap and put it on the chopping board. She reached for another one from the sack and her damp hand came out covered in dirt. With a grimace, she turned the tap back on to clean it. Dusting the particles that had fallen onto her jeans only turned it into a smear but that didn't matter. She'd probably be rolling around on the floor, playing with one of the toddlers, before long. This was the only place she ever wore jeans and it was an illicit pleasure that fitted right in with not worrying about the mess or the noise. She'd just have to make sure she left enough time to shower and change when she went home to collect the cake.

'So, how was the wedding?' Maggie sounded excited. 'Did you know we could see the fireworks from here? A couple of the boys sneaked out to watch them and we didn't have the heart to tell them off for getting out of bed. They were so pretty.'

'Weren't they? I got the best view from upstairs at the hall.'

'Upstairs? I thought that was out of bounds?'

'Hmm. The guy doing the fireworks show had permission, apparently. He needed to be where he could see everything in case there was a problem.'

'And he took you upstairs, too?'

'Mmm.' Penelope concentrated on digging an eye out of the potato she was holding. 'Upstairs' was the least of the places Rafe had taken her last night but, no matter how much she loved and trusted Maggie, she couldn't tell her any of that.

She knew what happened when you did things that disappointed people.

They stopped loving you.

This time, when she picked up a new potato, the mud on her hand got transferred to her face as she stifled a sniff.

'You all right, pet?'

'Mmm.' Penelope forced a smile. 'Bit tired, that's all. It was a big night.'

'Of course it was.' Maggie dampened a corner of a tea towel and used it to wipe the grime off Penelope's cheek. 'Let's get this food on the table. You can have a wee snooze during the play later. It wouldn't go down too well if you fell asleep during dinner, would it? Your folks are going to want to hear all about everything that happened last night. They must be very proud of you. I certainly would be.'

Penelope's misty smile disguised a curl of dread. Imagine what would happen if she told her grandparents absolutely everything? But could she hide it well enough? Her grandmother had always had some kind of sixth sense about her even thinking about something she shouldn't and she'd always been able to weasel out a confession in the end, and a confession like this one would make the world as she knew it simply implode.

Oh, for heaven's sake. She hadn't been a child for a very long time. Wasn't it about time she stopped letting her grandparents make her feel like one?

It was one of the classic saxophone solos of all time. 'Baker Street' by Gerry Raffety. Rafe had first heard this song when he'd been an angry, disillusioned six-teen-year-old and it had touched something in his soul. When he'd learned that it had been released in 1978, the year he was born, the connection had been sealed. It was *his* song and he was going to learn to play the sax for no other reason than to own it completely.

And here he was, twenty years later, and he could close his eyes and play it as though the gleaming, gold instrument was an extension of his body and his voice. A mournful cry that had notes of rebellion and hope. So much a part of him that it didn't matter he hadn't had time to take the sax out of its case for months at a time. It was always there. Waiting for an opportunity that always came when it was needed most.

And, man, he'd needed it tonight, to exorcise that prickle that had refused to go away all day. Even walking the expanse of amazing gardens he could now call his own, as he'd collected the last of the charred cardboard that had enclosed the shells fired last night, hadn't been enough to soothe his soul. Or floating on his personal lake to retrieve the barge. Memories of the fireworks display that had been intended to celebrate his ownership of Loxbury Hall would be inextricably linked to other memories for ever.

Of a woman he'd never expected to meet and would never meet again.

But never mind. He could let it go now. 'Baker Street' had worked its magic again.

'That was awesome, dude.' Scruff had given his all to his drum accompaniment to the song. So had the guitarists and Diversion's keyboard player, Stefan. Now the beer was cold and there was plenty of comfortable old furniture in this disused warehouse that was the band's headquarters for practice and parties.

'As covers go, it's one of the best,' Stefan agreed. 'But it's time we wrote more of our own stuff.'

'Yeah…' Rafe took a long pull of his beer. 'You know what? I've been toying with the idea of setting up a recording company.'

Stefan's beer bottle halted halfway to his mouth. His jaw dropped and his gaze shifted from Rafe to Scruff, who shook his head. Was it his imagination or did the boys take a step further away from him? Okay, so he had more money than he used to have. More money than most people ever dreamed of, but it didn't change

who he was, did it? Didn't change how much he loved
these guys.

He shrugged, trying to make it less of a big deal. 'I
could do with a new direction. Blowing things up is
getting a bit old.'

So not true. But there had been a moment today,
when memories of the fireworks and of Penelope had
seemed so intertwined, that the idea of taking a break
from his profession had seemed shockingly appealing.

'Get a whole new direction.' Scruff had recovered
enough to grin. 'Join the band again. Come and experience the delights of playing covers at birthday parties and weddings. You too could learn every ABBA
song in existence.'

The shout of laughter echoed in the warehouse rafters. He was forgiven for any differences and it felt
great. A cute blonde with a cowboy hat on her bouncy
curls and a tartan shirt that needed no buttons fastened
between an impressive cleavage and the knot above a
bare midriff came over to sit beside Rafe on the ancient
couch. One of the Twickenham twins. He knew they'd
been watching him closely all evening and their shyness
had been uncharacteristic enough to make him feel the
barriers were still there. Apparently, he'd just broken
through the last of them.

'Nothing wrong with ABBA.' She pouted. 'It's great
to dance to.'

'Yeah, baby...' Her identical sister came to sit on his
other side. Somehow she moved so that his arm fell over
her shoulder as if the movement had been intended. And
maybe it had been. 'Let's dance...'

Lots of people were dancing already, over by the jukebox that had been the band's pride and joy when they'd discovered it more than a decade ago—when Rafe had been part of the newly formed band. A pall of smoke fog hung under the industrial lights and, judging by what he could smell, Rafe realised he could probably get high even if he didn't do stuff like that any more. The party was getting going and it was likely to still be going when dawn broke.

The thought brought a wave of weariness. Good grief…was he getting too old for this?

'Can't stay too long,' he heard himself saying. 'Got a board meeting first thing tomorrow. We're making a bid for New Year's Eve in London again this year. It's big.'

'Oh…*man*…' Scruff groaned. 'We just find you and you're gonna disappear on us again?'

'No way. I've bought a house around here now.'

'For real?'

'Yeah…' Rafe wiped some foam from above his top lip. 'Given my advancing years, I reckoned it was time to settle down somewhere.' Not that he was going to tell them where the house was yet. That would put him back to square one by intimidating them all with his wealth and success.

The laughter of some of his oldest friends was disquieting. Stefan couldn't stop.

'House first, then a wife and kids, huh?'

Rafe snorted. 'You know me better than that, Stef.'

The twins snuggled closer on both sides. 'You don't wanna do that, Rafey. A wife wouldn't want to play like we can.'

So true. The connotations of a wife brought up images of a controlling female. Someone who made sure she got everything precisely the way she wanted it.

Someone like Penelope Collins?

The soft curves of the twin cleavages that were close enough to touch and inviting enough to delight any man were curiously unappealing right now. There would be no surprises there. It might be nice but it would be old. Jaded, even, knowing that it was possible to feel like sex was brand-new and exciting again.

Rafe sighed. He had to get out of there. The prickle had come back to haunt him.

'You're not the only one with something big coming up,' Scruff said into the silence that fell. 'We're gonna be a headline act at the festival next month.'

'The Loxbury music festival?' Rafe whistled. 'Respect, man.' Then he frowned. 'I thought they'd wound that gig up years ago. Too much competition from the bigger ones like Glastonbury.'

'They did. It's been nearly ten years but this year is the thirtieth anniversary. The powers that be decided it would be a great blast from the past and put little ol' Loxbury back on the map.'

'Sounds fun. You'll get to play some of your own stuff.'

'You could be in on it, mate. You'd love what we're doing these days. Kind of Pink Floyd meets Meatloaf.'

The other band members groaned and a general argument broke out as they tried to define their style.

One of the twins slid her arm around Rafe's neck. 'There's going to be a big spread in one of the music mags. That's Julie over there. She's a journo and she's going to be doing the story. Did you know a girl died at the very first festival?'

'No… Really?'

'That's not true,' the other twin said. 'She collapsed at the festival. She didn't die until a couple of days later. It was a drug overdose.' She raised her voice. 'Isn't that right, Julie?'

'That's not great publicity to rake up before this year's event.'

'There's a much better story.' Julie had come over to perch on the end of the couch. 'There's Baby X.'

'Who the heck is Baby X?'

'The baby that got found under a bush when they were packing up. A little girl. They reckoned she was only a few days old.'

'She'll be nearly thirty now, then.' The twins both shuddered. 'That's old.'

'Not as old as me.' But Rafe was barely listening any more. Penelope's words were echoing in his head.

My mother abandoned me as a baby and then died. I have no idea who my father is.

Holy heck… Was it possible that *she* was Baby X?

The idea that the renewed curiosity of this journalist could expose a personal history that had to be painful was disturbing.

He should warn Penelope. Just in case.

Not his business, he told himself firmly. And that would mean he'd have to see her again and that was the last thing he wanted.

He drained his beer and then stood up, extracting

himself with difficulty from the clutches of the twins. If he was going to believe what he was telling himself, he needed to get a lot more convincing.

He had to get out of there. He wasn't having fun any more.

The resolution to keep an adult poise along with any secrets she might wish to keep lasted all the way to the elegant old house in one of Loxbury's best suburbs. Her shower might have washed away the effects of so many sticky fingers but the glow of the cuddles and laughter was still with her. Her jeans were in the washing machine and she knew her new outfit would meet with approval. A well-fitted skirt, silk blouse and tailored jacket. There were no runs in her tights and she'd even remembered to wear the pearls that had been a twenty-first birthday gift from her grandparents, along with the start-up loan to start her small bakery.

A loan that was about to be paid off in full. Another step to total independence. She was an adult, she reminded herself again as she climbed the steps carefully in her high heels. The same shoes she'd worn the day she'd gone to the office of All Light on the Night. The same shoes that Rafe had tugged off her feet last night shortly after he'd unzipped that silver dress…

Penelope needed to take a deep, steadying breath before she rang the bell. She had a key to the kitchen door but rarely used it. By implicit agreement, being granted admission to the house she'd grown up in was the 'right' thing to do.

As was the kiss on her grandmother's cheek that

barely brushed the skin and, instantly, she was aware of the child still hidden deep inside. Having skinny arms peeled away from their target with a grip strong enough to hurt.

'Don't hug me, Penelope. If there's anything I detest, it's being hugged.'

'How are you, Mother?'

'Fabulous, darling. And you?' She didn't wait for a response. 'Oh, is that the cake? Do let me see. I do hope it's Madeira.'

'Red velvet.'

'Oh...' The sound would have seemed like delighted surprise to somebody who didn't know Louise Collins. Penelope could hear the undertone of disapproval and it took her back instantly to the countless times she had tried so hard to win affection instead of simply acceptance. Why did it still matter? You'd think she would have given up long before this but somehow, beneath everything, she loved her grandmother with the kind of heartfelt bond she'd had as a tiny child, holding her arms up for a cuddle.

It was a relief that the beat of silence was broken by the arrival of another figure in the entranceway. Maybe this was why she'd never been able to let go. Why it still mattered so much.

'Grandad! Happy birthday...' This time the kiss was real and it went with a hug. A retired and well-respected detective inspector with the Loxbury police force, the happiest times of Penelope's childhood had been the rare times alone with her grandfather. Being hugged. Being told that she was loved. Being taken fishing, or on a secret expedition to buy a gift for her grandmother.

The grandmother who'd never allowed the real relationship to be acknowledged aloud.

'For goodness' sake, Penelope. I was only forty-three when you turned up on our doorstep. Far too young to be called a grandmother.'

'I'll take the cake into the kitchen, shall I?'

'Let me have a peek.' Douglas Collins lifted the lid of the box. 'Louise, look at these roses. Aren't they fabulous?'

'Mmm.' Louise closed the box again. 'Don't stay nattering to Rita in the kitchen, Penelope. The champagne's already been poured in the drawing room.'

Rita always made you remember the old adage of 'never trust a thin cook'. Even bigger than Maggie, her hugs were just as good and her praise of the cake meant the most.

'Red velvet? Oh…I can't wait to taste it. Make sure there's some left over.'

'You should get the first piece, Rita. You're the one who taught me to bake in the first place.'

'Never taught you to do them fancy roses. I always said you were a clever girl.'

'I only *felt* clever when I was in here. It's no wonder I ended up being a baker, is it?'

'You're a sight more than that now. How did the wedding go?'

'It was fabulous. As soon as the magazines come out with the pictures, I'll bring some round for you.' The tinkle of a bell sounded from well beyond the kitchen and the glance they exchanged was conspiratorial. Penelope grinned. 'I'll pick a time when the olds are out and we can have a cuppa and a proper natter then.'

'I'd love that, sweet. You go and have them bubbles and enjoy your family time now. Go on…scoot before her ladyship rings that bell again.'

How ironic was it that 'family time' had already been had today. First with Maggie and Dave and then with Rita in the refuge of her childhood.

The messy places that were always warm and smelled of food.

The drawing room should have been overly warm thanks to the unnecessary coals glowing in the enormous fireplace, but somehow the perfection of every precisely placed object and the atmosphere of a formal visit created a chill. Tasting the champagne as they toasted the birthday didn't help either, because it made Penelope remember the taste in her mouth last night, when she'd emerged from the kitchen to take Rafe's hand and let him lead her upstairs.

The spiral of sensation in her belly at the memory couldn't have been less appropriate in this setting. Closing her eyes with a silent prayer, Penelope took another gulp.

'You look tired.' Her grandmother's clipped tones made it sound like she was excusing her lack of manners in drinking too fast. 'I hope you got some rest today instead of playing cook at that orphanage place.'

'Orphanages don't exist any more, Mother. Not like they used to.'

'I know that, Penelope.'

Of course she did. She'd probably gone searching for one as an alternative to doing the right thing and claiming their baby granddaughter.

'Charity work is to be commended, Louise. You know that better than anyone.' That was Grandad in a nutshell. Trying to keep the peace and protect his beloved wife at the same time. He'd always done that. Like the way he'd explained away some of the endless punishments and putdowns meted out by Louise.

She's only trying to keep you safe, sweetheart. We know what it's like to lose a precious little girl.

And now it was her turn to be soothed. 'Good on you, Penelope, if you went and helped when you were tired.'

'I wouldn't call it charity.' Oh, help. Why was she contradicting everything being said? She took another gulp of champagne and found, to her horror, that she'd drained her glass.

'Of course it's charity. Those children are riff-raff that nobody wants. With no-good parents that probably spend all their money on cigarettes and alcohol and have no idea how to set boundaries for themselves, let alone their offspring.'

'Mmm…' Penelope was heading for the ice bucket that held the champagne bottle. 'Bad blood,' she murmured.

'Exactly.'

The long pause was enough for the silent statement that was as familiar as a broken record.

'You can't help having bad blood. You just have to fight against it. Otherwise you know what can happen.'

Yep. Penelope knew.

She'd end up just like her mother.

Funny that the ice bucket was on the occasional table right beside the fireplace. And that family photos were positioned artfully on the top of the mantelpiece. There was Penelope in a stiff, ruffled dress, aged about three, clutching a teddy bear that the photographer had had available in his studio.

A not dissimilar professional portrait of another small girl was to one side of an equally posed portrait of her grandparents' wedding. This girl had the same blonde hair as Penelope but her skin was much paler and her eyes were blue. One of the few pictures of her mother, Charlotte—before she'd gone off the rails so badly.

It wasn't that the Collins blood was bad, of course. Charlotte had been led astray by the person who'd really had it. The unknown father whose genes had overridden her mother's to give Penelope her brown eyes and more olive skin. A permanent reminder to her grandparents of the man who'd destroyed their perfect little family.

Louise Collins rose gracefully to her feet. 'I'll go and let Rita know we're ready for the soup. Come through to the dining room, Penelope.'

'On my way.' Or she would be, when she'd filled her glass again. Heaven knew, she needed some assistance to get through the next hour or so of conversation without causing real trouble. Falling out with her grandmother any more than she had already this evening would only distress Grandad.

The worst thing about it all was that she had just learned what it was like when you lost the fight with the 'bad blood'.

And it was a lot more fun than she was having right now.

CHAPTER FIVE

NEARLY THREE WEEKS.

It should have been plenty of time to put any thoughts of Penelope Collins to bed—so to speak.

No...wrong choice of expression. Rafe Edwards closed his eyes for a moment to try and quell that surge of sensation that was inevitable whenever thoughts of Penelope and beds collided.

Maybe this was a mistake. He eyed the old building in the heart of Loxbury's industrial area with deep suspicion. Why had it even occurred to him that it might be a *good* idea?

Karma?

The amusement that was inherent?

Or was he being pulled along by some cosmic force he couldn't resist?

Fate.

With a dismissive snort, Rafe slammed the door of his four-by-four behind him. He didn't believe in any of that kind of rubbish. You made your own fate unless you were rendered powerless by youth or natural disaster or something. And success was sweet when it was earned.

Perhaps that was why he had grudging respect for Penny.

Oops...*Penelope*.

From the outside they were total opposites but there was a driving force at a deeper level that they both shared. Judging by the magazine and newspaper coverage of that wedding, Penelope was now poised for extraordinary success and she'd earned it. For whatever reason, she was carving her own niche in the world and she was doing it exceptionally well.

Plus...

Rafe rapped on the iron door that was the only entrance the building had to the street. No doubt there was a sparkling commercial kitchen behind the door with a team of loyal employees who could do their jobs with the kind of military precision Ms Collins would demand. Given how late in the day it was, however, it would be disappointing if the door was opened by someone other than the woman he'd come to see.

He wasn't disappointed. It was Penelope who opened the door.

'G'dday...' Rafe let his grin build slowly. 'I think you might owe me a favour.'

Oh...*no*...

She'd assumed it was Jack, who'd said he might drop in the new menus he was working on. She would never have opened the door otherwise. Not when she was wearing her pyjamas and slipper socks, with her hair hanging loose down her back. Funny how she'd never thought it might be a problem, with the only windows facing the street being on the next level where her apartment was.

How stupid was it not to have bothered using the peephole in the door? Not only stupid, but dangerous. It could have been anyone demanding entrance. A drug addict, for instance. Or an axe murderer.

Or…or…*Rafe*…

And he was calling in a favour?

He was still grinning at her. 'I realise you're probably beating off clients after getting so famous.'

'I… Ah…' Yes. Potential bookings were pouring in in the wake of the Bingham-Summers wedding. And part of that success had been down to its glorious finale with the fireworks. And, yes…Rafe had made that happen when he hadn't had the slightest obligation to, so she did owe him a favour.

But what on earth could he want from her?

The thought of what she might *want* him to want from her was enough to make her knees feel distinctly wobbly and that was more than a little disturbing. She'd got past that lapse of character. It had been weeks ago. Her life was back on track. More than back on track. Penelope tried to pretend that she was wearing her suit and high heels. That her hair was immaculate. She straightened her back.

'The thing is, All Light on the Night is booked to blow up a car on a movie set the day after tomorrow but the gig's about to be postponed, which doesn't suit us at all.'

Penelope had no idea where this conversation was going so she simply stared at him. Which was possibly a mistake. Beneath that battered hat she could see the tousled hair that her treacherous fingers remembered burying themselves in and below that there was a glint in those dark eyes that made her think he was finding this amusing. More than that—he was quite confident that she might find it amusing, too. Because he knew what she liked and he was more than able to deliver?

Penelope dragged her gaze away from his eyes. Dropped them to his mouth. Now, that really was a mistake. Staring at his lips, she could almost feel her body softening. Leaning towards him. Hastily, she straightened again.

'Sorry, what was that?'

'The catering company. It went on a forty-eight-hour strike today. Something to do with the union. Your workforce doesn't belong to a union, does it?'

'Um…not that I know of.' They'd started with only herself and Jack. Other employees had come via word of mouth and the company had grown slowly. They were like a family and there'd never been a hint of an industrial dispute.

'So you could take on the job? It's not huge. Just an afternoon and there'd only be a couple of dozen people to cater for, but film crews do like to eat and they like the food to be on tap. Catering for a movie set could be a whole new line of business for you. Could be a win-win situation for both of us, even.'

'In a couple of days?' Initial shock gave way—surprisingly—to a flicker of amusement at the way he was using the exact turn of phrase she'd tried on him in his office that day. Had he remembered that visit in the same kind of detail she had? 'We usually book that kind of job well in advance. *Months* in advance sometimes.' Her lips twitched. 'I could certainly give you a list of other companies that might be able to help.'

Rafe put an elbow up to lean against the doorframe. It pulled the front of his leather jacket further apart and tightened the black T-shirt across his chest. 'But I don't want another company,' he said. 'I have to have the best and…and I suspect that might be *you*.'

Penelope swallowed hard. She knew what was under that T-shirt. That smooth skin with just enough chest hair to make it ultimately masculine. Flat discs of male nipples that tasted like honey…

Taste. Yes. He was talking about food, she reminded herself desperately. *Food…*

'Have…have you got any idea what's involved with setting up a commercial catering event?'

'Nope.' He quirked an eyebrow and tilted his head. He could probably see into the huge kitchen area behind her anyway so did he really have to lean closer like that? Was he waiting for an invitation to come inside and discuss it?

Not going to happen. It was no help trying to channel thoughts of being dressed in something appropriate. She was in her pyjamas, for heaven's sake. At seven-thirty p.m. Any moment now and she might die of embarrassment.

'There's meetings to be had with the client.' Her tone was more clipped than she had intended. 'Menus and budgets and so forth to be discussed.'

'The budget won't be an issue.'

Another turn of phrase she'd used herself that day in his office. When she'd been desperately trying to persuade him to help her. Impossible not to remember that wave of hope when he'd said he might be able to do it himself.

She could do the same for him. Already, a part of her brain was going at full speed. Mini samosas and spring rolls perhaps—with dipping sauces of tamarind and chili. Bite-sized pies. Sandwiches and slices. It wouldn't be that hard. If she put in a few hours in her kitchen tonight, she could get all the planning and a lot of the prep done. She could use the old truck parked out the back that had been her first vehicle for getting catered food to where it was needed.

It might even be fun. A reminder of her first steps to independence and how far she'd come.

'Will you be there?' The query popped out before she could prevent it. What did it matter?

'Oh, yeah…' That wicked grin was back. 'I love blowing things up. Wouldn't miss it. The real question is…' The grin faded and there was something serious about his face now. 'Will *you* be there?'

That flicker of something behind the amusement told her that he wanted her to be there, but was it only about the food?

Penelope couldn't identify the mix of emotions coming at her but it was obvious they were stemming from that place she thought she'd slammed the door on. It would be a struggle to try and contain them and…and maybe it wouldn't be right.

Even her grandmother would tell her that she had an obligation to return a favour.

'Okay.' She tried to make it sound like it wasn't a big deal. 'Give me the details and I'll see what I can do.'

'How 'bout I email them through to you tomorrow?' He tugged on the brim of his hat and she could swear he was smirking as he turned away. 'Don't want to be keeping you up or anything.'

The flood of colour heated her cheeks so much that Penelope had to lean against the cool iron door after she swung it closed. Nobody knew that she liked to wear her pyjamas in the evenings when she wanted to relax. It would have been okay for Jack to find out but... *Rafe*?

Good grief. Penelope tried to think of something to make her feel less humiliated and finally it came to her.

At least he hadn't caught her dancing.

The thought was enough to get her moving. She needed to check supplies in the cold room and the freezers and start making a plan. The way to get over this humiliation was crystal clear. Even if it was only for an afternoon, this was going to be the best damned catering this movie company—and the visiting pyrotechnicians—had ever experienced.

Man, the food was good.

Rafe wasn't the only person on set to keep drifting back to the food truck and the long table set out beside it. Those delicious little triangles of crispy filo pastry filled with potato and peas in a blend of Indian flavours, along with that dark, fruity sauce, were irresistible. Just as well the platter kept getting replenished and he'd arrived just in time to get them at their hottest.

Just in time for Penelope to be putting the platter on the table, in fact.

'Definitely my favourite,' he told her. 'Good job.'

It was more than a good job. She'd not only made it possible for everyone to keep to schedule, there were a lot of people saying they'd never been so well fed on set. His praise brought out a rather endearing shyness in Penelope. She ducked her head and wiped her hands on her apron.

'Samosas are always popular. Try the spring rolls, too, before they run out. These guys sure do like to eat, don't they?'

She wasn't meeting his gaze. Maybe that shyness was left over from the other night when he'd caught her wearing her PJs.

And hadn't that been totally unexpected? About as strange as seeing this uptight woman dancing in the middle of his maze. There were layers to Penelope Collins that just didn't fit. It wasn't the things that were opposite to him that intrigued him. It was the opposites that were in the same person. Did she actually know who she really was herself?

Not that he was going to embarrass her by mentioning the PJs or anything. She'd returned his favour and he was grateful. And that would be the end of it.

'Won't be for much longer. We're all set for the filming and we only get one take.'

'Really? They seem to have been filming the same scene for ages.'

Rafe glanced behind him. They were in a disused quarry and the road had already been used for the sequence of the car rolling off the road.

'That was the hero getting the girl out of the car. I think they've nailed it now. He gets to help her run away from it next and when they hit a certain point is when we blow up the car. My boys are just getting the explosives rigged. It'll look like they're close enough to be in danger but they won't be, of course. All smoke and mirrors but we need the shot of them with the explosion happening behind them and that'll be it for the day.' He glanced upwards. 'Which is just as well. Those thunderclouds are perfect for a dramatic background but nobody wants their expensive camera gear out in the rain.'

'Is it going to be really loud?'

'Hope so. Should be spectacular, too, but you won't see much from here. Want to come where you will be able to get a good view?'

What was he thinking? The flash in her eyes told him she remembered agreeing to that once before and she hadn't forgotten where they'd ended up. The way her pupils dilated suggested that it had been an experience she wouldn't be entirely averse to repeating.

This was supposed to be the end of their association. Favours given and returned but, heaven help him, Rafe felt a distinct stirring of a very similar desire.

'No.' The vigorous shake of her head looked like she was trying to persuade herself. 'I can't. I'm here to do a job.'

'You can just leave it all on the table. Everybody's going to be busy for a while, believe me. Have you ever seen a car being blown up before?'

'N-no...'

'There you go, then. An opportunity missed is an opportunity wasted.'

It was more than a bit of a puzzle why he was trying to persuade her. It was even more of a puzzle why he felt so good when she discarded her apron and followed him to a point well out of shot to one side of the set. He used his radio to check in.

'You all set, Gav? Can you see the point they have to cross before you hit the switch?'

'All good to go, boss.' The radio crackled loudly. 'Reception's a bit crap. ...are you?'

'Other side. Raise a flag if you need me.'

'Roger...' The blast of static made him turn the volume down. 'Something to do with the quarry walls, I guess. They won't need me. I don't usually even come to gigs like this any more.'

Oops. Why had he let that slip? Not that Penelope seemed to notice. She was watching the actors being positioned for the take. Make-up artists were touching up the blood and grime the accident and extrication had created. Cameras were being shifted to capture the scene from all angles. The director was near a screen set up for him to watch the take on the camera filming the central action and the guy holding the clipboard moved in front, ready for the command to begin the take.

'Places, please,' someone shouted. 'Picture is up.'

* * *

This was a lot more exciting than Penelope had expected it to be. So many people who seemed to know exactly what they were doing. There were cameras on tripods, others being held, one even on top of a huge ladder that looked rather too close to the car, which must be stuffed full of explosives by now. A sound technician, with his long hair in a ponytail, was wearing headphones and holding a microphone that looked like a fluffy broomstick. The actors were waiting, right beside the car, for the signal to start running.

'That door's going to blow off first,' Rafe said, his tone satisfied. 'With a bit of luck it'll really get some air at about the same time both ends of the car explode.'

'I hope they're far enough away by then.' Penelope kept her voice down, although they were probably far enough away for it not to matter if they talked.

'See where that camera on the tracks is? There's a white mark on the ground well in front of that. When the actors step across that, it's the signal to throw the switch. There's no chance of them getting hit by anything big.' He shielded his eyes with his hand as he stared across the open ground between them and the car. 'There might not be that many rules I regard as sacred but safety is top of the list.'

Penelope's gaze swerved to his face. The anticipation of waiting for a huge explosion was making her feel both scared and excited. The notion that even her safety was important to Rafe did something weird and, for a heartbeat, it felt like she was falling.

But it also felt like she *was* safe.

Rafe was right beside her. He would catch her before she could get hurt.

As if he felt the intensity of her gaze, his head turned and that weird feeling kicked up several notches. A split second before the eye contact could get seriously significant, however, a loud clap of wood on wood and the shout of 'Action' distracted them both.

Game on.

The actors were doing a good job of making it look like a panicked struggle to get away from the crashed vehicle as flames flickered behind them. The girl was only semi-conscious, blood dripping down her face, and the guy was holding her upright and pleading with her to try and go faster.

Penelope could feel Rafe's tension beside her. He had his hand shielding his eyes again and was looking beyond the actors, who were getting closer to the white mark.

The vehement curse that erupted from his lips made her jump.

'What's wrong?'

But Rafe ignored her. He grabbed his radio and pressed the button.

'Gav? Abort…abort… There's a bloody *kid* behind the car.'

The only sound in return was a burst of static. With another curse, Rafe took off, taking a direct line from where they stood to the side towards the car.

The car that was about to explode…

'Oh, my God…' Penelope couldn't breathe. She stood

there, with her hands pressed to her mouth. Should she do something? Run towards the director and shout for help, maybe?

But Rafe was almost at the car now and surely someone had seen what was happening?

Her feet wouldn't move in any case. She'd never felt so scared in her life. With her heart in her mouth she watched Rafe reach the car. He vanished for a moment behind it and then reappeared—a small figure in his arms and half over one shoulder. Incredibly, he seemed to run even faster with his burden. Off to the side and well away from the line the actors had taken.

Were still taking.

In absolute horror, Penelope's gaze swung back to see them cross the white mark and then the first explosion made her cry out with shock. From the corner of her eye she could see the door of the car spiral into the air just the way Rafe had said it would, but she wasn't watching. Another explosion—even louder—and the car was a fireball. Big, black clouds of smoke spread out and she couldn't see Rafe any longer.

Couldn't think about how close he'd been to that explosion and that something terrible had just happened.

She was safe but—dear Lord—she didn't *want* to be safe in that moment. She wanted to be with Rafe. To know that *he* was safe…

And suddenly there he was. Emerging from the cloud of smoke, still well to the side of the set. Still with the child in his arms.

There was no missing what was happening now. All hell broke loose, with people running and shouting, coming towards Penelope from one side as Rafe came from the other. She was right in the middle as they met.

'What the hell's going on?' The director sounded furious. 'What in God's name is that kid doing here? Where'd he come from?'

'He was hiding behind the car.' The director's fury was nothing on what Penelope could hear in Rafe's voice. His face was grimy from the smoke and his features could have been carved out of stone as he put the boy down on his feet.

And Penelope had never seen a man look more compelling. Then her gaze shifted to the boy and she was shocked all over again. She'd seen this child before.

'Billy?' The name escaped in a whisper that no one heard but the boy's gaze flew to meet hers and she could see the terror of a child who knew he was in serious trouble.

A man in a fluorescent vest, holding a radio, looked as white as a sheet.

'Tried to call you to abort firing, Gav,' Rafe snapped. 'Reception was zilch.'

'We had security in place. Nobody got into the quarry without a pass.'

'He was with me.' Penelope cleared her throat as every face swung towards her, including Rafe's. 'In the food truck. I'm sorry...' She turned towards the boy. 'You knew you were supposed to stay inside, didn't you, Billy? What were you *thinking*?'

Billy hung his head and said nothing but Penelope could see the tremor in his shoulders. He was trying very hard not to cry.

Lifting her gaze, she found Rafe glaring at her with an intensity that made her mouth go dry. He knew she was lying.

'He was thinking he might want to get himself killed,' Rafe said quietly. 'He very nearly succeeded.'

'But he didn't.' Penelope gulped in a new breath. 'Thanks to you.'

'I'll have to file an incident report,' the director said, his anger still lacing every word. 'I should call the police. The kid was trespassing.'

'No.' Penelope took a step towards the boy and put her arm around his shoulders. 'Please, don't call the police. I take full responsibility. It's not Billy's fault. It's mine. I should have stayed in the truck with him.'

'You shouldn't have brought him on set in the first place.'

'I know. I'm sorry. But he knew a car was going to get blown up and it was too exciting an opportunity to miss.' She flicked a glance at Rafe. Would he hear the unspoken plea to get him on side by repeating the words he'd used to persuade her?

As if to underline her plea, a distant clap of thunder unrolled itself beneath boiling clouds. And then raindrops began to fall. Heavy and instantly wetting.

The director groaned. 'This is all we need.'

'Shall we start packing up, chief?' someone asked.

There was a moment of hesitation in which it felt like everyone was holding their breath.

'I'll deal with it,' Penelope offered. 'I'll see that Billy gets the punishment he deserves.'

'I think that's *my* call.' Rafe's voice had a dangerous edge. 'Don't you?'

The heat of his glare was too intense to meet but Penelope nodded. So did Billy.

'Fine.' The director held both hands up in surrender. 'It's your safety regulations that got breached. And it was you that brought this flaky caterer on set. You deal with it.' He turned away, making a signal that had the crew racing to start getting equipment out of the rain, but he had a parting shot for Rafe. 'You have no idea how lucky you are that no harm was done. You'd be out of the movie business for good if it had.' He shook his head. 'You're also lucky that your heroics didn't show up on screen or we'd have to be reshooting and you'd be paying for it, mate.'

The last person to leave was Gav.

'I'll pack down and clear the site,' he said. He cast a curious glance at Penelope and Billy. 'Guess you'll be busy for a while.'

The rain was coming down steadily now. The kid was visibly shivering in his inadequate clothing and the look on his face was sullen enough to suggest he was used to getting into trouble.

Rafe saw the way Penelope drew him closer. For a moment the kid resisted but then he slumped as if totally defeated. He wasn't looking at either of the adults beside him but Penelope was looking and she didn't look at all defeated. Her chin was up and she looked ready to go into battle. What was it with this kid? How on earth did Penelope even know his name?

'Want to tell me what this is all about?' Rafe wasn't about to move and any sympathy for how uncomfortable either of these people felt hadn't kicked in yet. 'There's no way this kid was in your truck when you got here.'

'The kid has a name,' Penelope shot back. 'It's Billy.'

'How did you get anywhere near that car, Billy?'

He got no response.

'He didn't know you were going to blow it up. He—'

'Billy's not a puppet,' Rafe snapped. 'Stop talking for him.'

Penelope's mouth opened and closed. She glared at Rafe.

'Billy? Or is your real name William?'

A small sound from Penelope told him that she got the reference to her own name preference. The kid also made a sound.

'What was that?'

'Billy. Only rich kids get called William.'

'And how do you know Penelope?'

'I don't.'

That made sense. Billy looked like a street kid.

Like he'd looked about the same age? Rafe pushed the thought away. He didn't want to go there.

'How does she know your name, then?'

'Dunno.' Billy kicked at the ground with a shoe that had a hole over his big toe.

'I help out at a local children's home.' Penelope's tone was clipped, as if she expected to get reprimanded for speaking again. 'I've met Billy there a couple of times in the last few years when things haven't been so good at home.'

That also made sense. A bit of charity work on the side would fit right in with the image that Ms Collins presented to the world. The image that hid the person she really was?

Rafe stifled an inward sigh. 'So, is that why you sneaked into the quarry? Trying to find a place away from home?'

'I was playing, that's all.' The first direct look Rafe received was one of deep mistrust. 'I saw them doing stuff to the car and I wanted a closer look. You didn't have to come and get me. It was none of your business, man.'

Whoa…did this kid know that he'd almost got killed and didn't care? The anger was still there. In spades.

'You don't get to make decisions like that,' he told Billy. 'Not at your age.'

An echo of something unpleasant rippled through him. People making decisions for him because he was too young. People making rules. Making things worse.

But this was about safety. Keeping a kid alive long enough for him to get old enough to make his own decisions—stupid or otherwise.

'I'm taking you home,' he said. 'I want a word with your parents.'

'No *way*…' Billy ducked under Penelope's arm and took off. If the ground hadn't become slippery already from the rain, he might have made it, but Rafe grabbed him as he got back to his feet. And he held on.

'Fine. If you don't want to go home, we'll go and have a chat to the cops.'

'*No.*' Penelope looked horrified. 'Don't you think

he's got enough to deal with, without getting more of a police record at his age?'

More of a police record? Good grief.

'I'll take him to Maggie and Dave. They'll know what to do.'

'Who the heck are Maggie and Dave?'

'They run Rainbow House—the children's home. They're the best people I know.'

There was passion in her voice. Something warm and fierce that made Rafe take another look at her face. At her eyes that were huge and...vulnerable?

'And how do you think you're going to get him to this home? In the back of your truck that he could jump out of at the first set of traffic lights?' The tug on his arm confirmed his suspicions so he tightened his grip.

Penelope faced Billy. 'You've got a choice,' she said. 'You can either come with me and see Maggie and Dave or go to the police station. What'll it be?'

Billy spat on the ground to show his disgust. 'You can't make me go anywhere.'

'Wanna bet?' Rafe was ready to move. It was easy to take the kid with him. 'Let's go back to your truck, Penelope. We can call the police from there.'

'No.' Billy kicked Rafe's ankle. He stopped and took hold of the boy's other arm as well, bodily lifting him so that he could see his face.

'That's enough of that, d'you hear me? We're trying to *help* you.'

'That's what they all say.' There was a desperation in Billy's voice that was close to a sob as he struggled for freedom. 'And they don't *help*. They just make everything worse...'

Oh, man... This was like looking into some weird mirror that went back through time.

'Not Maggie and Dave...' Penelope had come closer. Close enough to be touching Rafe's shoulder. Was it just the rain or did she have tears running down her cheeks? 'They can help, Billy. I know they can.'

'Then that's where we'll go.'

'We?'

'I'm coming with you.' He couldn't help his exasperated tone. 'You can't do this by yourself.'

Which was a damned shame because Rafe could do without a trip to some home for problem kids. Could do without the weird flashbacks, thanks very much. But he'd only get more of them if he left this unresolved, wouldn't he?

And this was supposed to be the end of his association with Penelope Collins. It would be a shame to leave it on such a sour note.

'Let's get going,' he growled, as another clap of thunder sounded overhead. 'Before we all catch pneumonia.'

CHAPTER SIX

IF PENELOPE HAD been a frightened child with a home she was scared to go back to, then Rainbow House was exactly the place she'd want to be. She knew she was doing the right thing here, but the vibes from the two males in the front seat of her little food truck told her they didn't share her conviction.

Penelope was driving and Billy was sandwiched between the two adults to prevent any attempt to escape. A sideways glance as they neared their destination revealed remarkably similar expressions on their faces. It could have been a cute 'father and son' type of moment, except that the expressions were sullen. They were both being forced to do something that ran deeply against the grain. Being punished.

Her heart squeezed and sent out a pang of…what? Sympathy? There was something more than the expressions that was similar. Had Rafe been a kid who had broken every rule in the book to get some attention? He still broke rules—look at the total lack of appreciation for the stated boundaries at Loxbury Hall. Not that he needed to do anything to attract attention now. He was the most gorgeous man she'd ever seen. He was clever and passionate about his work. And he'd just risked his life to save a child.

The memory of the wave of emotion when she'd seen him emerge from the smoke unharmed made her grip the steering-wheel tightly. It gave her an odd prickly sensation behind her eyes, as though she was about to cry—which was disturbing because she had learned not to cry a long time ago.

'Don't cry, for heaven's sake, Penelope. The only difference it makes is that your face gets ugly.'

There was no denying that Rafe Edwards stirred some very strong emotions in her and the fact that he clearly thought she was punishing Billy by taking him to Rainbow House was annoying. Hadn't he been prepared to deliver Billy to the police? He'd soon see that she was right.

His expression certainly changed the moment Dave opened the door and welcomed them in. They must have just finished dinner judging by the rich smell of food. Most of the children were in the playroom, watching television, and the sound of laughter could be heard. Maggie was on the floor in front of the fire, dressing a small baby in a sleep suit. She scooped up the infant and got to her feet in a hurry.

'Oh, my goodness. What's happened? Billy? Oh…' She handed the baby to Dave and enveloped Billy in a hug that was not returned. The boy stood as still as a lamppost.

'This is Rafe Edwards,' Penelope told her. 'He's the

pyrotechnician I told you about—the one who did the fireworks at the wedding?'

'Oh…' Maggie held out her hand. 'Welcome to Rainbow House, Rafe,' she said. 'I'm Maggie. This is Dave. And this is Bianca.' She dropped a kiss on the baby's head. Then it was Penelope's turn to be hugged. 'Good grief, darling. You're soaked. Come upstairs with me while I get baby Bi to bed. We'll find you some dry clothes.' She glanced at Rafe. 'I'm not sure there'd be anything in the chest to fit you, but Dave could find you something.'

'I'm fine.' The sullen expression had given way to… nothing. It was as if the Rafe that Penelope knew had simply vanished. This was a man with no opinion. No charisma. No hint of mischief.

'Stand over by the fire, then, at least. Dave'll get you something hot to drink. Billy? You want to come and find some dry clothes?'

'Nah.' Billy's head didn't move but his glance slid sideways. 'Reckon I'll stand by the fire, too.'

Maggie shared a glance with Penelope, clearly curious about the relationship of the stranger to the boy she knew, but she wasn't going to ask. Not yet. Best let her visitors settle in first. Penelope knew she'd accept them no matter what story had brought them here, and she loved Maggie for the way you became a part of this family simply by walking through the door. When Dave handed her the baby, she was more than happy to take her and cuddle her as she followed Maggie out of the room. Pressing her lips to the downy head was a delicious comfort. It eased the worry of glancing back to see Rafe and Billy both standing like statues in front of the fire.

Rafe had the curious feeling that he'd fallen down one of those rabbit holes in Alice's wonderland.

Had he really thought that Penelope came here occasionally as her contribution to society to read stories to the children or something? She was a part of this family. In this extraordinary house that felt exactly like a *real* home. It even smelt like one. The aroma of something like roast beef made his stomach growl. The heat of the fire was coming through his soaked clothing now, too. A sideways glance showed steam coming off Billy's jeans and the kid had finally stopped shivering. He kind of liked it that Billy had chosen to stay with him, instead of disappearing with the others to find dry clothes. Maybe he felt the connection. Felt like he might have an ally.

Not that Rafe had any qualms about leaving him here, if that was possible. This wasn't like any children's home he'd ever experienced. Hell, it wasn't even like any foster home he'd been dumped in. No point in wondering what kind of difference it might have made if there'd been a place like Rainbow House in his junior orbit. Water under the bridge. A long way under the bridge, and he still didn't want to go swimming in it again. The sooner he got out of here, the better.

Dave had gone to the kitchen and the silence was getting noticeable.

'So you've been here before?'

'Yeah...'

'Not bad, is it?'

'Nah…I guess.'

Dave reappeared with two steaming mugs. 'Soup,' he announced. 'Lucky we always have a pot on the back of the stove.'

Maggie and Penelope appeared by the time he'd taken his first sip and he almost slopped the mug as he did a double-take. What was Penelope wearing?

An ancient pair of trackpants, apparently. And a thick, oversized red woollen jersey that had lumpy white spots all over it. She was still rubbing at her hair with a towel and when she put it down he could see damp ringlets hanging down her back. She had *curly* hair?

She looked so young. Kind of like the way she'd looked in her PJs, only a bit scruffier.

Cute…

The power-dressing princess seemed like a different person. Of course she did. It *was* a different person. Just part of the same, intriguing package that had so many layers of wrapping.

A teenaged girl with improbably blue hair walked through the living room on her way to the kitchen.

'Hey, Billy. How's it going?' She didn't wait for an answer. 'Dave—John's got the remote and he's not sharing.'

A shriek was heard coming from the playroom. Dave shook his head. 'Excuse me for a moment.'

Maggie clucked her tongue as the blue-haired girl came back. 'Charlene, go back and get a spoon. It's bad manners to eat ice cream with your fingers.'

A snort of something like mirth came from Billy

and Penelope caught Rafe's gaze as she came closer to the fire. *This is good*, the glance said. *This is where this kid needs to be.*

She was right. Eventually, there was time to explain why they were here. They were listened to and questions were asked that got right to the heart of the matter.

'You live near the quarry, don't you, Billy? Is that where you go when you need to get away from home?'

Billy shrugged.

'You know it's breaking the law, don't you? The quarry's a dangerous place and that's why there's no public access allowed.'

Another shrug.

'Breaking rules just gets you into trouble, Billy,' Penelope added quietly. 'You *know* that.'

'We'd love to have you back here,' Maggie said, 'And, if you want, Dave'll give Social Services a ring in a minute. Do you think you'd like that to happen?'

The silence was broken by a sniff. Billy scrubbed at his nose, his head still bent so his face couldn't be seen.

'Yeah…I guess.'

'You'd have to follow our rules. Not like last time, okay?'

''Kay.'

'Any knives in your pocket?' Dave's voice was stern.

This time Billy glanced up. Rafe frowned at him.

A pocket knife came out of a back pocket and was handed to Dave.

'Matches?'

The packet of matches that was produced and handed over was too soggy to be a danger but the message was clear. Rules were to be followed and, if they weren't, there would be consequences.

But these were good rules. Rules that kept kids safe. Rafe nodded approvingly.

With a phone call made and permission given to keep Billy at Rainbow House for the time being, the chance to escape finally arrived. Weirdly, Rafe wasn't in a hurry any more. He stayed where he was, as Maggie bundled Penelope's wet clothes into a plastic shopping bag and farewells were made.

Penelope spoke quietly to Billy. 'I'll see you when I'm back on Sunday. Don't tell the others but I'll make a cake that's especially for you. What sort do you like?'

'Chocolate.'

'No problem. And, Billy…?'

'What?'

She was speaking quietly but Rafe could hear every word. 'You don't have to break rules to get people to notice you. It's when you follow the rules that people like you and the more people like you, the more likely you are to get what *you* want.'

What? At least the astonished word didn't get spoken aloud but Rafe had to step away and take a deep breath. Did she really believe that?

Probably. It might explain why this woman was such a complicated mix of contradictory layers. Whose rules was she following? And why did it matter so much that she was liked by whoever was setting those rules? Hadn't she learned by now that what really mattered was whether you liked yourself?

Self-respect. Self-belief.

Obviously not. Man...someone must have done a good job on her self-esteem at some point in her life.

Not his problem. None of what was going on here was his problem and he didn't want to get any more involved. He pulled a phone from his pocket.

'What's the address here?' he asked Dave. 'I'll just call a taxi.'

'No...' Penelope turned away from Billy. 'I can drop you home. It's the least I can do. You saved Billy's *life*...'

A look flashed between Maggie and Dave. A look that suggested she thought there was more going on between him and Penelope than met the eye. Oh, help... Had she heard *all* about the night of the fireworks?

'That's a much better idea,' Maggie said, turning her gaze on Rafe.

He almost grinned. It would be a brave man who went against what this loving but formidable woman thought best.

'Fine.' It came out sounding almost as grudging as Billy had about getting something he was lucky to be offered. He put an apologetic note in his voice. 'I'm a bit out of town, though.'

'No problem.' Penelope stuffed her feet into her damp shoes and picked up the bag of clothing. 'We've still got some samosas in the back if we get hungry.'

Penelope followed the directions to take the main road out of town and then the turn-off towards the New Forest.

'I've been here before. It's the way to Loxbury Hall.'

'Mmm.'

The only sound for a while then was the rough rumble of the old truck and the swish of the windscreen wipers. The heater still worked well, though, and Penelope was starting to feel too warm in Maggie's old jersey. The T-shirt she had on underneath wasn't enough to stop the itch of the thick wool. She couldn't wait to get home and put her own clothes on. Fire up her straighteners and sort out her hair, too.

Good grief…she must look an absolute fright. This was worse than being caught wearing her pyjamas. At least her hair had been smooth and under control.

'What was that for?'

'What?'

'That groan. I did tell you I was out of town a bit.'

Penelope cringed inwardly. And then sighed aloud. 'It's not that. I'm just a bit over you seeing me at my worst, that's all. A girl thing.'

There was another silence and then Rafe spoke quietly.

'Maybe I'm seeing you at your best.'

She tried to figure that out. Couldn't. 'What's that supposed to mean?'

'You do realise you broke the rules, don't you?'

'What rules?'

'The safety regulations that are a legal obligation for anyone who runs a business like mine. I should be filing a "Near Miss" incident report. Billy should have been charged with trespass.'

'And you think that would have helped him? For God's sake, Rafe. He's a kid whose home life stinks.'

'And you stood up for him. You were prepared to break the rules to stand up for him. I'm impressed.'

Impressed? With *her*?

Should she feel this pleased that she'd impressed a pyrotechnician cowboy her grandparents would probably consider riff-raff?

Moot point. The pleasure was irresistible and felt inexplicably genuine. And then he went and spoiled it.

'What were you thinking, telling him that people only like you if you follow all the rules?'

'It's true.'

But she could hear the note of doubt in her voice and this man, sitting beside her, was responsible for that. Rafe didn't automatically follow anybody's rules but he had the kind of charisma that no doubt had women falling at his feet with a single glance. He'd won over a small, troubled boy who had probably never trusted anyone in his short life so far. And even Maggie had fallen for him, judging by the way she'd acted when she'd taken Penelope away to find those dry clothes.

Instead of opening the old chest, she'd sat on the top and fanned her face with her hand, giving her a glance that had made Penelope feel she was in the company of young Charlene instead of the warm-hearted and practical woman who was in charge of Rainbow House.

'I'm not a bit surprised you went upstairs at Loxbury Hall with *him*. I'd have been more than a bit tempted myself.'

'Like' was far too insipid a word to describe how Penelope felt about Rafe but she wasn't going to try

and analyse those strong emotions. They were dangerous. The kind of emotions that led to trouble. Shame.
Sometimes, even death…

Rafe's voice brought the wild train of her thoughts
to a crashing halt.

'Did you follow all the rules today? Do you think I
like you less because you didn't?'

She didn't respond. There was a note in his voice that
suggested he didn't like her much anyway.

'Turn in here.'

'Are you kidding?' But Penelope slowed as the iron
gates of Loxbury Hall came up on the left.

Rafe pulled out his phone, punched in a few numbers and the gates began to swing open.

She jammed on the brakes and they came to a grinding halt.

It was quite hard to get the words out. 'When you
said you'd cleared it with the owner about going upstairs, you hadn't actually talked to anyone, had you?'

'Nope.'

'Because you *are* the owner?'

'Yep.'

Oh, no… Penelope let her head drop onto the steering-wheel on top of her hands. Now she felt like a complete idiot. Someone who'd been played like a violin.

'Um…Penny?'

She didn't bother to correct the use of the loathed
diminutive. 'Yeah…?'

'Do you think you could get us off the road properly
before someone comes along and rear-ends us? Just to
the front steps would be grand.'

* * *

The front steps belonged to the property he'd acquired by not following all the rules. He'd got to where he was in life because he'd believed in himself, not because he'd made other people like him.

Billy could do with a message like that.

Not that he wanted to go anywhere near Rainbow House again. It was sorted. This was it. Time to say goodbye to Ms Penelope Collins.

He turned towards her to do exactly that but then he hesitated. Rain beat a steady rhythm on the roof of the truck and it got suddenly heavier. A flash of lightning made Penelope jump and her eyes got even wider at the enormous crack of thunder that came almost instantly.

'The storm's right on top of us. You can't drive in this.' Without thinking, Rafe leaned over and pushed back a stray curl that was stuck to Penelope's cheek. 'Come inside till it blows over.'

She wasn't looking at him. And she shook her head.

He should have left it there but he couldn't. He knew an upset woman when he saw one. Had it been something he'd said? His hand was still close to her face and his fingers slipped under her chin to turn her head towards him. At the same time he was racking his brains to think of what it was that had sent her back into her shell. Revealing that he owned Loxbury Hall? No. That had nothing to do with her. Ah… As soon as Penelope's gaze met his, he knew exactly what it was.

'I still like you,' he murmured. 'Breaking the rules only made me like you more.'

Her lips parted and the tip of her tongue appeared

and then touched her top lip—as though she wanted to say something but had no idea how to respond. The gesture did something very strange to Rafe's gut. The look in her eyes did something to his heart.

She looked lost. *Afraid*, even?

He had to kiss her. Gently. Reassuringly. To communicate something that seemed very important. And, just in case the kiss hadn't got the message across, he spoke quietly, his lips still moving against hers.

'You're beautiful, Penny. Always believe that.'

A complete stillness fell for a heartbeat. There was nothing but the butterfly-wing softness of that contact lingering between their lips. A feeling of connection like nothing Rafe had ever felt in his life.

And then there was a blinding flash of light. A crack of thunder so loud it felt like the van was rocking. Penelope's body jerked and she emitted a stifled shriek.

That did it. Rafe moved without thinking, out of his seat and running to the driver's side of the van. He wrenched open the door and helped Penelope out. He held her against his body and tried to shelter her inside his jacket but even in the short time it took to get across the driveway and up the steps to the front door of his house was enough for them both to be soaked all over again.

Thank goodness for the efficient central heating in this part of the vast old house. But it wasn't enough. Penelope was shivering.

'I could get a fire started.' He was feeling frozen himself.

'Th-that would be n-nice…'

Was the fire already set or would he have to go hunting for kindling and wood?

'It could take a while.' Which wasn't good enough. And then inspiration struck. 'How 'bout a hot bath?'

'Oh…' She looked for all the world as if he'd captured the moon and was offering it to her in his hands. 'I haven't had a bath in…in for ever. I've only g-got a shower at my p-place.'

Rafe felt ten feet tall. With a decisive nod, he walked towards the staircase. 'You'll love my bath,' he said. 'It's well big enough for two people.'

At the foot of the stairs, he had to stop. Why wasn't she following him? Turning his head, he smiled encouragingly and held out his hand.

'You're quite safe. I wasn't actually suggesting that I'm intending to *share* your bath. I just meant that it would be big enough.'

When she took his hand, hers felt like a small block of ice. Weird that it made him feel so warm inside.

As if he was the one who was being given the moon?

CHAPTER SEVEN

HAVING RAFE IN a bathtub with her was crazy.

It also seemed to be the most natural thing in the world.

How had it happened? Penelope had been sitting there, on the closed lid of the toilet, with a big, fluffy towel around her like a shawl while Rafe supervised the filling of the enormous tub. The tap was one of those old-fashioned, wide, single types and the water rushed out with astonishing speed, filling the room with steam. Steam that became very fragrant when Rafe upended a jar of bath salts into the flow. Then he found a bottle of bubble bath and tipped that in as well.

'You may as well use them up,' he said. 'I'm not likely to.'

So the steam smelled gorgeous and the room was warm but Penelope could see that Rafe was shivering.

'You need that bath as much as I do. More… You've been in wet clothes for hours.'

'I'll go and have a shower in another bathroom.' But Rafe had turned his head on his way out and met her gaze and it felt like time had suddenly gone into slow motion. 'Unless…?'

And so here they were. Sitting at either end of this wonderful old, claw-footed bathtub, with Rafe slightly lopsided to avoid the tap and Penelope's legs between his. The bubbles covered her chest enough to be perfectly decent and she kept her knees slightly bent so that her toes didn't touch anything they shouldn't.

For the longest time they simply sat there in silence, soaking up the delicious warmth.

'I've never done this before,' she finally confessed. 'As soon as I got old enough, I wouldn't even let my nanny stay in the bathroom with me.'

'You had a *nanny*?'

Penelope swept some bubbles together with her hands and shaped them into a hill. 'Only because my grandmother didn't want to be a mother again. She'd done it once, she said, and that was enough.'

'I hope it was a nice nanny.'

'She was okay. Rita—our housekeeper—was better. She's the one who taught me to cook and bake, and by the time I was about eight I was spending so much time in the kitchen Mother decided that the nanny was superfluous so they fired her.'

'A housekeeper and a nanny. Your folks must be pretty well off.'

'We only had one main bathroom and my grandparents' room had an en suite that had a shower.' Penelope didn't want to talk about her family any more. Another scoop of bubbles made the hill higher. It wobbled but still provided a kind of wall and it meant she didn't have to look at Rafe directly. 'How many bathrooms have you got?'

'Haven't really counted.' He sounded vaguely discomforted by the query. 'A few, I guess.'

Penelope laughed. 'I'd say so.' Her laughter seemed to diffuse the awkwardness. 'What made you want to live here?'

Rafe tipped his head back to rest on the curved rim of the bath. 'I came here once when I was a kid. To a Christmas party. I thought it was the kind of house that only people with a perfect life could ever live in.'

'Were your parents friends of the owners?'

It was Rafe's turn to laugh. 'Are you kidding? I was one of a busload of what they called "disadvantaged" kids. The ones that went to foster homes because they wanted the extra money but then they'd get found out and the kid would get "rescued" so that somewhere better could be found. Somewhere they wouldn't get so abused.'

Shocked, Penelope slid a little further into the water. Her mind was back under that tree, as Clarissa and Blake's vows had been pledged. Seeing that sadness in Rafe's eyes as he'd told her she was one of the lucky ones.

'You know what it's like to have a family. Parents. You know what it's like to live in that safe place...'

Had he thought that a mansion was that kind of safe place when he'd been a little boy? That it would automatically give him a family and mean he was loved?

Penelope wanted to cry. She wanted to reach back through time and take that little boy into her arms and give him the kind of hug that Maggie would give.

She wanted to scoop him up and take him to Rainbow House—the way they'd taken Billy today.

That explained the hero-worship, didn't it? Had Billy sensed the connection? Somehow realised he was looking at a role model that he could never have guessed could understand what his life was like?

Maybe her thoughts were hanging in a bubble over her head.

'There weren't any places like Rainbow House back in my day,' Rafe said quietly. 'I wish there had been.' Something like a chuckle escaped. 'Maybe then I wouldn't have broken so many rules.'

Penelope's smile felt wobbly. 'Something went right along the way. Look at where you are now. *Who* you are…'

Her foot moved a little and touched Rafe's leg. His hands must have been under the water, hidden by the layer of foam, because his fingers cupped her calf.

'I'm wondering who *you* are,' he said softly. 'Every time I think I have it figured out, you go and do something else that surprises the heck out of me.'

'Like what?'

'Like breaking the rules. Not shopping Billy in to the cops. Going upstairs with me when you thought it wasn't allowed.'

Oh…help. His fingers were moving on her calf. A gentle massage that was sending tendrils of sensation higher up her leg. More were being generated deep in her belly and they were meeting in the middle in a knot that was both painful and delicious.

'Is not dancing in public one of your rules, too?'

'What?' The exclamation was startled.

'I saw you that day. Dancing in the maze. I was up on the balcony.'

Penelope gasped as something clicked into place. 'How did you know what song I was listening to?'

'You left your iPod on the table in the hall. It wasn't rocket science to check what was played most recently.'

'You were *spying* on me.' Penelope pulled her leg away from his touch. She gripped the side of the bath, stood up and climbed out.

Rafe must have climbed out just as fast because he was right there as she wrapped herself in a towel and turned around. Water streamed off his naked body, taking tiny clumps of bubbles with it. He caught her arms.

'Not *spying*,' he said fiercely. 'I was…intrigued.'

The nearness of him was overwhelming. Nearness and nakedness. She could feel the heat coming off his skin. Smell something masculine that cut through the perfume of the bath salts and bubble bath. His hair hung in damp tendrils and his jaw was shadowed by stubble. And the look in his eyes was…

'I still am,' he murmured. 'You intrigue me, Penelope Collins. No…when you get beneath the layers, I think it would be fairer to say you *amaze* me.'

Penelope forgot how to breathe.

She *amazed* him? On a scale of approving of somebody that was too high to be recognisable. Penelope had never amazed anybody in her life. The highest accolade had been her grandad being proud of her. A nod and even a smile from her grandmother.

Rafe had the world at his feet. He ran a huge, successful company. He'd just bought a house that very few people could ever dream of owning. What did he see in her that could possibly amaze him? It was true, though. She could see the truth of it in the way he was looking at her.

Was it possible for bones to actually *melt* for a heartbeat or two? She was still managing to stand but her fingers were losing their grip on the edges of the towel she had clutched in a bunch between her breasts.

Rafe was still dripping wet. His fingers felt damp enough to leave a cool trail as he reached out and traced the outline of her face but coolness turned into enough heat to feel like her skin was being scorched. Across her temple and cheekbone, down the side of her nose and then over her lips, and still they hadn't looked away from each other's eyes. She could feel the dip to trace the bow of her top lip and then his finger seemed to catch on the cushion of her lower lip.

She saw desire ignite in Rafe's eyes and his face came closer. She could feel his breath on her skin. Could feel his mouth hovering over hers—no more than a hair's breadth from touching—but it couldn't be called kissing.

This was something much deeper than kissing. Something that felt spiritual rather than physical. The waiting was agony but it was also the most wonderful thing Penelope had ever felt. The closeness. The knowing what was coming. The feeling of…*safety*? How amazing was that, that she could feel safe when she was so close to something that she knew could explode with all the ferocity and beauty of one of Rafe's fireworks.

The towel slipped from her fingers as his lips finally made contact. This wasn't just one kiss. It was a thousand kisses. Tiny brushes. Fierce bursts of pressure.

He caught her shoulders as her knees threatened to give up the struggle of keeping her upright. He lifted her. Carried her to where they needed to be.

In his bed.

Rafe didn't turn the bedside light off after he'd ripped the duvet back and placed Penelope in his bed. He wanted to see the look in her eyes as he made love to her. To see if he could catch an expression as extraordinary as the way she'd looked when he'd told her that she amazed him.

And he wanted this to be slow. To last as long as he could make it last because—incredibly—it felt like last time, only better. Still as new and exciting as if it had been the first time ever but familiar, too.

Safe...

She smelled like heaven. She *tasted* like heaven and it had nothing to do with all the stuff he'd tipped into that bath.

It was sex but not as he'd ever known it. This was a conversation that went past anything physical. It felt like simply a need to be together.

And even when the passion was spent, it didn't have to end, did it? He could hold her for a while longer. As long as she was willing to stay?

'Oh, Penny...' Rafe drew her more closely to his body, loving the way her head tucked in against his shoulder. 'Sorry.' His words were a murmur that got buried in her hair. 'Penelope. I forgot how much you hate that.'

'I don't hate it when you say it.' The husky note in her voice was full of the lingering contentment of supreme satiety.

'It's more you.' Rafe could feel his lips curl into a smile and it felt odd—as if he'd never smiled quite like that before. 'It's how I'm going to think of you from now on.'

'How do you mean?'

'It's like "Penelope" has extra layers of letters that hide the real stuff. And it sounds kind of...I don't know...stilted? All professional and polished, anyway. Like you were when you came into my office that day. And how you looked in that silver dress at the wedding.' His breath came out in a soft snort. 'Who knew I'd end up seeing you wearing your PJs? And trackpants and a jersey with big fluffy spots on it?'

'Don't remind me.'

He could feel the way her body tensed. He pressed his lips against her hair and willed her to relax. And it seemed to work. She sounded amused when she spoke again.

'I was so embarrassed when you caught me in my pyjamas. I only do that when I think no one's going to see me.'

'When you're being Penny instead of Penelope.'

He felt her breasts press against his arms as she sighed. 'My best friend at school called me Penny for a while but I made her stop.'

'Why?'

'There were some older kids there who knew more about me than I did. They told me I'd been called Penny because they're not worth anything any more. That nobody wanted me. That my mother had died because even she didn't want me.'

'Kids can be so cruel.' Rafe stroked her hair. 'What did you say?'

'That my name was Penelope and not Penny. And then I told the teacher about them breaking the rules and smoking behind the bike sheds and they got into a whole heap of trouble.'

'Did it make you feel any better?'

'Not really. And then I went home and started asking questions and that got me into a whole heap of trouble. My mother got one of her migraines and had to go to bed for three days and Grandad told me not to talk about it again. It became a new rule.'

'Sounds like you grew up with a lot of rules.'

'Yep.'

'Like what?'

'Oh, the usual ones. Doing what I was told and not talking back, getting good marks in school, not smoking or drinking. Only going out with nice boys that they approved of.'

Rafe snorted again. 'Would they approve of me?'

Penelope sounded like she was smiling but her tone was wry. 'After what we've just been doing? I doubt it very much.'

'Breaking another rule, huh? Lucky me.' He pressed another kiss to her tangled hair. 'Guess I'm a bad influence.'

'More likely it's my bad blood finally coming out. And you know what?' Penelope turned in his arms before he could answer. 'Right now, I don't even care.' She lifted her face and kissed him.

It was true. How could something that felt this right be so wrong, anyway? She waited, in that moment of stillness, to hear the old litany about her turning out just like her mother but, strangely, it didn't come. Maybe it would hit her on the way home, in which case she might as well stay exactly where she was for a bit longer. Maybe she could just go to sleep here in his arms. How perfect would that feel?

But Rafe didn't sound sleepy.

'Bad *blood*? What the heck is that?'

'Oh, you know. A genetic tendency to do bad stuff. Like take drugs or have wild sex with strangers.'

'I'm pretty sure you don't have "bad" blood.' He sounded amused now. 'It was probably one of the rules you grew up with. No bad blood allowed.'

'Pretty much. Nurture had to win over nature. Which is why I was never allowed to ask any questions about my father. That's where I got my bad blood from. He was the one who led my mother astray. Got her into drugs. Got her pregnant at sixteen. Made her run away from home so my grandparents never saw her again. Until she was dead.'

'I don't do drugs,' Rafe said quietly. 'And you're not going to get pregnant if I can help it. I do have a few rules of my own. In my case, nature probably won out over nurture.'

'I'm not sixteen. I get to do what I choose now.' It had been true for a very long time but this was the first time it *felt* true. She was choosing to be here and stay here for a bit longer because…because it felt so good.

'But you wouldn't tell your grandmother.'

'No. Only because it would hurt Grandad so much. He loves her. He loves me, too, but his priority has always been to protect Mother. And I get that. I think their lives got ruined when they lost their daughter. My mother.'

'What was her name?'

She hesitated for a long moment. She never talked about this. She'd never told anyone her mother's name. But this was Rafe and she felt safe. The word still came out as a whisper.

'Charlotte.'

There was a long silence then. Penelope was absorbing how it made things seem more real when you spoke them. How weird it was to have had a mother who'd never existed in reality as far as she was concerned.

Rafe seemed content to leave her in peace. Had he fallen asleep?

No. He must have been thinking about her. About her unusual parentage.

'Have you ever wanted to find out who your father was?'

'I know his name. It was on my birth certificate.'

'What was it?'

'Patrick Murphy. How funny is that?'

'Why funny?'

'They're probably the two most common Irish names there are. Imagine trying to search for him.'

'Have you…imagined, at least?'

'Of course. But maybe it's better not to know anything more.'

'What *do* you know—other than his name?'

'That he played a guitar in a band. Took drugs and got girls pregnant and then left town and never saw them again. Doesn't sound like a very nice person, does he?'

'There are always two sides to every story, darling.'

Darling…nobody had ever called her that before. It sent a weird tingle through Penelope's body. Embarrassingly, it made her want to cry. Or maybe there was more to the prickle behind her eyes than the endearment.

'He didn't want me,' she whispered. 'Any more than my mother did. She *left* me…under a bush. Who does that to their baby?'

'Maybe she had no choice.' Could he hear the imminent tears in her voice? Was that why he was holding her so close? Pressing his cheek against her head as if he could feel her pain? And more…as if he wanted to make it go away.

Nobody could do that. It was ancient history.

'There's something I should tell you. It happened a few weeks ago. The night after we…the night after the wedding here.' The pressure on her head was easing—as if Rafe was creating some distance because he was about to tell her something uncomfortable. 'I went to a party with some old mates. A band I used to be part of. There was a girl there…'

Oh, *no*… Was he about to tell her he was in a relationship with someone? That this was nothing more than a bit on the side? Penelope braced herself for something huge. Something that had the potential to hurt her far more than she had a right to let it.

'She was a journalist. Julie, I think her name was.'

Penelope didn't need to know this. Her muscles were bunching. Getting ready to propel her out of Rafe's bed.

Out of his life.

'Anyway, she's interested in a story. About a baby they called Baby X.'

Penelope went very, very still. There was relief there that he didn't seem to be telling her about a woman who was important in his life but there was fear, too. This was something that was supposed to be hidden. Long forgotten.

'Apparently Baby X was found under a bush. At the Loxbury music festival, nearly thirty years ago.'

There were tears running down Penelope's cheeks. 'That was me,' she whispered. 'It's going to be my thirtieth birthday in a couple of weeks.'

'I'm guessing you wouldn't want someone turning up on your doorstep, asking questions?'

'*No*…' Penelope squeezed her eyes shut. 'Or, even worse, chasing my folks. They'd *hate* that.' She swallowed hard. 'You don't think they'll be able to find out, do you?'

'I don't know. I'm surprised it's been kept such a secret for so long. It's the kind of story people love to know there's a happy ending to.'

'Grandad was pretty high up in the police force back

then. He might have pulled a few strings to have things kept quiet. People knew that my mother had died, of course, and that I was an orphan. But I'm pretty sure no one got told *how* she died or where she was at the time.'

'So there's no way to connect her to Baby X, then. You should be safe.'

But there was a note of doubt in Rafe's voice and Penelope felt it, too. Why hadn't anyone made what seemed like an obvious connection?

More disturbingly, what would happen if they did?

'I should go,' she said. 'Maybe I should have a word with Grandad and warn him.'

'Don't go. Not yet.' Rafe's arms tightened around her. 'It's still raining out there. Why not wait till the morning?'

How good would it be to push that all aside and not worry about it yet? If she stayed here and slept in Rafe's arms, would he make love to her again in the morning?

'Julie's actually coming to see me at the office to-morrow. I've offered to do a fireworks show at the close of the festival as a contribution to the charity they're supporting. I could find out how much she knows al-ready. Whether there's a chance they'll find out who you are. I could try and put her off even, if you'd like. Warn her that she could do some damage to people if she pursued a story that would be better left alone.'

He'd do that? For her?

'Thank you. I'd owe you a big favour if you could do that.'

'You wouldn't owe me anything.' Rafe was smiling. 'I told you, Penny. I like you. I like you a lot.'

'I like you, too.'

She gave herself up to his kiss then, and it was easy to put any other thoughts aside. So easy to sink into the bliss of touching and being touched.

Except that one thought wasn't so easy to dismiss. Again, 'like' was too insipid a word to have used when it came to Rafe.

She felt protected. Chosen. Loved—even if that was only a fantasy on her part.

It was no fantasy in the other direction. God help her, but she was in love with Rafe Edwards. She probably had been ever since he'd chosen the song she'd been dancing to for his fireworks show. Knowing that he had done so after seeing her dancing had shocked her, but now it made it all seem inevitable. How could you not fall in love with a man who'd chosen a song he knew would make you dance?

A man who was amazed by you?

The potential fallout of having her past and her family's shame made public was huge. And frightening.

But it wasn't nearly as big as how she felt about Rafe, so she could still feel safe while she was here. She could catch this moment of a happiness she'd never known existed.

Tomorrow would just have to take care of itself.

CHAPTER EIGHT

PENNY WAS GONE from his bed long before dawn broke. It was a downside of working in the food industry, apparently. If they had a large gig to cater, the kitchens opened for work by four a.m. She didn't go in this early very often now, because her role was changing to event management, but she'd told Jack she wanted to be in charge of this particular event.

It was a special occasion, apparently. Something to do with the Loxbury City Council and her grandfather would be there so she wanted everybody to be impressed.

'And I have to go home first. Can you imagine what people would think if I turned up in track pants and a spotty jersey, with my hair looking like *this*?'

She actually giggled and it was the most delicious sound he'd ever heard. No…that prize had to go to that whimper of pure bliss he'd drawn from her lips not so long ago.

But, yeah…he could imagine. They'd be blown away by seeing a side of their boss they'd never seen before. A glimpse of Penny instead of Penelope.

But she never let people see that side, did she?

Maybe he was the only person who'd ever got this close to her?

That made him feel nervous enough to chase away the possibility of getting back to sleep.

And his bed felt oddly empty after she'd gone anyway, so he shoved back the covers and headed for the shower.

The bath was still full of water from last night. The bubbles had gone, leaving only patches of scum floating on the surface of a faintly green pond. With a grimace, Rafe plunged his arm into the icy-cold water and pulled the plug.

Just like he'd have to pull the plug on whatever was happening between himself and Penny at some point down the track? His nervousness morphed into something less pleasant. He avoided looking in the mirror as he moved to the toilet because he had a feeling he wouldn't like the person he'd see.

Somebody who'd let someone get close and then leave town and never see her again?

The puddle of the towel on the tiled floor was in the way of getting to the shower cubicle. Rafe stooped and picked it up, remembering the way it had slipped from Penny's body as he'd been kissing her last night. He could almost swear a faint scent of her got released from the fabric as he dropped it into the laundry basket. He heard himself groan as he reached into the shower and flicked on the taps.

It wasn't that he was setting out to hurt her. He just didn't do anything long-term. What was the point of making promises that only ended up getting broken? That was when people got really hurt.

She was too vulnerable for him. And her belief that marriage was some sacred promise that made everything perfect was downright scary. She would probably deny it—he'd seen that magazine article where she'd said she was a happily single career-woman—but the truth was she was searching for 'the one.' The man who'd marry her and give her a bunch of babies.

And that man wasn't him.

No way.

Funny how empty his house felt when she'd gone. How empty *he* felt.

Well, that was a no-brainer. How had they completely forgotten to have any dinner last night? A fry-up would fix that. Bacon and eggs and some mushrooms, along with some thick slices of toast and a good slathering of butter.

By the time he'd finished that, he might as well go into work himself. He'd promised a show to remember for the anniversary Loxbury music festival and the pressure was on to get it planned and organised.

It was a weird twist of fate that the original festival had such significance in Penny's life but a seed of something that felt good came in thinking about that connection. He might not be able to give her what she wanted in life but he could do something to protect her right now. To stop other people hurting her.

Yes. By the time Rafe locked the door of his vast, empty house behind him and walked out into the new dawn, he was feeling much better.

He could fix something. Or at least make sure it didn't get any more broken than it already was.

Julie the journalist was young—probably in her early twenties—and she had an enthusiasm that made Rafe feel old and wise in comparison.

She was also cute, trying to look professional in her summery dress and ballet flats, with her hair up in a messy kind of bun.

Compared to Penny in professional mode, she looked like a child playing dress-up. She was a bit of a chatterbox, too, and giggled often enough for it to become annoying. Was she flirting with him?

If so, she had no idea how far off the mark she was. He couldn't be less interested but he kept smiling. He might need her cooperation on something important if the opportunity arose to put her off chasing the Baby X story. No, make that when. He'd make sure that opportunity arose.

There was plenty to show her and talk about before that. Video clips of old shows, for instance.

'This was the Fourth of July in Times Square. A bigger show than the one we're planning for the festival but we'll be using a lot of the same kind of fireworks. And this is a much more recent one.'

'Oh…isn't that the Summers wedding? I've seen that already. Love the hearts. And it's a cool song…' Julie's head was swaying and her hands were moving. He couldn't imagine any inhibitions about dancing in public with this girl. Any moment now she'd probably jump onto his desk and start dancing.

An image of Penny dancing in the maze moved in the back of his mind. Awkward. Endearing...

'That's one of the early challenges, picking the right song for a show. And it's important to get it locked in because that's when the planning really starts. Hitting the right breaks with the right shells. Making it a work of art instead of just a lot of noise and colour.'

'So have you chosen the song for the festival?'

'Mmm. Did that first thing this morning.'

'What is it?'

'I can't tell you that. If word got out, it wouldn't be a surprise and it would lose a lot of its impact.'

'Oh...*please*...?' Julie's eyes were wide as she leaned closer. 'I cross my heart and hope to die promise that I won't tell *anybody*.'

She was desperate to know. And if he gave her what she wanted, would she be more likely to return the favour?

'Okay...but this has to be a secret. Just between us.'

Her nod was solemn. Rafe made his tone just as serious.

'The first festival was held in 1985. The first thing I did was search for all the number-one hits for that year. And then I looked for ones that would work well with fireworks.'

'And...?'

'Strangely enough, Jennifer Rush's "Power of Love" was one of them.' And hadn't that hit him like a brick. How long had he sat there, the list blurring on the screen in front of him, as he relived watching Penny watching his fireworks that night. That first kiss...

'But you've already used that recently, yes?'

'Yeah…then I found another one and remembered something big that happened in 1985. In May. Only a few months before the festival so anyone who was there would remember it very well.'

'Bit before my time.' Julie smiled. 'You'll have to enlighten me.'

'The Bradford stadium fire? Killed a bunch of people and injured a whole lot more. It was a real tragedy.'

Julie frowned. 'Doesn't sound like a good connection to remind people of.'

'That's the thing. A group that called themselves The Crowd released a song to help with the fundraising effort and it's a song that everybody knows. An anthem that's all about exactly that—connection between people and the strength that they can give each other.'

'Wow…so, are you going to tell me what this magic song is?'

'Better than that.' Rafe clicked his mouse. 'Have a listen…'

A few minutes later and Julie was looking misty. 'That's just perfect…' She sniffed. 'I'd love to use it in my story but it'll still make great copy for a follow-up review.'

'There should be lots of great stuff to follow up on. Did you know that they've got a lot of the original artists playing again?'

'And current ones—like Diversion. Are you going to play with them? Matt really wants you to.'

Was there something going on between Diversion's lead singer and Julie? Rafe made a mental note to ask his mate what he thought he was doing when he saw the guys at the pub straight after this. Julie was too young. She'd end up getting hurt.

'I'm thinking about it. It'd be fun but I'll be pretty busy setting up the show.'

Julie folded her notepad and picked up her shoulder-bag. She looked like she was getting ready to leave.

'It can't be just the fireworks you're checking up on for your piece about the festival,' he said casually. 'What else is interesting?'

'Well, there's some debate about what charity is going to benefit from the profits. Last time it was the Last Wish Foundation for terminally sick kids and the time before that it was cancer research, but they want something local this time. It's all about Loxbury.'

'Mmm.' Rafe tried to sound interested instead of impatient. 'What about that other story? The girl who died?'

'Oh…' Julie's face lit up and she let her bag slip off her shoulder to land on the floor again. 'Now, that's *really* interesting. I had to call in a few favours to get any information but I finally tracked it down through someone who had access to old admission data at Loxbury General's A and E department. There were a few girls to choose from that day but only one who was really sick.'

'From a drug overdose?'

'That's the interesting bit. It was a bit of a scandal at the time because everyone assumed it *was* a drug overdose.'

'And it wasn't?'

'No. Apparently there was no trace of drugs. The coroner listed the death as being from natural causes. The poor girl had a brain aneurysm. She got taken off life support a few days after she'd collapsed at the festival.'

Why didn't Penny know that? Why had she been allowed to think that her mother had been some kind of drug addict who'd abandoned her in favour of finding a high? He'd suggested that maybe she'd had no choice other than to leave her baby under a bush. Having a brain haemorrhage certainly came under that category, didn't it? Wouldn't it have caused a dreadful headache or something? Scrambled thoughts enough for the sufferer to not be thinking straight?

'I got lucky.' Julie tapped the side of her nose. 'I got her name. Charlotte Collins. I've been trying to contact her family but do you know how many Collinses there are in Loxbury?'

She didn't wait for him to guess, which was just as well because Rafe was still thinking about Penny. How it might change things if she knew the truth. But, then, why hadn't she already been told? What kind of can of worms might he be opening?

'A hundred and thirty-seven,' Julie continued. 'And this Charlotte might not even have been local.' She paused for a breath. 'Mind you, I did get an odd reaction of this dead silence with one call. And then the phone got slammed down. The number was for a Douglas Collins. He got an OBE for service to the police force and now he's got some important job in the city council. I might follow that up again.'

'Don't you think it would be kind of intrusive to have someone asking about the death of your child?'

'But it was thirty years ago.' Julie looked genuinely surprised. 'I'd think they might like to think that someone remembered her. I might suggest some kind of tribute at the festival even, if I can find out a bit more.'

'I wouldn't.' Rafe summoned all the charm he could muster. 'I'd let the poor girl just rest in peace.'

'Oh…' Julie was holding his gaze. 'Really? But doesn't it strike you as too much of a coincidence that a girl died *and* there was an abandoned baby found? There's got to be a connection, don't you think?'

'Is that why you're chasing the story of the dead girl?'

'It's the only lead I've got. I can't find anything out about the baby. All I've got to go on is that they thought it was a few days old and there was a mention in the news that it had been reunited with family a short time later. Nobody ever said *why* it got left under a bush, though.'

'I guess the family wanted privacy. Maybe that should be respected.'

Julie didn't seem to hear him. 'Do you know how many babies get born in Britain?' She had a habit of asking questions she intended to answer herself. 'One every forty seconds or so. That's a lot of babies. Even if you have an approximate birth date you've got hundreds and hundreds to choose from, but guess what?'

'What?'

'Last night, I found one with the surname of Collins.

Born in London but guess what the mother's name on the birth record is?'

Rafe didn't want to guess. He already knew.

'Charlotte,' Julie whispered. 'But that's just between us, okay? I'll keep your secret about the song and you can keep mine.'

'So you're looking for this daughter now?'

'You bet. But I've got a long way to go. What if she got adopted and has a completely different name now?'

'What if she's adopted and doesn't know about it? You could damage a whole family.'

'She's all grown up now. I'm sure she could cope. She might even like her five minutes of fame.'

Rafe stood up. He couldn't say anything else but he needed to move. He wasn't doing a very good job of putting Julie off the scent, was he? How could he protect Penny?

He really, really wanted to protect her.

Somehow.

'As you said, it's a common name. I suspect you'll find a dead end.'

'No such thing in journalism.' Julie beamed at him. 'It just means there's a new direction to try. And I've got one to go and try right now. Thanks for the interview, Rafe. I'll look forward to seeing the fireworks.'

There might be fireworks of an entirely different kind well before the festival, Rafe mused, leaving his office to get to the pub where his old mates were waiting to have a beer and talk about whether he was going to join the band for a song or two on the day.

As soon as he'd had a beer or two he'd get away. At least he and Penny had exchanged phone numbers now. He could call her and warn her about how close Julie was getting to the truth. Apologise for not being more effective in throwing her off the scent, but how could he when she was so far down the track already? He could do it now, in fact, before he went somewhere noisy. Stopping in the street, he pulled his phone from his pocket. He dialled her number but, as it began to ring, another thought struck him.

Maybe he should also tell her that the truth was not what she believed it to be. But that wasn't something he could tell her over the phone. Cutting the call off, he shoved his mobile back into his pocket. It was a good thing he knew where she lived. A smile tugged at his lips as he pushed his way into a crowded Irish bar. Maybe there was a chance she'd be wearing those PJs again when she opened her door. If he stayed a bit longer at the pub with his mates, the odds of that being the case would only get stronger.

There was a good band playing and the beer was even better. Telling Scruff and Matt and the others that he'd like to get up on stage with them for old times' sake led to a lot of back-slapping and a new round of beer, this time with some whisky shots as well.

'You'll love it, man. Can't wait to tell the Twicken-ham twins. Bet they'll turn up with their pompoms as well as their cowboy hats. Hey, let's give them a call. They might like a night out, too.'

'I can't stay too long. Somewhere to be soon.'

'You can't leave yet. Band's not bad, eh? For a bunch of oldies.'

Rafe took another glance at the group on stage. 'They're no spring chickens, are they? Best place for Irish music, though. They wouldn't sound half as good at an outdoor gig.'

'Don't let them hear you say that. They'll be playing at the festival. They're one of the original acts that's being brought back.'

Rafe peered at the set of drums. 'What's with the name? The *Paws*?'

'Bit of a laugh, eh? I hear it got picked because it's the nickname of the lead guitarist but it got a lot funnier after the Corrs came along.'

'What kind of a nickname is Paws?' Rafe had another look as a new round of drinks got delivered to their corner. 'His hands look perfectly normal to me.'

'That's not normal. Listen to him—the guy's a genius. Paddy's his real name. Good name for an Irish dude, eh?'

'Don't tell me,' Rafe grinned. 'His surname's Murphy?'

Scruff's jaw dropped. 'You knew all along, didn't you?'

'No.' This time Rafe couldn't take his eyes off the guitarist. Paws. Paddy. Patrick. A Patrick Murphy who played the guitar. Who'd been at the Loxbury music festival thirty years ago? What were the odds?

Maybe Julie was right. Dead ends only led to a new direction. If the truth was going to come out, maybe the best thing he could do for Penny was to make sure that the *whole* truth came out. And this was too much of a coincidence to ignore.

Maybe he'd wait until the band finished for the night. Buy the guy a beer and at least find out if he'd ever known a girl called Charlotte Collins. Get a feel for whether there was any point in going any further.

In the meantime, there were drinks to be had. Conversations to be had along with them.

'Hey, Scruff? What did you do with that old set of drums I gave you way back? The ones I got given before I took up the sax?'

'They're still in the back of my garage. Bit of history, they are.'

'D'you really want to keep them?'

'Hadn't thought about it. Guess I should clean out the garage some time so I can fit my car back into it? Why?'

'Just that I met a kid the other day who looks like he could use a direction in life. A set of drums is a good way to burn up a bit of teenage angst, if nothing else.'

'True. Come and get them any time, man. They were yours in the first place, anyway.'

It was the buzzing in his pocket that finally distracted him from what was turning out to be a very enjoyable evening. He would never have heard his phone ringing but he could feel the vibration. When he saw that Penny was the caller, he pushed his way out of the bar again. Out into the relative peace of an inner-city street at night.

'Penny…hey, babe.'

'How *could* you, Rafe? When you knew how important it was…'

Good grief…was she *crying*?

'I trusted you…and then you go and do *this*…'

Yep. She was crying. Either that or she was so angry it was making her words wobble and her voice so tight he wouldn't have recognised it.

'What are you talking about? What am I supposed to have done?'

'Julie.' The word was an accusation. 'You *told* her.'

'Told her what?' But there was a chill running down his spine. He had a bad feeling about this.'

'About me. About my grandparents. She turned up on their doorstep, asking all sorts of questions… Oh, my God, Rafe… Have you any idea what you've *done*?'

'I didn't tell her anything. She'd already figured it out. I was going to tell you…'

'You really expect me to believe that? You told her and then she turned up and now…and now Grandad's probably going to die…'

'What?'

'They got rid of her but Mother was really upset. Rita called me. By the time I got there, all I could do was call an ambulance.' There was the sound of a broken sob on the other end of the line. 'He's had a heart attack and he's in Intensive Care and they don't know if he's even going to make it and…and this is…this is all… Oh, *God*… Why am I even talking to you about this?'

The call ended abruptly. What had she left unsaid? That it was all his fault?

It wasn't true. It wasn't even fair.

But standing there, in the street, with the echoes of that heartbroken voice louder than the beeping of the terminated call, it felt remarkably like it was, somehow, *his* fault.

CHAPTER NINE

THEY WERE TAKING him away.

Penelope watched the bed being wheeled towards the elevator, flanked by a medical team wearing theatre scrubs, the suddenly frail figure of her beloved grandfather almost hidden by the machines that were keeping him alive.

The elevator doors closed behind the entourage and Penelope pressed her hand against her mouth. Was this going to be the last time she saw him alive? He was the only person in her life she could believe still loved her, even when she messed up and broke a rule. Someone who could see some value in what Rafe called Penny instead of Penelope.

Oh, God…she didn't want to think about Rafe right now. About that shock of betrayal that had felt like a death and only made it so much worse as she'd watched the paramedics fighting to stabilise Grandad before rushing him to hospital.

A sideways glance showed her own fear reflected on her grandmother's face but the instinct to move closer and offer the comfort of a physical touch had to be suppressed.

'I'll take you to our family waiting room.' The nurse beside them was sympathetic. 'Someone will come and find you as soon as we know anything.'

'How long is this procedure going to take?' Louise spoke precisely and it sounded as though she was asking about something as unimportant as having her teeth whitened but Penelope knew it was a front. She'd never seen her grandmother looking so pale and frightened. Lost, even...

'That depends,' the nurse said. 'If the angioplasty's not successful, they'll take Mr Collins straight into Theatre for a bypass operation. We should know whether that's likely within the next hour or so. Here we are...' She opened the door to a small room that contained couches and chairs, a television and a coffee table with a stack of magazines. 'Help yourself to coffee or tea. Milk's in the fridge. If you get hungry, there's a cafeteria on the ground floor that stays open all night.'

The thought of food was nauseating.

The silence, when the nurse had closed the door behind her, was deafening.

Louise sat stiffly on the edge of one of the chairs, staring at the magazines. Was she going to pick one up and make the lack of conversation more acceptable?

'Can I make you a cup of tea, Mother?'

'No, thank you, Penelope.'

'Coffee?'

'No.'

'A glass of water?'

'*No*... For heaven's sake, just leave me alone.' Her voice rose and shook and then—to Penelope's horror—

her grandmother's shoulders began shaking. She was *crying*?

'I'm sorry,' she heard herself whisper.

What was she apologising for? Telling Rafe her story, which had been passed on to that journalist who'd been the catalyst for this disaster? How *could* he have done that? She'd felt so safe with him. Had trusted him completely. The anger that had fuelled that phone call had evaporated now, though, leaving her feeling simply heartbroken.

Or was she apologising for being the person her grandmother had to share this vigil with? For all the years that her grandparents had had to share their lives with her when they could have been enjoying their retirement together? Was she apologising for having been born at all?

Or was she just sorry this was happening? Sorry for herself and for Mother and most of all for Grandad.

Maybe it was all of those things.

'He's in the right place,' she said softly. 'And he's a fighter. He won't give up.'

Louise pulled tissues from the box beside the magazines. 'You have no idea what you're talking about, Penelope. This is precisely what *could* make him give up. Being reminded...'

Of what? Losing their daughter and getting the booby prize of a grandchild they hadn't wanted? Penelope didn't know what to say.

Louise blew her nose but kept the tissue pressed against her face so her voice sounded muffled. 'He gave up then. He was in the running for the kind of job that would have earned him a knighthood eventually. A seat in parliament, even, where he could have achieved his life's dream of law reform that would have made a real difference on the front line. There were two things Douglas was passionate about. His job. And his daughter.'

'And you.' Penelope sank onto the couch, facing her grandmother. Louise had never talked to her like this and it was faintly alarming. This was breaking a huge rule—talking about the past. Maybe that was why she was crossing a boundary here, too, in saying something so personal. 'He loves you, too, Mother.'

Louise had her eyes closed as she slumped in her chair. 'I gave him Charlotte,' she whispered. 'That was my biggest accomplishment…but I couldn't stop it happening. I tried *so* hard…'

Penelope's mouth was dry. Was Louise really aware of who she was talking to? It felt like she was listening to someone talking to themselves. Someone whose barriers had crumbled under the weight of fear and impending grief.

'What…?' The word opened a door that was supposed to be locked. 'What was happening?'

'The violin lessons. That was what should have been happening.' The huff of breath was incredulous. 'But, no…we found out she'd given up the lessons. It wasn't hard to have her followed and that's how we found out about the boy.'

Penelope's heart seemed to stop and then deliver a painful thump. 'My…father?'

'Patrick.' The name was a curse. 'A long-haired Irish

lout who'd given up his education to be in a band that played in pubs. He was living in a squat, along with his band and their friends—the drug dealers.'

'Oh…' She could understand how distressing that must have been. What if she had a sixteen-year-old daughter who got in with a bad crowd? A reminder of the anger she'd felt towards Rafe surfaced but this time it was directed at the mother she'd never known. A drug addict. Someone who'd made her parents unhappy and then gone on to abandon her own baby. There was something to be said for the mantra she'd been brought up with. Penelope didn't want to end up like her mother. No way.

'She threatened to run away and live with the boy if we tried to stop them seeing each other. They were "in love", she said. They were going to get married and live happily ever after.' For the first time since she'd started talking, she opened her eyes and looked directly at Penelope. 'How ridiculous was that? She barely knew him.'

Penelope had to look away, a confusing jumble of emotions vying for prominence. She barely knew Rafe but there'd been more than one occasion with him when she'd thought there was nowhere else in the world she'd ever want to be. A wave of longing pushed up through the anger. And then there was that hurt again and somewhere in between there was a flash of sympathy for her mother. A connection born of understanding the power of that kind of love?

'Douglas was in the final round of interviews for the new government position. Can you imagine how helpful that would have been? How could anyone think that he could contribute to law and order on a national level when he couldn't even keep his own house in order? When his daughter was living in a drug den?'

Penelope was silent. Maybe it could have been a point in his favour. Didn't a lot of people become doctors because they hadn't been able to help a loved one? Have the motivation to help because they understood the suffering that could be caused? Look at the way Rafe had been with Billy. He'd known what that boy was going through and he'd had to step up and help, even when it had clearly been difficult for him. There was something fundamentally good about Rafe Edwards. It was hard to believe he would ever do anything to hurt someone else deliberately. She didn't *want* to believe it but how could she not, when the evidence was right there in front of her?

'It wasn't hard to have the house raided with our police connections. Arrests made.' Louise sounded tired now. 'There wasn't anything that the boy or his band friends could be directly charged with but association was enough. They got warned to get out of town and stay out. *He* was told in no uncertain terms that if he tried to contact Charlotte again, charges could still be laid and they could all find themselves behind bars.'

'So he just left? Even knowing that he was going to be a father?'

Louise fluttered a hand as if it was unimportant. 'I don't imagine he knew. I'm not sure Charlotte knew. Either that or she kept it hidden until it was too late to do anything about it.'

Somehow this was the most shocking thing she'd heard so far in this extraordinary conversation and the words came out in a gasp.

'An abortion, you mean?'

She might not have existed at all and that was a weird thought. She would never have known the satisfaction of being successful, doing something she loved. Or felt the pleasures that creating beautiful food or listening to wonderful music could provide. She would never have danced. She would never have experienced the kind of bliss that Rafe had given her, albeit so briefly.

There was something else she could feel for her mother now. Gratitude at being protected?

'Of course.' The clipped pronouncement was harsh. 'Not that your mother would have cooperated. She became extremely…difficult. She stopped eating. Stopped talking. Your grandfather was beside himself. It was the psychiatrist we took her to who guessed she was pregnant.'

The long silence suggested that the conversation was over as far as Louise was concerned, but Penelope couldn't leave her story there.

'What happened then?'

'I found a boarding school that specialised in dealing with situations like that. She was to stay there and continue her schooling and then the baby would be adopted.'

That baby was *me*. Your grandchild…

But the agonised cry stayed buried. Instead, Penelope swallowed hard and spoke calmly. 'Was Grandad happy about that?'

Louise had her eyes shut again. 'It was a difficult time for all of us but there was no choice. Not if he wanted that promotion.'

A promotion that had clearly never happened.

The silence was even longer this time. Maybe they would hear soon about what was happening with Grandad. No doubt someone would come and talk to them in person but it was an automatic gesture to check her phone. Nothing.

Except a missed call from Rafe.

Hours ago now. Well before she'd called him.

The wash of relief was strong enough to bring the prickle of tears to her eyes. So he had been telling the truth? He had tried to call her? To confess he'd said something he had promised not to and revealed the identity of Baby X?

But why had those questions Julie had been asking had such an effect? Why was it still such a big deal, given that her grandfather had retired so long? This was only getting more confusing.

'How did I end up at the music festival? Do you know?'

Louise shrugged. 'There was a letter that came to the house. From him. Full of ridiculous statements like how he couldn't live without her. That he'd be at the festival and if she felt the same way she could find him there. I didn't forward it, of course, but I presume Charlotte found out somehow. She was in the hospital then, instead of the school, so it was probably wasn't hard to escape.'

Escape… As though she'd been sent to prison. How

hard would it still have been to get away? To take her newborn baby with her?

Penelope felt the ground shifting beneath her feet. She hadn't been abandoned. Her mother could have left her at the hospital but she'd taken her. To the festival. To meet her father?

'We got the call later that day to say she was in the intensive care unit. Right here, in almost the same place as Douglas. How ironic is that? It was obvious she'd recently given birth so we had no choice but to make enquiries about what had happened to the baby. It was your grandfather who insisted on bringing you home. You were the only thing that he cared about after Charlotte died. He gave up on his job and he…he blamed me for sending our daughter away…'

'He still did well. He got an OBE.'

'Hardly a knighthood.'

'He's a well-respected councillor.'

'Not exactly a seat in parliament or a mayoralty, is it? And the passion was never there any more.' Louise was struggling not to cry again. 'I tried to make the best of it. We pulled strings and managed to keep the story out of the papers. I did my best for you but the reminders were always there. And now there's a reporter trying to turn it all into tabloid fodder. Asking questions about why people had been allowed to assume it was a drug overdose when it wasn't. And it's all—'

All what? *Her* fault? Her own fault? What had caused her mother's death if it wasn't a drug overdose? Something that she could have had treated and survived? Had guilt been the poison in her family rather than shame?

The unfinished sentence was an echo of her call to Rafe. And he probably knew that she'd been about to tell him it was all *his* fault. But how could Julie have known it hadn't been a drug overdose? She hadn't told Rafe that because she hadn't known herself.

This was all a huge, horrible mess. And maybe none of it really mattered at the moment, anyway. The door to the room opened quietly to admit the nurse who had brought them here.

'It's all over,' she said. 'And it went very well. Mr Collins is awake now. Would you like to come and see him?'

Louise seemed incapable of getting up from her chair. She had tears streaming down her face. When she looked at Penelope there was an expression she'd never seen before. A plea that could have been for reassurance that she had just heard what she most wanted to hear.

Or could it be—at least partly—a plea for forgiveness?

Penelope held out her hand. 'Let's go,' she said quietly. 'Grandad needs us.'

'So that's about it. The rehearsal starts at five tomorrow. Let's all work together and make this a really family-friendly occasion.'

Rafe glanced at his watch. The meeting of all the key people involved in the organisation and set-up of the Loxbury music festival had filled an impressive section of the town hall. Scruff and Matt were here and he'd noticed Patrick Murphy at the back, no doubt here to find the time his band was expected to turn up for the rehearsal. Surprising how strong the urge still was to seek him out after the meeting and talk to the man who could well be Penelope's father, but he'd already done enough damage as far as she was concerned and he had no desire to get any more involved.

It was over. Or it would be, when he could shake this sense of…what was it? He hadn't done anything wrong in the first place and he hadn't even tried to contact Penny since she'd hung up on him so why did he feel like he was still doing something wrong? Making a monumental mistake of some kind?

'One other thing…' The chairman of the festival committee leaned closer to his microphone. 'We still haven't made a final decision about the charity that will be supported by the festival. If anyone has any more suggestions, they'll need to talk to a committee member tonight.'

Rafe found himself getting to his feet. Raising his arm to signal one of the support crew who'd been providing microphones for the people who'd wanted to ask questions during the briefing.

'I have a suggestion,' he said, taking hold of the mike.

'And you are?'

'Rafe Edwards. My company is providing the fireworks to finish the festival.'

A ripple of interest turned heads in his direction. The chairman was nodding. 'You've made a significant contribution to the event,' he said. 'Thank you.'

The applause was unexpected. Unnecessary. Rafe cleared his throat. 'The message we've been hearing to tonight is that you want this to be a family-friendly event. A mini-festival that isn't a rave for teenagers but something that could become an annual celebration that will bring families together.'

'That's right.'

'So I have a suggestion for the charity that you might like to consider supporting.'

'Yes?'

'The Loxbury Children's Home—Rainbow House—is a facility that this town should be very proud of. It's changing the lives of the most vulnerable citizens we have—our disadvantaged children—and, with more funding and support, it could do even more good for the community.'

A murmur of approval came from the crowd and the chairman was nodding again, after exchanging glances with the other committee members on the stage.

'It's local,' the chairman said. 'And it's about family. It's certainly a good contender.' A nod signalled that the evening's agenda was complete. 'Thanks, everybody. You'll find some refreshments in the foyer. I look forward to seeing you all again on Saturday evening. And, Mr Edwards? Come and see me before you go. I'd like to provide some free passes for the children at Rainbow House to come to the festival.'

Rafe hadn't intended staying to drink tea or eat any of the cake the Loxbury Women's Institute was providing, but there seemed to be a lot of people who wanted to shake his hand and tell him how appreciated the contribution of his fireworks show was and what a good idea he'd had for the charity to be supported.

One of them was Paddy Murphy.

'Kids are everything, aren't they?' He smiled. 'They're the future. Biggest regret of my life was not having any of my own.'

Close up for the first time, there was no doubt in Rafe's mind that this man *was* Penny's father. Those liquid brown eyes were familiar enough to twist something in his chest. About where his heart was. But he had to return the friendly smile. Say something casual.

'I'll probably have the same regret one day.' Oops. That wasn't exactly casual, was it? He shrugged. 'It's a hard road, finding the right woman, I guess.'

'Oh, I found her.' The Irish brogue was as appealing as the sincerity in Paddy's gaze. 'But then I lost her.' He slapped Rafe on the shoulder and turned away but then looked back with a shake of his head. 'Truth be told, *that's* really the biggest regret of my life. Always will be.'

Rafe watched him disappear into the crowd.

And it was right about then that he realised why he couldn't shake that nagging feeling of making some huge mistake.

He knew what that mistake was.

He just didn't have any idea of how to fix it.

CHAPTER TEN

WHAT ON EARTH was she going to do with all these cakes?

Chocolate and banana and carrot and red velvet. All iced and decorated and looking beautiful, and Penelope had no desire to eat a bite of any of them. The baking marathon had been therapy. Something comforting to do while she tried to sort through the emotional roller-coaster of the last couple of days.

She could take one of them in to the hospital for the lovely nurses who were caring for her grandfather so well. Maggie and Dave were always happy to have a cake in the house and her grandmother might like to take one home to help Rita cater for the stream of well-wishers that were turning up at their door. And maybe—the thought came as a gleam of light at the end of a dark tunnel—she could take one to Rafe.

To say sorry. Of course it couldn't make things right again but…it would be something, wouldn't it?

An excuse to see him one last time, anyway.

She chose the chocolate cake for the nurses in the cardiology ward of Loxbury General.

'You didn't need to,' the nurse manager told her. 'It's been a pleasure, caring for your grandad. We'll be sorry to see him go home tomorrow. But thank you...we *love* cake.'

She gave her grandmother the choice of the other cakes.

'Could I take the red velvet? I know your Grandad loved his birthday cake and it *was* rather delicious.'

'Of course. I'm sorry—I didn't think to make a Madeira one.'

'Do you know, I think I'm over Madeira. Such a boring cake, when you come to think of it.'

There was no farewell hug or kiss after handing over the cake but Penelope still felt good. There was something very different about her relationship with her grandmother now. Something that had the promise of getting better. Just like Grandad.

The smile stayed with her as she drove to Rainbow House. How good had it been to sit and hold Grandad's hand in the last few days? To talk to him about things they'd never discussed and even to tell him about that extraordinary conversation with her grandmother.

'She did do her best with you, you know. And she does love you, even if she doesn't let herself admit how much. She got broken by your mother's death, love. We both did. Nobody's perfect, you know. We all make mistakes but what really counts is who's there to hold your hand when it matters.'

'I know.' It was a poignant thought to realise whose hand she would want to be holding hers in a crisis.

Only she'd want more than that, wouldn't she? She'd

want her whole body to be held. So that she could feel the way she had when Rafe had held her.

'Loving people carries such a risk of getting hurt, doesn't it?' There had been an apology in her grandfather's voice as he'd patted her hand. 'Maybe neither of us was as brave as we should have been.'

Penelope's smile wobbled now as she turned into a very familiar street. How brave was she?

Brave enough to take one of those cakes to Rafe's office? To ask that receptionist if there was a chance that the terribly important chief executive officer of All Light on the Night might have the time to see her?

Not that he'd be at work this late in the day.

Maybe it would be better to take the cake to Loxbury Hall? To the place where she had fallen in love with him...

The place where he'd made *her* feel loved...

Phew... Just as well she had a visit to make to Rainbow House first. Some time with Maggie and Dave and the kids was exactly what she needed to centre herself before taking a risk like that.

How awful would it be if he didn't want to see her?

'Cake... And it's not even Sunday.' Maggie's hug was as warm as ever. 'Come in, hon. How's your grandad?'

'Going home tomorrow. His arteries are full of stents and probably better than they've been for a decade or more. Good grief, Maggie...what's that terrible noise?'

A naked, giggling toddler trotted past, with Dave in pursuit. 'I think we have you to thank for that racket.' He shook his head but he was grinning.

Charlene's hair was orange today. She went past with her fingers in her ears.

'I can't stand it,' she groaned. 'Someone tell him to stop.'

'Maggie?'

'Go and see for yourself. Out in the shed.' Maggie looked at the wet footprints on the hall floor. 'I'd better give Dave a hand with the baths.'

Bemused, Penelope put the cake in the kitchen and kept going through the back door to the old shed at the far end of the garden. The noise got steadily louder. A banging and crashing that had to be a set of drums, but they weren't being played by anyone who knew what they were doing.

Sure enough, opening the door and stepping cautiously into the cacophony, she saw it was Billy who was surrounded by the drum set. He was giving it everything he had—an expression of grim determination on his face. And then he stopped and the sudden silence was shocking.

'That was rubbish, wasn't it?'

Penelope opened her mouth to say something reassuring but someone else spoke first.

'Better than my first attempt.'

Rafe... She hadn't seen him in the corner of the dimly lit shed, sitting on a bale of the straw kept to line the bottom of the rabbit's hutch. Billy had his back to her but if Rafe had noticed her entrance he didn't show it. His attention was on the young boy he'd rescued from that imminent explosion.

'You're doing well all round, Billy. Maggie's told me how hard you're trying.'

Maybe she was interrupting something private. Penelope turned. The door was within easy reach. She could slip out as unobtrusively as she'd come in.

'I'm following the rules,' Billy said. 'Like Penny told me to. So that—you know—people'll like me.'

'Penny's an amazing lady,' Rafe said.

The tone of something like awe in his voice captured Penelope so instantly that there was no way she could make her feet move. Was it possible his feelings went further than merely being impressed by her? A smile tugged at her lips but then faded rapidly as Rafe kept talking.

'What she said, though…well, it's absolute rubbish, Billy.'

That stung. Without thinking, Penelope opened her mouth. 'How can you say that?'

Rafe must have seen her come in because he didn't seem nearly as surprised as Billy that she was there. The boy's head jerked around to face her but the shift in Rafe's gaze was calm.

'You've always followed all the rules,' he said. 'How's that worked out for you?'

'Just fine,' Penelope said tightly. What sort of example was Rafe giving Billy by saying this?

She glared at him. He had his cowboy hat on and the brim was shading his face but he was staring back at her just as intently. She could *feel* it.

'Sometimes you haven't followed all the rules. How's *that* working out?'

Oh…maybe he was providing a good example after all. What were those rules she'd broken? The only one she could think of right now was the time she'd gone upstairs at Loxbury Hall when she'd thought it was forbidden. When she'd given herself to Rafe.

She dropped her gaze to try and shield herself from the intensity of that scrutiny. 'Not so good.'

'You sure about that?' The quiet voice held a note of…good grief…*amusement*? As if he knew very well how well it had worked out.

Billy's foot went down on the pedal to thump the bass drum. 'I don't get it,' he growled. 'One minute you're telling me to follow the rules and then you say stuff about *you* guys breaking them. It doesn't make sense.'

Rafe leaned forward on his straw bale, his hands on his knees, giving Billy his full attention again.

'There are a lot of rules that are important to follow, Billy, but people will like you for *who* you are. You just have to show them who that really is and not hide behind stuff.'

'What kind of stuff?'

'Some people try to hide by being perfect and following all the rules.'

Penelope winced.

'And some people try to hide by making out they're tough and they don't care.'

Billy was twisting the drumsticks he still held. 'I *don't* care.'

'Yeah, you do.' The gentle note in Rafe's voice made Penelope catch her breath. 'We *all* care.'

'You don't know anything.' Billy's head was down. The drumsticks were very still.

'I know more than you think. I *was* you once, kid. I was tough. I didn't give a damn and I broke every rule I could and got into trouble all the time. And you know why?'

It took a long time for the reluctant word to emerge.

'Why?'

'Because I didn't *want* to care. Because it was too scary to care. Because that was how you got hurt.'

The long silence then gave the impression that Billy was giving the matter considerable thought but when he spoke he sounded offhand.

'Is it true we're all going to go and see the fireworks tomorrow night?'

Rafe didn't seem to mind the subject being changed. 'You bet.'

'You got us the tickets,' Billy said. He paused. 'And the drums.'

'The tickets are for everybody. The drums are just for you.'

'For real?'

'For real.' Rafe was smiling. 'And you know why I gave them to you?' He didn't wait for a response but he did lower his voice, as though the words were intended only for Billy. He must have known Penelope could hear, though. Without the drums, it was utterly quiet in there.

'Because I care. It's okay to care back, you know. It's quite safe.'

He got to his feet and took a step towards Penelope. But his words had been directed at Billy just then.

Hadn't they? Her stupid heart skipped a beat anyway. A tingle of something as wonderful as hope filling a space around it that had been very empty.

Billy's sideways gaze was suspicious. 'Do you care about her, too?'

The brim of that hat made it impossible to read the expression in Rafe's eyes but she didn't need to. She could hear it in the sound of his voice.

'Oh, yeah…'

Billy made a disgusted sound. 'You gonna get married, then? And have kids?'

'Um… Bit soon to think about anything like that. And I might have to find out how Penny feels first, buddy.'

Billy's tone was accusing now. 'You care, too, don't you?'

Penelope couldn't drag her gaze away from Rafe. 'Oh, yeah…'

The delicious silence as the mutual declaration was absorbed finally got broken by a satisfied grunt from Billy that indicated the matter was settled. 'Can I go and tell the other kids that the drums are just for me?'

'How 'bout telling them that they're going to have the best time ever at the festival tomorrow? And tell Maggie and Dave that you'll help look after the little ones. Fireworks can be a bit scary close up and I'm going to make sure you have the very best place to watch.'

It was still hard to tell if his words were just for Billy or whether he was reminding Penelope of when he'd taken her to the best place to watch his fireworks.

Billy was on his feet now, though—his skinny chest

puffed with pride. 'I can do that.' He put his drumsticks on the stool. 'I'm one of the biggest kids here.'

He had to walk between Rafe and Penelope to get to the door but neither of them seemed to notice because he was below the line of where they were looking—directly at each other.

His steps slowed. And then stopped. The suspense was getting unbearable. Rafe was going to kiss her the moment Billy disappeared and Penelope didn't want to have to wait a second longer.

But Billy turned back. He went back to the stool and picked up the drumsticks. 'I'm gonna need these.'

Rafe grinned. 'Practise on a cushion for a bit. That way you won't drive anyone crazy.'

'I think I might be going crazy,' Penelope murmured, as Billy disappeared through the door of the shed.

'Me, too.' Rafe pushed the door closed. 'Crazy with wanting you.'

But he didn't move any closer. They stood there, for the longest time, simply looking at each other.

'Me, too.' The words escaped Penelope on a sigh. 'I love you, Rafe…'

He held out his hand. Without saying a word, he led her over to the straw bale and sat down beside her. Then he took off his hat and held it in his hands.

Penelope swallowed hard. She'd said it first and he hadn't said it back. He hadn't uttered a single word since she'd spoken.

He could have kissed her instead. That would have been enough. But he hadn't done that either.

She was standing on a precipice here.

Teetering.

Feeling like she might be about to fall to her death.

She'd said she cared.

Not just the way you could care about a lost kid and want to do something to help put him on the right path, even though that kind of caring could be so strong you had to put yourself out there and maybe face stuff that you thought you'd buried a long time ago.

Penelope had gone further. She'd said she *loved* him. She'd just gone right out there and said the scariest thing in the world. Put herself in the place where you could hurt the most.

The weight of how that made him feel had crushed his ability to form words. To form coherent thoughts even, because what he said next could be the most important thing he ever said in his life.

No pressure there...

That weird weight seemed to be too much for his body as well as his brain. He had to sit down, but he wasn't going anywhere without Penny and she seemed happy enough to take his hand and follow along.

But now he had to say something. He heard the little hitch in her breath in the silence. A sound that made him all too aware of how scared she was.

He was scared, too. His hands tightened on his hat, scrunching the felt beneath his fingers.

'You know why I bought Loxbury Hall?' His voice sounded rusty.

From the corner of his eye, he saw Penelope nod. 'You told me. That night—in the bath. You said it was the kind of house that only people who had perfect lives could live in.'

'Yeah… That's what I thought through all those rough years when my life was like Billy's. If you were rich enough, you could make your own rules. Live in a place like that and have a family that stayed together. You called family a safe place once and I guess that's what a huge house that cost a bucket of money represented to me. That safe place. But you know what?'

Her voice was a whisper. 'What?'

'I was wrong. So, so wrong.' The whole hat was twisted in his hands now. It would never be the same. Dropping it, he turned his head to look at Penelope. His empty hands caught hers.

'The safe place isn't a place at all, is it? It's a person.'

Her eyes were huge. Locked on his, and it felt as if something invisible but solid was joining them.

'But it's a place, too. Not a place you can buy. Or even find a map of how to get there. It's the place that you're in when you're with *that* person.'

Her eyes were shining now. With unshed tears? Was he saying something that she understood? That she wanted to hear?

Even if she didn't, it felt right to say it. Maybe so that he could understand it better himself.

'It's a place that only that person can create with you. You can't see it but it's so real that even when you're not together you can still feel safe because you know where that place is.' He had to pause to draw in a slow, steadying breath.

This was it.

The thing he really had to say.

'You're my person, Penny.'

Yep. They had been unshed tears. They were escaping now.

Her voice was the softest whisper but he could hear it as clear as a bell and it felt just as good as if she were shouting it from a rooftop.

'You're my person, too, Rafe. For ever and always.'

CHAPTER ELEVEN

THE WEATHER GODS smiled on Loxbury for the thirtieth anniversary of their first music festival and the lazy, late-summer afternoon morphed into an evening cool enough for people to enjoy dancing but still warm enough for the ice-cream stalls to be doing a brisk business.

The gates had opened at five p.m. and the fireworks show timed for ten p.m. had been widely advertised as something people wouldn't want to miss—an exciting finale to a memorable occasion.

It was a music festival with a difference. Artists who'd been at the original festival were given star billing, of course, but there were many others. New local groups, soloists, dance troupes, a pipe band and even the entire Loxbury symphony orchestra. The appreciative crowd was just as eclectic a mix as the entertainment on offer. Teenagers were out in force, banding together far enough away from parents to be cool, but there were whole families there as well, staking out their picnic spots on the grass with blankets and folding chairs, prams and even wheelchairs.

Between the musical performers, the MC introduced the occasional speaker. At about eight p.m., when the crowd had swelled to record numbers, the person who came out to speak was the mayor of Loxbury, resplendent in his gown and chain.

'What a wonderful event this is,' he said proudly. 'A credit to the countless people who have given up so much of their time both to organise and perform. Thank you, all.'

The cheer that went up from the crowd expressed their appreciation.

'I came to the very first festival,' the mayor continued. 'And I remember how much opposition there was to it even happening. There was even a petition taken to the council to try and prevent it corrupting our young people.'

There was laughter from the crowd now. Penelope caught Maggie's glance and shared a smile. Rainbow House had several rugs on the grass. The younger children had all visited the face-painting booths and even Billy had been persuaded to have his face painted white with a black star around his eye to look like the lead singer of Kiss. Right now, he was sitting with the youngest children, righting the occasional ice-cream cone that threatened to lose its topping.

'I can't see any dangers here,' the mayor smiled. 'Just a heart-warming number of our families having a great time together.'

It was a poignant moment for Penelope. She'd never dreamed of attending such an event in her life because she'd grown up with the belief that terrible things did, in fact, happen at music festivals. She'd considered herself living proof of exactly that.

'I see parents and grandparents,' the mayor continued. 'And I see many of our youngest citizens, who represent the future of Loxbury. Some of you know the story of Baby X—the baby that got found when they were cleaning up after that first festival that we're celebrating again today. That baby got returned to its family but we all know there are some children that aren't always that lucky, and it's my pleasure to tell you that the charity chosen to benefit from this festival is a place that cares for those children. Rainbow House...'

The clapping and cheering were deafening this time but Maggie burst into tears. Dave took her into his arms and Penelope suspected he shed a few tears as well. She had to blink hard herself because she knew what this could mean. The roof getting fixed, along with a dozen other much-needed repairs. All sorts of things that could make life more comfortable and enable these people she loved to keep doing something so wonderful. She might suggest a minibus so that they could transport the children more easily when they had somewhere special to go.

Like the festival today, which had presented a logistical challenge. And the Christmas party that was going to take place this year at Loxbury Hall. It had been a joy planning that with Rafe last night, and she knew it would happen. She was going to talk to Jack this week about the catering they would be doing for it.

The other crazy schemes they'd come up with might need some adjustment. Turning a wing of Loxbury Hall into offices so they could both work at home might be a waste because he'd still want to travel to his big shows. And she might want to go with him. Making the hall and gardens available as a wedding venue again needed thinking about, too. It was very likely to become their home and would they want to share that with strangers—especially when they had their own family to think about?

But how much happiness could it bring? Maggie and Dave had never hesitated to share their home and some of the people cheering so loudly right now were probably those teenagers who had come to find Maggie and Dave from amongst the gathering just to say hello. Young people who had needed shelter at some time in their lives and had a bond that would never fade. They seemed to be heading in this direction again to share the joy of this announcement and her bonus parents were going to be busy giving and receiving hugs for quite some time. She made sure hers was the first.

How lucky had she been to find that bond herself? How lucky was Billy?

And something else made her feel that she could never become any luckier. After what Rafe had whispered in her ear last night, maybe the next wedding she was going to manage was going to be her own. That would certainly happen at Loxbury Hall. And there was her birthday in a couple of days. Not that she needed any gifts because she had everything she could possibly want in her life now, but a small party would be nice. One that could be an invitation for her grandparents to share her new life in a meaningful way?

The mayor had finished speaking and the MC was introducing one of Loxbury's newer talents. Penelope recognised the group instantly as Diversion—the band that had played at the Bingham wedding. Were Clarissa and Blake here somewhere? If they were, they were probably dancing with the growing number of people in front of the stage. It was starting to get darker and there were glow sticks in abundance as well as headbands that had glowing stars or flashing lights on them.

Billy was on his feet now, jiggling a little on the spot as he listened to the music with his whole body. Penelope could see his hands twitching as if he was holding imaginary drumsticks. But then he stopped to stare at the stage, his black lipstick making his open mouth rather comical.

'Is that…*Rafe*?'

The band was playing a cover of Billy Joel's 'Just the Way You Are'.

Penelope could only nod in response. She'd known that Rafe would be joining the band for this song. He'd told her about it last night, when they'd left the shed in the garden, excused themselves from sharing cake and had gone to the best place in the world to celebrate the declaration of their love—where it had first begun—at Loxbury Hall. The most magnificent place that wasn't as important as the place he'd found with her.

The tears were too close again now. He'd told her what song he was going to be playing. He'd whispered the words as if they'd been written for him to say and it was his voice she could hear now, rather than Diversion's lead singer as he sang that he would take her just the way she was. That he wanted her just the way she was. That he loved her just the way she was.

And each time these lyrics led to a saxophone riff from the black-clad figure in the cowboy hat that had Penelope's total attention. Every bend and sway of his body ignited an all-consuming desire that she knew would never fade. The words were exactly how she felt. This love would never fade either.

The jab of Billy's elbow prevented her from turning into a mushy puddle.

'What's that thing he's playing?'

'A saxophone. He started learning it after he stopped playing on those drums he gave you.'

'That's what I'm gonna do, too.'

'Good idea.' Penelope took a deep breath as the song finished. 'I'll see you later, Billy. I told Rafe I'd meet him after this song to see how it's going with setting up the fireworks.'

'Can I come, too?'

'You promised to help look after the little ones, re-member? You're in the best place to watch and it's not that far away.'

It was just as well there was an acceptable excuse not to take Billy with her. The setting up of the fire-works had been finished by lunchtime today. She was meeting Rafe near the stage simply so that they could be together and she couldn't have kissed him like this if there'd been anyone around to watch.

Couldn't have been held so close and basked in the bliss of all those feelings she'd had during the song that were magnified a thousand times by being pressed against his body. Being able to touch him—and kiss him—just like this.

But Rafe wanted to do more than kiss her.

'Come and dance with me.'

'No-o-o… I can't dance.' Penelope could feel the colour rising in her cheeks. 'You know that. You *saw* me trying to dance in your maze…'

'Ah, but you weren't dancing with *me*…'

And there they were. Among a hundred people dancing in front of the stage to the music from an Irish band that had been announced as one of the original festival artists, and it *was* easy. All she had to do was follow Rafe's excellent lead. They danced through the entire set the band played and then they stood and clapped as the band members took their turns accepting the applause.

The lead guitarist leaned in to the microphone and held up his hand to signal a need for silence.

'It's been thirty years since we played here,' he said. 'But my heart has always been in Loxbury.'

He waited for the renewed applause to fade.

'The love of my life was a Loxbury girl.'

Rafe's hand tightened around Penelope's and she felt an odd stillness pressing in on her. She was still in a crowd but she felt as conspicuous as if a spotlight had been turned onto her. Alone.

No, not alone. She had Rafe by her side.

'Who is he?'

'His name's Paddy Murphy.'

'*Patrick* Murphy?'

'I came to that first Loxbury festival hoping to find

her again but I didn't.' Paddy shook his head sadly. 'There's never been anyone else for me but that's just the way things worked out, I guess. Maybe you're out there tonight, Charlie, my darlin'. If you are, I hope you're happy. Here's one more song—just for you...'

People around started dancing again but Penelope was standing as still as a stone. 'Oh, my God...' she whispered.

Rafe led her away from the dancers before anyone could bump into them. Right away from any people. He took them into the area fenced off as the safety margin for the pyrotechnic crew by showing his pass to a security guard. Off to the edge of field that was crisscrossed with wires leading to the scissor lifts.

'Watch your feet. Don't trip...'

The music was fainter now and the people far enough away to be forgotten. Except for one of them.

'He's my father, isn't he?'

'I think he probably is. He looks a lot like you, close up. And he's a really nice person. Special...'

'Did you know about him being here?'

'I knew his name and that his band was going to be playing. And then I met him a couple of nights ago and he told me that losing the woman he loved was the biggest regret of his life.' Rafe drew Penelope close to kiss her. 'That was the moment I realised that I'd be making the biggest mistake of my life if I lost you. That you were the love of *my* life.'

'He doesn't know about what happened to my mother, does he?'

'Apparently not.'

'You know what I think? I think that she brought me here to meet him. That he was the love of *her* life, too.'

'He told me something else, too. That his other huge regret was never having kids of his own.'

Penelope had a lump in her throat the size of a boulder. 'Do you think he'd want to meet me?'

'How could anyone not want to?' Rafe kissed her again. 'To be able to claim a connection to you would make him feel like the luckiest man on earth. No...make that the *second* luckiest man.'

Oh...the way Rafe was looking at her right now. Penelope wanted to be looked at like that for the rest of her life.

'I think I'd like to meet him,' she said softly. 'But it's pretty scary.'

'I'd be with you,' Rafe told her. 'Don't ever be scared. Hang on...'

The buzz of the radio clipped to his belt interrupted him and Penelope listened as he talked to his crew. The countdown to the fireworks was on. The orchestra was in position.

'This is a show to live music,' Rafe told her. 'It's a complicated set-up with manual firing.'

'Don't you need to be there?'

'That's what I train my crew to do. I'm exactly where I need to be.'

'And the orchestra's going to play it?'

'Along with the bagpipes. Can you hear them warming up?'

The drone of sound was getting louder. The lights set up around the field were suddenly shut down, plunging the whole festival into darkness. Glow sticks twinkled like coloured stars in a sea of people that knew something exciting was about to happen. Penelope and Rafe were standing behind the stage, between the main crowd and the firing area. Rafe turned Penelope to face the scissor lifts and stood behind her, holding her in his arms.

An enormous explosion sent a rocket soaring into the night sky and the rain of colour drew an audible cry from thousands of throats. And then the music started, the bagpipes backed up by the orchestra.

'Oh…' She knew this music. Everybody did.

'You'll Never Walk Alone'. An anthem of solidarity.

Penelope had never been this close to fireworks being fired before. The ground reverberated beneath her feet with every rocket. The shapes and colours were mind-blowingly beautiful but flaming shards of cardboard were drifting alarmingly close to where they were standing.

And yet Penelope had never felt safer.

Here, in Rafe's arms.

They would never walk alone. They had each other.

'Wait till you see the lancework at the very end,' Rafe told her. 'It took us a long time to build.'

The intensity of the show built towards its climax. Blindingly colourful. Incredibly loud. How amazing was it to still hear the crowd at the same time? Surely every single person there had to be singing at the tops of their voices to achieve that.

Penelope wasn't singing. Neither was Rafe. She could feel the tension in his body as the final huge display began to fade and something on the highest scissor lift came to life.

The biggest red love heart ever. And inside that was a round shape with something square inside that. Chains and a crown on the top. It was a coin. An old-fashioned penny. It even had the words 'One Penny' curving under the top.

'For you,' Rafe whispered. 'For my Penny.'

It was too much. Something private but it was there for the whole world to see. Penny. The person she really was. The person she'd tried to hide until Rafe had come into her life. Her smile wobbled precariously.

'A penny's not worth much these days.'

'You couldn't be more wrong. My Penny's worth more than my life.'

Rafe turned her in his arms so that he could kiss her. Slowly. So tenderly she thought her heart might break, but it didn't matter if it did because she knew that Rafe would simply put the pieces back together again.

Every time.

* * * * *

HER PERFECT
PROPOSAL

LYNNE MARSHALL

Special thanks to Flo Nicoll who always makes me dig deeper. And to Carly Silver for being a bright light and for being there whenever I need help.

Chapter One

"Is this because I'm an outsider?" said the petite, new and clearly fuming visitor in town. She'd jaywalked Main Street in broad daylight, far, far from the pedestrian crosswalk. As if it was merely a street decoration or a pair of useless lines. Did she really think Gunnar wouldn't notice?

Dressed as if she belonged in New York City, not Heartlandia, she wore some high-fashion fuchsia tunic, with a belt half the size of her torso, and slinky black leggings. Sure, she was a knockout in that getup, but the lady really needed to learn to blend in, follow the rules, or he'd be writing her citations all day long.

He took his job seriously, and was proud to be a cog in the big wheel that kept his hometown running smoothly. Truth was he'd wanted to be a guardian of Heartlandia since he was twelve years old.

"I won't dignify that slur with an answer," Gunnar said, though she *was* an outsider. He'd never seen the pretty Asian woman before, but that wasn't the point. She'd jaywalked!

With the often huge influxes of cruise-line guests all

disembarking down at the docks, and now with the occasional tour bus added to the mix, he had to keep order for the town's sake. The tourists rushed to the local stores for sweet deals and to the restaurants for authentic Scandinavian food without having to fly all the way to Sweden or Norway. If he let everyone jaywalk, it could wreak havoc in Heartlandia. The town residents had to come first, and it was up to guys like him to regulate the influx of visitors. Plus, jaywalking was a personal pet peeve. If the city put in crosswalks, people should use them. Period.

He kept writing, though snuck an occasional peek at the exotic lady. Shiny black hair with auburn highlights, which she wore short, her bangs pushed to the side, and with the pointy and wispy hair ends just covering her earlobes and the top of her neck. *Interesting.*

Most guys he knew preferred long hair on women, but he was open to all styles as long at it complemented the face. The haircut and outfit were something you might see on a runway or in a fashion magazine, but not here. And those sunglasses... She had to be kidding. Did she want to look like a bee?

Even though her eyes were shielded by high-fashion gear, he could sense she stared him down waiting for his answer to her "Is it because I'm an outsider?" question. Not wanting to be rude by ignoring her, he came up with a question of his own.

"Let me ask you this. Were you or were you not jaywalking just now?"

"I'm from San Francisco, everyone jaywalks." She leaned in to read his name tag. "Sergeant Norling."

"You with the cruise ship?" It was too early for a new batch of tourists to set foot on the docks, though there was no telling when those buses might pull up.

She huffed and folded her arms. "Nope."

"Well, you're in Heartlandia now, Ms...." He stared at his citation pad waiting for her to fill him in. She didn't. "Name please?" He glanced up.

"Matsuda. Lilly Matsuda. Can't you cut me some slack?"

"I need your license." Gunnar stared straight into where he imagined her eyes were, letting her absorb his disappointment at her obvious lack of regard for his professional honor. Something he held near and dear. Honor.

She wouldn't look away, so he motioned with his fingers for her to hand over the license and continued, "Did you jaywalk?"

She sighed, glanced upward and tapped a tiny patent-leather-ultrahigh-heeled foot.

For the record, he dug platform shoes with spiky heels, and hers looked nothing short of fantastic with the skin-tight silky legging things she wore. Didn't matter, though. She was a jaywalker.

"Yes."

His mouth twitched at the corner, rather than letting her see him smile. The way she'd said yes, turning it into two syllables, the second one all singsongy, sounded like some of the teenagers he mentored at the high school.

She lowered her sunglasses, hitting him dead-on with deliciously almond-shaped, wide-spaced, nearly black eyes. Hers was a pretty face, once he got past the Kabuki killer stare.

He tore off the paper, handed it to her and waited for her response.

Snagging the notice for jaywalking she frowned, then glanced at it, and the discontented expression broke free with a surprisingly nice smile. "Hey, it's just a warning. Thanks." She suddenly sounded like his best friend.

"Now that you know the rules, don't jaywalk again.

Ever." He turned to head back to his squad car, knowing for a fact she watched him go. He'd gotten used to ladies admiring him from all angles. Yup, there was definitely something about a man in a uniform sporting a duty belt, and he knew it. Just before he got inside he turned and flashed his best smile, but instead of saying have a nice day he said, "See you around."

She had to know exactly what he meant—if she was sticking around this small city, he'd be sure to run into her again, and he'd be watching where she walked.

"Officer Norling?"

The petite Matsuda lady stepped closer, her flashy colorful top nearly blinding him. He gave his practiced magnanimous professional cop smile, the one he hoped to perfect one day when he ran for mayor. "Yes?"

"Know any good places to eat in town? Bars for after hours?"

"Just about any place here on Main Street is good. Lincoln's Place does a great happy hour." Was she planning on sticking around? Or better yet, was she trying to pick him up?

"You go there? Eat there? Drink there?"

His bachelor radar clicked up a notch.

She dug into her shoulder bag and brought out a small notepad and pen. "I'm looking for the best local examples of everything Scandinavian."

What was she doing, writing a book? Maybe she was one of those travel journalists or something. Gunnar stopped dead, hand midway to scalp for a quick scratch. Or maybe she was one of those annoying type A tourists, who had to know it all, find the best this or that, snap a few pictures while never actually stepping inside or buying anything, just so they could impress their friends back home. She looked like the type who'd want to impress her friends.

"Yeah. My favorite lunch joint is the Hartalanda Café. And you can't beat Lincoln's Place for great dining. Got a crack new lady pianist named Desi Rask playing on the weekends, too, if you like music."

She didn't look satisfied, as if he'd failed in some way at answering her query—the question behind the question. Too bad he hadn't figured it out. Maybe she was a food reporter for some big magazine or something and wanted some input from a local. "Well, thanks, then," she said. "See you around."

See me around? That's what I said. So is she new in town, planning to stay here, or just here on assignment? His outlook took a quick turn toward optimistic without any specific reason beyond the possibility of Ms. Matsuda sticking around these parts. An exotic woman like her would be a great change from the usual scenery.

But wait. He wasn't doing that anymore—playing the field. Nope. He'd turned a new page. No more carefree playboy, dating whoever he wanted without ever getting serious. If he wanted to be mayor of Heartlandia one day, he'd need to settle down, show the traditional town he knew how to commit.

Gunnar slipped behind the steering wheel, started the engine and drove off, leaving her standing on the corner looking like a colorful decoy in a *Where's Waldo?* book.

Lilly stood at the corner of Main Street and Heritage, watching the officer drive away, having to admit the man was a knockout. Yowza, had she ever seen greener eyes? Or a police uniform with more laser-sharp ironed creases? This guy took his job seriously, which was part of the appeal, and he'd already cut her some slack on the citation.

Hmm, she wondered, slipping her sunglasses back in place. *What's his story?*

She'd been in town exactly three days, started her new job yesterday at the newspaper, and was already hatching her plan to buy out the owner, Bjork, and breathe new life into the ailing local rag. She'd taken a huge risk moving here, leaving a solid job—but one without room for advancement—back at the *San Francisco Gazette* in a last-ditch attempt to finally win her parents' respect. Somehow, despite all of her efforts to overachieve, she'd yet to live up to their expectations. Why at the age of thirty it still mattered, she hadn't quite figured out.

In her short time in Heartlandia she'd noticed things from her extended-stay apartment in the Heritage Hotel— things like a nighttime gathering at city hall of an unlikely handful of residents. Oh, she'd done her homework long before she'd moved here all right, because that was what a serious reporter and future newspaper mogul did.

She knew the newspaper was on its last breath, mostly copying and pasting national news stories from the Associated Press, instead of doing the legwork or being innovating and engaging. She recognized an opportunity to start her own kind of newspaper here, for the locals. The kind she'd want to read if she lived in a small town.

Before arriving, she'd gotten the lay of the land, or should she say *landia*? She snickered. Sometimes she cracked herself up.

She'd spent several months getting her hands on everything she could about Heartlandia. Their city website told a lovely, almost storybook history that didn't ring completely true. Could everything possibly be that ideal? Nope, she'd seen enough of life, how messy it could get, to know otherwise. Or maybe San Francisco had jaded her?

She'd memorized the city council names and faces, noting they'd appointed a new mayor pro tem, one Gerda Rask. She'd also scoured old newspaper stories and dug up pictures of the locals, including police officers, firemen and businesspersons. The *Heartlandia Herald* used to focus on those kinds of stories, and there were many to choose from. Not anymore.

She knew more about this town than the average resident, she'd bet, which, if it was true, was kind of sad when she thought about it.

Turn and walk, Matsuda. Don't let on to that taller version of a Tom Hardy look-alike that you're watching him drive off. A man that size, with all those muscles, a cop, well, the last thing she wanted to do was get on his bad side.

Once the light changed, Gunnar drove on with one last glance in his rearview mirror. Lilly hadn't budged. It made him grin. That one was a firecracker, for sure.

He'd heard old man Bjork had hired a new reporter. It was to save his sorry journalistic butt since running the *Heartlandia Herald* into the ground with bad reporting and far too many opinion pages—all Bjork's opinion. He'd also heard the new hire was a big-city outsider and a she. *Could the she be her?*

Maybe the *Herald* did need a complete overhaul from an outsider since the newspaper he'd grown up reading was failing. Sales were in the Dumpster, and it bothered him. Over the past few years he'd watched his hometown paper slowly spiral into a useless rag. It just didn't seem right. A newspaper should be the center of a thriving community, but theirs wasn't.

Truth was old man Bjork needed help. Who cared what other people thought about world politics? Everyone got enough of that on cable news. *Keep it local and engag-*

ing. That's what he would have told the geezer if he'd ever bothered to ask for advice since they worked across the hall from each other, but the guy was too busy running the paper into the ground.

What with the new city college journalism department, why couldn't they save their own paper? Heartlandia had always stood on its own two metaphorical feet. Always would. Fishermen, factory workers, natives and immigrants, neighbors helping neighbors. The town had remained independent even after most of the textile and fishing plants had closed down.

Only once had the city been threatened from outsiders, smugglers posing as legitimate businessmen. His own father had fallen for it. Once the original fish factory had closed, he'd been out of a job. Gunnar had been ten at the time and had watched his mother take on two part-time jobs to help feed the family. His father's pride led him to take the job as a night watchman for the new outside company, and he'd turned his head rather than be a whistle-blower when suspicious events had taken place. The shame he'd brought on the family by going to jail was what made Gunnar go into law enforcement, as if he needed to make up for his father's mistakes.

It had taken two years before the chief of police at the time, Jon Abels, had taken back the city. Gunnar had been twelve by then, but he remembered it as if it had just happened, how the police had made a huge sweep of the warehouse down by the docks, arresting the whole lot of them and shutting down the operation. That day Chief Abels had saved the city and became Gunnar's personal hero.

He drove back to the station in time to check out, change clothes and grab a bite at his favorite diner, the Hartalanda Café—he hadn't lied to Ms. Matsuda about that—before he hit city hall for another hush-hush Thursday-night meeting of the minds. It had been an honor to be asked, and joining this committee was the first step on a journey he hoped one day to take all the way to the mayor's office.

Sleepy little Heartlandia's history lessons had recently taken a most interesting plot twist, and he was only one of eight who knew what was going on. The new information could change the face of his hometown forever, and he didn't want to see that happen. Not on his watch.

Gunnar held the door to the conference room for Mayor Gerda Rask. She was the next-door neighbor of his best friend, Kent Larson, and a town matriarch figure who'd agreed to step in temporarily when their prior mayor, Lars Larsson, had a massive heart attack. She'd also been the town piano teacher for as far back as Gunnar could remember, until recently when her granddaughter, Desi, came to town and took over her students.

The city council had assured Mayor Rask she'd just be a figurehead. Poor thing hadn't known what she was stepping into until after she'd agreed. And for that, Mayor Rask had Gunnar's deepest sympathy, support and respect. When he became mayor, he'd take over the helm and transform the current weak-mayor concept, where the city council really ran things, to a strong-mayor practice where he'd have total administrative authority. At least that's how he imagined it. Any man worth his salt needed a dream, and that was his.

The older woman nodded her appreciation, then took her seat at the head of the long dark wooden boardroom table. Next to her was Jarl Madsen, the proprietor at the Maritime Museum. Next to him sat Adamine Olsen, a local businesswoman and president of the Heartlandia Small Business Association, and next to her Leif Andersen, the contractor who'd first discovered the trunk that could change the town's reputation from ideal to tawdry.

Leif had found the ancient chest while his company was building the city college. Though he was the richest man in town, he chose to be a hands-on guy when it came to construction, continuing to run his company rather than rest on his laurels as the best builder in this part of the state of Oregon. He hadn't turned in the chest right away—instead he'd sat on the discovery for months. Once curiosity had gotten the best of him and he'd opened it, saw the contents, he knew he had to bring it to the mayor's attention. After that, Mayor Larsson had his heart attack, Gerda stepped up and this handpicked committee was formed.

Gunnar nodded to his sister, who'd beat him to the meeting. She smiled. "Gun," she said.

"Elke, what's shakin'?"

She lifted her brows and sighed, cluing him that what was shaking wasn't all good. He'd signed on to this panel, like he had to his job, to protect and serve his community. Since his family tree extended back to the very beginning of Heartlandia, and his father had slandered the Norling name, doing his part to preserve the city as it should be was Gunnar's duty.

So far the buried-chest findings had rocked the committee's sleepy little world. He'd heard how some places rewrote history, but never expected to participate in the process. He lifted his brows and gazed back at his kid sister.

As the resident historical maven and respected professor at the new city college, Elke's services had been requested. Her job was to help them decipher the journal notations from the ones dug up in the trunk during construction. Apparently, the journals belonged to a captain, a certain Nathaniel Prince, who was also known as The

Prince of Doom and who might have been a pirate. Well, probably *was* a pirate. The notations in the ship captain's journal held hints at Heartlandia's real history, but they looked like cat scratches as far as Gunnar was concerned. Good thing Elke knew her stuff when it came to restoring historical documents and deciphering Old English.

Across from Elke sat the quiet Ben Cobawa, respected for his level head and logical thinking, not to mention for being a damn great fireman. The native-born Chinook descendent balanced out the committee which otherwise consisted entirely of Scandinavians. But what could you expect from a town originally settled by Scandinavian fishermen and their families? Or so he'd always been led to believe.

Cobowa's Native American perspective would be greatly needed on the committee. They'd be dealing with potential changes to town history, and since his people had played such an important role in the creation of this little piece of heaven originally called Hartalanda back in the early 1700s, they wanted his input.

"Shall we call this meeting to order?" Mayor Rask said.

Gunnar took a slow draw on the provided water. Judging by the concerned expression on his younger sister's face he knew he should be prepared for a long night.

Lilly sidled up to the bar at Lincoln's Place. A strapping young towhead bartender took her order. But weren't most of the men in Heartlandia strapping and fair?

"I'll have an appletini." She almost jokingly added "Sven" but worried she might be right.

The pale-eyed, square-jawed man smiled and nodded. "Coming right up."

She wasn't above snooping to get her stories, and she wanted to start off with a bang when she handed in her debut news story, like her father would expect. She'd been casing city hall earlier, had hidden behind the nearby bushes, and lo and behold, there was Sergeant Gunnar Norling slipping out the back door. She'd watched him exit the building along with half a dozen other people including this new Mayor Rask.

She'd combed through old council reports on the town website and noticed a tasty morsel—"A new committee has been formed to study recently discovered historical data." What was that data, and where had it been found?

The website report went on to mention the list of names. The one thing they all had in common with the exception of one Native American, if her research had served her well, were Scandinavian names that went back all the way to the beginning of Heartlandia, back when it was founded and called Hartalanda. Of course, the Native Americans had been there long before them. Yup, her type A reporter persona had even dug into genealogy archive links proudly posted at the same website.

These people weren't the city council, but they had been handpicked, each person representing a specific slice of Heartlandia life.

She'd met the handsome and dashing Gunnar Norling today, and the idea of "getting to the bottom" of her story through him had definite appeal. Her parents had trained her well: set a goal and go after it. Don't let anything come between you and success. Growing up an only child in their multimillion-dollar Victorian home in Pacific Heights, Lilly's parents had proved through hard work and good luck in business their technique worked. As far as her father was concerned, it was bad enough she'd been born a girl, but for the past five years, since she'd left graduate journalism school, they'd looked to her to stake her claim to fame. So far she hadn't come close to making them proud, but this new venture might just be the ticket to their respect.

A half hour later, nursing her one and only cocktail, she was deep into conversation with the owner of Lincoln's Place, a middle-aged African-American man named Cliff. It seemed there was more to Heartlandia than met the eye once you scratched the Scandinavian surface.

"Looks like you get a lot of tourist trade around here," she said, having studied the bar crowd.

"Thank heaven for the cruise ship business," Cliff said, with a wide and charming smile. "If it wasn't for them, I'd never have discovered Heartlandia."

"Are you saying you cruised here or worked on a cruise ship?"

"Worked on one. Thirteen years."

"Interesting." Normally, she'd ask more about that assuming there might be a story buried in the statement, but today she had one goal in mind. She took a sip of her drink to wait the right amount of time before changing the topic. "So where do the locals go? You know, say, like the regular guys, firemen and police officers, for example." She went for coy, yeah, coy like a snake eyeing a mouse, looking straight forward, glancing to the side. "Where do they hang out after hours?"

He lifted a long, dark brow, rather than answering.

"I'll level with you, Cliff, I'm the new reporter for the *Heartlandia Herald*. I'd like to bring the focus of the newspaper back to the people. I've got a few different angles I'd like to flesh out, and I thought I'd start with talking to the local working Joes." Funny how she'd chosen "flesh out," a phrase that had certain appeal where that Gunnar guy was concerned.

He nodded, obviously still considering her story. And it was a tall tale...mostly. She did have big plans to bring the human interest side back to the paper, but first off, she wanted a knock-your-socks-off debut. Introducing big-city journalist Lilly Matsuda, ta-da!

"There's a microbrewery down by the river and the railroad tracks. To the best of my knowledge, that's where the manly types go when they want to let off steam." He tapped a finger on the bar, smiled. "Here's a tidbit for you. Rumor has it that in the old days, down by the docks in the seedy side of town, right where that bar is today, an occasional sailor got shanghaied."

"Really." The tasty morsel sent a chill up her spine. She had a nose for news, and that bit about shanghaied sailors had definitely grabbed her interest. Though it was an underhanded and vile business, many captains had employed the nasty trick. The practice had been an old technique by nefarious sea captains. First they'd get a man sloppy drunk. Then, once he'd passed out, his men would kidnap the sailor onto the ship and the unsuspecting drunk would be far out at sea when he came to and sobered up. Voilá! They had an extra pair of hands on deck with no ticket home, and they didn't even have to pay him. With Heartlandia being on the banks of the gorgeous Columbia River, a major water route to the Pacific Ocean, the story could definitely be true.

Wait a second, old Cliffy here was probably just playing her, telling her one of the yarns they told tourists to give them some stories to swap when they got back on ship.

"Yes indeed," Cliff said, touching the tips of his fingers together and tapping. "Of course, a lot of the stories we share with our tourists have—" he pressed his lips together "—for lack of a better word, let's say been *embellished* a bit. No city wants to come off as boring when you're courting the tourist trade, right? So we throw in those old sailor stories to spice things up."

She appreciated his coming clean about pirates shanghaiing locals. "I hear you. So you're saying the shanghaied stuff may or may not be true?"

He tilted his head to the side, not a yes or no. She'd let it lie, take that as a yes and try a different angle.

"Hey, have you noticed any after-hour meetings going on at city hall? Or am I imagining things?"

He cast a you-sure-are-a-nosey-one glance. "Could be. Maybe they're planning some big tercentennial event. I think the town was established around 1715."

"Tercentennial?"

"Three hundredth birthday."

"Ah, makes sense. But why would they keep something like that a big secret?"

"Don't have a clue, Ms.…." He had the look of a man who'd had enough of her nonstop questions—a look she'd often seen on her father's face when she was a child. Cliff suddenly had other patrons to tend to. Yeah, she knew she occasionally pushed too far. *Thanks, Mom and Dad.*

"Matsuda. I'm Lilly Matsuda."

He shook her hand. "Well, it was a pleasure meeting you. I hope to see you around my establishment often, and I think you've got what it takes to make a good reporter. Good luck."

"Thanks. Nice to meet you, too."

After Cliff moseyed off, attending to a large table obviously filled with cruise-ship guests on the prowl, she scribbled down: "Microbrewery down by the river near railroad." She'd look it up later.

She'd been a reporter for eight years, since she was twenty-two and fresh out of college, and had continued part-time while attending grad school. Had worked her way up to her own weekly local scene column in the *San Francisco Gazette*, but could never make it past the velvet ceiling. She wanted to be the old-school-style reporter following leads, fingers on the pulse of the city, always seeking the unusual stories, and realized she'd never achieve her goal back home, much to her parents' chagrin.

When the chance to work in Oregon came up, after doing her research and seeing a potential buyout opportunity, she'd grabbed it. Statistics showed that something happened to women around the ages of twenty-eight to thirty. They often reevaluated their lives and made major changes. Some decided to get married, others to have a baby, neither of which appealed to her, and right now, since she was all about change, moving to a small town and buying her own paper had definite appeal.

Lilly finished her drink and prepared for the short walk—no jaywalking, thank you very much, Sergeant Norling—back to her hotel.

Once she bought out Bjork, she could finally develop a reputation as the kind of reporter she'd always dreamed of becoming—the kind that sniffed out stories and made breaking headlines. If all went the way she planned, maybe her dad would smile for once when he told people she was a journalist and not a famous thoracic surgeon like he'd always wanted her to become.

Her gut told her to stick with those discreet meetings going on at city hall, and to seek out a certain fine-looking police officer partaking in them. He may have almost written her a citation, but he might also be her ticket to journalistic stardom.

Tomorrow was Friday night, and she planned to be dressed down and ready for action at that microbrewery. If she got lucky and played things right, she might get the decidedly zip-lipped Gunnar Norling, with those amazingly cut arms and tight buns, to spill the proverbial beans to the town's newest reporter.

Chapter Two

After a long week of rowdy tourists, teens in need of mentoring, plus last night's special council meeting, Gunnar needed to blow off some steam. He got off work on Friday, went home and changed into jeans and a T-shirt then headed out for the night. After downing a burger at Olaf's Microbrewery and Gastro Pub, he ordered a beer, and while he waited he thought about last night's meeting. Again.

Elke had uncovered a portion of the journals suggesting there might be buried treasure somewhere in the vicinity of Heartlandia, and until she could get through all of the entries, while carrying a full teaching load at the college, they wouldn't know where to look.

First pirates. Now buried treasure. What next? Was this for real or had they been set up for some kind of reality gotcha show?

"Thanks," he said to the short and wide Olaf, turning in his empty burger plate in exchange for that brew. The historic old warehouse by the docks had been transformed into a down-to-earth bar, no frills, just a wide-open place guys like Gunnar could go to let off steam, have a decent meal and be themselves. A workingman's bar, it had mismatched tables and chairs, open rafters with silver air-vent tubing, good speakers that played solid rock music, an assortment of flashing neon signs, posters of beer and burgers, and a few sassy photos of women. Nothing lewd, Olaf's wife wouldn't allow that, but definitely provocative shots of ladies, that and work-boot ads galore.

Olaf kept a huge chalkboard he'd snagged from a school auction and filled it with all of his latest microbrews. Tonight Gunnar was sticking with dark beer, the darker, toastier and mellower the malt, the better. He glanced around at the pool tables, card tables and dartboards there for everyone's entertainment, when they weren't drinking and talking sports or cars, that is. Very few women ventured into the place. The ones who did usually had one thing on their minds. Most times Gunnar avoided them and other times, well, he didn't.

Not anymore, though. That was all behind him since he planned to change his bachelor reputation.

He picked up the Dark Roast Special, first on the list on Olaf's blackboard, and headed back to the dart game where he was currently ruling the day. But not before hearing a lady's voice carry over the loud music and louder guy conversations in the bar. Somehow that high-toned voice managed to transcend all of the noise and stand out.

"Word has it there're some secret meetings going on at city hall," she said. "You know anything about that?"

"Do I look like a politician?" Jarl Madsen, Clayton County's Maritime Museum manager and fellow member on the hush-hush committee, said to the woman, doing a great job of playing dumb.

Gunnar cocked his head and took a peek to see who was being so nosey. Well, what do you know, if it wasn't Lilly the jaywalker with the sexy shoes, elbows up to the bar chatting up Jarl. He looked her over. She knew how to dress down, too, wearing tight black, low cut jeans and a black patterned girly top with sparkles and blingy doodads embedded in the material. In that getup she blended right in.

Right.

At least she'd traded her sexy heels for ankle boots, killer boots, too, he had to admit, and from this angle her backside fit the bar stool to perfection. Yeah, he knew it wasn't polite to stare, so after a few moments, and he'd memorized the view, he looked away. He glanced around the room. Only a handful of other ladies in pairs were in attendance, and this one appeared to be flying solo.

Gutsy.

Or dumb.

But dumb didn't come to mind when he thought about Lilly Matsuda. She seemed sharp and intelligent, and if he trusted his gut, her being here meant she was on task, not here for a simple night out. The task seemed to be related to the committee meetings.

If he were a nosey guy himself, it would be really easy to wander over to Jarl and insinuate himself into the conversation. But that could be considered horning in on another guy's territory, even though in his opinion Jarl and Lilly were completely mismatched. His honorable side won out over the curious cop dude within, mainly because he was off duty and loving it. So back to darts he went, ready to win the high score of the night, trying to forget about outlander Lilly at the bar.

A few minutes later he put his heart and soul into the second game with his latest victim, Jake Bager, a paramedic who was seriously low on bull's-eyes. All three of Jake's darts had made it into the inner circle, but were an inch or more away from the center.

On his next turn, solely concentrating on the game, Gunnar stepped up and threw one, two and three darts dead into the center of the board, the last one so close it nearly knocked the second one out.

Jake groaned. A person behind him clapped.

"Bravo," she said.

Gunnar turned to find Lilly with the fashion-model hair smiling, applauding his efforts.

"Well, if it isn't little miss jaywalker." Damn, she filled out those jeans in a slim-hipped petite kind of way he rarely saw. He knew that shouldn't be the first thing he noticed, but as sure as Mother Nature made little green apples, he had. Her mostly bare arms showed the results of gym workouts, not overly done, just nice and tight, and her nearly makeup-less face was as pretty as an ink-wash painting. He knew because he happened to like that Japanese art technique and had several posters in his home to prove it.

"Thanks," he said, thanking her more for looking nice than for her paying him a compliment. "And what are you doing here?"

She gave a coy smile, even though nothing about her personality that afternoon hinted at coy, lifted her shoulders and dug her hands into her back pockets. He had to admit the move put her perky chest on much better display. He knew he shouldn't focus on that, either, and tried not to notice for too long, but he was a guy and those dang blingy things on the shirt caught the light just right. He lingered a beat longer than he'd meant to, which seemed to be a pattern where Lilly was concerned.

If she'd noticed, she didn't let on. Or seem to mind. That was more like the lady he'd met yesterday afternoon.

"Since you went the touristy route when I asked for the bars where locals hang out," she said, "I had to find out where the action really was from Cliff over at Lincoln's Place."

He nodded. Solid fact-checking. She knew how to gather her information. He hoped she was a travel writer and not the new journalist, since that might complicate his resolution to quit playing the field. "You play?" He offered her the three darts he held.

She left her hands in her back pockets. "Not much. I'm better at pool."

He nodded. "Okay, well, if you'll excuse me, then," he said, deciding to stay put and let Lilly explore the joint on her own, "I've got to teach my man here, Jake, another lesson on darts."

Ten minutes later, Lilly was back at the bar chatting up Kirby, the local pet controller and town grump. Her non-stop questions, and choice of conversation partners, both well past middle age, made it obvious she wasn't here to get picked up. Which, surprisingly, relieved Gunnar.

"And what makes you outsiders think you can just walk into our bar like you belong here?" hairy-eared Kirby said, his voice loud and territorial, carrying all the way to the dartboards.

"The bar sign said Open, nothing about members only." She didn't sound the least bit fazed. Yeah, that was more like the lady he'd met yesterday than little miss coy snooping around a few minutes ago.

Even though she seemed to have things under control, Gunnar knew Kirby's sour attitude mixed with a few beers could sometimes take a turn for ugly and, never really off duty, he hightailed it over to them to keep the peace.

"Kirby, my friend, have a bad day?"

The man with iron-colored hair, in bad need of a barber, grumbled to his beer. "I liked it better when we only let locals in here."

Olaf noticed the scene and was quick to deliver a new beer to Lilly. "This one's on the house, miss. I hope you'll come here often." He smiled at Lilly first, then passed a dark look toward Kirby, who didn't even notice. Or, it seemed, care.

Lilly nodded graciously. "Thank you." She glanced at Gunnar, an appreciative glint in her eyes.

Gunnar turned back to Kirby, patted his back. "Cheer up. Why don't you try enjoying yourself for a change?"

The codger went back to mumbling into his beer, "If you had to deal with what I do every day…"

Gunnar was about to remind the old fart that he was a cop and had to deal with the tough stuff every day, too, but he cut him some slack. Being a cat lover, he understood it must be hard to deal with stray and homeless pets day in and day out, but that's what Kirby got paid for. And just like Gunnar's job, someone had to do it to keep order in their hometown.

He gazed at Lilly, ready to change the subject. "You said you were better at pool than darts. Feel like playing a game?" Mostly he wanted to get her away from Kirby's constantly foul mood because he had the sneaking suspicion she'd tell him where to stick it if Kirby made one more negative remark. And who knew where that might lead, and like he'd maintained all night, he'd come here to let off steam, not be the twenty-four-hour town guardian.

Her expressive eyes lit up. "Sure."

"What do you say I put my name in for the next table, and in the meantime, I'll show you around the bar?"

She got off the bar stool, lifted the toe of her left boot, grinding the spiky heel while she thought. "Sure, why not?"

The circular tour lasted all of three minutes since there wasn't much to show. He used the time to get a feel for

Lilly, pretty sure why she'd showed up here tonight. As he spoke, she studied him and seemed to be doing her own fair share of circling him. At this rate, in a few more minutes they might be dancing. He smiled at her, she smiled back. Seeing a shyer, tongue-tied version of Lilly was surprising, and didn't ring true with how he'd sized her up yesterday. Maybe she was putting on an act.

Gunnar waved down Olaf's wife, who worked as a waitress. "We'll have a couple of beers," he said to Ingé, then turned back to Lilly. "I'll get this one, okay?"

She gave an appreciative look and after perusing the blackboard ordered pale ale named after some dog Olaf used to own. She made a dainty gesture of thanks and accompanied it with a sweet smile. Beneath her tough-girl surface, maybe she was a delicate work of art, and he kind of hoped it was true.

There was something about those small but full lips, and her straight, tiny-nostriled nose that spoke of classic Asian beauty, and Gunnar was suddenly a connoisseur. Yeah, Asian beauty, like a living work of art, or just like those ink-washed prints back at his house. He liked it.

He pulled out a chair for her to sit near the pool tables while they waited, then one for him, throwing his leg over and sitting on it backward.

"You said you were from San Francisco, right? What's it like living there?" he asked, arms stacked and resting along the back rim of the chair.

She crossed her legs and sat like she was in school instead of at a bar. "You remembered."

"Part of the job."

"Well, for starters, it was a lot busier than I'm assuming living around here is." Under different circumstances— not giving her a citation—she was friendly and fairly easy to talk to.

"We're small all right, but there's lots going on. I wouldn't jump to judgment on life being any easier or less interesting here."

"Okay." And she seemed reasonable, too.

Their drinks arrived. He took a long draw on his, enjoying the full malt flavor. She sipped the nearly white clear ale. Things went quiet between them as he searched his brain for another question. She took another drink from her mug, and he could tell her mind was working like a computer. Before she could steer the conversation back to business, he jumped in.

"You have any brothers or sisters?"

"I'm an only child."

"So you're saying you're spoiled?"

She gave a glib laugh. "Hardly. There's a lot of pressure being the only child. When it's just you and two adults, well, let's just say sometimes they forget you're a kid."

"I guess I can see your point."

"If my dad had it his way, first I'd have been a boy and then I'd be a thoracic surgeon."

"I see. So what was your major in college?"

"Liberal arts."

Gunnar barked a quick laugh. "I bet Daddy liked that."

She went quiet, stared at her boots, took a sip or two more from her beer. "To this day I hate hospitals. Can't stand the sight of blood. Probably has to do with a Christmas gift I got when I was eight." She pressed her lips together and chanced a look in his direction, then quickly away, but not before she noticed Gunnar's full attention. That must have been enough to encourage her to go on. "I got this package, all beautifully wrapped. I'd asked for a doll and it looked about the right size, so I tore it open and found the ugliest, scariest, clear plastic anatomical 'Human' toy with all the vessels showing underneath."

He smiled and shook his head, feeling a little sorry for her, but she'd chosen the entertaining route, not self-pity. It made her tale all the more bittersweet. "If you removed that layer there was another with muscles and tendons, and under that another with the organs." She glanced up and held Gunnar's gaze. He sensed honest-to-goodness remorse for an instant, but she kept on like a real trouper. "It had this scary skeleton face with ugly eye sockets."

Under other circumstances, this might be funny, but Gunnar knew Lilly, under the guise of funny stories, was bearing her soul on this one, and he had the good sense to shut up and listen.

"Anyway—" she looked resigned and took another sip of beer "—all I wanted was a doll with a pretty face and real hair I could comb." She shrugged it off and pinned him with her beautiful stare. "What about you? You have brothers or sisters?"

"One kid sister named Elke."

"You close?"

He nodded. "It's just the two of us now."

"Sorry to hear that."

"Well, that's how it goes sometimes, right?"

Lilly tipped her head in agreement. "So what made you become a cop?"

He couldn't blame her for taking her turn at asking questions. But since he was on the hot seat, he went short and to the point—*Just the facts, ma'am*.

"My dad."

"Family tradition? Was he a cop, too?"

Gunnar opened his mouth but stalled out. How should he put this? "No." She'd been flat-out honest with him so he figured he owed her the same. "I guess you could say he was a bad example. Did some time for making really poor choices. Took our good family name and stomped it into the ground."

She inhaled, widening her eyes in the process. "I see. But look at you—you're an honest, upright citizen."

"That I am."

An old Jon Bon Jovi track blasted in the background, and to change the subject, he thought about asking her to dance, nearly missing when they called out his name for pool. "Oh, hey, our table's up," he said, relieved to change the subject. "You ready?"

She passed a smile that seemed to say she was as ready as he was to drop the subject of messed-up families. There was something else in that smile, too, like she might just surprise him tonight, and to be honest, he hoped she would. After that story about her father, he'd decided to go easy on the new girl in town, since it sounded like her childhood had been as rocky as his.

Chapter Three

Lilly followed the hunk with the sympathetic green eyes to the pool table against the back bar wall, the one closest to the bathrooms. What had gotten into her, opening up like that, telling a near stranger about her messed-up family? She could blame it on the beer and his Dudley Do-Right demeanor, but knew it was more than that. It was part of that scary feeling that had started taking hold of her in the past year, that twenty-eight-to-thirty-year-old-lady life-change phenomenon—and the desire to connect with someone in a meaningful way. The thought made her shudder, so she took another sip of beer before glancing up.

Holy Adonis, that man filled out those jeans to perfection. Out of his neatly ironed uniform, he still cut an imposing figure. Extrabroad shoulders, deltoids and biceps deeply defined, enough to make him an ideal anatomy lesson with every muscle clearly on display. Far, far better than that old plastic doll. With those thighs, and upper body strength, he could probably single-handedly push an entire football blocking sled all the way down the field. Or flip a car in an emergency. The guy was scary sturdy.

He'd stepped in when things had gotten sticky with Kirby at the bar, like it was second nature. Gunnar's family had been through the wringer with his father going to prison. Apparently that had influenced his career choice.

She continued to watch him. There was something sweet and kind about his verdant eyes with crinkles at the edges. He hadn't let the tough times or stressful job turn him hard. And his friendly smile. Wow, she liked his smile with the etched parentheses around it. That folksy partial grin gave him small-town charm, and the self-deprecating, beneath-the-brow glance he occasionally gave added to that persona, though nothing else about him gave the remote impression of being "small."

She finished her ale, had really liked the crisp, almost apple taste, and chalked her cue while he racked up the balls in the triangle. She'd played her share of pool in college dorms, enough not to humiliate herself, anyway.

"Eight-ball okay with you?"

She nodded. It was the only game she knew.

"Stripes or solids?" he asked.

"Stripes."

"Want me to break?"

"Sure. Thanks."

Once Gunnar set everything up, he waved the waitress over and ordered some chips and salsa with extra cheese. She'd eaten a salad for dinner, and the beer was already going to her head, so she wouldn't sweat the extra calories.

When Ingé brought the food, he joked with her and gave an extra nice tip. Lilly liked friendly and generous guys—guys who maybe wanted to make up for their pasts. A couple of cops, probably subordinates since they referred to Gunnar as "Sergeant," lined up nearby to watch the game, looking amused. "Go easy on her," one of them said.

"Don't worry, miss," said one of the other men sitting at the bar, who looked big like a construction worker. "He's a gentleman. Right Gun-man?"

From the way people talked to Gunnar, always smiling when they did, some calling him Gun-man, others Gun, and the way everyone responded to his casual style, she could tell he was liked and respected by his peers. She'd also noticed that Kirby had taken Gunnar's firm hint, and kept quiet. Adding up all of that, plus the company of the charming police officer, helped her relax and let her usual guard down. This Gunnar was a nice guy. Gee, maybe she'd actually have a good time tonight. Come to think of it, she already was!

"Did I mention he tried to give me a ticket for jaywalking?" She joined in the fun and chided his buddies.

Gunnar laughed. "A warning."

"Yeah, he's a stickler sometimes," said the dart player named Jake.

Could she blame a guy overcompensating for his father's wrongdoings?

Lilly suddenly wanted to be treated like one of the guys, so she glanced around at the half dozen men taking special interest in her playing pool with *Gun-man*, and decided to put on a show.

"The next round is on me," she said as Gunnar stepped back to let her take her shot. The call for more drinks went over well with the small audience, according to the assorted comments.

"Great!"

"Thanks!"

"Now, that's what I'm talking about."

Gunnar had, once again, set her up with some good and easy shots, if she didn't blow it from being a bit rusty and all, and she'd gotten the distinct feeling he'd done it on purpose. She leaned forward, and since he had an audience, she waited for him to step in and pull the oldest come-on in the book—to show her how to hold the cue stick and make the shot, meanwhile his hands running over her body for a quick and sneaky feel-up.

But he didn't. He stayed right where he was and explained the technique from there. He really was Dudley Do-Right.

"Try keeping your shoulder back and your elbow like this." He demonstrated. "See how my fingers are? Try that. You'll have more control."

He never got closer than two feet away.

She knew how to play well enough, but she'd let him school her, make him think he was helping her compete. Clicking back into her reason for being here tonight, she decided to play along for now, forget about her news quest. She did exactly as he'd said and made her shot. In the pocket. Yes!

She smiled at him and he winked. Uh-oh, that wink flew through her like a warm winged butterfly searching for a place to light. Good thing her fresh beer was within reach to give her an out to quickly recoup.

She smiled and made a quick curtsy, then got back to business.

She'd come here with the plan to find Gunnar, pepper him with drinks and get the information she wanted for her first breakout story. But after their surprising conversation, where they'd both shown a bit of their true colors, all she wanted to do was fit in. This was fun. To hell with the story. She could follow up on that later.

The pool game was the center of her attention, well, that and Gunnar and his every sexy move, and she had a nagging desire to impress him. Just like a kid. Eesh. If she could keep her head straight and concentrate on the game, not him, she'd do just fine.

As the game went on, he used his cue as a pointer to suggest where she should stand for which shot and she followed his every lead. As a result she had the best, most competitive game of pool in her life. Who knew how fun it was to play pool in a stinky men's bar?

Between the beer and chips breaks, and their undeniably steamy looks passing back and forth over the scraped-up, green felt-covered table, the game kept getting extended. Occasionally while changing places they'd brush shoulders, and the simple interaction made her edgy. Man, he knew how to rattle a woman with his laser-sharp gaze, too.

As she watched Gunnar make his shots, he seemed to ooze sexy. Whether it was her beer or his smoldering gaze—he was one hot guy—her knees turned to noodles. But he was also very human, just like her, with "issues" as she always jokingly referred to the pressure from her parents to be the best at everything she did.

Gathering her composure, Lilly called the pocket and sank the eight ball. More surprised than anyone, she put down the cue and jumped with hands high above her head. "Yay! I did it. I beat you."

Gunnar smiled, took a step closer and, being anything but poor sport, patted her shoulder in congratulations. "Good job, Ms. Jaywalker."

"Thanks." Every thought flew out of her mind when he touched her. Having him close scrambled her brain, twisting her thoughts into knots. She needed a moment to recover.

"I'm going to the ladies' room," she said, edging away from his overwhelming space invasion. This seemed far more intimidating than when his easygoing charm had gotten her to let her guard down and spill about her past.

While in the bathroom she gathered her composure and remembered why she'd come to the bar tonight, then returned to the game with new intent. But the first thing she saw was Gunnar. He leaned his hips against the pool table, long legs outstretched, ankles crossed, arms folded, talking casually to Jake. Could he give a better display of his biceps? Man, it was going to take a lot of effort to concentrate on the next game. And, uh-oh, there was another beer waiting for her.

"I always buy the winner a drink," he said, seeing her surprised glance when she got closer.

"Thanks." How could she refuse? Even though she rarely exceeded her two-drink limit, she'd take a sip or two just to be nice.

He'd already set things up for the next game. She broke, and watching the balls scatter to all corners of the table, she mentally chanted her personal promise for tonight's bar visit. It was time to get back on task, if nothing more than to get her mind off Gunnar.

"So, I've heard some mumblings around town about secret meetings going on over at city hall." She stopped midplay, stood up and gave him a perfected wide-eyed, play-it-dumb glance. "You know anything about them?"

He scratched the side of his mouth. His tell? "Can't say for sure I've heard about any secret meetings on the beat. What else have you heard?"

Liar. She'd seen him with her own eyes going into that building from her room at the Heritage, and later leaving, from the bushes where she'd staked out last night. Though she supposed the officer wasn't brazenly lying, saying he couldn't say "for sure," and using a technicality, "not hearing anything *on the beat,*" but he was definitely fudging. And he'd turned the tables on her asking what she'd heard. Lilly could feel in her journalistic bones there was a big story behind those meetings and her proof was his inability to admit to or deny them. Which only made her more curious about the after-hours comings and goings over at city hall.

What had she heard, he'd asked? She shook her head, again taking the dense tack. "Just that things are going on and it may be important to Heartlandia."

He touched her arm. The spot went hot. "Tell you what, if I hear anything from anyone in town about those meetings, you'll be the first to know." Again, he'd set up his phrase to keep it from being a bona fide lie.

Without warning, he leaned across the table for something that was behind her, and because she didn't budge, on his way back he brushed her cheek with his shoulder. "Chalk," he said, showing her the prize. Was this a ploy to throw her off track?

From this proximity she looked into his baby greens and, oh-baby-baby. Their eyes locked up close and personal and she thought someone had poured warm honey over her head. *Good move, Gun-man, I've forgotten my own name.* Close enough to smell his sharp lime-and-pine aftershave, she turned toward his face at the exact moment he'd shifted closer to her, and their lips nearly touched. What if she bridged the gap and snuck a quick kiss just for the heck of it? She'd bet her first paycheck there'd be a tingly spark when she made contact.

Their eyes met for an instant, and she didn't even need to make contact to get that zingy feeling again.

You're on the job, remember? She let the moment pass, but was quite sure she'd made her almost-intentions known, and there it was, she'd gotten to him. His eyes went

darker, and she sensed a surge in his body heat. He probably wondered the same thing about that potential kiss.

Don't overanalyze everything.

"Okay," she said, acting as if she almost kissed guys on
the run all the time, taking the proffered chalk. "Then I
start." After she chalked up her cue, and before she made
her shot, she sipped more beer as euphoria merged with lust
and tiptoed up her spine. Wow. She rolled her shoulders
and willed her concentration back, then made her next shot.

She needed to pace herself with the beer or, the way her
mind was buzzing all around from the nearness of Gunnar, she might get into trouble. She glanced at her wrist-
watch. It was only eleven.

Midway through the game, she made a decent shot
but, feeling a little tipsy, lost her balance. She leaned
against Gunnar since he was close by, and since he felt so
darn nice, she put her head on his chest for a second. He
wrapped a hand around her waist but immediately let go
once she was back on her own two feet.

*Do not make a fool of yourself. It's dishonorable to act
foolish.* Her father's mantra drilled through her thoughts.
Concentrate on the game. Win!

The game progressed. They spontaneously bumped
hips after his next good shot and high-fived on hers, but
he cheated. He pulled his arm in just enough so her chest
touched his when their palms met. Dirty trick, but *zing-
oh-zing*! She liked touching his chest with her breasts.

So Officer Dudley Do-Right played dirty with a few
beers under his belt. But she'd also noticed he'd forgotten
about his last beer. She needed to do the same, to stay on
her toes, but unfortunately his sex appeal was throwing
her too far off balance for that.

He won the game, and came around the table grinning
to collect a winner's high five. She had an overwhelm-

ing urge to forget the victory slap and surprise him with a full-on mouth kiss, but fortunately came to her senses before she acted on it.

As their palms slapped together, and he didn't pull his dirty trick a second time, their eyes met and held for several beats, the pool game all but forgotten. After lowering their now-interlocked fingers, neither of them moved, instead they stood staring at each other.

"Come on, come on, come on, you gonna play another game or stand there drooling on each other?" One of the guys impatiently waiting for a pool table broke the magical moment, which—considering Lilly's continuous urge to kiss Gunnar—could have gotten out of hand at any given second.

Gunnar cleared his throat, gestured for her to take the first shot then racked the balls. Thank goodness he was a gentleman because right about now she couldn't begin to remember what it was like to be a lady. *Sorry, Mom.* She must be out of her mind to think about making out with a practical stranger in a bar on her first Friday night in town. Yet it was foremost in her mind and completely doable if she deemed it. *Wasn't that what Daddy had always taught her? Set a goal. Go for it. Let nothing get in the way.*

Between her and Gunnar's lips?

"Okay, okay," he said to the impatient guy, sounding diplomatic as all hell. "The last game." But he nailed her with a heated look—it melted into her center and spread like warm fingers stroking her hips.

"Let's do it," she said, breathless, thinking she could be up for almost anything tonight as long as it included Gunnar Norling. "Can we get another round here?"

Olaf's wife was passing by but Gunnar intercepted and ordered a couple of waters and coffee instead.

Okay, she got his point, but that was taking his job too far. Was the guy ever off duty?

Truth was Lilly had no intention of drinking another drop of beer anyway—she knew her boundaries—but she needed Gunnar to get a little looser-lipped. Not that his lips and everything else about him weren't doing a great job already. But maybe next time when she brought up the meetings, if he had another beer, he'd at least admit to taking part in them. That would be a start. Then she could begin to slowly and meticulously strip him down to the truth.

She leaned on her pool cue as the journalistic euphemism morphed into pure, unadulterated sex thoughts with Gunnar stripped down and standing buck naked at the center of them. Almost losing her balance and falling off the stick, she swallowed and looked at her shoes, hoping he hadn't seen it, or couldn't read her mind, or notice *her tell*—burning, red-hot ears.

He scratched the corner of his mouth.

Before the water and coffee came she reached for her beer, but soon realized Gunnar had moved hers far out of reach. Was he worried about her? Heck, she was a big girl, could handle her liquor. If his gesture hadn't seemed so darn sweet and protective, she might have flashed her feminist membership card, ripped into him about being a chauvinist and suggested he mind his own business.

Instead, she took her sexual frustration and went all competitive. In the heat of the faster-paced game, they touched a lot, whether intentional or not, she couldn't tell and definitely didn't mind, but each and every time it kept her nerve endings on alert and craving more.

In between pool shots, she tried to dial things back a notch by bringing up old family pets. She told him her favorite pet story from when she was a kid. Her favorite pet was a Chihuahua from a puppy mill store that won her over with the offering of a tiny paw. She'd named it Chitcha, then explained that was Japanese for *tiny* and her grandmother still called her Chitcha to this very day. She liked how he repeated the name, Chitcha, as if memorizing the word.

His favorite pet turned out to be a stray cat named Smelly, whom he'd found while he walked home from school one day. The homeless cat was half-dead and hosting a dozen abscesses. According to Gunnar, that red tabby lived fifteen years with his family.

Knowing he was the kind of guy to rescue a stray cat made her go all gooey inside.

They played on, and she enjoyed getting to know a bit more about this man who, despite a couple of close calls, continued to act the gentleman—except for the high-five incident, which would really be unforgiveable if she hadn't enjoyed it as much as he apparently had.

Good thing he'd ordered the coffee because the drinking had definitely caught up to her. The bar had taken on the appearance of golden-warm tones, fuzzy around the edges and a little distant, and Gunnar looked like the sexiest man on earth—probably was.

Something about Gunnar made her edgy, though, like he was the kind of guy a girl could fall really hard for. Most men his age would already be married if they wanted to be. Her journalistic intuition told her he wasn't the committing kind. Nah, he was too charming and smooth around ladies, well, around this lady anyway, proving he'd had a lot of experience. Which would be par for the course in Lilly's world, since none of her boyfriends ever had the least bit of interest in commitment.

Nope. This guy could be trouble.

The best way to deal with Gunnar would be professionally, journalist to cop. She had to break him down, and after this game she'd make her move. She'd invite him somewhere closer to her hotel for coffee and quiet conversation. This time, instead of relying on a pool hall and beer, she'd use more of her hard-earned journalistic prowess and throw in a few more naturally acquired wily ways to get him to open up.

Charm didn't come second nature to her, like it did with him, but she could pull it off if she had to. For the sake of her story.

He won the game and since she was still feeling pretty darn good from her last beer, and was in close enough proximity, she decided to give him another high five. In order to do that, she had to move toward him. Shifting from where she stood to Gunnar felt the way slow-motion photography looked, with streaks of light trailing the object. Boy, she should have eaten more of the chips and salsa. She stopped, shook her head and regained her balance.

"Whoa, hold on there, Chitcha." He steadied her with hands on her shoulders. "You okay?"

Amused, she chose to think he'd called her the nickname her grandmother had given her, not her dog's name. "I think I'm a little tipsy."

She moved gingerly toward him, and he drew her close, wrapping around her like a warm rugged blanket. "I better give you a ride home. Is that okay?"

She'd never felt such strength in her life. Solid. Like a rock.

"But you've been drinking, too."

"Two beers," he said. "Didn't even finish the last one. I'm fine."

She dared to glance into his eyes again, and could tell he was perfectly okay. The biggest question was did she trust herself enough to let him take her home without falling all over him? One more glance into those dreamy green eyes and she made up her mind.

"Okay."

"I'll get my motorcycle."

She gulped as if he'd just suggested jumping off the bridge as he led her outside the bar.

The former warehouse covered in weathered wood with a rusted aluminum roof stood stark against the night sky and sat in the center of the crowded asphalt parking lot. The Columbia River rushed by behind the bar giving a calming effect after the noise from Olaf's. Lilly's car was a sporty red sedan and Gunnar's motorcycle was two aisles down. He led her to the bike.

"I can call a cab," she said, panic brewing in her dark eyes.

"I'm a safe rider. You'll be fine." He handed her his helmet.

Her decision to put it on seemed more about saving face.

Gunnar liked how Lilly threw her leg and spiky-booted foot over the pillion seat of his motorcycle. He twisted around and helped her fasten the helmet. She'd clearly never taken a ride on a bike before, so he decided to take the back route from the docks through residential streets. Whenever he leaned into turning a corner, her hands tightened around his middle, and it felt good. Beyond good. Going far slower than usual, never over thirty-five for her sake, they crossed the railroad tracks, a small houseboat cul-de-sac section of the harbor, and Fisherman's Park with its distinct fishy smell, then rode past the town library, grammar school and finally drove down Main Street to the Heritage Hotel.

Regretting the end of the ride with *Chitcha* nearly strapped to his back, he parked in front.

"Thanks," she said over his shoulder the moment he stopped.

He waited while she got off the back of the motorcycle, then shut off the engine and parked, leaning it on the kickstand.

"So, thanks for bringing me here." Again with the thanks business. "Guess I'll see you around." She seemed nervous and flighty compared to earlier, and as she headed for the rotating door he pulled her back and pointed to the helmet she'd forgotten to take off.

"Oh. Sorry," she said, flush-faced, removing it and handing it to him.

Her hair stuck out every which way, and it made her look even cuter. He didn't want to humiliate her, so he held back his grin, only letting one side of his mouth hitch upward the tiniest bit. He tried his best to make eye contact, but hers darted around as if planning a major escape.

What had happened to the bravado lady at the bar, the one who he could have sworn almost kissed him after one particularly successful shot?

Not wanting to make her uncomfortable, he backed off. He may be knocked out by the feisty Asian beauty, but the last thing he'd ever do was push himself on her. Or any lady. Hell, if history repeated itself, women always returned to Gunnar. He'd wait for her to come to her senses and make the next move, even though he wasn't supposed to be doing that anymore.

"Okay," he said. "So I'll see you around, I guess."

"Sure thing." Her expression turned all earnest and he braced for something awkward to happen, like an apology, but something much better than that came next.

Lilly went up on tiptoes, hands balanced on his shoulders, and bussed his cheek—his reward for being a gentleman. He thought he'd been kissed by a butterfly and liked the way tiny eyelash-type flutters marked the spot. It surprised him.

She must have picked up on that "something more" reflex she'd caused, because he stole a glance into her eyes and an open book of responses filled him in on the rest of the story. She was interested. Very interested.

So was he, and he was damn sure she could figure that out. For a few breathy moments they stayed staring under the light of the street lamp, trying to read each other. He could still detect her fresh and flowery perfume, and resisted taking a deep inhale.

Having spent the better part of the evening in Lilly's company, he'd already understood she liked to take the lead with questions, pool and drinking. If he read her right, and he liked to think that being a policeman had taught him how to read people, she'd prefer to make the next move. So he waited, counting out a few more breaths while taking a little excursion around her intelligent and thoughtful eyes…and getting lost. Her creamy skin contrasted the dark, straight hair and meticulously shaped eyebrows. And those eyes…

She wrapped her hands around his neck and drew him close. Her fingers cool on his skin, and with a twinkling glint in her night-like eyes, she carefully touched her mouth to his and kissed him as if she meant it. Her small but well-padded lips, soft and smooth, fit over his in petite perfection.

Beyond pleasantly surprised, he inhaled, catching that fresh scent again, found her waist and tightened his grip. The kiss felt right on-target and he liked that. Boy, oh boy, did he like it. His stout and her pale ale complimented each other perfectly as their tongues managed a quick touch here and there before going for more exploration.

Not stopping there, his hands cupped her face, his

thumbs stroking those creamy cheeks, and he kissed her lips, the delicate skin beneath her eyes, her neck, cheeks and ear. He brushed her jaw with his beard stubble, sending shock waves along his skin, driving his reaction inward and starting a slow burn. Not wanting to overpower her, since the kiss had been her idea, he let up the slightest bit, but pulled her body closer. She settled into his embrace, curled up and stayed there for several long tantalizing moments, basking as he planted more soft-lipped kisses on the top of her head, along her hair, the shell of her ear.

She let him kiss wherever he wanted, so he went back to her mouth.

It didn't feel like a first kiss. Nope. This felt more like a kiss that had been waiting a long time to be born and today was the day the right two people made it happen.

She tilted her head upward and their lips met again. Could she read his thoughts?

Things were working out just fine. He really liked his theory about the kiss taking on a life of its own, so he just went along with the sexy thrill...

Until she stopped kissing him.

"I'm sorry I got tipsy and that you had to give me a ride home."

He'd been so swept up in the moment he hadn't realized she'd been multitasking, kissing *and* thinking. And she'd finally gotten into her apology.

"You are? Because I'm really liking how things've turned out."

She gave a gentle-lipped smile, her arms edging away from his neck. "The fresh air's helped a lot. Oh, and thank you for not taking advantage of me."

"Would never do that." He wanted to make it clear he wasn't anything close to smarmy if that was what she thought. He wasn't that guy, not like his father, who'd say one thing then do another, and never would be.

Her gaze shifted from his chest to his eyes and registered some kind of sincerity. "I'm very grateful for that." They stared at each other for a couple more beats of his pulse, which was definitely thumping stronger than usual.

"I don't know what kind of guys they raise in your neck of the woods, but we're a mostly honorable bunch here."

"Good to know. Like I said, sorry for getting tipsy back there."

He liked looking at her pointy chin and long, smooth throat, and it made it hard for him to read the moment. Was she cooling off? "Don't worry about anything. You were fine."

"I don't want you to get the wrong impression about me."

"I haven't and wouldn't."

"Thanks."

"But maybe stay out of bars for a while." He thought a little teasing might loosen her up again. "Keep your nose clean. Stay under the radar." He disengaged his hands from her small hips and used one to demonstrate flying under the radar.

"Hey, I'm an adult, remember?" She'd taken it good-naturedly. "And I didn't exactly make a fool out of myself."

"In the bar or just now?"

She nailed him with a disapproving stare. "I'm an emancipated woman and I kiss whomever I want, wherever I want."

"Got it. In fact, you can do it again if you want."

He'd done his job, made her laugh against her will. "Let's make the next one a rain check, okay? I'm all kissed out for tonight."

All kissed out? They'd just gotten started. Maybe she wasn't as turned on as he'd hoped.

At least she'd said "the next one." Yeah, that was the spirit. "Definitely." He went along with the distancing process because he sensed she needed it, and underplayed his honest-to-goodness disappointment. Anything to make her comfortable with the fact she'd laid a pretty spectacular kiss on him right there in front of the Heritage Hotel entrance, yet didn't want to take things any further. "Your reputation's safe with me."

"My reputation is just fine, thank you very much."

Usually, after a kiss like that, the ladies invited him in, and even though she'd just asked for a rain check on the next one, she'd gotten her feathers ruffled over his playful comment, and it puzzled him. Maybe that's all he could expect from a lady who was supposed to be a thoracic surgeon but hated the sight of blood.

Gunnar had a strong hunch getting invited into her hotel room wasn't going to happen with Lilly the jaywalking journalist anytime soon. He wanted to let her know it was okay. He was fine with taking things slow. Especially if he could look forward to more spectacular kisses like that.

"Write some good stories for the newspaper, and no one will remember your pool-hall days." Her head shot up. "You didn't think I knew that, did you?"

Those pretty brown eyes lit up. "How did you know?"

Of course he knew she was a reporter. Hell, with all those questions about hush-hush meetings he'd have to be a damn fool not to figure it out. The lady wanted to know the secret so she could blab it all over the newspaper before the committee decided how best to handle things.

Well, she wouldn't find out from him, that was for sure, no matter how great she kissed.

"For one thing, the newspaper is right across the hall

from the police department and Bjork has a big mouth. For another, you're the nosiest lady I've ever met. I put two and two together."

As if she'd been outed, she went brazen-faced. "The thing is, I want to make a big impression with a breaking story. I feel like I'm on the scent of something."

She was, and it was his obligation to stop her.

"Stop trying so hard. Take some time to get a feel for Heartlandia first. You'll figure out some angle. It may not be a big splashy lead story, but you'll find a way to capture your audience. Maybe even the heart of the town." He could think of a few ways she'd already captured his attention, but he was starting to sound like a big boring town guardian and needed to back off.

She nodded infinitesimally. "You're probably right. I try too hard." For an instant she changed into a self-doubter, but before his eyes, she switched back to the overconfident woman from the first day he'd met her. "Well, thanks again for the ride. I'll catch a cab to my car in the morning. See you around."

All business. Any possibility of her kissing him again had been taken off the table, which probably meant there wouldn't be an offer to come inside, either. Funny how he had to keep reminding himself it wasn't going to happen.

Okay. He could deal with that. But she'd knocked him off balance enough to hesitate asking for her phone number, and he didn't want to ruin the memory of that perfect kiss if she didn't give her number to him. So, out of character, he let things lie and took a step toward the curb and his bike.

One thing he'd already learned—Lilly liked to be the leader.

Problem was so did he. But not today.

"Don't be a stranger. I work right across the hall from

you," he said, doing his best to forget the mind-boggling kiss and sound nonchalant.

She nodded. "Okay. Good night. I had fun." With that she headed for the entrance, waved goodbye and disappeared into the revolving door.

He started the bike and revved the engine. Forgetting his new resolve to quit playing the field, he'd wait for her to make the next move.

And if history repeated itself, the ladies always did.

Chapter Four

Saturday afternoon Lilly had a long talk with herself. Evidently her ethics regarding getting the story at all costs were in the tank. She never wanted to be caught in such a vulnerable position as getting tipsy in a strange bar, or having to accept a ride home on a motorcycle with a man she barely knew, again. But good thing Gunnar had been there like she'd planned.

He was a law-enforcement officer and from what she'd observed, a well-respected guy. A guy making up for the sins of his father? Maybe. Most important, he was a gentleman.

The problem was she'd lost focus on her plans drinking those beers. She'd shared far too much with Gunnar about her personal life. Did he really need to know about what a disappointment she'd been to her parents? And, as far as she was concerned—and she was sure her mother would agree with her—she'd nearly made a fool out of herself telling him the Christmas doll story, then followed that up with getting a little tipsy. What must he think?

It wouldn't happen again. Couldn't.

But she had to admit, she'd had a great time hanging out with Gunnar, and she'd surprised herself initiating the kiss, which had been more than she'd ever expected. Wow. That's why it couldn't happen again. She couldn't let Gunnar get in the way of her plans. So Sunday afternoon, when she'd absentmindedly picked up her cell phone to search for his phone number, she'd stopped. What was she thinking?

On Monday, she put her best foot forward with her new boss, Mr. Bjork. She'd come to work with a gazillion ideas, each of which he'd nixed until she'd brought up doing a human interest story about the local animal controller, Kirby Nylund. Carl Bjork's eyes lit up at the suggestion. Perhaps he had a soft spot for pets?

Bjork also put her on assignment regarding the local firemen and a slew of recent Dumpster fires around town and along the railroad tracks. Now she felt like part of the reporting team.

Unfortunately, the police department was just across the hall, and both the newspaper and PD offices were on either side of the lobby, their front walls being all glass, making it difficult to avoid Gunnar. Once or twice that morning she'd already seen him enter the building in all of that law-enforcement-officer splendor, filling out the perfectly ironed uniform, and sporting the low-slung duty belt, shiny badge and cop sunglasses. Totally out of character, after gawking at him she'd ducked down at her desk, below the chair-rail cubical partition in order not to be seen, and in the process had garnered more than a few odd looks from Bjork and his skeleton newspaper staff. What was it about Gunnar that caused her to repeatedly make a fool out of herself?

Until she figured out how best to handle the big friendly—and sexy—cop, she'd avoid him like a bad story. Since Gunnar might be the source of her future news flash,

Lilly couldn't risk getting personally involved with him, compromising the story.

But no matter how busy she'd kept herself over the past few days, bits and pieces from their fun night together— she really had to admit the bar had been the most fun she'd had in years—haunted her quiet moments. She remembered touching his face and kissing him, surprised how tender his lips were, and thinking wow, just wow, this guy was something else. He might look big and tough, but he kissed like she was the most delicate creature on earth. Then she remembered that big ol' red flag popping into her brain… *Careful, Lilly, this one could be a heart-breaker for sure.*

With all her big-city ways, she might give the impression of sophistication and world wisdom, but in reality she'd spent so much time and energy pursuing her studies and job, not to mention trying to please her parents, that she'd yet to figure out how to make time for relationships. Whatever "relationship" meant.

She'd dated a few men here and there, but nothing came close to being serious. Who had time?

Anyway, Lilly Matsuda had far more important things to do than get all infatuated with a bossy cop.

Just before lunch, grateful to hit the beat, she grabbed the strap of her purse, thrust her trusty notepad and mini recorder inside, and set out, taking the back exit to avoid the big Swedish sergeant with eyes the color of pine trees.

She'd learned well from her demanding parents that nothing must stand in the way of your goal, and Gunnar Norling was not her goal, no matter how appealing he was.

Even though Lilly lived in a hotel, it was an extended stay and she had a small kitchen with a half refrigerator, hot plate and a microwave. Just like in college. Since she'd run out of breakfast cereal and a few feminine items, Tuesday night she stopped in at the local market chain, the only place in town that didn't carry a Scandinavian name. She pushed her cart toward aisle ten. Having just grabbed the special hair gel she'd run out of that morning, she now loaded up on the items she needed for that time of the month. After that she'd buy some fruit and cereal, oh, and she couldn't forget the milk.

Just before leaving the aisle, something caught her eye. Condoms.

A certain handsome face came to mind. Gunnar.

Hmm…what if?

He's not your goal. Remember.

Another thought overrode the first.

She was a modern girl. Shouldn't she be prepared if the occasion ever arrived? Looking at the small box of extra fancy condoms, "ribbed with heating lubrication," on impulse, she picked them up, read the back cover, then tossed them into her cart and moved on.

Rounding the corner, focused on the task of groceries, she nearly ran into another shopping cart. "Oh, sorry!"

Lilly glanced up to see Gunnar holding a couple of packages of deodorant, one in each hand, as if making the biggest decision of his life, and looking as surprised as she must have running into him.

"Hey," he said. "Fancy meeting you here." He'd made his choice and put one brand back on the shelf.

"I needed a few things." She couldn't help herself, and looked into his cart loaded with food items and paper products. The guy obviously lived on his own, judging by the contents of his cart, not one feminine thing to be found.

"So how've you been?" He looked honestly interested.

"Very well, thank you. How about you?" *Hide the con-*

doms! How was she supposed to do that without being obvious?

"Not bad. Breaking into that new job?"

"Yes," she said, edging from behind the cart to alongside it, then standing in front of it altogether. Unfortunately, this put her in much closer proximity to him. Close enough to see those green, green eyes. "Bjork's teaching me the ropes and sending me out on assignments."

"Good. Good." The guy looked as if he wanted to settle in and have a real conversation, his expression inquisitive and his brows mildly furrowed, yet he held back. And she held her breath, preoccupied with the condoms and him not noticing them. Were they destined to discuss the weather?

"Anything new or exciting going on in the police department?" She broke the lingering moment of silence and as she spoke leaned against the front of the cart, surreptitiously moving her other hand behind her, searching around, hoping to make contact with the naughty little box. But the cart was too deep. The condoms were out of her reach. Whatever possessed her to buy them, anyway?

"No breaking news." He smiled, imparting the obvious— he wouldn't tell her anything if there was, and she could count on that. "How about you?"

"Nope. No breaking stories." She glanced at Gunnar, the handsome homegrown stud in fitted jeans and a blue plaid flannel shirt. Her cheeks warmed. She needed to get away from him. This was the guy she'd kissed with all of her heart the other night, and even though she'd been a little under the influence at the time, she'd really wanted to. That kiss had influenced her thoughts just moments ago. Now she'd been caught buying condoms. Wouldn't that go right to his head. Oh, not that head!

Her warming cheeks advanced into an all-out hot-from-the-neck-up affront.

Lilly shook her head, hoping to clear out all the crazy thoughts. *Get away. Go. Now!* "Well, I better get over to the produce aisle. A girl needs her five pieces of fruit a day."

"Sure thing." He glanced toward her cart, but couldn't see around her. "The apples are good this time of year. But here's a tip, they're much better at the farmer's market every Sunday afternoon. Our local growers are best."

Always up for a good story, she searched in her purse for the notepad, ready to scribble a reminder for that coming Sunday farmer's market, unmanning her cart. "Thanks, I'll do that."

He glanced into her cart and with a twinkle in his eyes nailed her when she glanced up again. Damn. He'd seen them.

He winked and scratched the corner of his mouth. She could read his face so easily it was sad—*Hmm, you planning on using those with me?*

"Well, I guess I better go check out," he said, making her squirm in her tracks.

"See you around the office building," she said. *Cringe.* Every assumption known to man must be elbowing its way into his already oversize masculine ego. She needed to stay away from him.

"Sure thing," he said, far more confident than necessary.

Just for the record, the one thing she wasn't was a *sure thing*.

So why did she have that little box with her other items?

She fumed, mostly at herself, and pushed her cart toward the back end of the aisle as he headed for the checkout clerk up front.

Ten minutes later, having calmed down and completed her shopping, distractedly putting the contents of her cart on the small conveyor belt at the checkout, she reached for the box. Lifting it, she saw the extra fancy, ribbed-with-heating-lubrication condoms and blushed again. Gunnar'd had a frisky look on his face when he'd said goodbye, and she'd put it there because of these.

"You gonna want that, miss?" the checker asked.

"Oh." Instead of letting her eyes bug out and making some excuse about having made a mistake the way she wanted to, just to spite Gunnar she handed the condoms to the clerk with her head high, looking straight into his eyes. "Yes."

She was a grown-up. If she wanted a box of condoms, she'd buy them, and it didn't matter what Gunnar thought about it. But an unwanted image planted in her mind—using one of the condoms on Gunnar—and it made the tips of her ears burn hot as she left the market, one bag of groceries in each arm.

Gunnar couldn't figure it out. It had been five days since he'd given Lilly a ride home and they'd kissed, and almost another day since she'd snuck the condoms into her grocery cart, yet she still hadn't called him. Sure she'd been embarrassed when he'd dropped her off at her hotel last Friday, but she hadn't been drunk or anything, just tipsy enough to need a ride home. No harm, no foul.

His mouth twitched into a partial grin. That kiss had been damn fantastic, and this wasn't the first time he'd thought about it since Friday night. Which was unsettling. Since when did Gunnar get all floaty-headed over the memory of a hot kiss?

When she'd opened up about her parents pressuring her into becoming a surgeon, and how instead she'd followed her heart in college, and then told the touching story about the little girl who'd only wanted a doll, not a science lesson, well, his chest had tightened with compassion. There was definitely more to Lilly than her sexy and sophisticated exterior.

Gunnar parked his unit that Wednesday midmorning and headed inside to the police department from the back parking lot. The close-to-retirement officer working the front desk waved him over.

"Got a message for you," Ed said, offering a sealed envelope to Gunnar.

"Thanks." Gunnar took it and noticed the feminine handwriting then smiled. Yeah, so he'd been right, sooner or later she'd come around.

He took the envelope back to his desk, sat and fished out his letter opener then tore that sucker open. He was a bit disappointed to see typing inside, instead of the handwritten "call me" note with a phone number and a real lipstick kiss he'd imagined.

He read on.

Hi Gunnar—I wanted to get your approval to use your heartwarming story about that stray cat you once gave shelter in a little piece I'm doing on our local pet control. It will run on Thursday. If you're okay with it, please let me know at…

She left her work phone number. That was a start. But she'd only signed off with her name. Not *look forward to hearing from you*, or *let's get together soon*, or any number of catchy coy phrases that would have made it easy for him to suggest they have dinner together that weekend. Nope, she'd gone the just-Lilly route. Very professional.

He dialed the number she'd given and it went straight to messages. *Bummer. Not even gonna get to talk to her in person.* After the beep, he used his charming voice and gave her permission to share his story and any other noble thing she'd like to share about him, but stopped short of asking her out. He'd decided to do that face-to-face the next time he saw her.

The mysterious outsider with the wide-spaced and beautifully shaped eyes, that when you looked closer were maybe a little sad from growing up with overbearing parents, wasn't making his job easy. Now he smiled full-out because, truthfully, he was looking forward to the challenge of getting Lilly Matsuda to go out with him.

Thursday morning Gunnar let his cat, Wolverine, out for his morning explorations then walked down the driveway to pick up the paper. Pulling it out of the thin plastic cover he headed back inside. Once he'd gotten his coffee together and a peanut-butter-and-banana sandwich on toast, he settled at the kitchen counter to read the news. Back on page five was an article written by Lilly featuring, of all people, Kirby Nylund, the curmudgeon himself, half smiling, half scowling for the camera.

Gunnar was impressed with Lilly's style of journalism. It included a little bit of folksy banter with Kirby, a bit of a history lesson on Heartlandia's approach to animal control, the current state of stray pets in Clayton County, and informative tips on where and when to have pets spayed and neutered at a reasonable cost. Then she did something that hit home with Gunnar, she threw the question out to the local readers: "Tell us about your personal pet-rescue story for a chance to see yours in print." After that she started things off with Gunnar's story about Smelly.

When he finished reading the article he had a big grin on his face. Yes, that's what the *Heartlandia Herald* had been missing, that personal touch, with the invitation to the locals to participate in the newspaper. If his hunch was right, there would be an avalanche of responses to her invitation.

Lilly might put up a tough facade, but beneath that stylish, modern-woman exterior she had a big heart. He'd experienced it firsthand the night she'd kissed him stupid in front of the hotel. Why she'd gone into hiding, he didn't understand.

Gunnar finished following up on the complaint about a disturbance in the city college parking lot later that night. Several such calls had come in almost simultaneously across town. Because he was closest to the college, he rolled on that one, leaving the other units to investigate the different areas.

Everything checked out fine at the college, no sign of disturbance at all, other than night students heading to their cars after class. He decided to take one more trip around the parking lot to make sure he hadn't missed anything when a call about a fire came through the radio just after 9:00 p.m. *Old warehouse. 300 block of First Street. The railroad tracks.*

Hell, it was Olaf's place.

He hit his emergency lights, sped off and, when he'd gotten onto the main road, seeing huge black clouds of smoke off in the distance, turned on the siren and raced toward the scene down by the river.

As a police officer his job at a fire was crowd-and-traffic control of the area, the biggest hazard being looky-loos swarming the scene and getting in the way. Within five minutes he arrived behind another police cruiser and jumped out.

Tactical planning was the sergeant's job, and he took it seriously.

"How many on the way?" he called to Eric, the other

police officer. Heat from the huge explosive flames at the brewery warmed his face even from this distance. Three fire trucks and dozens of men flocked to the blaze hitting the pavement at full speed toward the old warehouse.

"Six other units that I know of are on the way," Eric said.

Soon, several other blaring sirens made known their arrival and Gunnar had half a dozen units spaced evenly and parked in a line at the outskirts of the parking lot. Fortunately, the river acted as a natural boundary on the back side and was one less thing to worry about.

The police officers worked as a team, some marking boundaries with flares and bright orange cones and others taking to the streets directing and detouring what little traffic was out this time of night.

Like moths to light, employees from nearby businesses and residents from local neighborhoods poured outside to have their own up-close-and-personal view of the fire.

The crowd grew as the fire put on a diabolical performance in the night sky, and Gunnar concentrated on his immediate surroundings, the citizens, and fellow police officers, leaving the firefighting to the well-trained pros. There were more sirens, more police units to strategically place and also an ambulance, which he assisted through the crowd and police line.

Things could get out of control fast if they didn't demarcate the perimeter. "Get the traffic control unit out here and tell them to bring the sawhorse barricades," he said.

"Roger, Sarge." Eric headed for his unit to put in the request.

Gunnar got on his radio for the latest updates, wondering if his best friend, Kent, who ran the local Urgent Care, had been notified. Another ambulance arrived, and he hoped beyond hope that the injuries would be kept to a minimum, especially since the nearest hospital was the next town over thirty miles away, and there was only so much Kent and his staff could handle at his UC. As it was Kent would be inundated with smoke inhalation patients from the gathering crowd.

With his mind flitting to a hundred different thoughts, Gunnar saw a petite silhouette break from the main group of bystanders and head his way.

"Gunnar!"

It didn't take more than a second to recognize the lovely Lilly, and since it was the first face-to-face he'd had with her since that night at the market, a mixture of bad— Olaf's, the place they'd first gotten to know each other, had been decimated by the fire—and good—it was great to see her again—feelings took him by surprise. A single word popped in his head: *Chitcha.* On reflex he smiled.

She returned the smile, then flashed her reporter's ID. "Hi! This is horrible. Can you tell me what's going on?"

Gunnar gave her the general rundown of time and events while he took in her jeans, boots and half-off-the-shoulder purple sweater. "No word yet on how it started." But something had been niggling at the back of his brain ever since he'd received the call. Thinking back to the college parking lot disturbance that had been a false alarm, and which he'd rolled on, he remembered hearing several other calls, all with the same complaint, right at the exact time around 8:30 p.m. He wondered if all of those had been false alarms, too, like a widespread decoy. Putting that together with the recent onslaught of trash-can fires around the docks and train tracks the past few weeks, he also puzzled over whether there might be a connection.

"Has the fire captain issued a statement yet?" Lilly asked. "Anything I can use?"

"Not yet." Looking at Lilly, remembering how great

she'd felt Friday night in front of her hotel, wishing they'd had more time together since then, some protective instinct clicked on in his gut. "You shouldn't get so close. Who knows what toxic fumes might be spilling into the air."

"Like twenty feet will make a difference?" She had a point. "I'm here for the *Herald*, can you give me any information?"

"Nothing official. But all the alcohol in the bar and brewery is probably what made the huge blast about an hour ago. Did you hear it?"

She nodded. "I thought someone had dropped a bomb."

Gunnar glanced over his shoulder at the raging orange-and-red flames. Smoke plumes rose into the night sky like an ancient genie finally released from his bottle. "Kind of looks that way, doesn't it?"

He used his hand on her shoulder to direct her farther back and to the side of his car, thinking they may be able to hear each other better over there.

One of the rookie cops burst onto the scene, a cardboard multiple-cup holder in his hands. "The coffee shop insisted I bring some coffee. You want one?"

Gunnar looked at Lilly. "Coffee?" She nodded her thanks so he grabbed two. "Thanks, Darren."

Off the new officer went, spreading his good-coffee cheer to the other policemen working nearby. Something crackled over his radio in the car. "Excuse me," he said, handing Lilly his paper cup and hopping inside to listen. Lilly followed close behind.

"A fireman's been injured. Make space for medevac emergency landing. ETA ten minutes." Gunnar saw an upsurge in activity around one of the ambulances. His stomach cramped at the possibility of anyone getting killed tonight, and his hunch about the source of this fire plumed in his thoughts.

Getting right back on task, he gave an apologetic look to Lilly. "I've got to take care of this."

"Any word on who the fireman is?"

"Not at this time, I'll let you know as soon as I find out."

"Thanks. Hey, I was interviewing some firemen this week about the trash-can fires going on around town. Of course they said they were all intentionally set. Do you think there is any connection?"

He remembered from earlier reports how well planned all the trash-can fires that didn't pan out were. Someone had made sure to distract the police officers with bogus calls. "Don't know for sure." He looked around the scene again. "Though I've got to say—" he looked at Lilly, thinking of her as a friend "—my hunch is this fire and those trash cans might be related and this could be arson, too."

Her eyes went big enough for him to see the fire reflected inside the irises. She stepped back and he cut in front of her, heading back to the parking lot. "Cobawa. It's Ben Cobawa." The fireman's name crackled over the radio. "Looks like second-degree burns on his face and neck, which means smoke inhalation, too. Better hope that unit gets here quick."

Damn. "Ben's been injured," he said so Lilly could hear.

"Who's Ben?"

"One of our best firemen."

"I realize that, but what's he to you? You seem really upset."

He'd known Ben all his life. The gentle Native American was also on the pirate project at city hall. And sometimes, he could swear there was something going on between Elke and Ben, but he'd never had proof.

"A friend of my sister's." Gunnar sped up, leaving Lilly standing taking pictures of the fire as he threw out directions to his men left and right. He had a hell of a lot to accomplish in a short time, and from the looks of the angry fire across the way, things were going to get worse before they got better. And it would be another long, long night ahead.

He glanced over his shoulder, seeing Lilly's tiny frame in the shadows diligently scribbling notes and snapping pictures, and wished this latest meeting with her had been under completely different circumstances.

Gunnar rolled out of bed early Friday afternoon. He'd been up all night with the fire that had finally been put out around four. He'd stuck around doing his part to make the situation navigable until the morning shift, and more importantly until his lieutenant insisted he go home and take the day off.

His eyes still burned from the smoke, and even though he'd showered when he'd gotten home, the smell remained fresh in his nostrils. Wolverine snubbed him as if he were nothing more than a pile of ashes, until he got out the bag of kitty kibble. Then the cat acted as if Gunnar was the lion king himself and rolled belly-upward, allowing Gunnar to pet the softest fur. Gee, such an honor.

After he'd made his coffee and had thrown on his guy-type Japanese spa robe—otherwise he was naked—he tied the sash and went outside to get the newspaper to keep him company while he ate some cereal.

Around the fifth crunchy bite, he opened the paper and got hit with a headline that nearly had him spewing his honey and oats across the kitchen.

Arson Thought to Be at the Center of Brewery Fire. He hadn't given her the okay to print that!

He read on about how the fire captain had confirmed his hunch about arson, and lectured himself about jumping to conclusions regarding Lilly, then calmed down. She brought up the cluster of calls coming in as decoys just before the fire got set. That someone set Olaf's bar and brewery on fire on purpose, and wanted to make sure everyone was scattered around town when it happened. Then she'd covered the diligent firemen putting out the flames and the dramatic medevac of Ben Cobawa. Excellent reporting, in his opinion. Next she focused on the police force keeping order and protecting the local citizens who'd lined up for a firsthand view of the dangerous fire. His name popped up after that.

Concerned and giving orders, Sergeant Gunnar Norling put all of his efforts into manning the front line of this fire with his fellow officers. Norling, a ten-year veteran on the police force takes his job to protect and serve seriously. Giving orders and drinking donated coffee, he doesn't miss a detail. Perhaps he is driven by his own father's mistakes, occasionally overcompensating for being the son of an ex-con with his stiff, by-the-book attitude.

He blinked at the flaming wall of anger encircling him. He hadn't even known Lilly for a week and she'd already crossed into the forbidden territory of his past. In public! For the whole town to read and remember how his father was a common criminal, who'd done time...

Leaving his cereal bowl on the counter, he stomped to his bedroom, threw on some clothes and headed for the door.

He'd slipped up, made the mistake of thinking Lilly was a friend and talking honestly with her, sharing part of his painful past, and now he'd paid the price.

Well, lesson learned.

As he put on his helmet and hopped onto his motorcycle, he planned to chew Lilly out when he cornered her.

Lilly glanced up from the computer screen Friday afternoon and saw a human hurricane blowing her way. Gunnar.

She jumped up and steadied herself, meeting his glower by lifting her chin. "What's up?" she asked, bracing herself for who knew what, but from the looks of him, something unpleasant was about to go down.

He tossed the front page on her desk. "I'll tell you what's up, *this* is what's up." His usual affable masculine voice was tempered by a slow, hot simmer. He pointed to the headline. "I made the mistake of confiding in you about my father, and now you've pasted it all over the front page for the whole town to read."

His penetrating green-eyed stare could be unsettling for the average person, but she'd had to face the steely glares of her mother and father her entire life. Gunnar was no contest. "I added it to give a human interest side—hey, we can be better than our parents, look at Gunnar Norling."

"You had no business bringing that up without my permission." His voice was quiet, yet the words slashed at her confidence.

Out of habit, she donned her good-soldier attitude and stood straighter. "Do you remember the message you left me the other day?" She waited for him to remember, but he showed no sign of it. It was her turn to go on offense, and she played it to the hilt. He wasn't the only person around here who knew how to lean into an argument. "Then let me refresh your memory." She put her hands on her hips and glared at him. "'Sure—'" she tried to sound like Gunnar when he played it charming "'—you can use that information…*and any other noble thing you'd like to share about me…*'" She emphasized the last part.

He stopped briefly to digest what she'd told him. "I may have said that, but come on, you should have known better." Quiet yet cutting to the quick.

"Are you calling me dense?" Her voice rose and she failed at hiding her frustration.

"The last thing I'd call you is dense. How about insensitive." He failed at hiding his ire, too, but his tone was more of a molar-grinding growl.

She couldn't retort because it was true. She should have known his father was off-limits, and yet she'd let that part slip her mind when writing the article because it was good press—the son atoning for the father's sins. She'd been all fired up about the front-page story, and had given it her all, ignoring a couple of really important points. Never leave your source hung out to dry. Not if you hope to use them for future articles. Journalism 101.

Damn.

She blinked and took a quick breath, preparing to do something she was really lousy at. "I'm sorry." She said it quietly, biting back an ugly old feeling she used to get whenever her father called her on the carpet—shame. She cast Gunnar a contrite glance. Was she bound to spend her adult life trying to please the entire male population thanks to her father?

Gunnar went still, as if in the eye of the storm, taking time to pick up the newspaper and read the rest of the article. His jaw should have been making popping noises from all the gritting of teeth. He took in a long breath, glanced at her with less glaring eyes, then slowly let out the air. "I've got to be able to trust that when I talk to you, you won't go blabbing everything on the front page."

"I said I'm sorry. I get it. It won't ever happen again." What the heck did he want her to do, grovel?

He rolled his lips inward and rubbed his stubble-covered

jaw. His hair went every which way from wearing the motorcycle helmet, there were dark circles under his eyes from the long and stressful night and he still managed to look sexy as hell.

All she wanted to do was make him forgive her. Quick decision. Okay, so she would grovel. A little. "Let me buy you dinner tonight so I can give an official apology."

He torqued his brows and got that steely-eyed look again, then shook his head. "You don't have to do that."

"I want to. Please, Gunnar, let me buy you dinner." Against her better judgment, she'd been meaning to get in touch with him anyway. Something about a rain-check kiss she'd promised. "That is if you don't already have plans."

"No plans." He shifted his weight from one jeans-clad muscular thigh to the other, then ran his fingers through the mishmash of hair, still thinking.

"Then, let's do it." She walked closer, stood right in front of him, engaging his slow-to-trust gaze. Heck, she'd been trained by two of the toughest tiger parents on the planet. She could make him do what she wanted. "Have dinner with me. Come on."

Something twinkled way in the back of those green irises. "Okay, if you insist. I'll take you to *husmanskost* for a proper Swedish meal. I'll pick you up at eight."

She'd won the match, but was careful not to gloat, and he'd quickly taken over the plans. She needed to regain some control. "I'm paying."

One corner of his mouth twitched, the way it had the first day she'd met him when he wrote out her jaywalking warning and she knew he didn't want to smile. He scratched it, then turned to leave. "We'll discuss that later."

Chapter Five

Gunnar patted the aftershave on his cheeks and crinkled his nose over the initial potent spicy scent. Okay, so he hadn't opened it since his sister had given it to him two Christmases ago because that was the month his mother had died and Christmas hadn't seemed possible to bear that year. Had the stuff fermented or something? He fanned the air, grateful aftershave didn't last like cologne, then ran a comb through his short hair and took one appraising look in the mirror. Looked good enough for him, but would he look good enough for Lilly?

Since he was still ticked off at her for exposing something so personal about him, something he worked to make up for every single day of his life, it would take a lot of effort and charm on her part to make him forgive her. He shouldn't give a darn what she thought about how he looked.

Truth was it never took much to set off those horrible memories, to relive the mortification of a twelve-year-old kid who'd found out his father had broken the law and was going to jail. Gunnar brushed away the quick thoughts of panic and how he'd literally thought it meant the whole family would be homeless, but more importantly, how ashamed he'd been of his father, and how he wouldn't be able to hold up his head in Heartlandia ever again.

If it wasn't for a big Swedish kid two years older than him, one of the cool and popular kids named Kent Larson who, seeing how distraught, unpredictable, angry and explosive Gunnar had become, insisted on being his best friend, well, Gunnar may have very well followed in his old man's footsteps.

All he knew for sure was that not a day went by when he wasn't trying to make up for the shadow of shame on his family name and, damn it, Lilly had nailed that part, said it for everyone to read right there in the newspaper.

He took a deep breath and shook his head, walked shirtless to his closet and grabbed his favorite royal oxford shirt, fresh from the laundry and perfectly pressed, the way his mother used to do. *Gunnar, we may not have money for nice clothes like the other people around here, but we can keep what we do have clean and pressed, yes?*

The shirt was pale blue with navy pinstripes and he'd been told by a lady or two that it made his eyes look blue.

Not that he wasn't happy with his green eyes, it was just that they'd always reminded him of his father. Shifty sea green eyes. And the lies his old man had told. *I'm innocent*, he'd sworn. *Been set up.* The way he'd left his mother after she'd been so loyal to him. She'd never said a word against the man when he was in jail, while she worked two jobs to keep him and his sister fed. Her reward? The minute the man got out of the slammer he took off and was never heard from again. That was until he got sent back to jail ten years later and needed money for bail.

Some role model he'd turned out to be.

Gunnar shook his head. *Knock it off.* He was taking a

new lady out for dinner, his favorite pastime. Now was not the moment to get all morose about his father.

When he became a teenager, Gunnar had discovered that girls could take a guy's mind off his lousy family history and put it on much more entertaining things of the physical nature. Since then he was rarely without a lady. Yet these past few months, seeing Kent so happy with Desi, Gunnar had slowed down on the constant superficial dating. So why was he so hell-bent on going out with Lilly?

Because she was different? Or maybe because, since she'd let slip some pretty telling information about her own old man, Gunnar thought they might have something in common. Since when did he give a hoot if he and a lady had anything in common besides attraction?

Okay, he was starting to give himself a headache, so he looked into the mirror and said, "Dude, knock it off."

He buttoned and tucked, slipped on his best loafers. Tonight, like every other day of his life, he'd be the man he wanted his own father to be. And that was all there was to that. Gunnar grabbed a sports jacket and headed for the door. Wolverine made a disapproving meow.

He patted his head. "Oh, hush up. You'll be fine. Go take another nap or something."

But unable to get off the rough subject of his father, he admitted he had major issues with people who said one thing but did another. Lilly had run his name in the paper, said some strictly private information and made a very public connection between him and his dad without his official consent. She'd said it was an example of his honor and dedication to the job, but Gunnar wondered if it wasn't more to prove how good she was at getting a story so her own old man might cut her some slack.

For now he'd give her the benefit of the doubt, especially since she was taking him for an apology dinner. But he'd make it clear that from now on everything he said was strictly off the record and he expected to read in advance *anything* she intended to print about him. If she couldn't deal with that, then sayonara, baby.

He parked in the guest section at the Heritage and took the elevator up to the fifth floor—the top floor, because that was as high at it got in Heartlandia thanks to a hundred-year-old city building code. Truth was, he liked that there weren't any high-rises, like so many other coastal communities had, blocking the view of the water for those like him who dwelled on the hillside.

He tapped on her door and, wow, when it flew open she looked stunning. In pink. She greeted him wearing a loose-knit sweater that casually fell off one shoulder with a darker pink cami underneath, and a frilly girlie necklace. Once he pulled his gaze away from the smooth white skin of her shoulder he noticed she'd sculpted her hair in a sexy and fun way, and that her eyes were enhanced by mascara and perfectly applied three-toned eye-shadow. And those fine lips glistened, also in pink.

Which was beginning to be his favorite color.

"So how's it goin'?" he asked, sounding like a doofus even to himself.

"Pretty good. You hungry? Because I am. This is way past my dinnertime."

He'd noticed the black pencil skirt and black hose and pointy black heels, so his answer got delayed. "Oh, sorry. But the wait makes everything taste better."

"Well, I cheated and ate some cheese and crackers about an hour ago."

"Someone your size probably has a picky and fast metabolism, right?"

"I've never thought of it that way." She'd picked up her

purse from the hotel-style living room chair, leaving him waiting at the threshold rather than asking him in. The lady really was hungry.

She closed the door, which automatically locked shut, and they walked down the hall of the oldest hotel in town. With a replica of the original patterned wallpaper making the walls feel claustrophobic, and thick red carpet splattered in huge yellow-and-white hibiscus nearly lifting off the floor, he ducked on reflex thinking he might bump his head on the ceiling, then broke the silence. "The restaurant is just a couple of blocks away. It's really pretty out tonight, and I thought it would be nice to walk there. You up for that?"

She made a decisive nod.

"You going to be able to walk in those shoes?" With the sexy pointy toes...

"No problem. They're more comfortable than they look."

"Could have fooled me." He used the excuse of looking at her shoes to notice her legs and athletic calves. Okay, so he was ogling her, he admitted it, but he'd make up for it over dinner with pithy conversation, where he'd let her talk all she wanted.

Truth was, he really wanted to get to know more about Lilly.

The late-summer evening was crisp and cool, with the hint of moisture from the river, and it felt great on his skin. Others might complain about the weather in Oregon, but he loved it here. Of course, it was his home and the only place he'd ever lived.

She looked straight ahead. "So I hope you've had time to cool down." She looked up at him with earnestness in her eyes, like it was really important. "The last thing I ever wanted to do was make you upset."

"I don't want to rehash things, but when it comes to trusting, let's just say I have issues with people who aren't straightforward."

"I understand. I don't like to think of myself as not being straightforward, though. It's not a good quality."

"Is that the only reason?"

"No. Of course I don't want to be thought of as a liar."

"I didn't call you that."

"No, but that's what you implied."

"Not true. I was complaining about not being notified or giving approval."

"And so by skipping that part, I lied to you. Right?"

"Okay." They'd stopped in front of Hannah's Hand-made Sweaters, and he really didn't want to get stuck in an argument with Lilly all night, because something told him she wouldn't back down. "Hey, it's a beautiful night, let's not muck it up with semantics. What do you say we call a truce?"

"Sounds good to me."

"With the promise that we can trust each other from now on."

"Okay."

He encouraged her to walk again with a gentle touch to her elbow. "And whatever I say when we're together is *always* off the record."

She paused again, but smiled. "I get it."

"And anything you print about me in the future gets my approval first."

She saluted. "Yes, sir. Tell me whatever you want. My lips are sealed."

"Well, that's a shame because I was just thinking how kissable they looked."

She nailed him with a "seriously?" kind of glance, then trudged ahead of him. Okay, unsubtle, he got it, plus he might be behaving a little chauvinistically, but he was a guy and he was allowed now and then to slip up, and man, someone needed to remember their kiss.

She didn't pursue the kissing topic, which disappointed him a little, and thankfully after a few more steps they were already outside the restaurant.

He gestured to the door of the modest white building with the blue-and-yellow canopy.

She squinted at the sign out front. "What is *husman-skost*?"

"A style of Swedish cuisine. You're gonna love it." He swung the door wide open into a darkened dining room lit only by candlelight. Bringing Lilly here made him see it from another perspective. Tables for two were selectively arranged near plants and white-lattice-panel room dividers. All the tables were round with white tablecloths, with a hint of blue-and-yellow thread woven around the edges. The overall appearance was clean and modern. He liked it and hoped she would, too.

It had been a long time since Gunnar had brought someone here as he usually came by himself when he got nostalgic for his mother's cooking. The young waitress brought the menu with the night's supper specials, then left to retrieve some water.

"So how do you say it? Hus-mans-kost?"

"That's right."

"What does it mean?"

"It's traditional Swedish countryside cuisine made with local ingredients. You don't get to pick and choose from the menu, like at other restaurants. Basically we eat what they've made today."

She glanced at the long list on the day's specials. "All of this?"

He liked how her eyes lit up with wonder. "I'll help."

"I won't be eating animal brains or pickled eyeballs or anything, will I?"

He gently laughed. "Don't worry. I guarantee you'll like the food or I'll pay for dinner. How's that for a money-back guarantee?"

"I'm so hungry it won't be a problem."

When the waitress returned he ordered some dishes from the night's menu. *"Ärtsoppa, rotmos med fläsk."* He leaned toward Lilly. "Would you prefer potato dumplings or potato pancakes?"

"Dumplings sound good."

"Okay. We'll have *palt*. Oh, and why not, we'll have some *raggmunk*, too."

The waitress nodded. He glanced at Lilly. "You've got to try *raggmunk*."

She lifted her narrow shoulders in a "whatever" gesture.

"Oh, and you can warm up the apple cake now, because we're definitely going to have that."

"Share," Lilly said. "We'll share a piece."

Lilly obviously liked to take control. Problem was, so did he.

Once the waitress walked off, Lilly tapped Gunnar's arm. "What did all that mean?"

He smiled. "Pea soup with yellow peas, boiled and mashed carrots, rutabaga and potato with free-range pork tenderloin and, since you wanted potato dumplings, that comes with ground meat, also free-range. But I decided you had to try potato pancakes, too, so I ordered *raggmunk*."

"That's a lot of potatoes. I'll explode if I eat all that."

"We'll take it slow, and you can take the leftovers home."

"Sounds like comfort food."

"It definitely is." He took a moment to study Lilly, looking so pretty in pink, appreciating her being open to food she'd probably never try otherwise. "I know after your little incident at the bar last week you probably don't want to drink, but the best way to eat this food is with vodka."

"My incident at the bar?" She immediately bristled.

He used his thumb to imitate a person drinking from a beer bottle.

"I beg your pardon, but I was fine." She pulled her sweater up over her shoulder and sat straighter. "Well, almost fine."

Continuing to tease, he shrugged his shoulders and tilted his head, giving her some slack. She went quiet, but not for long.

"Vodka? Like a martini?"

"No. Just vodka. Straight," he said.

"Well, anything would taste good after that."

"It actually enhances the flavors. That is if you sip it. No guzzling like you and beer."

She playfully slapped his arm and he realized how much he enjoyed giving her a hard time, and being around her in general.

"Let's go for it, then. I may as well experience my first *husmanskost* the authentic way. Maybe I'll even do a piece for the paper on it. That is if it's okay with you?"

Did she ever get her mind off work? But in this case he really liked that angle—a human interest story spotlighting a local business, just what they needed more of these days.

He smiled. "That would be a great idea."

He waved the waitress over and made their drink orders, then not wanting the easy flowing conversation to go dead, thought up another topic. "So what's your favorite food?"

"I'm a California girl, sushi, what else?"

"That's it?"

"Sticky rice, teriyaki chicken, seafood. Oh, and avocados."

"Can you make sushi?"

"My sobo taught me to make *makizushi*." She played with the silverware on her napkin and he detected a nostalgic gaze.

"Maki sushi?"

"Close enough. Rice-filled rolls wrapped in seaweed. Mostly vegetarian, celery, cucumber, avocado, since she didn't trust me with raw fish."

"Who is Sobo?"

"My grandmother." There it was again, endearment in her eyes. All he remembered about his grandmother was that occasionally she'd pull him by the ear when he'd acted up.

"I'd love to try some of your maki sushi."

"Once I find a place with a kitchen I'll make you some."

"You're looking for a permanent place?"

"I'm planning on sticking around and making something out of that newspaper. Maybe even asking Bjork to sell it to me."

"Really?"

"Yes, really."

"Well, in that case, I know a man who has a guesthouse sitting empty. He built it about ten years ago for his mother after his father died. But then a few years later she died, and a year after that his wife died, so it's been sitting empty for two or three years now. Maybe he'd rent it to you."

Her eyes enlarged and brightened. "Can you ask for me?"

"Sure. His name's Leif Andersen." The excitement in her gaze doubled when he mentioned the name. "The best contractor in this part of Oregon. Built the city college. Sure, I'll put in a good word for you."

* * *

Lilly couldn't believe her good fortune. Leif Andersen was on that secret committee, and maybe he'd be her ticket to Big News so she could lay off Gunnar. "The sooner I can move out of the Heritage, the happier I'll be."

"I'll talk to him tomorrow, then."

Another secret meeting? She'd have to stake herself out in the bushes again.

As they ate, she watched Gunnar relax and his face brighten. Food could do that, bring back good memories.

"Good as Momma used to make?" she asked.

He nodded. "Almost." He smiled. "I always think about picnics and camping trips from when I was really young, when I ate cold potato pancakes." He gazed at her. "They travel well."

"Did you do a lot of camping when you were a kid?"

"Doesn't everyone?"

Not her. In fact, she couldn't remember a single family vacation until she graduated from high school and her parents decided it was time to take a trip to Europe. "Actually, I went to camp a lot, but never went camping."

He screwed up his face, not figuring out what she'd meant, like it was some sort of riddle.

She nibbled on some beef. "My parents always sent me away to these themed camps in the summer. They'd ship me off to Maine or Montana or Washington. All over the country. Every summer."

"Did you like it?"

The memories were sad and lonely, but she knew how to put a carefree spin on things so as not to make Gunnar feel sorry for her. "I learned a lot."

"Did you make friends?"

The question almost threw her out of breezy mode,

but she didn't miss a beat. "A few. Mostly other nerds and castaways like me."

His head popped up. "You? A nerd? Never."

She laughed. "The thing is, when I figured out my gift was writing and I'd proved it by getting my first C ever in science, and was only mediocre in advanced math, well, let's just say it didn't go over well with good old Dad."

She didn't want to lay a sob story on him, but she certainly had his interest so she forged ahead. "That year Dad found a science camp on Catalina Island off the coast of California. Though I did enjoy the outdoor activities, hiking and kayaking and snorkeling, it didn't set a fire in my heart for science. We suffered through a few more rocky semesters in school before I admitted I wanted to major in journalism."

"And Daddy didn't like that."

She shook her head, suddenly losing her appetite even though the aroma of the apple cake was out of this world. She picked at her share, claiming to be too full to eat more. One lonely memory forced its way out of the recesses of her mind, where she'd packed it away in her busy life. She'd entered a statewide writing contest and had taken first place. The day of the awards ceremony neither of her parents could be there, both claiming they had important appointments with clients that couldn't be rescheduled. What had started out as a moment of great pride had turned into one of the loneliest mornings of her life, and in the Matsuda household, there were many to choose from.

As if reading her mind about something much deeper going on than she'd let on, Gunnar reached across the table and wrapped his big warm hand around hers. The look in his eyes was both tender and understanding, and for an instant she wanted to give him another mind-boggling kiss.

Instead she gave a weak smile, hoping her eyes weren't welling up.

The waitress appeared. Evidently while Lilly was buried in her thoughts, he'd asked for the check and a small box to take the apple cake home in. Since things had gotten a little too heavy for her liking, she was grateful for the change in venue.

After a long and incredibly delicious meal, Lilly was glad they'd walked to the restaurant, desperately needing the exercise or she'd fall asleep from the overabundance of comfort food.

Gunnar had been right, the vodka did enhance all the different flavors. She definitely planned to write a spotlight article on the place, and had gotten the owner's name and phone number on her way out. Lilly looked forward to hearing more about the free-range ranchers and the local farmers the owner used for the ingredients. The man mentioned that many of the farmers came to the weekly farmer's market held right in the center of town. She'd already gotten a huge response from her shout-out regarding stray animal stories, and wanted to keep the human interest aspect of Heartlandia rolling in the newspaper. Who knew, maybe subscriptions might go up, too.

The minute they stepped outside into the fresh night air a fire truck zoomed down Main Street...toward the Heritage.

Gunnar looked at her. "I wonder what's going on?"

"Me, too."

They walked briskly and arrived at the scene. A small but growing crowd filled the sidewalk.

Gunnar went up to one of the firefighters he knew and she stuck to his side like seaweed on rice. "What's going on?"

She fished in her purse for her notepad.

"Someone set off all of the fire alarms. We're evacuating the entire hotel until we know for certain everything is safe."

"A prank?" she asked.

"We don't know yet. Just being cautious right now."

"But I'm staying here."

"We can't let anyone in until we've checked everything out." Where were they supposed to go? How long would they be stuck outside? She glanced at Gunnar.

"Guess that means you're coming home with me to wait things out."

She yanked in her chin, letting her shock register in her eyes. "But I need to submit this info for the Heartbeat on Heartlandia log. Ack, but my laptop is in my room."

"You can use mine."

There might not be any way around this. Regardless of what she'd told him about her shoes being comfortable, right about now her toes were aching, and the thought of hanging out on the street for God only knew how long, wasn't the least bit appealing. Plus she could upload her newspaper info on Gunnar's computer. He must have been reading her thoughts. Again.

"It's either that or stand around in those high heels on this cold sidewalk until they let you back in."

He made a solid point, and she was a reasonable person. Plus all that comfort food, and not to mention the vodka, had made her very sleepy. "Okay, but don't get any ideas."

He paused, as if some great plans had been dashed. "Okay—no hanky-panky...unless you ask nicely."

Chapter Six

Lilly was beyond impressed with Gunnar's semi-A-frame house. Modern-looking, built of solid wood with loads of windows and a wooden deck to sit and stare out at the river, the house nestled in the center of a tree grove. When he escorted her inside, she glimpsed his Swedish heritage in every room. There were clean white walls and light blond wooden floors, with pale gray club chairs and a white L-shaped couch, the only color contrast being a black throw rug under the glass-and-chrome coffee table. Oh, and the black modern-looking fireplace that hung a foot off the floor, extending like a triangular mushroom at the end of a long black vent pipe anchored high up the wall.

His taste in art seemed to be heavily Asian influenced with the exception of one modern art, pen-and-ink drawing that looked like a Picasso knock-off.

The spotless kitchen matched the white of the rest of the house with the only contrast being stainless-steel appliances and some surprisingly colorful yellow-and-blue curtains. Could a guy get any more Scandinavian?

Truth was, Lilly liked it. It was clean and well kept,

and it said something about this man. He was proud of his heritage, just like she was proud of hers.

"Hey," he said. "While you make your newspaper entry, why don't I open a bottle of wine?"

Even amidst the ultramodern atmosphere, Gunnar had still managed to pull off a homey feel, and when he put logs in the fireplace, she decided a glass of wine in front of a real fire sounded fabulous.

"Sure."

She got right down to business logging into the newspaper before the midnight print deadline and posted her information, then called Bjork who wore many hats in the small twice-a-week paper operation, including final copy editor, layout manager and printer. The jobs Lilly would have to learn and do if she wanted to become a small-town newspaper mogul. By the time Gunnar had opened the bottle of Pinot Noir and placed two glasses on the table in front of the fireplace, she was ready to join him.

As bossy as he seemed at times, she'd discovered over dinner he was also fairly easygoing. He'd bent over backward to make her feel comfortable both at the restaurant and now here at his house, and she couldn't ever remember a guy doing that for her in San Francisco. The vibes back home had always been "show me what you got, impress me," both with her parents and her dates. Except for Sobo. She could always be herself with her grandmother.

Before she would take her first sip of wine, she thought about checking with the Heritage to see if the evacuation had ended. "I'm going to call the hotel for an update."

He didn't say anything, just let her do her task. When she'd finished, keeping the fact to herself that the alarm was now all cleared, she headed for the couch.

"What'd they say?"

"They're still checking things out." Oops, she'd already

broken her promise to be straightforward with him. Did little white lies in her favor count?

Gunnar had taken off his sport coat and unbuttoned the collar on his shirt, even slid out of his loafers, and now gestured for her to join him on the couch. It looked inviting to slide under his shoulder and strong arm, and on a snap decision, she accepted his offer and snuggled into the alluring spot.

"Wouldn't it be crazy if that false alarm was just another decoy for the person who set the brewery fire?" She couldn't help thinking out loud.

"No shop talk on dates."

She sat straight in order to look him in the eyes. "We're dating?"

His head rested on the back of the sofa, eyes closed. He didn't bother to open them. "Yes. We are. Get used to it."

Just like that? She'd asked him out for an apology dinner and the next thing she knew they were dating. She stared at his eyes, which refused to open. Back home she'd take offense at any man making assumptions about her status. For some crazy reason Lilly kind of liked the idea of dating the Swedish-American cop. Just for the sake of being contrary, she could call him a chauvinist for telling her what she was or wasn't doing with him, but for once she decided to just go with the Zen of Gunnar Norling.

She took a quiet breath and went back to snuggling by his side.

"So this is nice," he said, all nonchalant, obviously not realizing what a big deal this was for Lilly.

She sipped her wine. "Yes. Nice place." She toed off the heel of first one pump, then the other, then crossed her ankles and rested her heels on the table next to Gunnar's.

"I meant cuddling, but thanks. I designed and built the house with the help of Leif Andersen."

"My future landlord?" The guy with the house she hoped to rent, who also happened to be on that secret committee. She shouldn't take anything for granted but Daddy had always said, go for your dreams, big or small. Take them. Make them happen.

"Yeah, we designed it with two sets of plans. One for right now, which is what you see, and the next for when I want to expand."

"You mean like adding on?"

"Yeah, with a couple more bedrooms, another bathroom, a rumpus room…"

"What the heck's a rumpus room?"

A lazy smile stretched across his lips, his eyes were still closed. "Like a big family room, or a man cave. I haven't decided which it will be yet."

The more she learned about Gunnar the more she was impressed. Somehow, during the conversation about how long he'd been living here—five years but with plans to expand for what, a family?—and in between more sips of wine, she battled covetousness. She wanted a house of her own and to know exactly where she wanted to be and what she wanted to do with her life, just like Gunnar. To settle for something, instead of always striving for the next big dream. But so far all she had was a sketchy idea about wanting to own her own newspaper in a town she wasn't even sure she liked yet or fit into. A stepping-stone gig. And after that, what? A bigger paper? Another city? More fitting in? Who knew?

She drank the end of her wine and laid her head back on Gunnar's shoulder. Natural as can be he leaned down and kissed her. Not a hungry, crazy kiss like their first one, but a soft and comforting kiss, as if they were a couple who'd been dating awhile. And just like the Swedish comfort food, the kiss made her all warm inside. She relaxed into his now familiar mouth and let her thoughts drift away to a little island in her head known best for sexy slow kisses and expansive chests that welcomed her with strength and amazing pectoral muscles.

If this was what it was like to date Gunnar Norling, which he'd already assured her she was, she wanted to sign up for the whole package.

After they kissed for a while, like a gentleman he offered her another glass of wine, and because she felt so darn good from the first one, she accepted. Except she was really tired and experiencing carb overload from that huge dinner. When he got up to refill her glass he took a little too long, going to the bathroom first, and since she could hardly keep her eyes open…she…closed…them.

She'd been shanghaied to heaven.

Lilly woke up in a bed she'd never been in before—in a clean, midcentury, modern, Scandinavian-style bedroom. It was minimalist in design and decor, just like the rest of Gunnar's house. Pale gray walls with ink-washed Japanese prints in black frames lined the room. The same blond wooden floors as in the living room were covered in intricately patterned and muted-colored throw rugs, a white duvet draped over her on the bed with icy blue sheets. The A-framed bedroom ceiling had two large windows and the bed was positioned to look onto a hillside where pine trees and wild flowers grew. No need for curtains.

Little drills seemed to be working on her temples from all of the rich food, not to mention the vodka topped off with a glass of red wine she'd enjoyed last night. She heard clanking around outside the door, as if maybe Gunnar was opening cupboards and drawers in the kitchen. Something smelled great.

Streaks of daylight cut across her face. She squinted

and turned on her side in the big cozy bed. How had she wound up in Gunnar's bed? Or was this a guest room?

A tapping came from the door. "You decent?" Gunnar's smoky smooth voice said on the other side.

Was she decent? She hadn't a clue. She peeked under the covers, finding she was still completely dressed, thank the stars, but man, with all the wrinkles she'd have to ask Gunnar for the name of a good dry cleaner.

Good to know the guy was a gentleman.

More knocking. "Hello?" he said.

He was going the gentlemanly route this morning, too, knocking before entering. She wanted to pull her hair out in confusion about what exactly had gone on after that first kiss on the sofa last night.

Oh, right, she'd fallen asleep. *He wouldn't take advantage of me while I slept, would he? Completely dressed, remember?*

He tapped again.

She cleared her throat. "Sure. I'm *decent.*" *Whatever that means at this point.* "Come in." She tried to sound calm and upbeat, like yeah, sure, she was a modern woman who spent the night with all her dates.

So not true.

With cheeks and ears blazing hot, wondering how to handle things—feeling more like a lady who'd worn out her welcome after the first date—she waited for the godly and obviously well-mannered Gunnar to come into the room.

She sat in the center of his bed like a delicate water lily in a rippling blue-and-white pond, looking bewildered. He smiled at her widened eyes and mussed-up hair. Damn she was cute, even with raccoon-like makeup smudges under her eyes.

"Good morning," he said. Wolverine ran into the room before him and jumped on the bed with a thud.

"Ach!" She pulled the covers over her head again.

"Sorry. That's my cat." Who hadn't bothered to check in last night, but only showed up for food this morning.

She peeked over the top of the blanket. "Big boy."

"Yeah, he's what we call a Maine Coon cat. Weighs over thirty pounds. One false move and he'll lick off your face."

That didn't garner the kind of response he'd hoped for. She hadn't relaxed a bit, but slowly lowered the covers while staring down his big old gray tabby as if he was a bobcat. Looking at Wolverine, could he blame her?

He crossed the room carrying a breakfast tray with scrambled eggs topped with cheese and basil, a toasted and buttered English muffin, sliced tomatoes fresh from his yard and a mug of coffee.

"About last night, uh…" Getting right to the point she insinuated the rest of the question with those kissable pouty lips, as she reached for the coffee.

He placed the tray across her lap. Yeah, not many people knew he had a bed tray, but what the hell—he'd been known to go to great lengths to impress a girl.

She sipped nervously.

"Nope," he said. "Nothing happened."

The answer did what his cat couldn't—it changed her tense expression to one of tremendous relief. But it didn't stop there. Her pretty pointy features registered something along the lines of *Wow, this food looks and smells great, and I'm famished.* She put the mug down and reached for the fork.

"Thanks for breakfast."

"You're welcome."

"Gorgeous tomatoes."

"I grow them myself."

"Seriously?"

"Most definitely."

She dug in. He liked watching her. And he was still smiling.

Stopping midreach for the toast, she narrowed one of her eyes, sneaking a peek at him. "So we didn't get married or anything last night, I take it?" It was nice that she was lightening up.

"No, ma'am, we did not." He scratched the morning stubble on his cheek. "It's not every day a lady falls asleep in the middle of making out with me, though. I guess that's what I get for going to refill your wine." He poked the side of his cheek with his tongue. "Kind of hard on a guy's ego."

Alarm flew back into her gaze and the tips of her ears turned red. "I fell asleep after making out with you?"

"Frankly, judging by your enjoyment at the time, I'm surprised I have to remind you—" He raised his palm. "One moment you were kissing me like you meant it and after I come back with more wine, you're making these little purring sounds. At first I thought it was my cat, then I realized you were out cold."

"Are you serious?"

"I swear. Want me to cross my heart?"

"And that's all we did?"

"Honey, if I made a move on you, you'd remember every detail. I guarantee."

She started to breathe again, shook her head and finally picked up the fork, then played around with the eggs. He sat on the edge of the bed.

"I stayed up really late Thursday night covering the fire, then worked all day yesterday."

"Unlike me who got the day off so I could sleep?"

"You said it, not me."

"Gee, thanks, now I don't feel like such a failure putting you to sleep with my kisses."

"Oh, God. I hope you don't get the wrong impression, but, honestly, I'm not usually like that."

"A narcoleptic kisser?" Her list of titles kept growing—jaywalker, Tipsy Tina, narcoleptic kisser.

Her eyes nearly doubled in size. "How embarrassing." She shoved another bite of eggs into her mouth and chewed quickly. Her cheeks went pink and her ears lit up again.

"How'd I get in here?"

"I carried you."

Now she ate like she'd been doing gymnastics all night. Stuffing food into her mouth and avoiding his gaze.

His face must have given half of his thoughts away because Lilly suddenly looked suspicious as all hell. "The thing is, I don't remember anyone else in the bed…"

"I slept on the couch."

The tiny worry line between her brows softened. "Thank you for not undressing me."

"I have to admit I thought about it, only so you'd be more comfortable, you see, but even then it seemed too cheesy." He stretched out beside her on the bed, crossed his ankles and leaned on one elbow, took half of her toasted muffin and crunched into it. He stared at her making a silent promise that the first time they got undressed together would be something neither of them would ever forget.

Avoiding his gaze, and after a few more deliberate bites of breakfast, Lilly pushed the tray away. "Oh, man, this is embarrassing," she said. With her sudden move, Wolverine scrambled off the bed and headed for the living room.

Gunnar took her delicate hand and kissed the back of it. "No it isn't. You're an amazing woman, and if you were going to conk out anywhere in Heartlandia, I'm glad it happened at my house."

He put out a special unspoken invitation through his gaze, hoping she'd pick up on the meaning. If she felt like sticking around, the morning was young and the bed, which they just happened to be laying on, was ready for the taking. That is, if she was interested, now that she'd had a good night's sleep...

Instead, she hopped out from beneath the covers, suddenly all business, smoothing out her wrinkled clothes, searching for her shoes. "I'm pretty sure the hotel evacuation is all clear by now."

Disappointment hit like a punch to the solar plexus. He wasn't used to a lady being so hard to get. They'd had a nice date last night, called a truce on their argument, he'd brought her home so she didn't have to hang out in the cold on the street for who knew how many hours, and now this sudden need to get out of here.

Now that she was awake he'd had high hopes about his day off, but he was a man of honor, and if she wanted to go home, he'd take her there. Not the place he'd had in mind, but that's how life played out sometimes.

"Do you have to work today?" she asked.

"Not until the evening shift."

"Once I go home and shower and dress, would you mind taking me to see that guesthouse?"

"I'll give Leif a call. If he's around, then sure."

It wasn't the ideal way for his day to go, after seeing the vision of Morning Lilly in the middle of his bed, but he wasn't complaining about the chance to spend part of his day with a lady who'd rolled into town and held his undivided interest for going on two weeks.

Heck, in Gunnar's world, it was almost a new record.

Chapter Seven

Gunnar called Leif Andersen from the cell phone in his car while Lilly ran into the Heritage to shower and change clothes. He explained how Lilly was the new reporter in town and that she was looking for a permanent place to live. Surprisingly, Leif was available and not opposed to renting out his guesthouse, and agreed to meet Lilly and Gunnar at noon.

While he waited he thought how different Lilly was from his usual ladies. She was big city, big university, big cash—from her well-to-do parents—everything about her was big except her. *Chitcha*. She was petite and *sweet* when she let down her facade of urban tough chick. The more he got to know about her childhood disappointments and her tough-as-nails father, he liked her vulnerable side— she was someone he could relate to, someone who could understand him.

He liked helping her get settled in town, too, but most of all, he liked how it'd felt holding her in his arms last night and carrying her to his bed. If he got lucky, and they got to know each other better, if they trusted each other more that is, maybe the next time he carried her to his bed she'd be naked.

Once Lilly came barreling out of the hotel in jeans and yet another bright-colored sweater, this one kelly green, she caught him midgrin. To cover for his naughty thoughts, he scratched the corner of his mouth and suggested they take a drive out to the Ringmuren. The famous wall had been built by the Native Americans and the Scandinavian fishermen over three hundred years ago.

Once there, the photogenic wall gave her a spectacular view of the Columbia River, the Heartlandia basin, and also gave him a chance to spout a little history lesson he'd learned about the Chinook and his Scandinavian forefathers from his bookworm college professor sister, Elke.

"The Chinook people nursed the shipwrecked sailors back to health and taught them the secrets of hunting and fishing these waters. Back then, I guess the Columbia River could get really treacherous. In thanks, the Scandinavians, now calling themselves fisherman instead of sailors and who'd been bringing their families over from the homeland, helped the Chinook build the wall." Since he had her rapt attention he continued. "The purpose was to delineate the sacred Chinook burial ground for thousands of souls from the outer edge of town. And to this day, we still respect their land. The barrier has always been honored."

"This is amazing!" Lilly affirmed with her arms out, twirling around as if starring in her own version of *The Sound of Music*.

"I told you you'd like it up here."

"I'd like to do a column on Ringmuren."

"The city would love it."

Suddenly still and serious, she connected with his gaze. "Thank you for bringing me here. I can almost feel the

ancient souls in the air. Look, I'm getting goose bumps."
She pushed up one of her sweater sleeves to show proof.

Gunnar loved coming here, but he'd never gotten any
woo-woo feelings from it, just a deep sense of tranquility and renewed respect for the beauty of his hometown.
Lilly's gooseflesh made him feel like an underachiever.

Truth was she'd gotten him all worked up with her display of feelings, and since he only knew one way to process heady reactions like that, he went the physical route
and cupped her face, looked deeply into her eyes, then
dropped a simple kiss of appreciation on her lips.

Bam, there it was again, a kiss riding a zip line straight
through the electrical grid in his body. What was it about
Chitcha that got to him so quickly?

After he ended the kiss, she gazed up at him all dewy-
eyed with gratitude, and maybe with a little heat in the
depths of those dark brown eyes.

Instead of pushing for more, like he really wanted to, he
stepped back, letting her soak in the display of affection,
and to trust that he wasn't a single-minded guy. Though,
for the record she was certainly doing her part to turn him
into a single-minded guy. Only so she wouldn't get the
wrong idea, he'd fight off that part at every turn.

Luckily the honorable side of him, the side that set him
apart from his father, wanted Lilly to understand that he
knew how to take things slow, and how to be a companion
and a friend first. A damn good companion, too, especially
when it came to showing people around his hometown.

They stood there watching each other for a few more
moments, Gunnar admiring her porcelain-like complex-
ion and wanting to touch her more. The lingering morning
might have taken a different route if he hadn't glanced at
his watch. It was twenty to twelve, and Leif lived on the
other side of this mountain at the opposite end of town.

He grabbed Lilly's hand. "We've got to run if we want to make it to the house on time." Like a track star, Lilly, having worn far more sensible shoes today, kept up with his trot back to the car, and Gunnar only wished he'd parked a little farther away so he'd have the excuse to hold her hand longer.

At one minute to noon Gunnar pulled into the circular driveway of the most opulent house in Heartlandia.

The Andersen contracting company had been established by Leif's father fifty years ago. When his father developed debilitating arthritis and his parents moved to Sedona, Arizona, twenty years ago, Leif, a mere twenty-two years old at the time, had taken over the business with the help of his father's trusted foreman, who had since retired. Leif rode the wave of his father's success and doubled it, stepping into the twenty-first century as a competitive construction force to be reckoned with.

A hands-on guy, Leif had also found himself in the middle of the incident that had spawned the secret committee sorting through the contents of a buried trunk from an infamous sea captain, after he'd discovered it while breaking ground for the city college.

Lilly nearly gasped when they drove up the long and winding drive to the main house. "This is unbelievable!"

"Oh, it's real, Chitcha, all four thousand square feet of it."

"I can't wait to see the guesthouse." She clapped like an excited kid.

Gunnar had watched this house being built twelve years ago just before Leif got married. Most people started small and worked up to having their spectacular homes, but being in construction, he built the house of his wife's dreams right off.

A half-room-size bay window pushed out from the front

of the two-story, gray-and-white-painted contemporary house. Matching gables bookended the main house, with large windows everywhere, and balconies for every bedroom, of which there were four or five, Gunnar wasn't sure.

He had only been inside a few times, but was struck by the wide-open floor plan and pristine craftsmanship. The guy knew how to build top-notch homes.

Leif met them at the door dressed more like a contractor than a comfortably rich man. He wore jeans and a blue polo shirt that had seen better days with a misshapen collar half up and half folded at the back of his neck, like he'd just grabbed it out of the dryer and thrown it on. Trim as ever, his tanned arms wore the muscles earned from hard work when he reached for Gunnar's hand for a shake.

Leif's nearly white brows gave him the appearance of being world-weary, and his piercing blue eyes made Gunnar feel the guy was reading him, even the parts he wanted to keep hidden. But that must have been the skills a man picked up who'd lost all of the most precious people in his life—first his father, then his mother and then his beautiful wife.

"This must be Lilly," Leif said, offering his hand and giving a worked-at, dutiful smile.

"Hi." She stepped forward and gave a firm handshake, and to her credit Leif was an imposing figure.

"I hear you're looking for a place to call home?"

"Yes. I want to make Heartlandia home for now, and living in a hotel gets old really fast."

"Well, I don't know if this guesthouse will be convenient enough for you, it's a bit of a drive to downtown, and I'm fairly secluded up here."

She smiled. "I've commuted in San Francisco all my life, a winding drive through the hills is a piece of cake, and I like the idea of peace and quiet."

"Well, let me show you the place, then."

They followed Leif through his entryway and grand room and straight out French doors to a professionally landscaped yard beside a swimming pool complete with a mini waterfall. There was an overgrowth of gorgeous plants and flowers beside the pool, and the interlocking pavement pattern lead to a cozy path and a picture-perfect cottage.

This time, Lilly didn't hold back her gasp. "Oh, this is beautiful."

"It's completely furnished, but if the furniture doesn't suit you and you'd like to use your own, we can store it in the garage."

"I don't have any furniture, so that's great, but I'm afraid I won't be able to afford this cottage. What do you usually charge?"

"I've never rented it before, but money isn't an issue. We can work something out, all I'd ask is that you pay the utilities."

Lilly grabbed Gunnar's forearm and squeezed hard, her excitement radiating through her fingers. "What do you think is a fair price?"

"Just throw in a few extra bucks."

"Why so cheap?"

"You're a friend of Gunnar's. We Swedes stick together." For the first time, Leif gave an honest-to-goodness smile before winking at Gunnar.

Lilly smiled back. "I'll throw in the same amount I'm paying monthly at the Heritage, how's that?"

"Whatever that is, cut it in half." Case closed. Leif had spoken.

Lilly raised her brows, but being on the winning side of the decision like any smart person would do, she didn't argue. She accepted his kindness in stride by keeping her mouth closed and protests to herself, other than saying, "Thank you."

"You're welcome." He'd studied Lilly like he'd looked at Gunnar earlier, sizing her up and most likely deciding she'd passed his character test.

What wasn't to like about Lilly?

"By the way, I enjoyed that piece you wrote about animal services. My dogs have always come from shelters."

She looked flabbergasted that the man had read one of her articles. As she thanked him, Gunnar noticed Leif's comment was about the human interest story, not the headline news about the recent fire.

He was also stunned by the great deal Lilly was getting, and feeling pretty damn good about leading her to it. "Is there a side entrance?" Back to practicality, Gunnar was curious if he'd be able to come and go without Leif always seeing him. That is, if Lilly let him visit, which he seriously hoped would be the case. Often.

"Yes. She'll have her own private entrance and parking spot." Leif pointed to the right. "Over there." He unlocked the door and they entered a homey cottage with top-of-the-line amenities from ten years back—wood floors, granite countertops and upgraded appliances in the kitchen, and a doorless shower in the bathroom alongside a soaking tub. There was an abundance of windows throughout the four rooms with views of foliage, hillsides and even a glimpse of the Columbia River in the distance from over the sink in the kitchen.

"Sold. I'd like to rent this on the spot," Lilly said.

"But you haven't even seen the bedroom." Gunnar couldn't think of anything practical to say, he just wanted to make sure Lilly wasn't making too snap of a decision. Though, as far as he was concerned, he was right there with her on the sold part. The place was perfect for a single lady. Thinking like a cop though, there were things to consider, like would she feel safe here all secluded and alone? And on other fronts, would the winding hillside commute get old? Would she feel out of the pulse of the city, and wasn't that important for a journalist?

Maybe when they were alone she'd want to bounce some of those issues off him. Get his feedback, but unless asked, Gunnar would leave the decision completely up to her.

Leif opened the double doors to the single bedroom and Lilly emitted another gasp.

"How did you know what my dream bedroom was?" There she went again, acting as if the hills were alive with the sound of music.

It wasn't a huge room, but spacious enough for a queen-size bed, a desk, a loveseat and chaise lounge, and French doors out to a private patio complete with a small wrought-iron table and chairs, and a trellis overrun with morning glories.

"This is heaven!"

"You'll have to arrange for cable TV and internet access. We get good cell phone reception out here, though."

"Mr. Andersen, if you are willing to rent this to me, I would love to move in right away."

"Sure. Let me get my cleaning staff in today, and as far as I'm concerned it's yours tomorrow."

"Don't I need to sign anything?"

"Gunnar's vouching for you. That's all I need."

And that was that.

Gunnar had to fight off all of Lilly's hugs and kisses as they drove back down the hill, and he loved every second of it. She squealed like a teenager meeting a rock star, and thanked him over and over again for suggesting the place. He grinned and laughed all the way back to the Heritage, quickly forgetting his concerns. Surely Leif had state-of-the-art surveillance for his home, she'd be safe up there secluded and cut off from the rest of the city.

"I've got to get to work, but how about I meet you around ten tomorrow, and we can load up all of your stuff and move you in?"

Once they were out of the car and on the sidewalk, she rushed him like a contestant on a shopping-contest show. Her arms encircled him and held him tight. "Thank you, thank you, thank you, Gunnar. You're a prince. I've never been more excited about living somewhere in my life."

He laughed, receiving a contact high from her joy mixed with a few typical guy-type reactions stirring inside whenever touched by the pretty lady. "Every once in a while I come up with great ideas. I'm glad I could help."

Her arms moved upward from his middle to around his neck. She pulled him down to connect with her mouth, and without another thought, they both showed how glad they were to know each other with some major lip gymnastics and tongue contortions. She kissed great under normal circumstances, but wow, right now flying high from renting her new place, she made out phenomenally, working his blood from simmering to nearly boiling in record time.

Too bad they were once again in the middle of the sidewalk with Saturday-morning tourists and residents zipping by all around them. Too bad he had to go get ready for work, because he had it in his mind to sweep Lilly up and carry her into the elevator and right up to her room so she could show him exactly how much she appreciated his helping her find her dream cottage. Not that that had been the reason he'd done it.

But she broke up the kiss in the middle of his fantasy, looking as ruffled up and titillated as he felt. Good to know they were on the same page in that department. "I'll see you tomorrow at ten, then, okay?"

He needed a second to get his thoughts together before he could respond. "Sure."

She popped another quick kiss on his overstimulated lips. "Thank you with all of my heart."

The sincerity oozing from her eyes cut through his chest forming a warm pool beneath his breastbone. "You're welcome, Lilly," he said, really meaning it.

It seemed as if she wanted to say a lot more, but now wasn't the time or place, and when she finally did get around to telling him exactly how she felt, he wanted to be alone with her, and in a place where she could take all the time she needed.

"Now I've got shopping to do!"

"See you tomorrow," he said, smiling, and with his feet seeming incredibly light, he walked back to his car.

Careful, Norling. Don't be such a pushover with this lady who might just throw you under the bus for a good news story.

Chapter Eight

Lilly waited eagerly for Gunnar to show up Sunday morning. She'd spent the rest of yesterday afternoon shopping for items she'd need in her new place. Sheets. Towels. Bathroom rugs. A set of ceramic dishes and flatware, service for four. Because her bank account was already feeling the strain, and there was no way she'd ask her parents for a loan, she'd bought the bare minimum of pots and pans. After she moved in she'd hit the grocery store and stock up on food.

At five minutes before ten there was a knock at her door. She'd already discovered that Gunnar was a stickler about being on time, and her type A personality liked that about him. But that wasn't all she liked about him—he was proving to be an all-around great guy. Her hunch that he put a lot of effort into making up for his dad's wrong deeds had panned out. She'd hit a raw and exposed nerve when she'd written about it in the news article. To offset the imbalance, she'd exposed to Gunnar more about her own insecurities and the messed-up relationship she'd had with her father over dinner than she'd shared with most of her good friends the entire time growing up. Understanding his sense of dishonor made her less ashamed about her own situation. In her opinion, they were good for each other.

"Coming!" She swung the door wide and allowed a moment or two to take him all in. He'd come ready for work in old jeans and a nearly threadbare T-shirt that hugged his torso and put all kinds of ideas into her head. If she got lucky, maybe he'd offer himself as a housewarming present.

She'd gotten used to his always-serious eyes, looking as if they drilled right through her, but it knocked her a bit sideways when he came bearing a smile, like this morning—his idea of a smile, anyway. His version was kind of like a grammar-school class picture, a bit forced yet still genuine.

"Do I need to feed you before we get down to business?" he asked, always on task, wanting to do the right thing.

"Nope. I ate some cereal."

He leaned in for a quick cheek buss. "Good morning."

When he pulled back, she followed suit dropping a light kiss on his lips. "Morning."

After the kiss, those intense eyes eased up, taking on a playful glint and maybe something more. "I wish I could help you all day, but my shift begins at three. You'll just have to use me while you can."

She could think of ways to "use" him right now, but that wasn't the plan. "I don't have that much to move." She'd organized her things into a few significant piles: kitchen items, bedroom items, clothes, more clothes, bathroom items. "I lucked out that the place came furnished."

"Absolutely. Okay." He clapped his hands, all business. "I borrowed my buddy Kent's pickup truck so we should be able to get most of this stuff moved in one trip."

"I'll put all the clothes in my car."

"Will you be able to see out the windows?"

She delivered a frisky punch to his arm. He acted as if it hurt. "I'm just being practical here."

And that was another thing, since when had she ever been this playful with a guy before?

After several trips up and down the elevator, sneaking sexy smiles whenever they passed in the hallway, the truck was full and so was her car and amazingly, nothing of hers was left in the extended-stay hotel room.

After the last item was put in place, Lilly tugged the air. "Yes!"

Gunnar slid on his serious-as-hell sunglasses, the kind that made him look like a motorcycle cop holding a grudge. "Let's hit the road."

"I've got to check out first, but I'll meet you up there."

A half hour later, she used the key to her very own cottage and they reversed their duties from the hotel. By one o'clock, not only had they brought every last item inside, but they'd almost had the kitchen and bathrooms set up. What a team.

She tossed her new sheets onto the mattress.

Gunnar's eyes lit up. "Those are nice."

She glanced at the mauve-colored sheets. "I found all this stuff at Helga's Home and Hearth. What a cute little department store."

"Yeah, we pride ourselves on not allowing the big chain stores into Heartlandia, so folks like Helga have a fighting chance to keep their doors open."

"I could have bought a lot more, but I decided to wait and see what else I'll need." She'd run out of money and refused to ask her father to spot her a loan. He'd never let her hear the end of it. *You're thirty years old and still can't manage your finances.*

Before she could make her bed, Gunnar flopped onto the mattress and flapped his arms and legs, sort of like making snow angels without snow. "This feels good. You should try it."

She wasn't sure what came over her, maybe it was the fact that Gunnar had bent over backward to help her find this place and move her in, that he was the most decent guy she'd met in a decade and that, well, he was sexy as hell. Most important, she liked him, she really liked him. But she crawled onto the bed, catlike, until she looked down on his face, then hiked up one leg and slowly moved her hands and knees on both sides of his body.

On reflex, his hands went to her waist as he looked her dead-on in the eyes, communicating they weren't horsing around anymore, that her climbing over him like that was as serious as sex in the afternoon.

The message he sent both scared and excited her, and she didn't want to let this chance pass her by. She made a half pushup pose, lowering her face to his, and kissed him with the intent of exploring every possibility. Her breasts pushed against his solid chest as his hands found her hips and edged her flush to his lap. She'd worn shorts today, and his palms made a pattern over her rump and down the sensitive skin on the backs of her thighs. The gesture made her skin wake up with prickles.

They kissed like that first night, though this time they were fueled completely by each other and not beer. She let all her weight drop onto him, amazed how spectacular he felt. His hands continued an exotic exploration, caressing areas she'd never thought of as erogenous zones before, but under his touch, oh, yeah, every little curve and canyon apparently was.

Slipping under her top, his fingertips kitten walked across her back, making her contort with tingly pleasure. As their kisses deepened, and their breathing grew more ragged, his hands grew rougher, kneading her skin, pulling her tight to him, making her fully aware of his complete reaction to her.

Totally out of character, she broke away from his kiss, straddled his hips and pulled her top up and over her head. That smile returned to his face, looking nothing like a grammar school kid, but more like a man intent on having his way with her. Her excitement kicked up a notch, nerve endings tightened, she was ready for anything as heat pooled between her hips.

Gunnar sat up to do the honors of removing her bra. She was far from busty, but the way he looked at her made her feel like the most perfect woman on earth. She grabbed his cheeks and kissed him hard, enjoying the feel of the tips of her breasts rubbing against his old worn-out and scratchy T-shirt. But she wanted to feel his skin and, like magic, and with excellent teamwork, his shirt disappeared.

Heat radiated from his skin and she rubbed tight against the dusting of hair on his chest as they made out like ravenous lovers. His hands covered every part of her in their never-ending explorations. The warm pool in her center coursed down between her legs, readying her for him. Still straddling him, she moved over his erection beneath his jeans. Strong as steel, his wedge thrilled her, but their clothes were in the way and something needed to be done about that.

An attentive lover, Gunnar read her mind and soon made sure that first her shorts then his jeans both disappeared. She finished by pulling off her thong while watching him release his fully extended self from his briefs. The sight instantaneously became tattooed in her mind. He literally took her breath away with his muscles and sinew and full erection, and she needed to feel him again. It was his turn to crawl onto the bed and she went back on her elbows welcoming him.

She dropped back her head when he found her breasts, kissing and taunting them with his tongue while his fullness prodded her belly. She clung to his back and repositioned herself to capture his erection between her thighs, savoring the smooth steely feel of him.

The kissing never stopped as their bodies heated to near boiling point. He probed with his fingers, gently opening her, making sure she was ready for him. Hell yeah, she was. She bucked underneath him, impatient to feel him inside.

He came up from a particularly exciting kiss, a questioning look on his face. "Do you have condoms?"

"I think you know the answer to that," she said, remembering that glint in his eye when he'd noticed her little naughty box in the cart at the market the other night.

"They'd come in handy right now, right?" He grabbed and kissed her before she could protest.

She pointed, speaking over his lips. "They're in that box labeled Bathroom."

He zipped to the box, ruffled through the items inside until he found the box labeled "ribbed with heating lubrication for extra pleasure."

On the condom went and after another rough and hungry kiss, Gunnar entered her one blissfully consuming inch at a time.

Soon they were completely lost in each other, taunting, teasing, pleasing and generally driving each other crazy. Slowly but steadily over several minutes their lovemaking built to a frenzy and onward to the most unbelievably intense orgasm Lilly had ever experienced.

She gasped and clung to him, the sensations surging inside her and fanning across her entire body in tingling heat waves as he made another powerful thrust accompanied by a groan, then he followed her off the cliff to free-fall into paradise.

After a moment's reprieve, he rolled onto his side, still tucked deeply inside her, and brought her along with him as if she was weightless—which she pretty much was seeing that she'd essentially catapulted out of her body with the thrill he'd just provided. Once he caught his breath, he said the one word that would keep Lilly flying for days to come.

"Wow."

She wanted to jump up and dance around the bed saying yes, yes, yes! Never before in her adult life had she made a man say wow after having sex. Granted she'd only dated a few guys, and her experience was very limited, but still…

As far as her end of the deal went, well, for a journalist she should have been able to come up with something better than "Double wow," but at least it made her point, and Gunnar seemed to like it.

There was that bright grammar-school grin crossing his face again, but this time with the addition of blue-ribbon pride for outstanding athletic performance.

Chapter Nine

Gunnar hated that he'd had to leave Lilly naked in her bed in order to shower and leave for work on time Sunday, but he never missed work unless a hospital or doctor's diagnosis demanded it. Sure, it was part of "making up for the past" but it also was because of his total respect for the job and his fellow officers. His sister had once accused him of being married to his job, and truth be told, he didn't argue with her. For the past ten years, being a cop was as much his identity as being a Norling.

Monday he stopped by Greta's Garden and bought a Kalanchoe indoor flowering plant for Lilly that Greta promised anyone could care for. Though he enjoyed growing his own vegetables, he didn't have a clue whether Lilly had a green or black thumb, so he went with easy care and surefire blooming. Plus the planter was made by a local potter and the flowers on the plant were small but bright pink and reminded him of Lilly.

In his experience with women, he knew they liked to be thought of after the big night, or afternoon in their case. Buying flowers may be general etiquette where Gunnar and dating were concerned, but this plant, designed to last, seemed different. It made him think of Lilly and new possibilities, and that made him smile until he started to squirm at what those possibilities might be. Trusting someone was paramount for being together. At this point, Lilly still had some proving to do, but that didn't stop him from being a gentleman about their first time together.

She wasn't at her desk when he delivered the gift on his way into work that afternoon.

"I sent her out to the college to cover the story about the search for an artist to paint the city college mural," Bjork said.

Gunnar knew the administrative board of the college and the city council had agreed to hire an artist to tell the history of Heartlandia in pictures on the college campus walls. It would be a huge undertaking, and if Leif Andersen hadn't contributed bucket loads of cash, either the project wouldn't have moved forward, or they'd have had to settle for a local artist or the art majors at the college to complete the task. Who knew what quality of art that would have turned out? Last he'd heard they were down to a handful of finalists from all across the nation.

"Then she said something about interviewing a guy who raises free-range chickens after that," Bjork said.

It sounded as if Lilly's day was completely booked up. Gunnar packed away his disappointment at not seeing her, and scribbled out a quick note—"Lunch tomorrow? G."—then headed for his department and signed in for duty.

On Tuesday he took Lilly to his favorite lunch place, the Hartalanda Café. It was right across the street from their building, so they could walk over. She knocked him dead in a smart-looking business dress that he guessed would pass for sophisticated back in San Francisco. It had fine black plaid on the bottom with the top half being cream-colored with lacy trim and black pearl buttons down the front. He dug the schoolmarm-style collar, especially after knowing what a wild kitten Lilly had turned out to be in bed. Plus she wore a thin cardigan in an odd shade of green with pushed up sleeves and a little flare out at the bottom since it was end-of-summer cool and overcast.

When he first saw her, a weird dip deep inside his chest made him pause. Then she gave a bright smile that matched the pink flush on her cheeks, and he forgot about the odd sensation, having become completely wrapped up in her. He leaned in and kissed her, setting off a cascade of memories that they'd made so far, and after that the first-time-seeing-each-other-since-making-love nerves vaporized.

"Did you know they're down to choosing from four famous artists for the city college mural?" she asked as they walked to the diner.

"I haven't been keeping track, but I'll be sure to read your article to stay up-to-date."

She grinned at his subtle message reminding her they'd made a pact not to talk shop with each other. If he let her talk about her stories, she'd expect him to share about his job, and that might be a conflict of interest, plus it could overtake their time together. He wasn't going to let that happen, not if he wanted to get to know Lilly, the real Lilly, even better.

The waitress sat them immediately, since she'd been saving Gunnar's favorite table for him. He didn't need to look at the menu, so he sat back and enjoyed the view of Lilly in decision mode perusing the daily choices. She wound up asking the waitress to recommend something and went with the soup of the day—Scandinavian summer soup, even though early fall was already upon them, and half a turkey sandwich.

After the story on *husmanskost* came out in the newspaper Monday, word was people in town looked forward to having their establishments featured, too. In his opinion, the Hartalanda Café was deserving of a public review, but he'd let Lilly make that decision.

"My sobo sent me some seaweed so I wanted to invite you over for dinner Thursday for sushi, since you're off."

"Remind me who Sobo is again?"

"Oh, sorry. My grandmother."

"Ah, how nice of her to send you seaweed."

"Don't make fun. She wants to make sure I don't forget my roots."

"Can we make that Friday?" He had another special meeting on Thursday night and didn't want her to know. Elke had been visiting Ben Cobawa in the hospital while he recovered from his second-degree burns and smoke inhalation, and had been discussing her findings from the journals. With Ben's help she'd figured out approximately where the buried treasure might be located and she wanted to run it by everyone, so they were having an emergency meeting.

"You have another hot date Thursday?" she asked in a playful, teasing manner.

"Uh, I've got something I have to do."

She lifted one pert brow but didn't say a word. He wished he could tell her why, but knew she'd been asking around about the committee meetings. The last thing he wanted was to leak the story after all their efforts to control the information.

"Okay. Friday," she said, not pursuing the point. Surprising him.

After a great lunch, he found a tree they could stand under to hug, since it had started to drizzle. Lilly smelled like roses and expensive soap, and he inhaled deeply when he snuggled into her neck. He'd missed holding her, and from the way she was hugging back, maybe she'd missed him, too? The thought made him grin.

They glanced into each other's eyes, hers sparking with intent, before sharing a kiss, this one a real kiss, not one of those flimsy hello deals. Nope, this was a "Welcome back, where've you been?" kiss. Man, he'd been waiting ever since Sunday for it, too, and she didn't disappoint.

There was something about Lilly's mouth fitting perfectly with his that sent him on a sexy mental detour every time they kissed. And she nested right into his arms, as if she belonged there. He needed to watch himself or he'd be falling for this one, and…well, while kissing her he couldn't think of any reason why that would be a bad thing. But usually where women were concerned, it always got sticky down the line. They'd start complaining about his job taking up too much of his time, and he'd begin to think they weren't nearly as amusing as he'd thought in the beginning.

"Lunch tomorrow?" he asked.

"Okay. Can I pick the place?"

"Sure."

"Then let's go to Lincoln's Place."

"I love that place."

"I'm thinking about writing an article about how he came to Heartlandia, and why he likes it here."

"That'd be a great idea. Oh, and sometime you should think about interviewing his pianist, Desi Rask, too. She's got an interesting story."

Lilly nodded. "I'll make a note of that."

"Well, I've got to get back. We're working some burglary jobs related to the cruise ships."

"Hmm," she said, sudden interest gleaming in her gaze.

"I wonder why Borjk doesn't keep a police radio scanner in the office. We miss out on all of the interesting stories."

"Probably has to do with the fact we'd arrest him if he did for using information he's heard on it for personal gain—i.e. the newspaper."

"Ah, okay, so I learned something new today."

"You can pop into the department anytime and ask to see the police log, though."

"I can?"

"Sure. Hey." He reached for and held her shoulders to look square into her eyes. "I learned something new today, too." He tugged her close for a hug. "I miss you when you're not around."

Her body language showed she liked that, as she held and hugged him back. "How much longer are you working evenings?"

"Another week, then I'll be back on days."

She kissed him lightly. "Good. I get lonely in that cottage all by myself at night."

"Leif isn't good company?"

"He's more like a ghost. Sometimes I see him standing at his big old bay window staring out toward the river for a really long time."

"He's been through a lot."

"Well, you know me, I want to know the story. And why isn't a man like him married?"

"I told you he was, didn't I? Or I meant to."

"Really?" She wiped the quizzical look off her face when she noticed Gunnar's disapproving gaze. "Yeah, I know that's none of my business."

"It's not like it's a secret. His wife died about two or three years ago from cancer. He built that house for her, now has to live without her. I'm surprised he stays there. Don't know if I could."

"Wow. That's sad."

"Yeah." It was time to lighten things us. "By the way, the whole town already knows that story so don't get any ideas."

She socked his chest halfheartedly. "Can't I find out about my landlord?"

"Sure you can, just don't print it."

"Besides, I've got half a dozen human interest stories lined up for the next few days." She ignored his jab. "I'll be learning how to make cheese with the Svendsen brothers tomorrow morning, and Hilde Pilkvist promised to demonstrate collecting wool from sheep, dyeing, spinning and weaving it at Hannah's Handmade Sweaters." She tossed him a glance showing her frustration. "Not everything's a story for the newspaper, Gunnar. I know that."

Now he'd ticked her off, and he hated ending their lunch on a bad note so he kissed her until she quit squirming and started kissing him back. Then her cell phone rang, and she broke away from the kiss. "That's my father's ringtone. I've got to answer."

He needed to get back on the job anyway, so he kissed her forehead and took off. "Good luck," he said over his shoulder.

Thursday night, Gunnar thought he saw something in the bushes while heading from his meeting at city hall. He shook his head when he added up the probabilities. Lilly. Did she really think she could get answers from hiding in the bushes?

He walked Gerda Rask and his sister to their respective cars, noticing Lilly's red two-door way at the end of the parking lot. Did she really think he wouldn't notice? What kind of a cop did she think he was? Once the ladies had both left the lot, he got an idea.

Feeling perturbed about Lilly's snooping around after he'd specifically asked her not to, he strode to his car, which was near the bushes, and made a fake phone call, talking extra loud. "Yeah, the information we got tonight will blow your mind. I'm heading over there right now." Then he got into his undercover police car and started the engine and drove extra slowly out of the parking lot to give Lilly time to get in her car and follow him. At least that was his cheesy plan, and what do you know, surprisingly, she bit.

He'd been using the undercover unit while working the cruise-line-burglary case, and had been up so late last night he'd driven it home. He'd planned to trade it in for his own car after the emergency meeting tonight, but now that Lilly was trailing him—just like he'd planned—he decided to hold off.

He made a wicked grin, turned onto an isolated road ready for a game of cat and mouse, and headed for his favorite secluded beach. Lilly tailed him all the way along the high cliff roads and turning into the hillside canyons. What could she possibly think she could find out? Was she expecting a secret meeting of the local wizard coven or something?

In his gut, he didn't feel comfortable leading her on a wild-goose chase—in fact he kind of felt like a pompous jerk. Here he was concerned he couldn't trust her, and then he pulls a stunt like this. What if she thought he was mocking her? That wouldn't exactly help them learn to trust each other, but at this point he'd have a lot of explaining to do no matter what he did. This wasn't right. What the hell had he been thinking? He decided to put an end to this little caper and come clean.

Gunnar made a snap decision to take a turnout just around a tight bend and take the consequences. He deserved them. He planned to turn around and stop her, put an end to his little game. He'd confront her on why she insisted on breaking a big story about the secret committee when she had all these really great stories lined up with the locals. *Give it up*, he'd tell her. *You're not going to find out anything from me.*

It seemed like a good enough plan, anyway.

Except when he made his U-turn and got back out onto the road, she'd already passed where he'd turned out and was heading farther up the secluded coastal road.

She sure wasn't very good at trailing people. She'd made a completely wrong turn and would end up on a dark dirt road to nowhere if he didn't stop her. Thinking fast, he put on his police lights and sped up behind her. There wasn't any place to pull over, so she stopped dead in the middle of the narrow road.

He brought his heavy-duty flashlight along and got out of the car. Lilly stayed in her car, using common sense and probably big-city precautions. Good thinking.

Between the flashing undercover police-unit lights and his flashlight, he could tell she was staring straight ahead and was ticked off. His heart sank a little thinking he'd given her a fright. Sometimes he came up with bonehead ideas. Now he'd have to fix the fallout.

He tapped on her window. She cautiously turned her head. "It's Gunnar. Open your door."

"No."

"It's me. Come on. At least open your window."

"No. You lied to me."

Oh yeah, she was pissed, but not about what he thought she'd be angry about—his playing a juvenile game on her. She'd homed in on the fact he'd never been straight with her about his involvement in the secret meetings, even when she'd asked him point-blank at the bar that first night.

Truth was, it wasn't her business. She'd find out when the rest of Heartlandia found out, but now he needed to deal with the situation at hand.

"I hardly knew you then, and you were being too nosy."

Finally she turned on him, and between his flashlight and her facial expression, the picture wasn't pretty. Anger turned her normally lovely features into sharp lines and shadowed angles, reminding him of the Japanese folklore ghosts called *yurei* he'd often read about.

Through the closed car window she sounded muffled, yet he understood every single word. "You lied, and you continue to lie. And now you tried to scare me and trick me, and make me feel foolish. And I especially don't appreciate your taking me on a wild-goose chase."

She put her car in gear and drove off leaving Gunnar standing in the road kicking himself for his insensitivity. He'd really screwed up; now what the hell was he supposed to do to make things better?

One thing was for sure, he knew she was heading to a dead end and didn't have a clue how to find her way home from this location. He also knew this was the only way in and out of this particular canyon and she'd have to retrace her path straight to him. Moonlight dappled the surface of the Columbia River as it lapped the rocky shoreline, and he waited for Lilly to return so he could grovel and beg for her forgiveness.

Less than five minutes later, her headlights came barreling down the bumpy road. He'd turned his car around while he waited, so he jumped inside and with his flashing lights led the way for her out of the canyon. He switched them off when they drove across town straight to her cottage door. Once there, he waited for her to park and get out of her car, then he jumped out of the cruiser when she approached.

Lilly's furious expression clued him that he was still in deep doo-doo.

She socked him in the chest. Unlike usual, this one was meant to hurt but fell far short of the mark. He'd need to teach her some defense techniques for her safety.

"I'm not a game. How dare you humiliate me."

"I'm sorry. I messed up." Admitting his stupid mistake seemed like the only tack to take.

The admission made her pause a half beat but she recouped quickly, anger coloring her disposition.

Gunnar stepped in front of her, and tensed his muscles in preparation for another sock, but she didn't hit him. "I'm not a game, either," he said. "You can't know everything I'm involved in, and you just have to accept that for now."

"That was a dirty trick, Gunnar. You made me feel like an idiot."

Ah, jeez, he'd messed up beyond what he'd thought, made her feel like an idiot, never his intention, and he didn't have a clue what to do. Daring to gaze at her, he had a hunch there was more on her mind than his taking her on a detour for his own amusement. Her usual good-sport attitude had evaporated somewhere back in that dark canyon and maybe she wanted, no, needed, to talk about it.

"You're not an idiot. Couldn't be if you tried."

She folded her arms and huffed, studying the ground as if it was covered with diamonds or something.

He could wait it out. No matter how strong his urge to comfort her was, instinct told him to give her a chance to open up. But, ah jeez, her eyes were welling up and she bit her lower lip to fight off the tears. And since he was the source of her tears of humiliation he wanted to kick his own ass. "I'm the idiot. Not you."

She'd launched off into another time, it seemed, as she

looked over his shoulder and stared at the poolside waterfall.

"No one can make me feel like an idiot like my father. No one." She wiped away the first wave of tears spilling over her lower lids with a shaky hand. "I could never do anything right enough for him. No matter how hard I tried, he'd find the flaw somewhere, someway." She shook her head. "He was big on teaching me lessons. Showing me the error of my ways. Humiliating me. And he didn't give a damn who was around to hear or see it, either." She took a deep breath, held it then blew it out. "When I graduated in the top ten percent in my high school class, he wanted to know why I wasn't in the top three percent. When I got accepted to one of my top two university choices, he wondered why I couldn't get into an Ivy League university, then said it must have been because of my SAT scores. When I landed a job at the *San Francisco Gazette*, he asked why I didn't try for the *Chronicle*." She pressed her palms against her temples. "I have racked my brain and cannot ever once remember him praising me."

Gunnar wanted to hunt down Lilly's father and coldcock him right here and now. But more so, he wanted to rip his own heart out for bringing on this walk down nightmare lane because of his stupid and careless actions.

"I've been so wrapped up in all of these local folks' interviews for the newspaper," she said "I'd forgotten about your stupid meetings. But my dad called yesterday."

Gunnar remembered the cell phone call that interrupted their most excellent kiss after lunch.

"It took him less than ten seconds before he asked when I was going to break my big story. Then I realized I'd gotten off track." For the first time she nailed Gunnar with her tortured gaze. "I tried to tell him about all of these wonderful interviews I've been doing, but he reminded me that nothing should derail my goals. Nothing. Then I remembered you'd said you were busy tonight, and I put two and two together. Followed you. And where did it lead? To you teaching me a lesson.".

"That wasn't my plan, Lilly, I swear. I just wanted to mess with you for snooping around. I didn't know how… How could I know?" He stepped closer, wrapped her in his arms in apology. She didn't fight it, and he was grateful. "I really am the idiot."

"My father was the master of teaching by humiliation. I don't need that junk from the man I'm dating."

Oh, man, he'd pegged her so completely wrong. Her tough big-city-woman persona was nothing but a shield for a vulnerable girl, and his desire to protect and serve had never been stronger.

"I'm sorry. I'm so, so sorry." He hugged her tight, wishing he could take back the past hour, trying desperately to make things better. Hell-bent on being the opposite of his father, he'd acted nothing short of a bully tonight, apparently just like Lilly's father. It would never happen again. Ever. "I'm sorry, Chitcha, please forgive me."

The soldier-like tension in her body relaxed. She leaned into his chest and rested her head on his shoulder. "I shouldn't have been following you. I wasn't even that interested."

He kissed the top of her head. "Agreed. You absolutely shouldn't have been following me. So no more games, okay?"

"No more games." She looked up.

"No more snooping?"

"No more secrets?"

"Touché," he said just before capturing her mouth for a long and tender kiss as they stood under the light of the perfect half-moon. He was in a sticky situation being on a committee that Lilly was dying to find out about, and just now promising not to keep secrets. How was he supposed to juggle that double-edged sword and not get injured, or worse yet, injure her?

Soon, the kiss heated up and his body stirred. Lilly must have felt the same way. She broke up their heady outdoor make-out session, took Gunnar by the hand and, without the need for another word, led him to her door.

On the way, he thanked his lucky stars for makeup sex.

Chapter Ten

Things were going great with Gunnar. Even though he'd taunted Lilly like a child that Thursday night—she'd gotten her feelings hurt, gotten furious and in his face, recalling far too many bad memories—he'd apologized like a prince and the next thing she knew she'd invited him in and they were having makeup sex. The next night he'd sung praises over her homemade sushi, even though she knew she'd done a mediocre job compared to her sobo. They'd gone out for breakfast on Saturday before he went to work, and Sunday he'd driven her to interview a fascinating young woman named Desi Rask. Of course that gave Gunnar the excuse to visit with his best friend, Kent, and his son, while she did. He'd spent the next week showing her around the county like she was an out-of-town relative. And she'd loved every minute.

Falling for him would change her focus in town. Her father had warned her about that. She could think of a million reasons why she shouldn't get involved with him while she was at work and out from under his spell, and that's pretty much what she'd decided he did whenever they were together—spin some kind of magic. They'd been dating almost four weeks, the longest relationship she'd ever had.

Sad but true.

Her parents' faces popped into her head, looking tenser and tenser. Gunnar wasn't her goal. He wasn't the reason she'd come to Heartlandia. She needed to stay focused on her plan to own and run her own newspaper. Having a relationship with the police sergeant would only complicate things.

So why was she smiling and going all gooey inside thinking about how he liked to snuggle with her while they slept, and how no man had ever used her nickname from her grandmother before—Chitcha—until Gunnar. It scared her how drawn she was to him, all of him, not just his made-for-work body, and his no-nonsense attitude, but his down-home personality and surprising gentle side, too.

She shook her head, as if that might jiggle some sense into her brain, and stared at the computer screen on her desk.

Over the past couple of weeks Gunnar had taken it upon himself to be her own personal guide around Heartlandia. Through the point of view of someone who'd lived here all his life, she'd developed a new respect and fondness for the place. What worried her the most was how much she genuinely wanted to be friends with the townsfolk, and how easily they accepted her. Which was a very foreign feeling coming from her family background. Some of her greatest ideas for articles came while touring the out-of-the-way spots in town with Gunnar. Yet she remained a little homesick for her sobo.

All mixed up with these mostly good feelings, she stared at her desk computer in the newspaper office, nearly squirming in her chair from the lack of inspiration that Monday morning. How could she make her mark at the

Herald? The most feedback she'd gotten was when she wrote stories about the locals. The townsfolk never seemed to get enough of those kinds of stories. Plus, she'd been told by a couple of the cruise-liner captains that they'd started buying and distributing to their guests her stories as a point of reference while touring Heartlandia.

Emil Ingersson had told her just the other day that his tourist trade had almost doubled since she'd written the article about his bread factory on the outskirts of town. How he'd had to hire a couple of the local housewives to help serve the samples and collect the sales. In fact, his monthly production had increased by a quarter, and he pointed to Lilly as the reason.

Since she'd shared Desdemona Rask's interesting tale of returning home to a family she never knew she had, Lilly'd heard that Lincoln's Place was packed on the weekend when she played piano there. And that Desi's estranged father had become her biggest fan.

She smiled, remembering how she'd choked up hearing about Desi's search for her father and the loss of her Heartlandia-born mother. She wondered what it would be like to have a special relationship with her father, for her father to be her biggest supporter. As if that could ever happen.

But she could pat herself on the back for other reasons. Truth was since she'd become the main reporter, the newspaper subscriptions had definitely increased, and deep in her heart she knew it wasn't because of Borjk's boring op-eds. But her father had always told her to remain humble in personal achievement, to never settle and always strive for more.

She'd wanted to tell him the last time they'd spoken on the phone how excited she was about the newspaper's recent surge, but knew it wouldn't be enough. He wouldn't get it, not something that subtle. Until she purchased the paper, she'd keep her mini steps of success to herself.

Sobo's soft-featured face came to mind, and Lilly had a yearning to make sushi with her. Maybe she'd share a personal profile about her roots and influences with the people of Heartlandia. Suddenly her fingers flew over the computer keyboard: I Dream of Sushi in Storybook Land. An Outsider's Perspective of Heartlandia.

Besides sharing a little about herself in the column, she could think of a dozen people to feature off the top of her head, starting with the mayor. The stories would be as plentiful as the population. And, *bam*, just like that she'd created her new column. Now all she had to do was convince Bjork the idea was a winner.

All the lectures in the world about single-minded goals didn't keep Lilly away from Gunnar that Thursday night. She tapped on his door at nine-thirty, knowing he'd had yet another meeting at city hall. No, she wasn't there to break him down and finally get the lowdown on those darn meetings. She'd promised and they'd called a truce; she was there to tell him her big news about the new weekly column.

Funny how Gunnar's face was the first and only one to come to mind once Bjork had given her the okay to run with the column.

He opened the door, wrapped in a towel, looking surprised. "Hey, I was going to call you in a few minutes. What's up?"

"I've got a great idea and I wanted to run it by you. Have you got a moment?" The guy was wrapped in a towel, maybe it wasn't the best time...

"I was just going to jump in the shower." He opened the door wide to let her enter. "Have a seat. I'll only be a few minutes." He pecked her on the lips and turned to mosey down the hall toward the bathroom. "Unless you want to join me? You can tell me all about it under the shower head.."

"I'm good thanks," she called after him. Girl! Why not take him up on it? She'd come here for one reason, to tell him about her new column, and showering with Gunnar wasn't her goal. Maybe she should reevaluate that.

"Make yourself comfortable," he said, closing the bathroom door.

She sat on the couch and briefly closed her eyes. She was too excited to settle down, so she glanced around the room. Wolverine mewed from his favorite spot on the rug by the elevated fireplace. Her gaze continued on toward the kitchen. Gunnar must have just finished a sandwich, judging by the crust sitting on a plate on the island counter. Leaning against the counter was a mailing tube, the kind that usually held blueprints.

Her mind drifted back to the first night she'd been here, when Gunnar had told her about Leif and him working on the house design together, and how this was just the first phase. What would the rest of Gunnar's house be like? Curiosity got the best of her.

She walked across the room and, seeing that the tube wasn't sealed, opened the lid, turned it upside down and pulled out the contents. Instead of the blueprints, like she'd expected, she found an aerial view of the portion of town that thanks to Gunnar she'd come to know as the Ringmuren, the great wall surrounding the northernmost corner of Heartlandia. The second page seemed like the same area, but it looked like some kind of heat map, like you'd see on those weather maps on TV.

Intrigued by the pictures, and forgetting about the blueprint idea, she sat on a kitchen stool and studied them. A bright red spot stood out in the upper left corner on the far side of the long and ancient wall. What in the world did that represent?

Completely engrossed, she jumped when Gunnar touched her arm. "What are you doing?"

"Oh! I'm looking at your pictures."

He didn't look happy. Nope, the guy looked disturbed and maybe a little angry judging by the creases between his brows. "Who gave you permission to go through my stuff?"

Oh, gosh, he'd taken it all wrong. She wasn't being snoopy, well, maybe she was, but it wasn't for the usual reasons, those secret meetings. "I thought this might be your house-upgrade blueprints."

He took the documents from her, rolled up the aerial photographs and put them back into the tube. "You know, if we're going to have a shot at a serious relationship, you've got to quit this stuff. Give it up. I'm not ever going to tell you about the meetings."

"I had no idea this had anything to do with the meetings."

He flinched. Now he looked ticked off at himself. Had he accidentally given away a big clue? He may have tried to put out a fire, but now he'd only made her more curious.

"Does it?" she asked, his ironman stare looking right through her. She didn't let it intimidate her. "Have to do with the meetings?"

He popped the lid back on the tube and put it on top of the high refrigerator, a place Lilly would need a stepping stool to reach. "None of your business." He turned toward her. "Did you even hear what I just said? About us?"

About having a shot at a serious relationship? Of course she had, and her knees had gone rubbery, but he'd buried the statement deep in his reprimand and then she'd gotten caught up with those special meetings again.

"Being exclusive? Yes, Gunnar, but first I need you to understand that I wasn't trying to go behind your back about anything just now. I made an honest mistake thinking that blueprints were inside that tube. I got curious about your house addition…maybe because I *was* thinking about us…and the future. Can you accept that?"

She'd stepped over the line and insinuated herself into his future. Talk about a turnoff to any guy, especially a contented bachelor like Gunnar.

He inhaled, his broad chest going even wider beneath his tight white T-shirt. "Because of your history of snooping around my meetings, Lilly, you can't fault me for thinking the worst."

She felt upset and huffy—a normally foreign feeling to her—but to add insult to injury the guy just blew off her admitting she was curious about their future. So right now, ticked off and not going to take it anymore, she blew off his willingness to be exclusive with her and decided to tell him how she felt about everything else. "Well, if all you can think is the worst about me, then I guess there's no point in…"

He grabbed her and dropped a quick kiss on her lips to shut her up. "I'm sorry," he said, then took the follow-up kiss to the next level. She wanted to resist, to recite her full-blown speech about her hurt feelings and his riding roughshod over them, but her heart wasn't in this fight, and he felt too damn good to stop kissing. By the time he'd made her go all dreamy-eyed, he ended the kiss. Tease! Why did he always have to take charge of things?

"Let's start over," he said. "I'm sorry I accused you of snooping, even though technically you were."

Why could he make her crack a smile at the craziest

moments, especially when she was upset and didn't want to? He'd given her a mini ultimatum—either forgive or make a big deal out of it. Hot off his superkiss, smelling the sporty soap on his clean skin, having just run her fingertips over his ultrasmooth, fresh-shaven jaw, she'd be nuts to go with door B. "I promise to never snoop around your stuff without your okay, again."

Crap! She'd just become Christine to his Erik in *Phantom of the Opera*. Somehow he'd gotten her to do exactly what he'd wanted.

He watched her for a few moments, those green eyes invading all of her barriers, as if studying her face for the first time and liking what he saw. "You know I'm nuts about you, right?"

He was? Well, sure, they'd been sleeping together about every other night since she'd moved into her place, and they'd been spending just about all of their spare time together, too. But he'd never, ever talked about being exclusive. Besides, that wasn't the way of the modern San Francisco woman whose profession came first. This was all too confusing.

Wait a second, wait a second, did he just say he was nuts about her?

"You are?" Could she sound more lame? Why not be honest and tell him she was crazy about him, too, but suddenly her tongue had knotted up.

"Against my better judgment, I am." He moved one longer lock of hair behind her ear. She knew her ear tips gave her true reaction away, feeling hot and probably being bright red.

"Oh, man. This changes everything." Without giving it a second thought, in a very un–San Francisco sophisticated woman way, she leaped into his arms, straddling his hips with her legs. Catching her didn't even faze him.

It felt like hitting a boulder, he was that rock solid. She kissed him as if she'd never wanted anything more in her life. She might not be able to tell him how she really felt just yet because something about saying the words scared her witless. She sure could show him how she was feeling, though, how she was falling…*gulp*…in love with him.

Gunnar sat in roll call Friday morning a bit stunned. He'd left a sleeping Lilly in his bed, and had taken a few extra moments standing and watching her before he'd left. This wasn't good. If his plan was to become chief of police down the road and move on to mayor once he was in his forties, he needed to show he was a solid Heartlandia citizen. Which meant he should get serious, settle down and quit sleeping around. In his mind he and Lilly were exclusive. He just hadn't gotten around to saying anything about it until last night. When he had, from her reaction, she was very receptive to the idea.

The take-out coffee turned bitter in his mouth. Yeah, he was crazy about Lilly, but he had to face it, Lilly wasn't a "stand behind your man" kind of woman the way his mother had been. Lilly was out for Lilly—and honestly a little of that mind-set sure would have been helpful for his mother. But Gunnar wasn't like his father, and if he wanted to become chief of police then mayor one day he needed a woman who'd support him all the way. A woman he could trust with every single secret. Was she capable of that? Was she capable of saying one thing and doing another, like his father who'd sworn his innocence right up until they'd led him off to jail? Later, the Norling family had learned how involved his father really was, taking hush money and turning his head while the smugglers did their transactions, nearly running the legitimate factory into the ground.

As a type A personality himself, Gunnar recognized an overachiever when he met one. Lilly was single-minded about taking over the newspaper—how proud she'd been to tell him last night amidst crumpled sheets fresh with the scent of their sex, about her new column with the catchy name. I Dream of Sushi in Storybook Land. It was also clear that she treated the *Heartlandia Herald* as a stepping stone to her future—which meant her future might not be around these parts.

Either the coffee or the day's police log had made Gunnar queasy. If he were to bet the feeling had more to do with a pair of perfectly placed dark eyes, and short, crazy-to-run-his-fingers-through hair. Not the ongoing dock mayhem and cruise-line robberies.

Was he ready to let himself completely fall for someone? To completely trust her?

Though making inroads with Heartlandia, Lilly was still an outsider with big plans for her future. Would having a real relationship, like Kent and Desi had, with a lady like Lilly be wise, considering his goals? Or the dumbest venture in his life…

He knew how his body felt about her, but it was time to check in with his mind and figure this out. Maybe Kent could set him straight since he'd been through a lot worse, getting divorced and feeling abandoned, yet he'd still managed to fall in love again. With an outsider. To look at Kent and Desi these days, they were the perfect pair planning their wedding and seemed nothing short of a miracle.

Was it out of the question to think Gunnar and the tiger lady, Lilly, might be right for each other?

"You ready?" Paul, his partner, prodded Gunnar's foot with the tip of his boot.

"Huh? Oh, yeah, sure. Where're we heading?"

"I knew you'd checked out. You were all but drooling."

"I was not." Gunnar stood, ready for the day. They walked in friendly banter out to the car.

Like radar, Gunnar's eyes went right to the red car pulling into a parking space, and the woman who expunged herself from behind the steering wheel. Lilly. He'd never admit it in a court of law, but his pulse did a little blip at the sight of her. Wearing a girlie version of a suit—straight-legged, tight-fitting black pants showing off all the right parts, and a waist-length matching jacket looking more like something Michael Jackson might wear back in the day, with gold epilates and brass buttons down the front, totally San Francisco—she walked with her usual good posture toward the newspaper office.

Warmth spread across his chest as he waved. Her serious face brightened the moment she noticed him and waved back. Damn, she was something.

Who knew what would pan out between them? All he knew for sure was he liked being with Lilly. Loved being with Lilly. And yeah, he was crazy about her on more levels than in his bed. She was a go-getter, just like him, she had goals, just like him, she was confident in her abilities despite her old man, just like him. And nothing would stand in the way of her getting a story. That was the part that got stuck in his throat.

And that's where they were different. His father would always be his point of reference for making a choice or going too far. He hoped Lilly's conscience knew when to stop her, too.

He believed she'd made an honest mistake looking at the latest bombshell from the committee—buried treasure smack in the middle of sacred Chinook burial ground, according to Ben Cobawa.

Leif had funded the special aerial study using something called infrared thermography. The way he'd explained it, the special camera recorded the energy emitted from objects. No one wanted to invade the burial ground, but the next step would be utilizing a high-tech metal detector to gauge whether the dense infrared image was in fact a sea captain's trunk, and if so, precisely how far down in sacred land it was located.

Paul started the police unit and backed out of the parking spot. Gunnar watched Lilly open the door and go inside the building, realizing a broad smile stretched across his face again.

There was just something about Lilly...

"What're you smiling at?" Paul chided, knowing full well the direction Gunnar had been looking.

He didn't bother to answer.

For a guy with a questionable track record as a player, maybe he'd surprise everyone and work something out for the long term with Chitcha.

Chapter Eleven

Lilly thumbed through the Rolodex—yes, Bjork was antiquated enough in his record keeping that he still used a Rolodex—looking for the contact information for Mayor Gerda Rask.

What better way to kick off her new column than with an interview with the mayor pro tem?

To her surprise the mayor, who insisted Lilly call her Gerda, graciously invited her over for tea that very Tuesday afternoon. Lilly parked in front of a huge Victorian-style house painted bright yellow and with soft green trim, reminding her of the colorful painted ladies back home. The house was on a huge lot with plenty of space between it and the next house, unlike San Francisco. As she knocked, she glanced across the yard to Gerda's neighbor, a bland white Victorian house in the early stages of being brightened up with jazzy lavender trim.

The stunning mocha-colored young woman she'd interviewed for the newspaper a couple of weeks ago opened the door. "Hi." Desi hugged Lilly like they were old friends. "Come on in." Desi was Gerda's granddaughter.

The warm welcome fueled the first-meeting excitement Lilly always got at interviews.

They briefly exchanged small talk as Desi showed her down the hall, across creaky ancient wooden floors to the sunroom, where Gerda and a fresh pot of tea awaited.

"Grandma, Lilly's here."

Lilly shook Gerda's bony hand, surprised by her warmth. Her aging blue eyes brightened as they smiled at each other.

"I've been looking forward to interviewing our mayor ever since I came to Heartlandia. Thanks so much for agreeing to see me."

"Oh, I'd much rather talk to you than deal with all the headaches going on at city hall these days," Gerda said, looking resigned and sitting back down in her classic oak rocker, as if she had the weight of the world on her narrow shoulders.

"Well," Desi said, "I've got my first piano student in five minutes. I'd better go get ready."

"Nice to see you again, Desi."

"You, too."

"I'd like to do a follow-up article on you and your dad sometime."

"Hmm, I'll have to think about that," the tall and lovely woman said as she closed the door, somewhat noncommittal.

Glancing at the pale, nearly colorless grandmother compared to the warm-toned granddaughter, Lilly knew there was a lot more to Desi's story to tell.

Gerda poured them both some tea and Lilly got right down to the interview, beginning with the mayor's genealogy going all the way back to the first founders of Heartlandia three hundred years ago.

Her previously bright eyes softened and seemed to drift far away as she told her more recent family history. Pain crossed her face when she spoke about her daughter, Ester, and how she'd run away as a teenager and had never re-turned home, and how Gerda hadn't gotten to really know Desi until after Ester had died from cancer.

If Lilly wasn't sure before, she was positive now about interviewing Desi from a different angle, not just about being the new town music teacher and favorite piano bar player at Lincoln's Place, but the rest of her story, too.

"These days, with Desi being engaged and planning her wedding to Kent, I should be thrilled. And don't get me wrong, mostly I am, but being mayor came with a lot of surprises."

"Like what?" Lilly sipped her tea, trying to keep her cool while hoping Gerda might tell her more.

"Oh, just a few things about our city that I'd never known before."

She'd already gotten in trouble with Gunnar for bad-gering him about the secret meetings, and he'd basically admitted they were going on. Plus, since she'd stumbled upon the aerial pictures, she knew they had something to do with the sacred burial grounds. She decided to go for it, bait Gerda with the little information she'd already ac-quired to see where it might lead. Wasn't that what any journalist worth their salt did?

"Do the things you never knew about city hall have any-thing to do with the secret meetings going on over there?"

Gerda's thin white brows tented. "You know about those meetings?"

"Am I not supposed to know about them?"

Gerda's brows dropped low over her eyes. She seemed in a quandary. "Well, we haven't gone public with any of our findings yet, but there will come a time when we'll be forced to, I guess."

"Care to elaborate on what those findings are?"

"No." Gerda put down her teacup and folded her hands in her lap. "Sorry."

"May I quote you on the other part?"

"Which part?" She knotted her hands together.

"On your surprise about some of the 'things about city hall you'd never known before' and the need for a special committee and time-consuming meetings."

Gerda leaned forward. "Just how much do you know about our special committee?"

Lilly sat straighter, not wanting Gunnar to get blamed if Gerda found out they were dating. "Anyone who reads the town website can figure it out."

"Really?" Gerda snatched up a nearby pencil and note-pad, scribbling out a quick sentence. Evidently she hadn't checked out the town website lately.

"Are these meetings about Heartlandia's upcoming birthday? Are you planning a celebration?"

"Our tercentennial, you mean?"

"That's three hundred, right?"

Gerda nodded. "I wish that was the reason. No. We're dealing with a glitch in our history that needs to get ironed out. Once we've worked it out, we'll let the community know everything."

"And may I quote you on that?"

Gerda's thumb flew to her mouth. She chewed her nail while thinking. Her previously serene face was now etched with crisscrossed lines and beetled brows. "I guess that's okay, just maybe only mention we're ironing out some is-sues regarding our town records. I don't want to get over-run with questions I'm not able to answer at this time."

"That's fine. Any idea when the community will be in-formed about what's going on?"

"It's too soon to say, but hopefully in the next month or two? Maybe I'm being too optimistic, but I'm hoping this won't be anything too earth-shattering to report. We just have to work out the particulars, present it in the right way and maybe..." Gerda's gaze shot up. "Oh, goodness, I've said too much already. Please disregard everything I just said."

"So I can't mention that you hope to have resolved the issue in the next month or two?"

Gerda shook her head. "I'd rather you didn't, in case we need more time."

"Okay, you have my word on that, but is it okay if I still mention the glitch in the town history being ironed out in the special meetings?"

Lilly could tell she'd talked the poor woman in circles, and by now she wasn't sure what would be okay to say or not, yet she pressed on.

"I guess that part would be okay."

"I must say you've really piqued my interest."

"Oh, goodness, that was the last thing I wanted to do."

Lilly didn't want to leave Gerda in a dither, so she changed tack and asked her what a typical day at city hall as mayor pro tem was like. That seemed to smooth out Gerda's concerned expression as she explained the many duties of a sitting mayor.

Fifteen minutes later, with a boatload of notes, Lilly finished her tea. "Well, thank you for your time, Mayor Rask. I truly appreciate it."

"My pleasure, Ms. Matsuda. By the way, I've really enjoyed your stories about our local entrepreneurs."

Knowing people were reading her little articles never failed to please Lilly, even though they weren't big breaking-news stories. But in her bones, she knew she was on to something with those up-close-and-personal stories.

Gerda showed Lilly out by way of the back deck, and as she trudged around the house, hearing the clunky piano playing of one of the young students through an opened window, she also overheard Gerda call out to Desi. "Do you know where my stomach medicine is?"

Lilly hunched her shoulders, figuring she'd been the cause of the mayor's stomach upset with her pointed questions, and a pang of guilt accompanied her thoughts about pushing the line with the dear lady. Was a breaking story really worth the discomfort it caused those involved? It wasn't as if they were common criminals trying to hide something horrible, not if Mr. By-the-Books Norling was on board.

Gunnar had volunteered to work the evening shift again on Wednesday night due to the continued illegal activities down at the docks. He'd dressed in shabby jeans, a ripped T-shirt and a pea jacket and would drive an undercover car. He'd changed to lead the surveillance task force for the evening. This would be a double shift, since he'd been in uniform all day doing the usual job. Three other undercover units were assigned to the watch. But things weren't set to officially begin for another hour.

He hitched a bun on the corner of another officer's desk in the department, and noticed the *Heartlandia Herald*, so he picked it up and began to peruse. Quickly, he discovered Lilly's lead story in the I Dream of Sushi in Storybook Land column. The subtitle nearly made him choke on his coffee.

What's So Secret about the City Hall Meetings?

She'd interviewed Mayor pro tem Gerda Rask and though the article started off with the usual personal history and charming anecdotes from the interviewee, Lilly had quickly veered off into another direction.

"Word has it around town that there are secret meetings going on with a special panel. Would you like to tell us about them?"

Looking uncomfortable with my line of questioning, the white-haired matriarch of Heartlandia, and acting mayor, commented, "[We're] ironing out some issues regarding our town records."

When asked how soon before the town would find out the reason for these meetings, Mayor Rask declined to answer, but she assured the meetings didn't have anything to do with the upcoming three-hundredth birthday of Heartlandia.

A lightning bolt cut through Gunnar's chest. His fists tightened and released as he used all his will not to wad up the newspaper and throw it in the trash. He counted to ten then strode out of the department, clomped across the black-and-white tile in the building foyer to the newspaper office entrance.

Bjork and three other employees were milling around working, but Lilly was nowhere to be seen. Having caught on to Lilly and Gunnar's relationship over the past few weeks, Bjork intercepted Gunnar's question.

"She's taking a late lunch break at the Hartalanda Café."

Having gotten the information he'd come for, Gunnar left the office without uttering a single syllable.

He counted to ten again before opening the door to the café. She'd really pushed things too far this time, especially after the incident with the aerial photos and promising him she wouldn't blab about those meetings. Evidently his feelings on the matter didn't mean squat to her.

She glanced up from her salad, a smile beginning but ending just as quickly when she noticed his dead-serious stare. He approached her table, and she sat straighter, as if steeling for a fight.

He wouldn't give her the satisfaction of arguing. Nope. She'd taken things too far and needed to hear him out. If he got in her face, she'd tune him out, and it was really important for her to hear what he had to say.

He sat across from her, determined to keep his voice down. "So let me get this straight. First you trick me into admitting I was involved in the meetings, I tell you I need to be able to trust you, you promise me I can, then you print the information for the whole city to read. What gives?"

She blinked. "I printed what Mayor Rask said. I wasn't quoting you."

"And that makes a difference how?"

"Two sources. One verified the other. Plus the mayor said it was okay to quote her."

Still keeping his voice quiet, the intensity went up a notch. "So it doesn't matter to you what I ask?"

She reached across the table and grabbed his fisted hand. He didn't pull away, just stared at their hands, wondering why he'd ever let himself get involved with a girl like Lilly. A single-minded reporter.

"Of course it matters to me what you want. What's the big deal if there's a glitch with the town records and you've all been assigned to a committee to work it out? What's the big deal, Gunnar? The people want to know and this should satisfy them until you make the big announcement."

Her voice wasn't nearly as quiet or controlled as his. She had no idea how big of a deal it was, and still she was determined to report it and risk putting the entire town in a tailspin. Not to mention all the questions poor Gerda would have to stave off. At least Lilly hadn't named the entire committee.

He removed his hand from under hers and gestured for her to keep her voice down. "What about trust?"

"You can trust me. This interview had nothing to do with you and me."

"So you think tricking someone into disclosing private business is okay?"

"I didn't trick her. She brought it up. Look, I'm a reporter. That's my job. I respect our mayor and asked her on two different occasions if I could quote her. One she okayed, the other she didn't. The second comment wasn't in the paper."

He wondered how much more Gerda had told Lilly and it caused his stomach to twist with the possibility she'd exposed everything before they'd ironed out their line of action. But more so, it stung like hell to realize he simply couldn't trust Lilly with everything in his life. "You need to let this go. Just leave this alone. Focus on the human interest stories."

"This *is* a human interest story." She sat back in the booth and folded her arms, her brows tense and her mouth pursed. "You're the bossiest man I've ever met."

He leaned forward. "And you're too nosey for your own good."

"You call it nosey, I call it doing my job."

"If you'd just realize you don't have to be the person your dad tried to make you." Gunnar shook his head, thinking how his own father's actions had shaped his life, making him an overcompensator and a stickler on rules and regulations, and sometimes rigid where his personal life was concerned. How he functioned in black-and-white with Lilly being in the gray area. He thought how Lilly's father had pushed and pushed and pushed her to become a tougher person until her gentle spirit had given in. Her judgment was damaged.

"Our fathers really jacked us up, you know?" he said. "But we're in charge of our lives now, and you don't have to play by your father's rules anymore."

"Old habits" was all she mumbled as she tore off tiny pieces of paper napkin. "And you don't have to be so rigid."

They played out a staring duel. He tried to read behind the steady set of her eyes, hoping she'd see his way of thinking, but he couldn't see past the glare. Yes, making up for his father's actions had made Gunnar inflexible at times but in his mind, trust meant everything.

"On this one point, I can't back down, Lilly. If I can't trust you, there's just no reason for us to be together, you know?" He cleared his throat, sad yet angry as hell to say what he knew he had to next. "I think it's best for both of us if we quit seeing each other."

Her chin shot up. He detected a fleeting flash of sadness in her eyes, perhaps a tinge of moisture gathering making her irises shiny, but she quickly toughened up. "Fine." Faced with his challenge, she put on her armor and turned as angry as he was sad.

Tension simmered between them for the next few moments as he breathed deeply yet had trouble getting air into his lungs, studying her, trying with every brain cell to figure her out. She wouldn't back down from the challenge and neither would he. Stalemate. Everything they'd shared, all the great moments, had been shot down because of a news story. That forced things into perspective for him.

If she was incapable of seeing that, there was nothing left to say, so he stood. "Go ahead and print our breakup on the front page, why don't you?" he said quietly struggling to sound nonchalant, as if his heart wasn't squeezing so hard he thought it might pop. Tucking his lower lip inward and biting on it to keep from saying another word, he turned and left the diner.

"Maybe I will!" she said in a strained whisper that broke at the end.

His step faltered. Chitcha didn't know how to back

down. Her father had seen to that. He briefly closed his eyes and shook his head. Breaking up with her was the last thing in the world he wanted to do…

But he couldn't trust her.

Lilly's stomach seemed to sit on her shoes. Her breathing came in spurts, and a panicky feeling that she'd just blown the best relationship of her life over a stupid snip of a story made her tear up. She was in public, she couldn't melt down here. She pushed away her half-eaten salad and pretended for the sake of the waitress and the couple sitting at the adjacent table that absolutely nothing wrong had just happened. It was always important to save face according to her parents. Never show weakness. Never.

Guilt ate at the edges of her thoughts. *You don't have to be the person your dad tried to make you.* Her stomach went queasy. Was she so success-oriented and hardhearted that she'd betray Gunnar's trust?

She curled her lower lip and tensed every muscle in order to not lose it in public. Slowly, her mind stiffened up, too.

How had she let a small town guy like Gunnar get under her skin in the first place? She'd lost sight of her goal. Why had she let that happen?

She knew exactly why. Gunnar was the truest, most honorable and dependable person she'd ever met. Sure, he'd been trying to make up for what his daddy had done, but in his case, it was a good thing. Everyone trusted and respected him.

It wasn't just Gunnar who made her feel like kitty litter at the moment. Once she'd ventured out and put names and faces on the people of Heartlandia, she'd lost her edge. The entire town had found a way into her heart through trust and innocence.

And she'd blown it all.

Her self-control nearly gone, she picked up the tattered napkin, and with a trembling hand dabbed at the corners of her mouth and, when she knew the couple at the next table wasn't watching, the corners of her eyes. Crying in public, showing weakness, failing in her father's ways, made her mad. She had to brush Gunnar out of her mind in order to survive the moment.

An inkling of fight returned.

She'd concentrate on something else, anything in order to make it out of the café without making a scene. With her napkin thoroughly shredded, she squeezed her brain to think. Something was going on with the town history. The people in power had decided to keep it quiet. It was so big her boyfriend had just broken up with her over it.

Stay focused, Lilly. She heard her father's voice.

As a reporter it was her job to bring the story out into the open. Full disclosure. *Transparency.* Wasn't that the buzzword of the decade?

As she reached for her purse and paid her bill at the counter, the guilty feelings gathered momentum again and invaded her breath. *Do not cry. Do. Not. Cry.* She had trouble inhaling, as if a blockade had been set up in her throat.

She'd just ruined any chance of ever having a relationship with Gunnar. Was the kind of success her father taught her really all about the goal and doing anything to achieve it? Maybe Gunnar was right, she didn't have to be that way.

Maybe it really was as easy as making a conscious decision to back off the story.

In a massive conflict of interest, she'd thrown over her best guy and set the town up for a confrontation with city hall, all for the sake of one stinking, smug, I-know-something-that-you-don't story lead.

She'd hate to look in a mirror right now. An overwhelming sense of failure enveloped her as she left the café.

Her father might be proud of her for breaking a major town story, but a gaping black hole had just opened up in the middle of her self-respect. She owed Gunnar and the entire town her heartfelt apology.

While trolling the dark streets of the docks with his lights off, Gunnar saw the first flames on the far side and drove toward them. It looked like the Maritime Museum had been hit. He parked, followed protocol and alerted his task force, then notified the fire department. He could wait for backup and risk losing his lead or jump out of his car and run for the scene. In his mind he did the right thing, lunging out the door and sprinting toward the fire.

A hundred yards out, a flash in his peripheral vision grabbed his full attention. It was someone dressed all in black running like a speeding shadow. He made a U-turn and hit the asphalt in full pursuit chasing down his target. The suspect dived behind some bushes, and Gunnar flattened himself against a shack, drawing his weapon and listening over his ragged breath for a clue where the suspect was hiding.

He edged to the corner of the wall, readying his heavy-duty flashlight with his left hand like an ice pick in the Harries hold, his gun hand resting on the wrist of the other hand for stability. He counted to three and stepped around the corner, his flashlight scanning the bushes. He saw movement and turned toward it at the exact moment a shot rang out. He rapidly returned fire and heard a loud groan, having hit his mark. Only then did he feel the white-hot pain in his left shoulder.

The police backup was right on his heels and the officers swarmed the bush, finding the guy curled into a ball hugging his right thigh.

Searing pain shot up Gunnar's shoulder and into his neck. His vision doubled and he had to sit down. Unable to hold up the flashlight any longer, he let go of it and low-ered his gun, then dropped first to his knees then onto his butt. The jolt of hitting the pavement sent sharp nauseating pain up to his shoulder. His head felt swimmy. He put it between his spread legs and bent knees and concentrated on breathing through the raging sting zinging along the nerve endings in his shoulder.

Sirens sounded from all directions, coming for the fire no doubt, but hopefully an ambulance was on its way for him, too, since the sticky wetness from his gunshot spread quickly across his chest and dripped down onto his stom-ach.

His peripheral vision going dark, Gunnar shivered and clinched his eyes closed.

Chapter Twelve

Lilly was still in her office peering through the ceiling-to-floor windows into the building's foyer, trying her best to get her mind off the saddest day of her life, when she noticed a couple of officers run out the door and in to their cruisers. Thankful for distraction, she scurried over to the PD's front desk.

"Anything special going on?"

"Another fire at the docks," the older man reported.

Lilly rushed back to her cubicle, grabbed her purse and headed for her car. Ten minutes later she showed up at the scene, which was easy to spot from several blocks away. Flames ate through the Maritime Museum as several fire units fought them back. Just like the last time, the police took over the scene blocking off all entrances to the activities. She looked for Gunnar, not that he'd want to see her or anything, but he was nowhere in sight.

She recognized one of the younger cops named Eric and headed straight to him. "What time did the fire start?"

"About a half hour ago."

She flashed her reporter ID. "Is arson suspected again?"

"Don't know yet." Eric recognized her, probably as Gunnar's new girl, not a journalist. "But Gunnar saw someone running from the scene and chased him. Took a bullet. But we got the suspect in custody."

"Who took a bullet, Gunnar or the suspect?" Worry and fear converged and rushed through her veins at the thought of Gunnar being hurt.

"Both."

The news of his being shot hit her like back draft, nearly knocking her over. "Is Gunnar okay? Where'd they take him?"

"Got shot in the shoulder. Wanted his buddy Kent to take care of it."

Lilly had been dating Gunnar for a month, and though she'd heard all about his best friend, Kent, she'd only briefly met him once when she'd interviewed Desi. Fortunately, she knew where his Urgent Care was, since it was the only medical facility in Heartlandia.

"Thanks," she said, gathering all of her wherewithal to think straight and keep moving, just before she snaked through the gathering crowd and sprinted to her car.

Ten minutes later, she rushed the entrance of the UC and ran to the reception area. "I'm looking for Gunnar Norling," she said, nearly breathless.

"We can't disclose any names of patients. State law," the full-bearded, college-aged receptionist said, looking distracted by whatever he was inputting on his work computer.

"Did a gunshot wound just come here?"

"Sorry. Can't disclose anything."

"I'm his girlfriend, damn it!"

The kid finally looked up. His gaze swept over Lilly head to waist, since she stood at the low reception counter. He thought a few seconds and then picked up the phone. "I have Sergeant Norling's girlfriend at the front desk. Can she come back?"

Oh, God, he'd just broken up with her, now she wanted special privileges to see him. Would he let her?

She folded her arms, fueled by adrenaline, nervous pangs running the length of her body as she tapped her toe.

"Okay." The receptionist put down the phone. "Dr. Larson will be right with you. Wait over there." He pointed to a secluded area by another door.

She did what she was told, fearing that Gunnar was too injured to see her, or worse yet, never wanted to see her again. Oh, God, she could barely take the anxiety zipping around her stomach, making her feel as if she might hurl.

She swallowed, and swallowed, forcing herself to shape up.

"Lilly?" A deep and soothing voice said her name from behind.

She spun around to see the huge guy, at least a foot taller than her, in a white coat, and like so many of the other men in town, a regular Nordic god.

"I'm Kent, Gunnar's best friend, remember me?"

"Yes, of course. Hi. Good to see you again. Well, not under these circumstances…" *Get a grip!* She inhaled. "Is he okay?"

"He is. Got a nasty bullet lodged in his shoulder and I don't have an adequate procedure room here to remove it. We've taken X-rays and now we're cleaning up the wound and getting him ready for transport to Astoria for surgery."

Her hand flew to her mouth, and tears pooled and overflowed onto her cheeks. "May I see him?"

Kent's lips tightened into a straight line. "I'm sorry, but he really isn't up to seeing anyone just now."

Damn, damn, damn, she'd ruined everything and Gunnar had sent his friend out to blow her off. He obviously didn't want anything to do with her. She dropped her head, not wanting Kent to see her cry. How many more people in town could she bear to see her cry?

His huge hand clasped one of her arms and he gave a gentle squeeze. "I gave him a pain shot and he's practically out to the world." He took out his prescription pad and wrote on it. "Here's the address of the hospital we're sending him to. He'll be going to surgery once he gets cleared in the ER there, but you can stick around if you'd like."

"Thank you." She took the paper, wanting to fling her arms around Dr. Larson, for giving her hope. Maybe Gunnar really didn't know she was here. Maybe he really was out cold from a pain shot. Maybe he hadn't said the most despicable words she could think of—I don't want to see her—after all.

Kent nodded, then ducked back behind the private door as an ambulance arrived in the parking lot.

She went outside and hung around in hopes of glimpsing Gunnar.

Five minutes later she got her wish. Out he rolled on the narrow gurney, eyes closed, chin slack. He was shirtless with a large dressing on his left shoulder, getting rolled toward the back of the vehicle.

She rushed to his side and took his hand, squeezed, before the paramedic could stop her. "Gunnar, it's Lilly. I'm here. I'll see you after surgery." It might have been her imagination, but she thought there was a faint squeeze in return.

The EMTs loaded him into the back of the ambulance and she stood and watched until they left the parking lot, hit the road and started the siren.

Fingers crossed, he didn't know she was here, and he hadn't banned her from the procedure room. Maybe she could mend the mess she'd made with him. There had to be some way to win back his trust.

She stood watching as the red light flashed farther and farther in the distance and the piercing sound of the siren faded.

The drive her father and mother had instilled in her since she was a child took over, and instead of following the ambulance to the hospital—since Gunnar would probably be going to surgery ASAP after clearance in the ER—she went to the newspaper to input her report first. She rationalized that she wouldn't be able to see Gunnar until recovery anyway, and the story would only take half an hour to write. This second fire story inside of one month needed to make the front page.

The instant she pressed Send on the story and attached photograph to Bjork, she got back into her car and drove to Astoria to find out about Gunnar.

She'd tell everyone at the hospital she was his girlfriend, and since he'd be unconscious, they'd have to believe her.

Nothing would stop her from being by his side when he came to.

The tall, thin blonde named Elke Norling called all the shots at the small Astoria hospital. A fierce sister, taking charge, she questioned Lilly the newspaper reporter like a prison guard in the surgery waiting room.

"How do I know you're not only here to get a story?" Her features reminded Lilly of a young Meryl Streep with a pointy nose sitting crooked on her face.

"I've been dating Gunnar for a month now."

"He's never mentioned you to me."

That sort of said it all, didn't it? He'd never told his only living family member about her. Her earlier optimism from Kent sank to the pit of her stomach like a bag of sand.

A racket ensued behind her. She turned to find a middle-aged man, dressed all in black including a hoodie, hand-cuffed to a gurney, getting rolled into the ER. His leg was bandaged and it appeared he hadn't been given the pain relief that Gunnar had when she'd seen him.

Two policemen followed the emergency medical technicians pushing him on the gurney to the emergency department.

The wild-eyed man looked right at Lilly. Recognition flashed through his eyes. "Her. I want to talk to her."

One of the policemen accompanying him she'd met at the last fire, and he noticed her. "Why do you want to talk to her? Do you even know who she is?"

True, her picture ran beside all of her stories in the paper, and Heartlandia wasn't exactly running over with Asians, but did anyone really know who she was?

"Sure. She's the lady from the *Herald*." There he went again, staring her down like a wounded feral animal with a plan. "I want to talk to you."

The look creeped her out.

"You're going to see a doctor first," the wise cop said.

A young head nurse met them at the ER entrance. Wearing an unearthly color of green scrubs, she stopped them. "I'm sorry, but we're out of rooms. Put him over there for now." She pointed to a long hallway at the back of the hospital entrance. One other gurney complete with patient was already parked along the wall. "We'll have to do the intake from there."

Lilly turned her attention back to Elke, who hadn't moved, pleading with her eyes. "I'm in love with your brother. He doesn't know it because I haven't told him yet." Elke seemed to stare into her soul, and Lilly stood with her head tall letting her. She made a snap decision to confess. "He broke up with me tonight." She connected with Elke's gaze, hoping with every breath the woman could understand the situation, and that she'd believe her. "You've got to let me see him, though. Please."

Something had softened in Elke's eyes. Maybe she did believe Lilly. She nodded. "Once he's out of recovery and assigned to a room, I'll make sure your name is on the list of visitors."

Without a thought, Lilly dived for Elke and hugged her. "Oh, thank you. Thank you. I've got to straighten things out with him."

Another ER nurse popped her head out the door, apparently searching for Elke. Then she found her. "Your brother's on his way to surgery now. It will be a few hours. Why don't you go get some coffee or something?"

Elke nodded. She looked at Lilly. "Come with?"

"Sure."

The only way to the hospital cafeteria was down the long hallway. Lilly and Elke walked past the man on the gurney. "I need to talk to you. You need to hear my story. I know things!"

She tried to ignore him, but couldn't. She stopped in her tracks. "About what?"

"Heartlandia's all a big lie. I have proof."

Was the guy off his psych meds? What the hell was he talking about? But why did it seem to tie in with the recent secret meetings and the "glitch in the town records" they needed to iron out?

And why was there a startled expression on Elke's face? "I know that man. He's been attending extension classes at the college. He's never been in any trouble or anything that I know of, but we do get our share of kooks at school."

Lilly's hard-earned "better judgment" took over and she ignored the fanatical patient and continued on with Elke for some coffee.

* * *

Two hours later, head slack against the chair in the waiting room, someone tapped Lilly's shoulder. It was that young ER nurse again. She'd come all the way upstairs to the surgical waiting room. "Roald Lindstrom asked to talk to you rather than call a lawyer. He's in the ER. Do you want to come?"

Lilly shook her head to wake up. The man on the gurney with the crazy accusations about Heartlandia? "The guy with the leg wound?"

The nursed tipped her head. "Said he might not get the chance again. Wanted to talk to you instead of a lawyer."

Lilly glanced at Elke sitting quietly and peacefully next to her.

"Go if you want to," Elke said. "I'll text you the instant I get any word."

Lilly gave Elke her cell phone number, then grabbing her bottled water, followed the nurse into the elevator and headed for the ER and the crazy alleged arsonist with a story to tell.

Lilly was officially introduced to Roald Lindstrom while he was under custody with the police, and under the influence of a sedative. He'd calmed down since the last time she'd seen him. His beady blue eyes gave her the willies, so she concentrated on his receding mousy-brown hairline instead.

Evidently the gunshot had hit the side of his thigh and had been a clean in-and-out wound. The nurse said they'd only used a local anesthetic for the wound care, but had given him something to calm him. Now he was all bandaged up and ready for transport back to jail. They were waiting for an available ambulance, since the fire had kept all units tied up most of the night.

A police guard sat just outside the ER cubicle, and seeing that Roald was still handcuffed to the gurney, she felt okay going in alone. The guard checked her purse, made her leave the bottled water with him and did a halfhearted frisking before she could enter. When she entered the cubicle, she kept a safe distance from the prisoner.

"You wanted to talk to me?"

"You need to know some things."

"About?"

"Our bogus town history. Heartlandia, my ass."

"Why don't you tell me a little bit about yourself first?" Lilly wanted to know whether or not this guy was totally nuts or if he might actually have some insight into what was going on at city hall. From the looks of him, she suspected it would be somewhere in between.

"I've lived here all my life. My people go back to the beginning."

"I mean, what do you do? What is your job?"

"I'm currently unemployed. Used to work at the fishery, but they closed up a couple years back, so I took early retirement."

This was a guy with a grudge. She wondered if he was out to sue the city, or was money even what he was after? Then why burn down a building and go to jail? Nothing made sense with this one.

"I heard you're attending classes at the college," she said.

"Yeah. I'm an adult student in the genealogy extension course. That's how I discovered all the right places to look for information." He quirked one shaggy, gray-tinged brow. "Did you know the Maritime Museum was the original immigration holding area for the state?"

She shook her head wondering what that had to do with him burning down the building, and while talking to her, would he also implicate himself in the microbrewery fire? This guy needed representation not a newspaper reporter. "Are you sure you don't want a lawyer?"

"I want you to tell this story. You need to write it. Everyone thinks Heartlandia is the perfect little town, well, it's all a lie. One of my distant relatives got shanghaied from a bar that used to be where the microbrewery was."

Oh, gosh, the guy was as good as confessing he'd pulled that job, too.

Roald kept his voice down, so the guard would have to strain his ears to hear the story. Did she want to be in the middle or have information like this on her shoulders while protecting the confidentiality of her source? And wouldn't everyone know who it was, since they were in a public place, and the guy was arrested? He really should have called a lawyer.

"Do you know what shanghaied means?" He broke into her thoughts.

"Yes." She'd heard that term in regards to Heartlandia before, but more in a fanciful way, more like an urban legend from Mr. Lincoln at his grill. Now this guy was insisting it was true.

"My relative had come through immigration not more than two weeks earlier. See, the pirates who ruled this place, not those peaceful fisherman and Indians like everyone yaps on about, found their marks in the holding area. They all worked for the captain who discovered the inlet here. They controlled everything and looked for young men with muscles. Then they'd crimp them by getting them drunk, so drunk they didn't know they were getting sent out to sea. Work them half to death and not give a damn."

So Roald was exacting revenge for his relative three centuries later? Was the ancient building that housed the microbrewery the place where his relative had been shanghaied? Her head was twirling with the wacky information. Pirates?

Where had this dark past come from? Certainly this wasn't the history she'd read about Heartlandia.

Under different circumstances Lilly would be salivating to research and run with a story like this, but her conscience and newfound fondness for the Heartlandia people, and loving one over-bossy resident in particular, sobered her. Too many things needed to be checked out first. This wild story could be a figment of the arsonist's twisted imagination.

She should have asked the ER nurse if the guy had been given a psych evaluation before agreeing to hear him out. Of course, since Elke confirmed they had genealogy classes at the college, Lilly could ask what the source of their information was. If anyone would know, a historian like Elke would.

Wasn't it interesting that this new information came on top of the secret meetings at city hall, meetings that were important enough for Gunnar to break up with her over?

Snap! Elke had been attending those meetings, too. She'd seen her with her own eyes when she'd spied on Gunnar.

A police officer entered the room with an ambulance technician and broke up her powwow with Roald the avenger. Thank goodness!

"You've got to believe me," he pleaded as the officer asked her to leave when he unlocked the handcuffs.

"I'll look into your story, Mr. Lindstrom." Though unlike her usual self, she felt completely halfhearted about the promise.

Without trying she'd stumbled upon the meatiest information of her career—provided it was true. Could those secret meetings be about pirates? Then where did those aerial views at Gunnar's house come in? They were of the sacred burial ground. How did one have anything to do with the other? That was the question of the day.

This could be the huge story she'd been hoping for! This could seal her reputation as a top-notch journalist. This story, if she could parse it out, and if it was true, could even get national coverage or go viral on the internet.

Sleepy Little Oregon Town Founded by Pirates. Or better yet, Ancient Revenge!

It could be her ticket to stardom. Damn it. Her father had taken over her conscience again.

Her stomach was tied in a knot and she felt a little sick at the thought. *You don't have to be the person your dad tried to make you.* Was she so success-oriented and hard-hearted that she'd betray Gunnar while he was injured and in the hospital, and ruin any chance of ever getting back together with him? What about being in love with him? Was success really all about the goal and doing anything to achieve it? Just how big a price was she willing to pay for recognition?

Her parents may have raised her to be this way, but after meeting Gunnar, did she really want to hold on to the tail of a dragon and miss out on the important things in life, like the love of a good man?

She wasn't sure how she'd get to the bottom of this potential news-breaking story, but it was her duty as a journalist, and she knew she'd start by talking to Elke.

Not tonight, though. Nope.

Tonight was all about Gunnar. The man she loved.

After Lilly stepped out of the patient room, she strode back to the elevator. Her head still spun from the crazy story, but her mind immediately compartmentalized the information. Thinking only of Gunnar, his surgery and, more importantly, his recovery, she rushed back to see him. Hopefully, this time he'd want to see her, too.

Chapter Thirteen

Elke was exactly where Lilly had left her in the waiting room. She sat quietly reading a decade-old magazine from a nearby table piled high with them. The blonde woman glanced up and smiled. "Anything interesting?"

Lilly inhaled and raised her brows. "You wouldn't believe what that guy told me."

"Try me." Elke glanced at her watch—it had only been a couple of hours since Gunnar had been taken to surgery. "We've got time."

"You said he went to Heartlandia CC, right?"

"Yes."

"Well, according to him that genealogy extension class your school offers gave him the key to finding out a lot more than he expected." Lilly took out her bottled water and took a sip. "Have you ever heard about people getting shanghaied here in Heartlandia?"

Elke went quiet briefly, as though planning what to say. "Oh, we've got a rich supply of seafaring stories to pass along to tourists, if that's what they're after. They're more like urban legends than truth, though."

"So you think this guy's story is off base."

"Could be."

Lilly wasn't sure if Elke would lie straight-faced to her or if she was the sane person who Lilly should believe, rather than the whack-job arsonist. She'd always prided herself on being a solid judge of character, and her gut told her Elke was the one to trust. But those darn secret meetings stirred up all kinds of doubt about who she could believe or why.

Lilly shuddered and rubbed her arms.

"You okay?" Elke asked.

"I hate hospitals."

"Most people do."

"My dad wanted me to be a surgeon. I was afraid if I ever set foot in one he'd lock me inside and never let me out. Made for quite a struggle when I needed my tonsils out at twelve." Lilly gave a doleful laugh and was surprised when Elke reached over to hug her.

The phone in the surgery waiting room wall rang and Elke jumped to answer it. Her eyes widened and overflowed with relief as she listened to the person on the other end. She hung up. "He's out of surgery. Everything went great, and I can see him as soon as they get him settled in recovery."

What about me?

Elke must have read the disappointment on Lilly's face. "After I see him, I'll see if you can go in for a quick visit, too. Okay?"

Lilly grabbed her forearm and squeezed. "Thank you so much." Maybe the anesthesia would make him forget they'd broken up just hours earlier. A girl could always hope. "I'm not just his fly-by-night girlfriend, you know."

"You're not." Elke's kind expression and confident words reassured Lilly, even though technically she wasn't

Gunnar's girlfriend *at all* anymore. At least until she could change things.

"He's a great guy, and maybe a little hotheaded when it comes to Heartlandia." Lilly leveled a gaze at Elke. "You may as well know that he thought I was snooping when I wasn't. Not on purpose anyway. I swear on a stack of Bibles I wasn't."

"Didn't you write that article mentioning how he may have become a policeman to make up for our father being a criminal?"

"I did." Lilly winced, now realizing firsthand the implications her story had had, the very ones Gunnar was so upset about.

"And the story about Mayor Rask?"

"Yes, but…"

"He was probably ticked off about that, too," Elke said.

"Tell me about it. He broke up with me over it!" That wasn't the whole reason, but for the sake of conversation, she'd leave trust out of it for now.

But that was only half of her problem. She'd let herself fall in love with him. He could always make her laugh, and he was a great match of wits with her. He'd opened up a whole new world showing her around Heartlandia and introducing her to the inhabitants. He made her feel protected and cherished, and above all accepted for who she was—such a foreign feeling. And their lovemaking was like nothing she'd ever experienced. The list went on and on.

The hole in Lilly's chest widened as she thought about actually losing Gunnar because of her mistakes. It wouldn't be fair. Her first blunder was before she'd completely fallen for him. Then the mix-up about the aerial views of the sacred burial ground was completely unintentional.

If he loved her he'd believe her. She'd thought that mailing tube had held the blueprints for the next phase of his house, that's all. That was the honest-to-God truth, yet she'd never managed to convince him. His natural instinct to mistrust people until proven otherwise had driven a wedge between them. Soon enough she'd pushed everything over the ledge. She'd run the article on Mayor Rask, heavily hinting at town secrets.

She'd ruined everything—broken his trust.

Since the scene in the restaurant, she'd had time to calm down and come to her senses. Gunnar had driven home some very important points. Success at all cost was a loser idea. *Gee, thanks, Mom and Dad.*

The big question was, could Gunnar think things through and decide what they had was worth keeping?

Of course not! He didn't have time! He'd had to rush off to a fire and he'd gotten shot.

Every thought must have played across her face because she snapped out of it and noticed Elke's empathetic expression. Lilly decided to lay it all out there.

"I love your brother, and I kind of thought he'd fallen for me, too. That is until this afternoon when he read me the riot act and walked off."

"He has a way of flying off the handle. Basically, he likes to be in control, has ever since our father left. He's got a lot of pride, too." Elke smiled. "Give him some time. If I know my brother, falling in love would mean he'd lost control of his heart. The last thing he ever wants to be is out of control. He'd be primed for finding ways to avoid it." The smile changed to a sad downward turn of her lips. "You picked a guy who prefers to be married to his job, trusts only himself and insists on testing people all the time, so it won't be easy, but something tells me, with your determination, you'll work this out."

The phone rang again, and in a flash, Elke had answered

it. "Okay. Thanks." She turned. "I can go see him now. Give me a few minutes to make sure he's okay, then I'll ask them to let you in."

"Thanks."

Lilly watched Gunnar's sister disappear behind a door operated by pressing a metal plate on the wall. Elke had decided Lilly was determined enough to make things right again. She only hoped Elke was right. But at the moment, the last thing she felt was determined. Truth was, she felt defeated and hated every second of not being in charge of her life the way her parents had taught her to be. She'd have to throw everything she ever knew out the window in order to regain his trust.

She and Gunnar weren't exactly a match made in heaven, with his lack of trust in her and her old habits tripping her up at every turn, yet she'd finally found a guy to be crazy about. Too bad he'd dropped her on circumstantial evidence.

Fifteen minutes later Elke reappeared looking relieved. "He's doing great. Still pretty out of it from the drugs, but he's coming around. They said you can see him for five minutes." She pointed to the double doors she'd just come through. "Push that plate and once you're inside, he's in recovery bed four."

"Thanks." After a quick squeezing of each other's hands, Lilly set out to see Gunnar, her heart tap-dancing inside her chest. What if he kicked her out? How could she save face after that?

The thought was too painful to consider. She trudged into the recovery room pasting false confidence onto her face.

Gunnar nearly took up the entire hospital bed. His eyes were closed and a huge white dressing covered most of his chest. His left arm was in a black sling. A little round bulb hung from the middle of the bandages. It was some kind of drain, and it was half-full of bright red blood already. His blood. Her heart squeezed.

An IV machine with several plastic bags in varying sizes attached took up one side of the bed, and assorted medical equipment filled most of the rest of the space on the other side. The sight of him looking so vulnerable made her dizzy. She found a wheelchair nearby and pushed it forward to sit on. But she couldn't sit and wait for him to notice her. She only had five minutes. She'd hoped to look into his eyes. To see if he truly hated her or if there was a chance he could forgive her. Since he was under the influence, maybe his true feelings would show.

She ran her hand down his forearm, the side without the IV. His thumb twitched.

He was okay, and the knowledge filled her heart with gladness. She exhaled her relief, not realizing until then she'd been holding her breath. His safety and health were all that mattered right this moment. She studied him with a huge bubble of love welling in her chest.

One of his eyes cracked open. It took a moment for him to focus on her.

"Lilly?"

"Yes. I'm here."

He went silent again for a few moments. "I thought we broke up." His voice was raspy from surgery and whatever they must have shoved down his throat to help him breathe.

She couldn't let on how shook-up she was, so she kept face. "That's your side of the story."

A tiny smile stretched his lips. "Just like Wolverine."

"What do you mean?"

"He won't go away."

She'd seen the way Gunnar adored his huge cat. This hard-ass facade was just an act. "I'm not going to go away, either, until you forgive me." She took and squeezed his hand. He gently squeezed back.

He inhaled deeply as if unable to fight off sleep. "We'll see about that," he mumbled and finally gave in to the sedation.

At least she knew he'd made it through surgery. He was all right. And hopefully he'd remember she'd been here by his side.

"I'll take care of Wolverine. Don't worry," she said, then let go of his hand leaving him to sleep.

She nodded her thanks to the nurse and left the recovery room, finding Elke right where she'd left her.

"I'm going to go to Gunnar's house and feed Wolverine."

"Thanks. I'm staying here until they transfer him to his room. I'll text you the number."

"Great. Thanks."

Lilly approached Elke, she stood, and they hugged, like new friends. Two people who both cared for the same man. One as a blood relative, the other as a crazy mixed-up blabbermouthed lover.

Riding down the elevator, Lilly felt trembly. Her world had been knocked on its head tonight. Though, having Elke put things in perspective on the Gunnar side of the equation gave Lilly a flicker of hope. His being married to the job didn't have nearly the benefits of a living, breathing warm body. Surely he knew that.

It wouldn't be easy to get a guy like him to forgive her, especially if he was looking for ways to avoid getting attached to anything outside of work, but she wouldn't give up. She'd find a way to get back into his good graces no matter what it took. There had to be a way to make Gunnar trust her again.

Right now she'd start by taking care of his cat.

* * *

Gunnar woke to sharp, stabbing pain in his shoulder. It took him a moment to realize he was in the hospital. He nearly knocked over a Styrofoam cup of ice reaching for the bedside call button for the nurse so he could get some relief. He'd had crazy dreams all night. Starting with visions of fire and chasing after someone. He remembered getting shot, stun-gun-level pain and feeling helpless, a feeling he hated more than anything. Then the smell of a hospital, and clattering noise, people talking over him as if he wasn't there.

His sister's face came into view, her voice sounding as if she were under water.

And he'd seen Lilly, or maybe he'd only imagined it. Yeah, it was probably a dream. She'd stood beside him and said something sassy. Wasn't that just like her, too? But having her near had settled him down, seeing her face warming his aching chest.

He shook his head, still trying to fully wake up. Why had Wolverine come into his thoughts? Oh, yeah, someone needed to feed him.

He massaged his temples with his one good hand. Ah, right. Lilly would. Feed Wolverine. Yeah.

But he'd broken up with her. She'd gone over the line printing that information about the meetings, even though Mayor Rask said she could, and he couldn't trust her. Wasn't trust the most basic element for any successful relationship?

So why did he trust her to feed his cat?

The nurse appeared and he was grateful to be distracted from his jumbled-up thoughts. "What day is it?"

"Friday."

He'd lost a day. "I need something for pain."

"Sure. I'll be right back."

Gunnar opened and closed his left hand, tried to bend his elbow just to make sure he could still use it, but the sling prevented him. When he tried to lift his entire arm, sling and all, he let out an involuntary groan.

A doctor who looked like a teenager appeared. "Sergeant Norling? How're you feeling today?"

"I could be a lot better, thanks."

"You're a lucky man. The bullet lodged in the lateral pectoralis major muscle and went through the scapularis."

"Whoa, whoa, Doc, come again?"

"Bottom line, we were able to remove the bullet and all of the fragments in your left outer shoulder. However, the impact of the shot did fracture your clavicle. You'll need to wear a sling for several weeks."

"So my shoulder socket's okay?"

"Amazingly, yes. I'll see about having you released for home by this afternoon."

"I'm in a lot of pain."

"That's to be expected, and we'll send you home with pain relief."

Kent entered the room and Gunnar's spirits immediately lifted. "Hey, man."

"How're you doing?"

"I could be better. Doc, this is my best friend, Dr. Kent Larson."

"Nice to meet you."

"Can you tell him what you just told me?"

He repeated the information for Kent then, all business and no doubt with a long list of patients yet to see, the junior-aged doctor prepared to leave. "I'll need to see you back in a week for a wound check and follow-up X-rays."

"Can I follow up with my friend here? His office is in Heartlandia."

"I run the Urgent Care there."

The kid curled his lower lip, looking at Kent and thinking. "I don't see why not," Dr. Too-young said. "You'll need to do another X-ray to see how the bone is healing, though."

"I can do that, we have radiology equipment at my Urgent Care, too," Kent said with maybe a hint of insult. It wasn't as if he ran a little country clinic in the middle of nowhere. Gunnar knew Kent worked hard at having the best and newest of everything, nearly going into debt to do it on more than one occasion.

"I'll be glad to consult with you over the phone when you're ready," Dr. Kid said.

"Great. Nice to meet you, Doctor." Kent shook the fresh-faced doctor's hand and went immediately to Gunnar's bedside. "So you made it."

"I did. Damn, I don't ever want to be shot again."

Kent smiled. "I don't blame you." Since he'd been dating Desdemona he'd grown a stylish beard, and Gunnar still needed to get used to it.

"What about the turd who shot me?"

"He's in custody. From what I hear, he's a whack-job."

"Attempting to kill an officer of the law, and arson, he'll be put away for the rest of his life."

Kent nodded solemnly.

After a few moments of silence, Gunnar realized how worried his friend had been about him—why else would he show up here on a Friday morning when he probably had a full clinic back home? Gunnar decided to change the topic from near-death experiences. "So, how are the wedding plans coming along?"

Kent's face brightened. "I wanted to talk to you about that. You'll be my best man, right?"

"Damn straight, I will." Gunnar tried to sit up more and tugged on his shoulder wound. "Ouch."

Kent rushed to help him adjust his position. "Hey, take it easy. You're going to need a lot of help when you get home. Maybe you should go to Elke's."

"Yeah, maybe for a few days." Gunnar's mind quickly drifted to Lilly, wondering if it was okay to ask an ex-girlfriend to help out.

"I'm going to need you in tip-top shape to be my best man."

"You name the day and place and I'll be there."

The happiness he read in his friend's eyes sent a sudden pang to his chest. Lately he'd been walking around looking that happy, too, all because of Lilly.

"How come you and Lilly never doubled with Desi and me?"

"Busy schedules. My job. Never had time." Gunnar had to stop for a second and think why Kent would bring up Lilly this morning. Oh, right, she'd shown up at the Urgent Care last night wanting to see him. Truth was he had been keeping Lilly all to himself instead of sharing her with his friends. The timing just never seemed right to make plans, but he really just wanted what little time they had together to be all his. Right now he didn't have the heart or inclination to explain they'd broken up.

"When you get better, we'll all have to go to *husman-skost* for a midnight supper."

"Deal." Gunnar nodded, even though his whirlwind love affair with Lilly might already be over before it had hardly gotten started.

Thinking about Lilly sent him off in all kinds of directions.

Yeah, she was aggravating and contrary and really nosy, but she was also someone he could respect on a professional level. She'd achieved a lot on her own and wasn't waiting around for some man to make her life complete.

She was reaching for her dreams. The only problem was sometimes she needed someone to reel her in when she went overboard. He'd be perfect for the job, too.

Except he couldn't completely trust her. How could he love her if he didn't trust her? Round and round his thoughts went.

"Hey, where'd you go?" Kent said.

"Aw, sorry. I'm still groggy."

The nurse entered the room with a syringe and asked Kent to step aside. Gunnar wanted him to do a favor, and called out from behind the closed bedside curtain. "Will you let Elke know I'll be going home this afternoon?"

"Sure. In fact, I was planning to stick around and drive you to her house."

So, he'd left his own clinic to be by Gunnar's side, but that was the kind of friendship they had. Solid. Always there for each other.

The nurse positioned Gunnar on his right side, opened the back of his hospital gown and rubbed his hip with something cold.

Gunnar stayed deep in his thoughts to avoid what he knew was coming. Why had he kept this love affair mostly to himself?

Was it because he didn't want her thrown in with the list of names, faces and figures he'd serially dated over the past several years? Was it because she was special and he wanted to make sure the feeling was mutual before they spent more time with his best friend?

Was it because he loved her?

"Ouch!" Medicine delivered.

Gunnar clinched his jaw, absorbing the blast of pain, thinking he'd just gotten a kick in the butt.

So if she was so damn special, why had he broken up with the best thing to ever happen to him?

Because someone needed to teach her there was a line, even in journalism, that a person instinctively knew not to cross.

The lady needed some fine-tuning, and now with his gunshot wound, he wouldn't have the time or opportunity to help her out.

But the thought of losing her completely felt as lousy as his aching bum shoulder.

Lilly tapped on Elke's front door after work Friday evening. Elke smiled when she saw her, but the expression changed to disappointment. "Oh, too bad, Gunnar just went to sleep."

Like osmosis, Elke's disappointment shifted to Lilly. "I should have called first, but I was afraid he'd refuse to see me if he knew I was coming."

Elke invited Lilly inside her small but comfortable home. "It's been a rough day for him. I think just about everyone from Heartlandia Police Department stopped by at one point or another. But I think we finally caught up on the pain, so that's a start."

Gunnar had once told Lilly that his sister had lived with his mother in their family home until she'd died a few years back. Being in his childhood home gave Lilly the oddest sensation, as if she could feel his entire history here. Humble beginnings begetting big dreams of being a police officer, of becoming a guardian for his city—and she knew without a doubt that was how he felt about the job.

Married to it. That's what Elke had said.

Wondering if there was any room left for her in his heart, or if she'd never be anything but second place, Lilly followed Elke into the kitchen.

"Let me make some tea."

"You've had a long day, too, so no need. I just basically wanted to know how he was doing."

A mischievous glint flickered in Elke's eyes. "Well, we've had some time to talk, and since he is basically under the influence with the pain meds, he's more talkative than usual."

That got Lilly's attention. She sat on the edge of a kitchen chair, waiting to hear more. "And?"

"My brother isn't simply suffering from a shoulder wound. Apparently he's also got a broken heart."

"What?"

"He'd kill me if he knew I was blabbing my mouth, but the poor guy went on and on about how you were the best thing he'd ever met, how well matched you were for each other. He sounded just like a drunk at a bar moaning over his ex. Then he said the strangest thing, he said he had to break up with you for your own good."

"What?" Wow, even in sickness and on drugs the guy was full of himself. Her usual impulse to play tit for tat stayed at bay. Truth was, he had a point. In his world she'd betrayed him. In hers, she'd done her reporter's duty. Somewhere in between there was the bigger pill to swallow—trust. She'd betrayed his trust.

"Elke!" a raspy and obviously weak voice came from the back room.

"Yes, Gunnar?"

"I need some water."

"May I bring it?" Lilly asked.

"Sure." Elke took a plastic glass from the cupboard and filled it with water from the refrigerator then handed her the chilled glass. The look of assurance in Gunnar's younger sister's eyes gave Lilly the courage she needed to take that glass and walk through that bedroom door.

The room was dark, but a window in the corner was

opened wide enough to keep the air fresh and circulating. Even ill in bed, Gunnar struck an imposing figure.

"Here you go," she said in a hushed voice, handing him the glass.

He shifted his head on the pillow to get a better look. "It's you." He took the water and drank a big gulp.

"Mind if I sit with you for a while?"

"I won't be much company. I'm pretty much doped up."

"We don't need to talk."

After a couple of moments' hesitation he set the cup on the bedside table, almost missing. Lilly rushed to prevent the glass from falling off.

"Oh, yes, we do need to talk," he said. "But not now. My head is spinning."

She took his hand and sat in the cushioned chair beside the bed, a chair that seemed like something his mother may have sat on once upon a time. He let her hold his hand, even ran his thumb over her fingers a few times. They sat like that for several minutes, not uttering a word, just being there, together. Then she felt him relax and his breathing went even. He was asleep.

A most precious feeling curled up inside her. Love. Not just infatuation or sexual chemistry, but real love, the kind she had for her grandmother, deep and abiding. The kind that could grow and weather the rough patches in life. Like the one they were in right now.

Lilly wanted to share everything she had with a man who couldn't trust her. There had to be a way to earn that back.

Thinking of Gunnar and love and how she cared for him in the same way she held a special place for her grandmother, a bright idea popped into her head. Sobo would know how to make things right again, she always did.

Lilly placed Gunnar's limp hand softly on his stomach

and bent to kiss his brow. His nose twitched in response. She took an extra moment to study him while he slept now that her eyes had adjusted to the dark. Strong features, proud jaw, short out-of-control hair that promised to be thick and wavy if he ever let it grow out. Eyelashes thick like a child's. Warmth drizzled through her chest. She loved this guy, and maybe he didn't know it yet, but they *were* going to be together.

All Lilly needed was some advice from her sobo so everything could get sorted out.

Chapter Fourteen

"You must do good, Lilly-chan. Show him," Sobo said

"But I'm afraid I've already ruined his trust in me."
Lilly sat curled up on her overstuffed lounger in the small
guesthouse living room talking to her grandmother on the
phone, gazing out the window onto the night-lighted swimming pool. It had been a week since she'd last seen him,
choosing to let him heal in peace at his sister's house, all
the while feeding Wolverine for him.

"If you respect yourself, you'll find a way."

Lilly wanted Gunnar's respect, yet all her life her sobo
had taught her that self-respect was the most important
respect of all. She had a point.

"Remember the way of *chanoyu*—*wa*, *kei*, *sei*, *jaku*."

Having been schooled in the traditional tea ceremony,
Lilly understood when her grandmother suggested the way
of tea. *Wa*—harmony, *kei*—respect, *sei*—purity, *jaku*—
tranquility. But what was Sobo getting at?

"Show him humility and your imperfection with a tea
ceremony. Show him your desire for respect and to be honorable. If he loves you, he will forgive you."

How could her grandmother know this, and how could a traditional Japanese tea ceremony mend her broken relationship with Gunnar?

"I'll think about it," Lilly said.

"Thinking is waste of time. Do."

With that, they said their goodbyes and Lilly made herself some herbal tea, nothing like the tea she'd need for a real tea ceremony. And speaking of tea, where in the world could she find an authentic Japanese tea set or *matcha*, the ground green tea powder, in a Scandinavian town like Heartlandia anyway?

Maybe in Portland? She picked up her cell phone again and used her voice to request information. Within seconds the phone brought up the Portland Japanese Garden, including directions on how to get there. Surely, she'd find what she needed at the gift shop there.

It was a crazy idea, and her heart fluttered even considering it. Could her grandmother be right or would this wind up being the most humiliating moment of her life? She went to bed, unable to sleep realizing she could have lost Gunnar if that gunshot had been just a little lower. The thought sent fear quaking through her. Her eyes stung and soon moisture brimmed, slipping out the corners and coursing toward her ears. He was alive and she still had a chance of getting him back.

They needed to wipe the slate clean, then start over. He'd argued that she should use discretion when publishing her stories. She felt it was her duty to report everything of interest for her paper. He made a good point, not everything belonged in the news, and she didn't know the half of the secret meetings story. There was probably a very good reason why a whole committee of people who loved and lived in Heartlandia wouldn't want their news pasted across the headlines. Maybe it was for the best for now.

Being tenacious wasn't always the answer, and trusting Gunnar about keeping the story quiet didn't diminish her power as a reporter. It just made her levelheaded, willing to compromise, a wiser person, not a news-at-all-cost hothead. Gunnar was right, it was time to mature in both her professional and personal lives. If she didn't she'd lose him. She couldn't lose him.

She rolled onto her side and practiced the movements for the tea ceremony in her mind, remembering every step her grandmother had once taught her, striving to be precise yet simple in every detail. She'd need a scroll to hang with the right thoughts written on it, and she remembered the proper placement and cleaning of the utensils she'd use. Soon, big thoughts of how to prove her love to Gunnar formed in her brain. In fact, this guest cottage was the perfect setting for working the miracles she needed in order to win him back.

The way of tea or *chanoyu* had never been more significant in her life. Now, if she could only shut off her mind so she could get some sleep because she had a big day tomorrow.

The next morning, being Saturday, she was tired but planned her trip to Portland, anyway. First she had another idea up her sleeve.

Lilly drove to Gunnar's house, and Wolverine, being a smart cat, had already figured out what her showing up meant. Food! But she had bigger plans for him today, plans that would hopefully also put a smile on Gunnar's face.

"Here kitty, kitty, kitty…" she cooed, food in one hand, a borrowed dog leash from Leif's collection in the other. All she had to do was click it to the cat's collar and drag him to her car for a field trip to see his owner.

Wrong! That nearly thirty-pound cat wanted nothing

to do with her or the leash, and he was a lot quicker than she'd expected. She lunged and he ran farther away, ignoring the food and distrusting her.

Good thing she had plan B.

Lilly trudged back to the car and found the can of tuna, then depending on his hunger, popped the top open and set it on the passenger seat of her two-door car. No matter how long it took, she'd get Wolverine inside and bring him to Gunnar for a visit. She knew how attached they were to each other, whether the big guy would admit it or not.

Lilly moved to the front bumper and leaned against the hood of the car, the passenger door left open, folded her arms and prepared to wait things out. Wolverine evidently had a weakness for smelly tuna. He ventured closer to her car, and she acted like she didn't notice or care. A couple minutes later, with Lilly pretending to be a statue, the cat got up on his back legs and put one paw on the seat where the opened can rested. She held her breath and slowly slid to a squat, then peeked around the front bumper. He must have jumped inside the car. Yes! She crawled as quietly as she could, praying the cat would remain distracted with the tuna, which he did, then she slammed the door closed. Rushing around to the driver's side she saw her fatal flaw.

Her window was down!

She sprinted to get there before Wolverine could jump out.

His big old face and front paws were halfway out, and though she feared being scratched, she used her best basketball defense pose to stop him. He meowed his thoughts about being trapped in her car, and growled his discontent as she pushed him back toward the passenger seat. His ears were back and he swatted her hand but his claws, in contrast to his given name, weren't out.

He was one scary mass of gray fur with furious eyes, but she held firm.

Lilly sucked in her gut and managed to slide inside a six-inch door opening, figuring he was too fat to make it through. Wolverine looked as if he wanted to eat her face off, but she stared straight ahead, started the engine and closed the window, then drove off with the cat meowing and walking over her as if she was a pile of laundry. Other than a couple times when he perched on the dashboard and completely blocked her view out the windshield, she managed to make it to Elke's house in ten minutes without further incident.

"Nice boy. Good kitty," she repeated over and over as she tried once again to put Wolverine on the dog leash. Since he had nowhere to run, she wrestled with him inside the car for a few minutes, but he was a slippery guy. Then she offered him a tasty morsel of the leftover tuna to distract him. Success!

She opened her door and just before dragging Wolverine out of the car, he backed up and with a quivering tail sprayed her driver's seat, leaving his mark. That would show her for messing with a Maine Coon cat.

She huffed out a breath, spitting more than a few cat hairs out in the process, and dragged the belligerent cat to Elke's front door. Being that it was a lovely late-summer day, she only had to call through the screen door.

"Elke? Can you let me in?"

Surprising her, Gunnar appeared with bed hair, arm in that black sling, shirtless and wearing gray sweatpants. It was probably too hard to tackle putting on a shirt under the circumstances with the sling and all… She dragged her gaze away from his chest. "What's up?" he asked just before noticing his loud protesting cat at the end of the leash.

Not exactly the greeting she'd hoped for, but under the circumstances…

"I thought you might like some company?" Had she done the right thing? Or was she completely out of her mind?

He opened the screen door, his disbelieving expression nailing her, then shifting toward his cat. He shook his head and his features smoothed out until a smile stretched across his face. "You've got to be kidding me." He squatted and petted his cat, who'd recognized his owner and exchanged his griping for walking back and forth so Gunnar could pet him, then rubbing against his legs. "Hey, buddy, I missed you. Were you worried about me?"

So Lilly hadn't been totally off her rocker with this bright idea after all.

Gunnar shifted his gaze up toward her and bowled her over with his grin. "Thanks. This was really thoughtful of you."

She wanted to blurt out, *Does this mean you forgive me?* but checked herself. "No problem."

He stood, she handed him the leash, and the cat followed him inside. "Do you want to come in?"

Yes, of course she did. She wanted to beg him to give her a second chance and spend the day with him, and help him in any way she could. Instinct told her to take it slow, to keep her distance, let him wonder what was going on since he broke up with her.

"Actually, I have to take a trip into Portland today. Is there anything you need before I go?"

"Elke's got everything under control, thanks. I'll text her and tell her to buy some cat food."

"Okay, good. You feeling any better?"

"Still in a lot of pain, but I'm getting by."

Though wanting to throw her arms around him and

take care of him and love him with all of her might, she kept her distance. "Well, don't push yourself. Take it easy for a few days, okay?"

He looked surprised, and maybe a little disappointed that she wasn't sticking around, and that boosted her confidence a little. Without giving it a thought, Lilly went up on her tiptoes and kissed Gunnar's cheek. "May I call you later?"

"Sure." He looked a little bewildered, but she could tell he liked it.

She could have sworn he wanted to reach for her and give her a proper kiss, but she didn't give him a chance. Elated with hope, her mind spinning, she turned and walked away, getting into her tuna-smelly car, and sat. Eew! Right in the stinky urine spot Wolverine had marked on her leather upholstery.

Ugh. Now she'd have to go home and change clothes and clean her car before she drove to Portland.

She pasted a smile on her face, though the cat's sticky gift gave her the heebie-jeebies, waved at Gunnar, who still filled up the door frame, and drove off as if she did this sort of thing—kidnapping cats and delivering them to their owners—every day.

The good news was, he hadn't thrown her out.

Gunnar took the clean shirt Elke handed him and let her help him gingerly put his arm through the sleeve without the sling. Damn it hurt. Then quickly she reapplied the sling for support of his broken clavicle. A week of healing had made a big difference in the pain.

"I've wanted to talk to you about something," Elke said, "but with everything going on, I wasn't sure when it was a good time."

"What's up?" He buttoned the last of his shirt and followed his sister into the kitchen for lunch.

"According to Lilly, the arsonist told her a lot of uncanny information that relates to our committee." Elke handed him a plate with a sandwich.

"And?"

"She's a journalist! She could blow all of our efforts to keep this pirate stuff quiet."

Gunnar sighed and sat, took a long drink of the lemonade she'd already put at his place. He hadn't heard about the arsonist talking to Lilly before now. "When did he talk to her?"

"The night you were in surgery. I played down his claims saying we had plenty of seafaring stories to tell our tourists for entertainment. But combine that with our mayor all but telling her we had some big news to share, and I think a smart reporter like Lilly can run with a big story."

"I haven't seen any stories in the paper other than reporting on the partial burning of the Maritime Museum."

"So far," Elke said.

"Your point is?" Gunnar had quickly lost his appetite.

"I think it's time the committee makes an announcement. Our town deserves to know what we've discovered."

"She saw the aerial views of the Chinook burial ground, too," Gunnar said. "Even the heat images." Elke's eyes widened. He put his one good elbow on the table and leaned on it rather than take a bite of sandwich. "You're right. She could put two and two together and run with it on the front page. That would sell a few extra newspapers."

"It would be better for us to come out first." Elke leaned against the kitchen counter, playing with the ends of her long braid.

"Agreed."

"Should I call a meeting to discuss how best to do it?"

Gunnar nodded, trying to act nonchalant and lifting his sandwich as if his stomach wasn't tied up in a baseball-size knot. Lilly stumbling onto bits and pieces of the evidence was enough for any hungry journalist to dive into a meaty story. The committee definitely needed to beat her to the punch in order to ward off some of the sting.

It was going to be bad enough to tell the town their lovely little history lessons had all been wrong. Heartlandia had been discovered by a pirate who killed the natives and hoodwinked fisherman into working his ships. It was only after the first people, the Chinook, joined forces with the fed-up fisherman and their families that a major uprising occurred. Not to mention the sinking of Captain Prince's ship and his subsequent murder. Then the pirates settled down, got sick and died, or moved on, leaving Heartlandia to the Chinook and the Scandinavian immigrants. Heartlandia's history had only been recorded from that point on, whose idea that had been they'd never know.

Elke made some calls finding Leif and the others. Then making sure Ben's second-degree burns were healed enough for him to go out in public, she discovered his respiratory condition from smoke inhalation was the biggest problem. He wouldn't be able to attend a meeting until okayed by his doctor, which meant the meeting couldn't take place until early the next week. That left the weekend up for grabs at the *Heartlandia Herald*. The tight feeling in Gunnar's chest wasn't from the wound or broken bone. This time it was from the thought of Lilly blowing the whistle before they were ready.

He shouldn't have broken up with her. At least he could have kept better track of what she was doing that way, and picked her brain about what she knew. Like, where had she run off to today?

He couldn't exactly call and ask her to keep the lid on the story because he wasn't sure if she'd connected all the dots and he didn't want to tip her off more.

But if she had put it all together, it was highly unethical to ask a journalist, looking for a way to make a name for herself, to sit on the biggest breaking news in the history of Heartlandia.

Later that afternoon, a beautiful Japanese invitation arrived at Elke's house exclusively for Gunnar, hand delivered by a local middle schooler.

Under the circumstances, Lilly having him over the barrel with information, the fact she'd been incredibly sweet since he'd broken things off with her, and not to mention he still had feelings for her—big feelings—it was an invitation he couldn't refuse.

Gunnar did as he was told, arriving at Leif Andersen's residence around three on Sunday afternoon. He hadn't been cleared to drive yet, but since his left arm was the issue, he felt confident to drive himself over using only his right arm, rather than feel like a teenager with his sister dropping him off.

Leif was out of town, but the lock on the gate to the cottage had been left unlatched. He entered along the side of the guesthouse, overrun with ivy, purple potato vines and grape leaves pressing inward on the narrow pass. As Lilly had instructed in her note, he sat by the pool in a large wingback wicker chair she'd placed dead center on the interlocking pavement tiles. Since no other chair was around, he figured this one was meant for him.

A mild breeze tickled a delicate rice-paper-and-shell wind chime dangling from the roof over the front porch. It made a light tinkling sound that felt calming and intimate. He rested his head against the wicker and, though he hadn't had a pain pill since yesterday, felt as though he'd taken a tranquilizer as the sun warmed his face and tender shoulder. He closed his eyes and thought about what he intended to ask Lilly today. *Are you planning to run with a patchwork story? Wouldn't it be better to get the information straight before shouting it to the world? Would you be willing to wait a few days?*

A shadow quietly crossed before him. He cracked open his eyes. Lilly stood in front of the wicker chair, a soft and beautiful vision outlined by the clear powder-blue sky. Her hair was slicked back and she wore a morning-glory-blue kimono with a white sash making her look like a modern-day geisha. The sight rocked him to the core and nearly knocked him out of the chair. She smiled and Gunnar responded with a dumbfounded grin. Subtle warmth spread from his gut outward to his limbs as he could no longer deny that this crazy big-city sophisticated lady-gone-geisha was the woman he wanted in his life more than anyone.

The vision of loveliness combined with the lazy-afternoon sedation he'd just slipped into caused him to react slowly and dreamily. Overwhelmed by her presence, he struggled to find his voice. "Hi,' he said. It sounded harsh, breaking the peace that had settled between them. Completely out of character, Lilly bowed, her silence beckoning him back toward serenity.

"I'm so happy you're here," she whispered, handing him a pair of white socks with a pocket for the large toe. "These are called *tabi*. Please put them on."

She wore similar "socks" but with wooden sandals and matching morning-glory-blue brocade thong straps. He had a picture hanging in his bedroom of a geisha and he knew the term for the shoes was *zori*. He liked them. A lot. "What's up?"

His mind reeled at the thought of spending an afternoon with a gorgeous geisha who happened to be his ex-girlfriend.

She placed a long and delicate finger over her lips and waited patiently for him to remove his shoes and socks, which was awkward with one hand. When she saw him struggle, she came to his aid and removed the shoes. Her touch sent a flash flood of sensations through his body, wiping out the trance he'd just been in. What was she up to?

"Please remove your watch," she softly continued.

It wasn't like she was bossing him around or anything, but she'd made it known right off who was in charge. Honestly, he liked it, and under the circumstances, a beautiful woman giving all of her attention to him, he'd go along with the program. No problem.

The watch was on his left wrist so he took it off and handed it to her. She directed Gunnar along the garden stepping stones toward the back porch where she had placed a large basin of water to wash his hands. He washed the right one, well, splashed it around in the warm water anyway, and she helped him with the one in the sling then handed him a small towel. He managed to dry both hands on his own.

"What is all this?" he asked.

"Please, no talking. Just follow me."

Gunnar liked the little fantasy his personal geisha was taking him on. He consciously stopped his mind from wandering in the direction it was leaning. But a quick glimpse of him in a huge tub with Lilly washing his back managed to sneak past his guard. With the fantasy pressed firmly in his mind, he smothered a smile and followed her inside to the back room of the cottage, enjoying every trickle of gooseflesh she unknowingly tossed over him just by wearing that getup.

He stepped inside. Lilly had been busy transforming her guest cottage. A simple and unpretentious setting greeted him: a small ceramic fountain sat bubbling in the corner. Large pillows were carefully arranged on each side of a low-lying table with a single, near-perfect red camellia placed in a delicate porcelain vase at the center. Sandalwood incense wafted through the room. Koto music played softly and serenely in the background.

A scroll hung on the wall with a haiku written out in calligraphy. It read: "Tonight I am coming to visit you in your dream, and none will see and question me—be sure to leave your door unlocked! Anonymous."

Gunnar's skin prickled in response to the cryptic and ancient poem. He'd definitely be waiting for her tonight. No woman had ever come close to this display of, well, he wasn't sure what this whole thing was about, but figured it might have something to do with their breaking up.

He needed to stop thinking like a cop, just go with the flow, let Lilly take charge. Like the poem said, leave your door unlocked.

A floodgate opened in his chest and it filled with a new sensation he wasn't prepared to name out loud. How much time had they spent dancing around their feelings for each other the past six weeks? And when things got tough, Gunnar had snapped the budding relationship in two.

Lilly motioned for Gunnar to sit. Once again, he forced his mind back into the moment. She brought him a bowl of tofu in broth, helped him hold it with one hand and drink from the traditional Japanese bowl. Next came a simple meal of fish, stir-fried vegetables and steamed rice. The scene felt surreal, his geisha serving him, no conversation required, any guy's dream. Had all the pain meds he'd taken over the past few days come back to cause a hallucination? He smiled to himself. If so, she was one hell of a beautiful delusion.

Lilly joined him at the table, her fresh lemony scent overtaking the food, and they ate in silence, her helping him whenever he had trouble, since chopsticks weren't his forte. The atmosphere was perfect and he wanted to comment on it to be polite. But he also didn't want to break the magic of the moment by speaking, plus she'd warned him not to, so he went against his impulse for etiquette and respected her desire.

Lilly looked at him, smiled and, appearing far more humble than usual, she blushed. Enjoying her coy geisha persona, he grinned back. Wow, those dark eyes made him a little crazy in the head. He especially liked how the shells of her ears turned pink—her tell—to compliment her beautiful lips.

What would make her go out of her way to do all of this just for him? Was it because he'd been shot? Because they'd broken up? All the nights they'd made love came rushing back into his thoughts. Or that?

When the meal was done, she once again escorted him back outside to sit in the garden.

Disappointment surged. "Is that all?"

"Sit there. Wait for me." She put her finger over those beautiful lips again, turned and left him. He wanted to ask if there was anything he could help out with, but was afraid this pleasant dream of an afternoon might disappear if he did. And she was in charge. For once in his life, he'd step back, let go and let Lilly do her thing. He sat in the waning sun wondering what would be next, excited by the possibilities.

She appeared at the back door looking as beautiful as before, inviting him back inside. Once again, she led him to the table, which was set up for tea. He sat on the comfortable cushion and watched in silence as she placed the tea powder into a fine porcelain bowl, placed a dipper into a kettle of boiling water and filled it. Graceful and perfect in manner, she used a bamboo whisk to carefully whip the tea. Gunnar felt transported back in time, a regular shogun tea ceremony moment. Lilly bowed and presented to Gunnar the tea in a tiny, red-patterned ceramic cup.

He made an amused bow in response and accepted the cup, taking one sip while fighting off the constant stream of chills circulating his skin. The tea tasted tart at first then surprisingly, sweetness lingered.

Lilly reached for the cup and turned it slightly then handed it back for a second sip and, repeating the same ritual, then a third sip. Each movement was repeated exactly as the first. She'd studied her art of serving tea well, and he suspected her sobo'd had a lot to do with the tradition. Seeing this humbler side of Lilly went straight to his heart. What kind of a jerk would break up with her before completely getting to know her?

A guy who'd thought she'd betrayed him, that's who. At least, that was how he'd seen it, always thinking in black and white.

Yet she'd sworn it wasn't true.

When she finished serving his tea, she offered and fed to him a small jellied sweet, which had a distinct apricot flavor.

Lilly then wiped the rim of the cup with a white cloth before repeating the same tea-drinking practice herself. Gunnar watched the ceremony with admiration. It struck him that in this way they partook of their own personal communion and that unnamed feeling flying around in his chest grew stronger. Was this her way of apologizing, or was she trying to tell him that she loved him? Unsure of the particular message, the power of the endeavor was coming through loud and clear. He was special to her... as she was to him. But how had he shown it to her? By breaking up with her over a news article.

The Koto music ended.

They finished sipping their tea in silence. Every time Gunnar looked at her, her eyes danced away making it hard to read her game plan. Why was she lavishing all of this attention on him when he'd been rude and pigheaded and had broken things off in that coffee shop?

She'd had him so dazed with her beauty and the sensations she'd conjured up, he'd forgotten the obvious reason for all of this. In her own humble way she was trying to rebuild his respect and trust. She'd shared the cup with him, wiping their troubles clean. At least that was how he'd interpreted it. Who knew what the real ceremony was supposed to represent? Maybe it was just about sharing tea with someone special.

Wasn't it about time for him to learn to yield graciously? Lilly's time and effort with the ancient ceremony had rubbed off on him, making him think about the future.

Lilly cleared her throat, placed her hands on her thighs and finally broke the solitude. "I want to explain something." Her voice sounded thin and wavering. She sat on her heels moving her hands to rest in her lap. She paused and seemed to struggle for composure, fighting back emotion.

He wanted to reach out for her, yet he knew she had something important to say and didn't want to interfere or ruin anything.

"In my family, honor means everything. I had a lot of making up to do just by being born a girl as far as my father was concerned. He taught me the consequences of dishonoring the family name, browbeat it into me, and now that I'm independent of him, I still give him power over my life.

"My sobo showed me that being true to myself was honorable. She gave me the courage to claim journalism as my major, no matter how upset my father was about it. But I never completely broke free of my father's hold. And I've made bad choices because of that.

"Whether I think of his form of honor or my grandmother's, I see now that I dishonored you with my duplicity. I wanted that big story. I wanted to make a name for myself, no matter what the cost. And I tricked myself into believing I was just doing my job, that it was expected of me. Now I've lost you and your trust in me and the cost is greater than I can bear. I want more than anything to earn it back."

She reached for his hands, grasped them and squeezed.

"Gunnar, what I've learned these past several weeks from knowing you, and how you've risen above your father's example, is I can do that, too. You've shown me that it isn't about being in the spotlight, it's about doing what's right.

"Please forgive me, Gunnar. I will change. I am changing just from knowing you and being here in Heartlandia."

He couldn't keep quiet another second.

"Lilly. Sweetheart." He tightened his grip of her hands. "I'm a hard-nosed SOB sometimes because of my father, and I've been thinking I've been way too hard on you. I can't dictate what you should or shouldn't report. It wasn't convenient for me if you broke the story, and I was being selfish. I threw around the word *trust* like a pompous jerk, expecting you to do all the changing. The thing is, I can't be in control of everything, and I don't want to control you. Will you forgive me?"

"Forgive you? Of course I will. I love you, Gunnar," she

said with a quivering voice. "I love you so much I don't know how I'd breathe without you."

The words burst into his chest and scattered, forcing his heart open to the root. She loved him, too.

Lilly rose up on her knees, let go of his hands and reached across to hold his face. Her hands trembled as she drew him near and gently kissed him. This one special kiss, knowing she loved him, bonded them like nothing else could. Talk about giving someone a second chance, and by Buddha, this time he'd handle things completely different. He'd learn from his mistakes and do everything right...the way she deserved.

"I've made some mistakes," she said, "but I want to make things right with you."

Her soft, warm lips were eager to take his again. So hungry for her, he was more than willing to oblige. He wrapped his arm around her and drew her close. A flame of passion sparked in every part of his body. She'd taken a huge risk by going first. It seemed only fair to tell her his plans, too.

Breathless, he broke away just long enough to get the words out. "Sweetheart, I've loved you since the day at the hospital when you came to see me even though I'd just broken up with you. I couldn't have been happier to see you." He covered her mouth and kissed her lightly.

This time Lilly broke away. "You love me, too?"

He nodded, smiled. "Oh, yeah." Then he moved to kiss her again.

Lilly pulled back from his embrace and looked directly into his stare. She must have felt his ragged breath against her cheek, saw the raw desire in his eyes since he reeled with longing.

He lifted her hand to his mouth, kissed the palm and squeezed her fingers tightly trying to harness his hunger.

He continued to breathe heavily, yet he never wavered from her stare.

"Let me make love to you," she said. "Trust me."

He swallowed, using every last ounce of power to resist her. "I do." He kissed her quickly again, then looked around the room hoping to find the right words to express these overwhelming feelings.

Lilly backed away and stood quiet, biting her lower lip, seeming to hold back what she wanted to say. He stepped closer and tenderly cupped her face with his good hand. He traced his fingertips across her cheek and ran his thumb along her lower lip then down to her chin, cherishing each centimeter. His gaze followed the path, and he'd never seen a finer face. He'd never felt someone else's pain as easily, or shared in the simple joy they'd found together. He'd never loved anyone like this. "If we're getting back together, I want to make sure we do everything right, but with my bum shoulder it will be tough to make love the way I want."

"Let me take care of everything," she said.

What was she suggesting? "I can't exactly lay back and let you do all the work."

"Do you trust me?"

Ah, gee, she'd used the trust card, and wasn't that what all of this was about—regaining his trust? He couldn't exactly put his foot down and be his usual overbearing self. Hell, he'd just promised to change, too. He wanted to be with her more than ever, but one handed lovemaking... damn. She was waiting for his answer, and he'd probably made her think he had to think about whether he trusted her or not, which wasn't the case at all.

"Of course I trust you," he blurted without further thought. For the first time in his life he was thinking about spending the rest of his life with one special person. Wasn't it about time, like he'd thought just a few moments ago, that he learned to compromise…to bend? And most important, learned true grace.

Lilly didn't say another word. Neither did he. She took his one good hand and led him into the bedroom.

Chapter Fifteen

Lilly had thought up a part to the tea ceremony her grand-mother would probably never imagine. She brought Gunnar into her bedroom, the bedspread already folded back, fresh silk sheets scented with roses, and felt his hand tighten in hers—a promise of things to come. Sandalwood-candle aroma filled the room as she'd lit the multiple votives just before she'd served tea. Out with the old. In with the new.

Gunnar stopped her, turned her toward him and kissed her again, his lips firm and hungry, melting through her like one of those candles.

She unbuttoned his shirt and tenderly pulled apart the Velcro sling, loving the sight of his chest and muscles, aching over the bandaged wound on the left shoulder.

She could tell he fought showing the pain that the simple act of lowering his arm brought on, so after removing the shirt, she quickly reapplied the black sling, leaving him otherwise topless. She kissed his right shoulder and the opposite side of the broken clavicle, then the notch at the base of his throat before walking him backward toward her waiting bed. She'd clicked the remote on the dining table and started the Koto music again, its strange ancient plucking sound being somehow perfect for the moment. Using one finger to push his chest, she forced him to sit on the edge of the bed then removed the *tabi* she'd given him earlier for his feet. Next came his jeans. Without being asked, he stood to help her out with a wink, a very cooperative partner.

Down came the jeans, then his briefs, fully exposing him, proving he was already coming to life. "What about you?" he asked.

She resorted to the gesture she'd used several times already this afternoon, placing one finger to her lips, looking deep into his eyes.

She gestured for him to lie down, and he did, smack in the center of her bed, curiously watching her every move. She walked to the right side of the bed and removed her *zoris* and *tabis*. Next she tended to the sash from her kimono, unwinding it over and over until the satin belt hung free, loosening the kimono in the process. She took his right hand, kissed the palm then put a slipknot around his wrist and before he realized what she'd done, tied his one good arm to the bedpost.

He looked amused, not the least bit concerned.

With a demure smile she slid the kimono over her shoulders revealing she'd been completely naked beneath for the entire tea ceremony.

Seeing the desire flaming in his stare, her breasts tightened. She got on the bed and sat primly on her heels as she had throughout the ceremony, exploring the skin on his torso, thighs and chest. He hissed in breath after breath as her explorations deepened, while adding kisses and nips wherever she pleased.

Gritting his teeth throughout, over the next several minutes Gunnar let her do any- and everything she wanted to him, showing complete trust.

He was already fully aroused and tall and she took her time, enjoying the feel of him, the smooth, the rough, the slick. One firm squeeze sent him sucking in more air, and even deeper breaths when she first kissed, then filled her mouth with him.

He moaned and squirmed on the mattress. "I can't take much more of this."

Hearing his plea, she sheathed and straddled him. Even though both were at the height of excitement already, they took their time, her hips gently rolling over him, rising and falling in sweet counter rhythm. It seemed every nerve ending inside worked overtime forwarding thrilling messages to all points north and south, all the way down to her toes and to the top of her head. He dug his heels into the mattress, pumped up the pace, and finding her special spot, she moaned. Then he homed in on it, sending hot jets through her center up and over her hips and back, growing the intensity to nearly unbearable, and soon giving her release.

Her fingers dug into his chest; senses completely overloaded she gasped, and he joined her as they tumbled together in what seemed like slow motion over the brink of paradise.

She collapsed on top of his taut, warm body and for several moments she basked in the afterglow of his love, gathering her breath, feeling her pulse return to normal.

"Are you going to keep me tied up like this or let me hold you now?"

She pecked his lips with a flighty kiss then undid the sash. One strong arm gathered her close making her feel secure and loved. Both exhausted, they cuddled in the bed surrounded by candlelight at dusk.

* * *

Gunnar needed to tell Lilly a few things. They'd forged into a completely new phase of their relationship this afternoon thanks to her taking the risk. Now it was his turn to take a risk and prove beyond all doubt that he trusted her. With everything.

He cleared his throat. "The reason I got so mad at you running the article on Mayor Rask was because you were getting too close to our secret."

Lilly's head bopped up faster than a jack-in-the-box. "Your secret?"

"Heartlandia's secret. At least that's what we've been trying to do with the information, keep it a secret. Until we're ready to tell the whole town everything we've found out, that is."

"Are you sure you want me to know this?"

"More than I've ever been in my life." He refused to throw in the term "off the record."

She gave a tender smile, almost solemn, indicating the significance of what he was about to do. "You're talking about the committee?"

"Yes." He nodded.

"The one I've been spying on."

"So you finally admit you've been spying on me." He softened the tease with a quick smile.

Totally focused on the carrot he dangled before her, she obviously chose to ignore his little dig. "The meetings at city hall?"

"Correct." He took Lilly's face in his hand and looked her square in the eyes. "Only because I trust you with everything I have, I'm going to tell you what's going on." Then he kissed her forehead, but not before noticing her eyes dancing with candlelight and wonder.

Was he making a mistake? If he loved her and she loved him, he couldn't be.

After shifting his position in bed, moving up so his head and shoulders rested on the headboard, he proceeded to tell her the whole story. How Leif Andersen had discovered the trunk filled with a sea captain's journals, small treasures, nautical artifacts, guides, charts, compass and chronometer when breaking ground for the city college. How his sister, Elke, had pored over the journals deciphering the notations, and discovering that Captain Nathaniel Prince, also known as The Prince of Doom, was a pirate who'd stolen men from up and down the Oregon coast, forcing them to work on his ships, until he crashed off the shore of what was to become Heartlandia and settled in. How he had continued his unscrupulous practices from this very spot until the night the Scandinavian fisherman teamed up with the Chinook and overtook their suppressors. They'd pieced together the rest of the information and figured out he was murdered by one of his own men shortly thereafter.

Gunnar explained the unfortunate timing of their mayor dying and Gerda Rask stepping in as mayor pro tem without knowing any of this, only then to be hit with the outlandish news. How the committee had been formed to figure out what they'd discovered in the trunk, and what to do about the information they'd unearthed. How at first they'd thought the whole incident amusing, something to add to the Maritime Museum to draw more visitors. Then how they realized this was a huge part of their history that had been suppressed and left out of the schoolbooks and needed to be addressed.

He watched Lilly, who sat rapt listening to his tale, hoping beyond hope she wouldn't pounce on the story of her lifetime before the time was right.

"To make matters worse, Captain Prince had hinted at buried treasure, and unfortunately, his handmade map and legend points to a spot located in our sacred Chinook burial ground. That's our current problem, and that was the picture you stumbled onto at my house. The infrared thermography shows what might be the trunk smack in the middle of those grounds."

Lilly rolled onto her back holding her head as if it would explode if she let go. "This is crazy!"

"Tell me about it."

"No wonder you didn't want me snooping around."

"In a twisted kind of way you've forced our hand, made us think about bringing this information out in the open. Letting our citizens help decide what to do next."

"It only seems fair." She'd come up on her elbow and pinned him with an earnest gaze. "But then, I'm an outsider, what do I know?"

"You're not an outsider anymore. You've become one of us."

"Then I say, tell the people. See how they feel."

"It does blow our perfect little history right out of the Columbia River, you know?"

She chewed her lower lip and nodded, eyes intense. "But it's the right thing to do, and you always do the right thing."

He put his hand on her forearm and squeezed. "And that's why we need to find the best time to announce the news and have our plans firmly in place for handling the results before we do." He made his pitch to Lilly for holding back on releasing the information. The rest was up to her.

"When's that?"

"We don't know yet."

"Wow, so that arsonist wasn't crazy after all, just criminal."

"Yup. And turns out the fun 'urban legends' that have always floated around, the ones we've used to amuse our tourists, have always been based in truth."

She sat up and stared at him. "Talk about a major cover-up."

"A centuries-old cover-up."

She bobbed her head in agreement. "And ancient revenge." Referring back to the recent fires.

He got lost in her brown depths, wondering what was going on in her mind. He also couldn't help but notice her ears were bright red, which usually meant she was excited or thinking extra hard.

His throat tightened. He loved Lilly, and because of it, he couldn't dictate what he thought she should do, he could only suggest. "That's why I'd like to ask you to write the story…but not until we're ready to tell the town."

"Really?"

"I know you'll be careful, sensitive to detail. Tell it the way it needs to be told."

"You trust me to be the town mouthpiece?"

"With all my heart, but the story isn't quite ready to be heard yet."

"I get it." She took his hand. "It's not always about my timeline. In this case, I understand how important it is to wait until your committee is ready to come out with it."

Trusting her with everything, Gunnar reached out. "Come here, Chitcha."

She obliged, snuggling close to his chest, kissing him sweetly.

Lilly respected the rock and a hard place the committee had been put in. He knew it down to his bones. If she sat on the story for just a while longer, respecting the mayor's wishes, being sensitive to telling the details at the right time, she'd have the major story of her lifetime and he'd have one last and very important question to ask her. And it had something to do with spending the rest of their lives together.

She'd spent the afternoon impressing upon him that she was worthy of his trust. Through her tea ceremony they'd wiped the slate clean. Right now, all he wanted was to get lost in Lilly's love again, to show her how he felt about her, and forget anything and everything that had to do with the town secret.

She must have read his mind, because her expression changed. Those brown depths only focused on him. He couldn't be one-hundred-percent sure if it was him or the story that had suddenly turned her on again, making her ears light up and all, but right this moment with her kissing him crazy, he really didn't care.

Monday morning Gunnar took a deep breath and opened the newspaper. No headline about the committee. Not one word buried in the back of the *Herald* about the story, either. Whew. It was his first day back at work, where he'd be on desk duty for at least a month, and he was glad to be on the job again. Hell, he'd had to twist Kent's arm to sign him off medical leave, but last Friday, after agreeing to only work inside, his buddy had given him the okay. He'd felt lost the whole week at Elke's. Recuperating had been a pain in the…well…shoulder, and had driven the point home how much his job had to do with his identity.

Until yesterday when Lilly had taken him on a surreal trip to ancient Japanese tradition.

He drove and gulped some coffee from his traveler's cup and forced his mind back into the moment, and the day ahead.

It might be boring working the desk, but it was better

than sitting at home feeling sorry for himself. Plus, an emergency meeting for the city hall committee had been called that night, which would surely be interesting. He'd prepared himself to take the fall if Lilly took the story and ran with it, and honestly, he was still holding his breath but choosing to believe in her promises and honorable intentions. She'd changed. Hadn't she proved it to him with the tea ceremony? A woman couldn't very well personify harmony, purity, tranquility and respect one moment then make a play for headline news in the next, could she?

As he parked his car and walked into work, he texted Lilly:

Have I told you lately that I love you?

He entered the building and there stood Lilly at the door to the newspaper, dressed in a pencil skirt, open-collared white blouse with a single, simple string of pearls around her neck, and hair back to its short, springy, fun style, her cell phone in hand.

After Sunday afternoon, they'd stayed away from each other last night. It had been hard, but he needed to move back home from Elke's, and Wolverine needed some extra attention. To be honest, she'd worn him out with her traditional "tea" ceremony, and he realized the gunshot had taken more out of him than he'd thought.

Lilly smiled and waved. Making a snap decision, he strode directly toward her and kissed her as if he hadn't seen her in weeks. After, she had that discombobulated gaze, which he always dug, and her ears pinked up. "Meet for lunch?"

"Sure," she said.

"I'll text you when I know what time."

By the time he walked through the police department door he got her reply text.

Love you, too.

He grinned and walked straighter.

So far, the day had gotten off to a great start.

Later, over yellow pea soup and mixed baby greens in the Hartalanda Café, he told her about that night's meeting. Her eyes widened, but she didn't pursue the subject. This was a welcome change and it forced Gunnar to realize they'd both grown since they'd broken up and he'd gotten shot. He understood her perspective better as a news reporter, and she seemed to appreciate the need for Heartlandia to remain the town with a storybook history.

As they left that topic behind, they alternated between eating and gazing at each other. Things had definitely changed between them for the better. They'd both needed some major attitude adjustments and all of the events of the past couple of weeks had forced that on them. He drank his soda and remembered the first day she'd arrived, all fashion model and attitude, and right now, how especially glad he was that she'd jaywalked.

Seven o'clock at night Monday, Gunnar entered city hall and headed to the conference room. Everyone but Elke and Ben were there, and surprisingly, a few minutes later, they came in together. Ben's second-degree burns from the first arson fire were still noticeable but healing around his neck and jaw. His frequent cough proved his lungs were still in the process of healing. Elke looked happy, and Gunnar wondered what was up with that?

Come to think of it, she'd gotten a few phone calls while he'd stayed at her house, which she always went into the other room to take. He'd assumed it had something to do with the city college, but maybe he'd been wrong.

At 7:05 p.m. Gerda Rask called the meeting to order. "I think we all know why we're here tonight," she began. "Before we get started with our discussion, does anyone have any new business?"

Gunnar smiled inwardly. Did falling in love count?

Elke raised her hand. "I wanted to inform everyone that we've selected the artist to paint the city college mural. Her name is Marta Hoyas and she is the great-great-granddaughter of the sculptor who created our town monument. She comes from Sedona, Arizona, and plans to arrive in Heartlandia next month."

"That's great news," Gerda said, the others joining in with quiet applause. "It's good to hear something positive for a change."

"We'll need to find a place for her to stay, though."

"That's something we can decide when the time grows closer." Gerda's expression quickly changed, growing serious again. "Now I'd like to open up a discussion about our problem and how best to handle it."

"I think we should hold a town meeting and inform our citizens about the error in our town history," Adamine Olsen, the business woman on the committee said.

"I agree, but this should be a two-phase deal," Leif Andersen chimed in. "Tell the first part now, but hold off on the buried treasure part until later. Let them take in the first part before we bowl them over with more crazy news."

"Agreed," Gunnar said.

"Maybe we can distract them with the shipwreck information," said Jarl Madsen, the director of the half-destroyed-by-fire Maritime Museum. "They can concentrate on finding that for a while, then after things calm down, we can bring up the sacred burial ground issue."

This brought on a long and drawn-out discussion about how best to handle the shipwreck along with all of the other information.

When the committee had talked and argued about their sticky situation, and finally come to a consensus, Gerda stepped back in. "Our first order of business is making a public statement about our findings at the college. Then holding a town meeting for those interested telling more about it."

"We could use the *Heartlandia Herald* as a source of information," Gunnar said. "Getting the complete story out there, but holding back on the buried treasure at this point. Lilly Matsuda would be perfect for the job."

"Once the dust has settled on the pirate part, we can reveal the shipwreck, maybe invite teams to search for it," said Jarl. "Make it a fund-raiser to help rebuild our Maritime Museum."

"Great idea," said Adamine. "That could help our local merchants, too."

"I don't think we should mention the buried treasure." Ben's soft-spoken voice drew everyone's attention to him and squashed the swell of enthusiasm over rebuilding the museum. "It will upset too many people. Just keep the secret."

"We could have a vote whether or not to dig up the treasure or leave it there. What do you think?" Adamine continued.

"I don't think we should," Ben insisted. "It will divide our town."

The room fell silent.

"Let's call a vote on the first part," Gerda said. "We'll deal with the buried treasure at a later time."

Gunnar nodded. Hopefully that vote would come at a much, much later date.

* * *

Wednesday morning, Lilly's bi-weekly column—I Dream of Sushi in Storybook Land—was on the second page as usual, her bright-faced picture right beside it. The good news was, the front-page headline was about Heartlandia choosing the artist for the city college mural, and nothing about the meetings.

They'd decided to unfold the news in three parts. First, announcing a citywide meeting at the community college auditorium, then the mayor's speech and finally Elke discussing the historical authenticity of the journals.

Of course there would also be a question and answer component including all of the committee members, but all had agreed to hold off on disclosing the whereabouts of the potential hidden treasure for now. They all hoped to distract from that with the possible shipwreck.

Gunnar had secured Lilly and the *Heartlandia Herald* as the main source of information for the town. It was a huge responsibility that Gunnar knew without a doubt Lilly could handle. Smiling, he began reading today's column.

Heartlandia has grown on me. Two months ago I arrived in town as an outsider looking for a way in. Today, having had the opportunity to meet and learn about so many of the wonderful citizens in town through this column by telling your stories, I feel like one of you. Yes, I still dream of sushi and hope Cliff Lincoln of Lincoln's Place will add it to his menu one day alongside his soul food, and I miss my roots in San Francisco, but there's one thing I don't miss. Feeling anonymous. It's easy to exist in the shadows of big cities, to get lost in the daily routine, focused on navigating the streets instead of getting to know the inhabitants. Here in Heartlandia, that's impossible. You've invited me into your lives through sharing your jobs, recipes, family stories and rich Scandinavian and Chinook history. You've initiated me into the wealth of Heartlandia with smiling faces, pride for your heritage and a willingness to learn about mine. More importantly, you've taught me honor, honor that is earned by keeping tradition alive, by taking the skills passed down from ancestors and putting a personal touch to them. By carrying out time-tested chores without seeking glory. I finally see that I don't have to blow the top off of Heartlandia with an earth-shattering story to make my name. I can celebrate the people of this community who embrace the simple, everyday joys in life, which is a sure sign of down-home wisdom. Thank you for sharing and showing me that.

Most of all, one person in particular has taught me there is more to life than a great news scoop. Thank you, Sergeant Norling, for teaching me about the hazards of jaywalking, for opening my heart, for teaching me to work with others and for setting me back on the right path.

Today, I salute the people of Heartlandia for helping me find my new home. Thank you for adding me to your roll call.

Grinning, thinking what a great gal he'd fallen for, Gunnar paged through the rest of the newspaper. Something on the next-to-last page snagged his attention: "Maritime Museum Arsonist Rants About Ancient Revenge, by Lilly Matsuda."

With the arrest of Roald Lindstrom, accused arsonist of Olaf's Microbrewery and the Maritime Museum, come claims of justification for starting the two fires. The accused was enrolled in the Heart-landia City College extension program, studying genealogy when he found, what he insists, is evidence of his relatives being shanghaied by pirates three hundred years ago, citing this as his motive for setting the two fires. Mr. Lindstrom will be arraigned on charges of arson and attempted murder of a police officer once he has been found of sound mind and able to face trial. At the time of this publication, the accused unemployed factory worker stands by his story.

Perfect. She'd handled the information like a true journalist, not a writer for a gossip rag flaming the fire of controversy, though in this case she certainly could have. The focus on the man's mental instability was the perfect ending to the brief article, casting doubt on Roald's motives and putting the onus back on him instead of his relatives possibly being shanghaied by pirates.

Gunnar checked his watch. It was only nine-thirty on his midweek day off, since he was scheduled to work that Saturday. But it wasn't too early to take his best gal out for a ride. He'd made a trip to Sven's Jewels on Tuesday and something was burning a hole in his pocket. Maybe if he asked real nice, Bjork would let him borrow Lilly for the rest of the day.

An hour and a half later they drove in silence up the hillside to his favorite lookout spot. He'd stopped at the market and picked up some fruit, cheese, crusty bread, and chocolate, plus some fancy bottled tea to share, something to draw out the moments while they enjoyed the view of the Columbia River off in the distance.

It was a crisp, clear, last-of-summer kind of day with twinges of fall making the sunshine more golden than bright. He parked and grabbed the grocery bag of goodies, wishing he could take Lilly's hand and lead her to the bench, cursing the sling, even though right now it served a perfect and important purpose.

She sighed when she sat and looked out over the pine trees below and outward to the body of water. In the far distance was the superlong bridge connecting Oregon to Washington.

He'd come here throughout his life whenever he'd needed time to think things over. He'd hidden out up here the day his father had left, the day he'd had his first kiss, when he'd finally saved up enough money to buy his first car, the night before he'd graduated from high school, the afternoon he'd applied for the police force and the day before he'd made up his mind to purchase the land and build his house. This weathered old wooden bench had seen him through many deep thinking sessions. Always seeking the wisdom and solitude of Heartlandia, he'd never, in all the years, brought someone with him.

It wasn't as if the place was a secret or anything. Plenty of people knew about the spot. But to him, it was almost sacred ground.

"It's so beautiful here," Lilly said, drawing him out of his memories.

"I knew you'd like it."

"Wow. I could use a place like this to run away to on tough days."

"Or great days. Milestone days. That's why I've always come here." He opened the bag and placed the contents, as best as he could with one hand, between them to share. "Feel free to borrow it anytime." If she picked up on the significance of bringing her here, she didn't let on.

Instead she stared out over the vista nibbling bread and cheese, then popped a grape into her mouth.

They sat in silence, enjoying the weather and view, and each basking in the comfort of the other. They'd come a long way in six and a half weeks, from strangers to lovers to today. A very special day by all standards.

For the sake of not seeming nervous, though he really was, he ate and drank some tea. "I'm planning on taking the lieutenant's exam next month."

"That's great."

"Have I mentioned I also plan to be the chief of police before I turn forty?"

"No, but I think you'd be perfect for the job."

"And mayor after that?"

She paused from eating some bread. "Seriously?"

"I've wanted to be mayor since I was a kid, like my favorite chief of police was. He's my role model."

She studied him, munching on another grape. "You can do it."

The way she'd said it, there was no doubt she believed in him, and it felt damn great.

He gulped another drink of the flavored bottled tea, finally deciding to broach the foremost subject on his mind. "Will you be able to put up with a guy that driven?"

"Oh, that's right, you haven't met my parents yet, have you." She wasn't making it easy on him, playing dumb on the one hand and self-deprecatingly snarky on the other.

Gunnar laughed anyway, her smart-alecky remark helping to take the edge off his nerves. He'd never done this before, had never had the slightest desire to. He looked toward the river to calm his jitters and gather his words.

Lilly must have picked up on his silence. "I'll put up with your being the mayor if you'll put up with me as a newspaper mogul."

Now they were getting somewhere. "Only seems fair."

"Bjork told me he plans to retire next year, and I already told him I want to buy him out when he does. The guy looked so excited that I think he might be revising his plans for earlier."

"That's fantastic, Lilly." So she was definitely sticking around, a really good sign, considering what he wanted to ask. "Did I also mention I've given Leif the okay to start building the next phase of my house?"

"You've been doing a lot of thinking and planning while you recuperated."

"Yeah, so I'm thinking about getting a roommate."

That grabbed her attention. Her head snapped toward him.

"You interested?"

The corner of her mouth twitched, and she scratched it. "Only if you put a ring on that offer."

"Why, Lilly Matsuda, are you asking me to marry you?"

She tossed her gaze at the sky in frustration. "You're the one who brought it—" stopping midsentence she noticed him fish something out from his sling. He'd kept the small, velvet box hidden there in case the perfect moment cropped up, which it just had "—up." She snapped her mouth closed appearing dumbfounded.

When he knew he had her undivided attention, he started the short speech he'd rehearsed all morning after reading the newspaper.

"I don't have a beautiful tea ceremony to show you how much I love you, but I do know one tradition." Gunnar stood then dropped down onto one knee. He opened the box, exposing a simple white-gold band with a solitaire diamond surrounded by tiny emeralds. Taking out the ring, he reached for her hand, then slid the delicate ring onto an equally delicate finger. "Will you marry me, Lilly?"

She'd grown oddly quiet, but from the sudden gushing of tears, followed by her flinging her arms around his neck, almost knocking him off balance and nearly squeezing the life out of him, he figured she'd heard every word.

As if on cue, a Western Meadowlark sang from the shelter of a nearby tree.

Gunnar grinned, feeling all was right with the world, holding the woman he loved and trusted with all his heart, and having a pretty darn solid hunch what her answer to his marriage proposal would be.

* * * * *

COMING SOON!

We really hope you enjoyed reading this book. If you're looking for more romance, be sure to head to the shops when new books are available on

Thursday 10th January

To see which titles are coming soon, please visit

millsandboon.co.uk/nextmonth